# REGENT'S MATE

### BOOK FOUR

OF THE HOUSE ADAMANT SERIES

Faolan's Pen Publishing
22 King St. S, Suite 300
Waterloo, Ontario
N2J 1N8 Canada



A record of this book is available from Library and Archives Canada.

Printed in the United States of America
1 2 3 4 5 6 7 8 9 10
First edition
ISBN 978-1-989674-88-8 (Trade Paperback)
ISBN 978-1-989674-87-1 (Amazon Paperback)

♛ **HOUSE ADAMANT**

# REGENT'S MATE

## BOOK FOUR

### OF THE HOUSE ADAMANT SERIES

## GLYNN STEWART

FAOLAN'S PEN
PUBLISHING
faolanspen.com

# ONE

"Incoming fire. Eighty shells. Defenses are active."

Nikola Adamant stood in the middle of Planetary Defense Center Mithral's Command Center like a statue carved from iron. Months inside the mountain containing Mithral had robbed his skin of much of its usual natural shadow, which only added to the impression of black-and-white stone.

His hair and uniform matched, with only the four gold pips of his rank interrupting the otherwise insignia-less black fatigues. That was an arrogance in itself, he knew. Only one Colonel in PDC Mithral didn't have unit patches and other insignia on their uniform.

Only one Colonel in PDC Mithral was in command, despite the presence of seven senior officers in the mountain.

"Four shells got through," a new report echoed through the intentionally quiet space.

The Command Center was kept at a steady fifteen degrees Celsius, with just enough airflow to keep the humans inside paying attention. From there, in theory, a General of the Royal Kingdom of Adamant Army could command the defense of the entire homeworld of the Kingdom.

All of the cables required for that had been cut months earlier, of course. Nikola did not command PDC Mithral as an RKAA—pronounced "Ar-Kah"—officer.

He commanded it as First Pentarch, the most senior of the five heirs who *should* have run for Election to replace his mother as King. Except that his uncle Benjamin, *Fifth* Pentarch until all of this began, had killed his entire family and claimed power as Regent.

Without even a fake or fixed Election, Nikola had to believe Benjamin Adamant's reign was doomed. At that moment, though, Benjamin controlled the government of the Star Kingdom of Adamant... and Nikola only controlled the largest and most powerful PDC on the planet.

"Damage report."

General Tóki Dam was an immense blonde behemoth of a man, with long hair and a beard kept neatly braided and maintained despite none of them having left PDC Mithral in months. Dam was the official commander of PDC Mithral and the divisions assigned to the mountain, but he'd sworn his service to Nikola's protection the moment the prince had touched down.

"We lost half a dozen sensor emitters in grid one-six-three-five," a technician told Dam. "We can get drones out to replace them momentarily, but we're watching for a second wave."

"Do we have a location on those guns?" Dam growled. "The Black Regent's people should know better than to poke the bear with that little firepower."

"They're testing us," Nikola observed. "After the last big bombardment, they want to know how much they weakened our defenses."

"Then let's not give them a second round. Coordinates?"

"Two-eighty-six-point-four-four degrees, eighty-six kilometers," someone reported. "We don't have an exact target; they're outside our reach for overhead. I can send in drones, but we'll lose them."

Mithral's guns were larger than anything the Regent's forces could bring to bear, but their two-hundred-kilometer range depended on their ability to find their targets. Normally, a mix of satellites and aerial drones gave RKAA a bubble of visibility that made the guns effective to their maximum range.

The Regent's forces had realized that. There were more antiaircraft and antidrone weapons in the slowly advancing positions than there was artillery.

"Then we don't try for an exact target," Nikola told the technician.

Every eye turned to him. He was always there. At least fifteen hours a day, listening, observing. He made a point of only interrupting Dam's authority in the Command Center if he needed to, which made his silence a clear and visible sign of support for the General.

"Your suggestion, Prince Nikola?" Dam asked.

"Were the shells of a type that could change their vector?" Nikola asked the techs.

"Negative, Your Highness," one confirmed. "The angular is exact. We just can't be certain of the radial. Variance is almost six hundred meters."

"At that range, that gives us a zone twenty meters across and twelve hundred meters long," he pointed out to Dam. "How much fire would it take to level the entire zone?"

"Minimum of one hundred guns," the General replied instantly. "They'd be well dug in. Making sure we take out the guns and any fortifications..."

"I estimate three hundred and fourteen Mark Forty-Five Dragon Shards," Nikola said. "Master Sergeant!"

The artillery NCO standing a step behind and to his left braced to attention. She was the senior noncommissioned officer in the entire mountain—General Dam's personal aide and keeper prior to this mess.

"I will have a team run the numbers immediately," Ivory Dustin promised. "We should be ready for a fire mission in twenty minutes."

Nikola looked back at her and nodded, all the permission she needed to march forward into the Command Center and corral a set of techs and computers for her task.

Dam stepped over to stand next to Nikola, close enough that he could have whispered. Instead, he spoke silently over their shared neural link.

*"Is this wise, Nikola?"* he asked. *"The Dragon Shards are one of our most powerful subnuclear munitions. We don't have many of them left."*

*"And by using them, we make my uncle think we have* more *left than we do,"* Nikola replied. *"More, we respond to this test with overwhelming force, demonstrating that we are far from beaten."*

"Incoming fire. Eighty shells. Defenses active."

The echo of the earlier report drew every eye to the main display. PDC Mithral was built into the largest mountain on Bastion's southern continent, also named Mithral. The Command Center itself was almost five kilometers above the surrounding valleys, and the summit was almost two kilometers above them.

None of the advancing Regent's forces had even entered the mountain range holding PDC Mithral, but that would change. It had taken them almost nine months to fully reduce PDC Ironhand, the other defense station on the southern continent, but Mithral had been able to support her sister installation.

Mithral had no such support. For two months since Ironhand's fall, Nikola had watched his uncle's forces close and tighten the noose around the people who'd sworn loyalty to him.

There *was* a way out, he knew. The problem was that so many of its pieces were out of his control.

"Five shells made it through. One hit in grid one-six-three-five again. The other four landed in one-six-four-six and one-six-four-five."

"Their fire is focused on those grid squares," Dam said. "That's strange. What game are they playing?"

"Unclear, ser. There's nothing special about that sector," a tech replied. "If their third salvo is as focused, we'll have a better chance if we angle our defenses around them—but that does make us more vulnerable everywhere else."

It was a gamble. Exactly the type of gamble that Benjamin Adamant would try to make them guess wrong on—though for all that the Admiral-turned-Regent was held up as the best tactician the Kingdom of Adamant had produced in a generation, Nikola was seeing evidence the man struggled outside his specialty.

Just not enough to change how the grinding civil war across Mithral had gone.

"Keep the focus spread," Dam said before Nikola could say anything.

The General had probably gone through the same thoughts, just faster. He had thirty years of experience on Nikola, after all. Nikola had earned his Colonelship, he believed firmly, but he'd been young for it—and had only *just* got his fourth pip a few months before everything went to hell.

"Or we could just not let them get a third shot in," Sergeant Dustin said, turning to look at her two superiors with an expression that reminded Nikola of his childhood teachers.

"Fire pattern is locked and loaded. One hundred twenty guns, two shots each. Two hundred forty Dragon Shard rounds."

The information hit Nikola's neural link as the NCO spoke. It took him only a few seconds to arrange it in a form his link could show him virtually and skim through the data. Centuries of expensive genetic engineering, starting with the trillionaire ancestor who'd founded the Kingdom, was good for some things.

"It looks good to me, Sergeant," he told her. "A bit conservative, honestly. We do want to make sure these guns stop shooting."

*"That's over seventy percent of our remaining Dragon Shards,"* Dam said through the neural link, pinging them both. *"I would rather not commit the remaining sixty to make a likelihood a certainty."*

"Any heavy fortifications will be shredded by the shards," Dustin said aloud. "We don't need them after the second salvo. We could bring in two more batteries firing conventional shots and have a third salvo of pure conventional shells."

The file Nikola was studying morphed as she spoke, suggesting that she'd already had that as a potential plan. Sixty more of the PDC's five-hundred-millimeter cannon firing regular high-explosive shells would add a notable degree of mess to the first two salvos, but it was the added salvo of a hundred and eighty guns dropping half-meter shells across the target zone that would probably finish the job.

Nikola nodded toward Dam.

"They're your guns, General," he said. Both of them knew that the real discussion had been the silent one between them. Dam *would* pull him up short if the General thought there was a real danger in one of Nikola's decisions, but they'd have their arguments in the most private place possible: their heads, and the network between their own implants.

"Pass the orders. I want that fire mission on its way before those howitzers fire again," Dam ordered.

Not that the Regent's guns were pushing themselves. Assuming the unit was using the same guns Nikola was familiar with—likely, since the Royal Adamant Marine Corps hadn't *had* their own mobile artillery, and the Government didn't seem to be relying on RAMC troops anymore—they could be firing every ninety seconds.

Not every ten minutes. Like he'd told Dam before, the Regency troops were testing them.

"Fire pattern downloaded. Batteries West Alpha, West Bravo, West Charlie, North Alpha, North Bravo and South Charlie are standing by for your order, ser," Dustin announced.

"Maximum fire rate. Commence in T-minus ten from *now*."

Half of Dam's commands were silent, flickering out over the network where Nikola was aware of them even if he couldn't hear them. The pause between order and execution certainly didn't *feel* ten seconds long, but it was there to make sure that all one hundred and eighty guns fired at the exact same moment.

Even after eleven months buried in the PDCs, Nikola expected to feel or hear something when the immense five-hundred-millimeter weapons fired. A full half of PDC Mithral's guns sounded at once, but the tremor in the ground was so gentle, he wasn't sure if he was imagining it.

Thirty seconds later, just before the first shells even landed, the second salvo fired. This time, Nikola assured himself that yes, he *could* feel the tremor.

Ninety-two seconds after the first gun fired, the last shell struck home.

"Last salvo included surveillance shells," Dustin reported, before Nikola or Dam could ask if she knew how much damage had been done. "Showing visuals while we work on the damage assessment."

The visual made Nikola shiver. Dragon Shards were designed to destroy fortification complexes much like the ones the Regency forces had hidden their guns inside. The Shards were armor-piercing cluster munitions, intended to punch through concrete, dirt, or vehicle armor with equal efficacy before detonating inside their target.

There was a lot more *explosive* in a standard five-hundred-millimeter shell, but the Dragon Shards applied their destructive force over a larger area and with far less concern for defenses.

An area over a kilometer long and a hundred meters wide looked like an angry god had taken a trowel to it, *cutting* a slice of earth from Bastion's crust and tossing it in the air.

The surveillance shells would have arrived a few seconds later than the rest, which gave the watching Command Center crew a bird's-eye view of the third salvos impacted. It didn't look like there was much *left* for those immense projectiles to wreck, but Nikola knew the reality was starkly different.

That was the point of the concrete bunkers and jammers and armor panels and everything that made up the bunkers they'd just devastated, after all. It wasn't just about stopping lesser munitions from breaking through. It was also about reducing the impact of what did make it through to a level where, say, a mobile artillery vehicle's armor could handle the blow.

Nikola forced himself to watch as the shells detonated, tearing the soil of his homeworld to the same pieces as his orders had torn the flesh of his people.

"Damage assessment is total, ser," Dustin said quietly. "Some of the scans from the surveillance shells suggest that there were several mobile guns trying to make a break for it when the third salvo landed, though. Turned out we did need those extra—"

"Breach!"

Nikola froze. That was impossible. They might have lost their satellite connections and have difficulty getting drones more than sixty kilometers from the PDC's perimeter, but *inside* that sixty-kilometer radius, nothing moved without them knowing.

"Report, Lieutenant Major," Dam growled. Experience meant he didn't dwell on what was impossible, Nikola realized. He just dealt with what was in front of them.

"Surface-integrity scanners in grid one-six-three-six have flagged red," Lieutenant Major Emmanuel Burns replied. The officer who'd spoken was probably one of the most junior officers in the room, Nikola realized—but he was steady under the direct attention of every *other* officer in the Command Center. "Something breached the exterior shell of the PDC—we're working on exact location and—"

"They came through the air intake," a different officer interrupted. "Apologies, Emmanuel," Lieutenant Colonel Amaterasu Fontaine told the junior officer, placing her hand briefly on Major Burns' shoulder. "We would never have seen it without you flagging the integrity-scanner blip."

Fontaine, Nikola realized, was in charge of PDC Mithral's life-support systems. It probably *should* have been her who caught the breach of the air intakes, but he figured it was a good thing she gave the credit to Burns.

"Who came in through the intake?" Dam demanded.

"I have no idea," Fontaine admitted. "There are visual scanners on all exterior intakes, along with everything else the designers could think of. None of them show *anything*—except that the intake cover was removed, which triggered the surface-integrity alert."

"Show me," Nikola ordered, a shard of ice taking up residence in his chest.

One of the nearby screens switched over, showing the air intake. It was almost invisible from the outside, built into a cleft of stone carved in such a way as to be obscured from all but exactly the right angle. A metal grill had been shifted aside and not put back, but otherwise, there was no...

Nikola had spent several years as a teenager obsessed with the concept of tracking and hunting. He'd never actually hunted a live creature—hunting for sport would be anathema to his family—but he'd done a *lot* of virtual simulations and training, including going out into the wild with a zoology specialist and learning how to track in the real world.

"Footprints," he told everyone, inserting his link into the control feed and zooming in on the markers of human passage. "They left footprints in the dirt."

"The scanners show *nobody*, Your Highness," Burns told him. "Which means they're capable of circumventing both our scanners and cameras."

"Nothing the Kingdom has could do this," Dam noted. "But that does not mean it's impossible."

"No," Nikola agreed. The frozen shard in his chest wasn't moving, and he pulled up the map of PDC Mithral that lived in his link. "And that intake puts them only four hundred meters from the Command Center, General.

"What's in position to cut them off?"

"We can't even locate them," Fontaine said. "I'm running internal sensors all over the place, and we don't see *anyone* who isn't cleared to be in here."

"There." Burns interrupted, pulling up a schematic of the PDC and highlighting a spot. "They moved through the air intake until they either couldn't progress or thought they were inside our heavy-sensor perimeter.

"They just breached the wall between the air-intake venting and the nearest corridor. It's one of the narrower spots—they have to have schematics."

"Of course they have schematics," Dam told the young man. "But that's a damn fine catch. We can't see them, but we can see where they breach doors and walls because of the integrity network."

"Close every door around them," Nikola ordered. "And every door between them and the Command Center. If we can only track them by what they break, we make them break as much as we can before they reach us."

His words killed any remaining conversation in the room, and every eye was suddenly on him.

"They're coming here," he reiterated, sweeping his people with a calm gaze that didn't reflect his own feelings. He wasn't afraid—he hadn't been *afraid* since the day most of his bodyguards had died getting him clear of an assassination attempt ordered by his favorite uncle—but he certainly wasn't *calm*.

"Again, General, what's in position to block them?" he asked. "We can assume we're looking at a relatively small group of special ops troops, probably equipped with gear smuggled from the United Worlds.

"They won't have the numbers for any major resistance, but if they can take this room, they can shut down *everything*."

They wouldn't hold it for long, but they wouldn't have to. The Royal Adamant Marine Corps, like the Royal Kingdom of Adamant Navy, seemed to have put their faith in the Admiral who'd commanded them and followed the Regency without question.

RAMC assault shuttles could make it from Home Fleet to PDC Mithral in less than ten minutes. If this was at all planned, the shuttles might already be in space, just waiting for the signal.

"There's nothing in the way, Your Highness," Dam finally told him. "The closest troops are at Nexus Five-Sixty-Two, almost half a kilometer away—and they're light infantry, intended for internal security more than withstanding any kind of breach."

Nikola *still* wasn't afraid, though he could feel the fear in the room. Instead, he turned to the Command Center entrance, where two men in the gray-on-gray uniform of the Adamant Guard stood silent sentinel.

"There may not be troops, General, but it's not true that there is nothing in the way," he told Dam. "Alexei!"

Major Alexei Krupin stepped away from the wall, animating into a deadly hawk-faced soldier at the First Pentarch's word.

As dark-haired as his Prince but even more sharply featured, Krupin had stood behind and beside Nikola Adamant since he'd been five years old. Nikola was certain Krupin was the only reason he'd survived the Regent's coup attempt.

"What do we have?" he demanded from his Guard.

"I have Ten Guard and fifteen Companions in the immediate area, Your Highness," Krupin told him. The Companions were a strange addition, volunteers from Nikola's old brigade that Krupin had accepted as necessary for the Pentarch's security—but had been unwilling to name Adamant Guards.

At least partially because it was the Adamant Guard who had nearly killed Nikola. Even several Guards of Nikola's own Atilla Detail had joined the attack.

"We have armor." It wasn't a question.

"We do."

"Then lead me to my gear, Major. We have a mountain to protect."

"Ser, this is—"

Nikola cut Dam off with a raised hand.

"*There is no one else,*" he told his friend silently, keeping the conversation silent so neither of them undermined the other. "*One man in armor may make all the difference.*"

"*You are the Pentarch!*"

*"And I am Adamant,"* Nikola countered. *"Our Realm. Our House. Our Will. Adamant.*

*"I will not let this mountain fall because I refused to take up arms in my own defense."*

# TWO

Nikola's armor was waiting for him, its limbs and chest plate wide open to allow him to step into the suit. Normally, there would be a dozen preparatory steps, at least, before he even triggered the opening protocols, but there was no time.

Not with invisible raiders inside PDC Mithral and already on their way to the Command Center.

The powered battle armor was a comforting shell, even the faded scent of washed-away sweat and lubrication feeling like home as the panels closed around him. This was *his* armor, the suit that had been made for him twelve years earlier when he'd completed the Advanced Armored Infantry Curriculum.

That thought brought up old memories he tried to suppress. His grinning little sister—seventeen at the time to his twenty, still six months from entering the Navy Academy—stepping up to him and inflicting the ceremonial "first scar" on his suit with a paintball gun.

Any memory of his family was painful. Lorraine was gone, just like Taura and Daniel and their parents, King Valeriya Adamant and her husband Frederick Adamant-Griffin.

His nieces, the daughters of his eldest brother, lived. They were the only members of his immediate family he *knew* lived.

There were questions about Lorraine. The Regency's strictly controlled media had latched on to her as a scapegoat for the coup, blaming the deaths of their family on her. But Nikola would not allow himself false hope.

The only hands that would save the Kingdom of Adamant were his. He had fought and sacrificed and promised to bring about that salvation, and he would not weaken himself with the faint dream that his sister had somehow succeeded in her part of their mother's fall-back plan.

Her part had been the Exodus Protocols, to flee and bring back help, but it had been *Nikola* who'd made contact with their father's people, the Five Families of the Concordat of Amal Jadid. They hadn't heard from her, and that told him she was dead.

She would have been briefed on the Masada Protocols, on the arrangements made for him to stand and fight until relief arrived. He knew, in his heart, that Lorraine Adamant would never have left him to this fight alone. Since neither he nor their closest allies had heard from her, he knew she had died.

And that had only made her an easier scapegoat for their uncle.

"Your Highness."

Without even a conscious thought, Nikola reached out to take the heavy blaster rifle offered to him. The RKAA Sergeant handing him the weapon was from the First Armored Division's Second Strike Brigade, the unit that Nikola had commanded before this.

He owed his life to the Second-of-First. There was a *reason* the "Companions" were drawn from that brigade—and most of them had been on the landing pad that awful day when one of his own body-guards had cleared the landing of a death squad coming for him.

She'd *also* pulled a gun on him herself before the death squad had arrived, but that didn't really make it any better.

The Sergeant hooked the control and power umbilicals from the rifle into Nikola's suit. Like the suit itself, there should have been a checklist before that was done, but there was no time.

"Report," Nikola said into the tactical network as the indicators flashed across his screen. The armor had configurations that would allow him to run for miles and leap medium-sized buildings. They weren't set up in that mode today.

Today, he had twelve hours of power, dispersal shielding that would stand up to the primary weapons on most combat vehicles—once—and a portable "rifle" that could punch through the armor of anything lighter than a main battle tank.

They were going to make a giant mess of wherever they met the raiders, but he was taking no chances.

"All fire teams locked and loaded," Krupin told him. "We're ready to move as soon as we have a target."

"Understood."

A thought switched his radio channel over to a link back to General Dam.

"General, have we located them yet?"

"We still can't *see* them," Dam told him grimly. "But locking all the doors was a damn good idea, Nikola. We're tracking them by the breaches—they are *definitely* headed our way.

"I've ordered the evacuation of anyone in their route. A few dozen clerks with sidearms are just going to get killed, not stop this mess."

"Link me to a schematic tracking their progress," Nikola instructed. It popped up in his neural link and his helmet display a moment later—the Command Center team had only been waiting for the word.

"Got them. One last ask, General," he said.

"I'm guessing it's not to get you somewhere to hide."

It was literally Alexei Krupin's job to keep Nikola alive, and Dam was still more of an overprotective mother hen than the bodyguard. Nikola wasn't going to hold it against Dam, though.

If Nikola died, everything Dam had sacrificed his command and his troops for died with him.

"When I give the order, trigger full fire-suppression protocols in whatever corridor segment the raiders are in," Nikola told his friend. "There are only a few ways they can be making themselves invisible to our sensors like this—and I don't think any of them will stand up to the bastards being covered in foam."

"NOW."

The bulkhead in front of Nikola's Companions was heavier-duty than most of the hatches they'd forced the intruders to breach. This was a blast door, part of the segmentation intended to keep the PDC online and firing even faced with ground-penetrating nukes.

It wouldn't have held the raiders for long—but it had stymied them for a few minutes. Enough minutes for Nikola to put twenty-six suits of battle armor in heavy-combat mode on the other side.

And since being able to both open and close the blast doors swiftly had been a key part of the design, the raiders were *not* ready for what happened at his order.

A solid wall of battleship-hull-grade composites slid smoothly and speedily into the ceiling—and at the same moment, every square meter of ceiling on the other side produced its own spray nozzle and began dispensing foam.

Nikola had a few moments to be stunned at how effective the smart camouflage the Regency troops were using was—even knowing they were there, with the full power of his armor's sensors, he *still* could only pick out a few outlines—before they were drenched with suppressant foam and suddenly *very* visible.

"Open fire."

Even with the foam making the targets clearly visible, Nikola's suit still struggled to identify them as hostile humans. Normally, the computers and servomotors in the suit combined to do at least half of the work of aiming for him—but like any good RKAA trooper, he'd also made sure that he could fire any weapon in his personal arsenal with no aid whatsoever.

The leading foam-shrouded figure took a blast from Nikola's rifle full in the chest, a perfect center-mass shot that should have gone clean through almost any personal armor. It hurled them backward several steps with visible force, but they were still moving, bringing up their own weapon.

A hail of energy fire swept down the corridor from his Companions, but only a handful of the raiders went down. Whoever these people were, their gear not only made them invisible, it did a *hell* of a lot better of a job dispersing energy than the Adamantine armor.

Instinct drove Nikola forward, left, and down. He hit one knee just in time for a pulse of laser fire to tear through the air where his head had been—a powerful-enough pulse that he heard the *crack* of air vaporizing as the beam flared.

He locked his attention back on the raider he'd hit. They might have survived, but their stealth system had been degraded enough that his suit *could* pick them out now.

He fired his rifle again—and, in the same moment, mentally triggered a command to his secondary systems. His target sidestepped the blaster shot—unlike the lasers, the plasma packets from the heavy weapons weren't lightspeed, though that *still* shouldn't have been possible—but couldn't dodge the half-dozen seeker missiles that launched from his shoulder.

The armor-piercing weapons could only lock on to a twenty-five-centimeter-wide chunk of the raider's breastplate. All six of them hammering into that spot would probably have broken the armor from full strength. Against plating already degraded by a direct heavy blaster hit, the poor bastard never stood a chance.

Nikola knew he was losing people. His neural link flashed an alert each time one of his troopers was hit, but this was a knife fight in a hallway. There was nowhere to dodge, nothing else he could do. He'd given his people the only chance they had against hostiles with invisibility, and now all he could do was find and shoot down targets.

He found a second target and fired at them—and realized that Krupin and at least one of the Companions were following his targeting data. The enemy suits were clearly running some kind of active dodge routine to keep their occupants alive, but what could dodge one shot couldn't dodge three.

Two of the plasma bolts hit home, close enough to each other to breach the armor and send the raider collapsing to the floor.

"Sync your fire," Nikola barked. "Attack by fire team."

He should have given that order before opening the damn blast door, he realized. It might have been micromanaging, but clearly, none of them had anticipated super-tech invisibility armor to also be tougher than anything they'd ever faced.

The laser weapons the raiders were using were brutally powerful. The Companions they hit went down, and most of them stayed down —but there were twenty-five troops with Nikola and only a dozen of the raiders.

The fight should have been over the moment it began, but it only lasted eighty-seven seconds per his suit's computer before the last shots fell to silence.

"Check in," Nikola ordered. The status reports filled half of his helmet, and he was glad for the fact that no one could see his face. Four more of his Adamant Guard were dead, another three wounded.

Nine of the Companions had joined them in death, along with five more wounded. Of the twenty-five troops he'd brought to the fight, only four were unwounded.

A number that did not include Major Krupin, he realized grimly.

"Dam, we need medical help up here immediately," he told the General. "And then the best forensics and technicians you've got. This was something new, and I need to know exactly what the Regency has dug up to throw at us."

He already knew that whatever the techs dug out of the foam-covered dead raiders in the hall, it was going to be bad news.

There was no way those suits had been built in Adamantine. The Regency had outside help—and the *best* case he could think of was that it came from the Bright Dream Republic, the most advanced state in their cluster.

Bright Dream was months' travel away, but their power came from holding the wormhole that led back toward Sol and the heart of human space.

And the worst case Nikola could see was that the armor came from the other side of that wormhole.

# THREE

"Honored guests, I present Her Royal Highness, Second Pentarch of our Kingdom of Adamant, Princess Lorraine Alexis Elouise Nala Adamant!"

The herald's voice boomed across the ballroom without an ounce of technological assistance, yet no one in the gilded space could possibly have missed his words.

Certainly, it felt like every eye in the room was on Lorraine as she stood in the massive double doors, two gray-uniformed Adamant Guards flanking her. The Grand Hall of Ominira House was easily two hundred meters wide and half again that long, with floating orbs hanging throughout to provide light even with the roof open to the late-evening sky above them.

There was nothing in Lorraine's clothes to draw the eyes, but she was unsurprised. She wore an unmarked version of an RKAN flag officer's uniform rather than the elegant dresses, robes and suits covering many of the guests in the space, but she needed no insignia.

She'd been in the Ominira System and on Ife Tuntun, the main habitable planet, for three days. For most of those days, she'd been met everywhere she went by cheering crowds—and her Adamant

Guard had been working overtime handling the covert agents of her uncle's Regency.

If there was anyone on the *planet* who hadn't known the Second Pentarch by sight before she'd arrived, they did now. Duty and politics dragged her out to this formal reception for the ambassador of the Kingdom of Aabo, even if Aabo's single star system was utterly irrelevant to the civil war she was facing or the other problems she knew were coming after it.

Major Vigo Jarret gave her a small smile as he stepped past her to lead the way into the Grand Hall. She needed that smile, and it gave her strength to follow him.

The massive, darkly colored Major was the senior officer of Archangel Detail, the Adamant Guard detachment tasked with keeping her alive. She wouldn't have managed to *leave* the Kingdom without him, let alone reach Earth, complete her mission and return.

The strange way she'd completed said mission had required not only his seemingly infinite strength and support but also his flexibility. Even on the surface of Ife Tuntun, there was a humming connection in her neural link, a permanent connection to Val, the powerful synthetic intelligence running her flagship.

The United Worlds Navy battlecruiser *Valkyrie* had been equipped with a Command Intelligence Routine, a capable but nonsapient computer system intended to give the crew and officers a whole new level of flexible automated support.

Except that the CIRs had emerged as true synthetic intelligences —and instead of dealing with the new people they'd accidentally created, the UWN had buried them.

And then Lorraine had found them and made friends.

"Your Highness, I am delighted that you were able to join us this evening," a familiar voice said from her right as Deputy Governor Gianna Mazza slid into step next to her.

Close work with the other woman had proven her both competent and friendly, but her dark hair and ice-pale skin left new acquaintances with a chilly first impression. A first impression Mazza was clearly willing to lean in to if she thought it would serve her purposes.

"Every part of this evening has been choreographed to the millimeter, Gianna," Lorraine murmured. Mazza's other hat was as Minister of Security, which left her tasked with making sure Governor Olusola Afolayan, his various officials, his guests and his Princess survived the night unscathed.

And with doing much of the choreographing of Lorraine's presence there.

"Now, now, none of this is new to you," Mazza replied, her voice equally soft. They could communicate by link, but both of them seemed to draw some amusement with the conversation. "One quick chat with Ambassador Abioye to start. It wouldn't do to offend our guest of honor."

"Of course not," Lorraine agreed, allowing Mazza and Jarret to subtly guide her toward that worthy, a towering figure with inhumanly onyx-black skin and eyes of nearly emerald green.

Lorraine was no stranger to genetic modification. Every piece of her genome that her ancestors could modify to give themselves an edge had been touched. The truth was that there were few clear "wins" in such genetic augmentation, but everyone always seemed to think they'd found the acceptable trade-offs.

Her own height, gold-green hazel eyes, and permanently lightly tanned skin were products of that modification, as were her high compatibility with cybernetics and a few other useful abilities. She paid for them with both a higher caloric intake and a number of food sensitivities only barely managed by her cybernetics.

She wasn't certain what Ola Abioye's ancestors had thought they were buying with the uniquely inhuman coloring of the ambassador, but Abioye clearly knew how to make use of their standout appearance.

They didn't tower as much over Lorraine as most of the rest of the crowd, which helped them see her coming. A few words in Yoruba dismissed several hangers-on, and they bowed deeply when Lorraine stepped into their immediate circle.

"Your Highness, my Kingdom is honored by your attention," they told her. "The unfortunate affairs sweeping your nation have drawn our eyes. While my journey to the Kingdom of Adamant has been planned for some time, we had hoped for it to have happier purposes and take place in better times."

*"Does Aabo not have a permanent embassy?"* Val asked in Lorraine's link. The SI had absorbed every piece of hard data on the region she could find, but Lorraine knew that wasn't the same as knowing the area and the people intimately.

*"They find themselves in an awkward position between us and the Richelieu Directorate,"* Lorraine replied. *"They trade more with us and—I'm told—prefer us. But the Richards are significantly closer, and only performative neutrality keeps Aabo from being threatened.*

*"So, they 'allow' both us and the Directorate to keep embassies there, but only send embassies out every two or three years to either of us."*

"Few of us wish to live in times like these, of course," she told Abioye calmly. She knew that no one could tell she'd been speaking to Val, but she still needed to focus on the man. "I understand, of course, that Aabo could hardly spare vessels from her own defense to assist against my uncle.

"Even if you were prepared to take a side in what you must see as an internal matter."

They bowed their head in acknowledgement, their gemlike eyes studying her intently enough to put a spike of discomfort through even her diplomatic training.

"We appreciate your understanding," Abioye agreed. "I hope to be able to speak with the new King once they are elected, but duty to my King requires me to speak with those... representing all sides in this question."

Thankfully, the Aabo courier was only capable of eighty-eight times the speed of light—a fast ship by the standards of even a first-order cluster like theirs but far slower than Lorraine's *Valkyries*. Abioye wouldn't beat her to Adamantine.

"As it is my duty to end my ill-fated uncle's coup and restore the traditions and constitution of my people," she assured him. "I see no likely change to our relationship with Aabo under either regime, I must admit."

Aabo's only capital ships were castoffs from the Richelieu and Adamantine navies. They refitted them extensively, but their three battleships were old ships that couldn't stand up to their neighbors.

"Such changes are what I was originally supposed to seek," Abioye admitted. "Though the affair was more... personal than it will be now, I fear."

That didn't fit the briefing Mazza had given Lorraine, and she gave the Ambassador a questioning look. The every-two-years embassy was mostly a touchpoint, a renewing of relationships and an opportunity to discuss high-level trade disputes before they could become serious conflicts.

"I'm not sure how personal an embassy visit can be, Your Excellency," she allowed.

Abioye smiled.

"That is because your family has at least *attempted* to avoid some of the inevitable segregation of noble houses other systems embrace," they told her. "My King finds himself surrounded by families that have not been so wise, and as such, his position is difficult."

Lorraine didn't *quite* catch where Abioye was going until she heard Mazza's sharp inhalation.

"King Olawale is only a year younger than you, of course, Princess Lorraine," they noted. "Meeting with you tonight fulfills a task that was to be a major part of my commission, Your Highness, to judge whether you would be a potential marriage match for him."

That left her almost literally flat-footed—and thankful for the choreographing of her evening that was going to move her on shortly. She knew her eldest brother, Daniel, had ended up in an arranged marriage with the heir of a wealthy Adamantine industrial family to make certain there was a new generation of heirs—but he'd *volunteered* for that after his love match had exploded in his face.

And while Lavender had been even unluckier in love than Daniel prior to their wedding, it had worked out well for them.

Lorraine had never even considered anything resembling a state wedding for herself! Though, given that she'd had to shoot the last man she'd loved...

"I do not believe that those are the times we live in," she finally told Abioye. "I do not know how a Lorraine that had not lived through the last year would have greeted your King's interest, but I must focus on my own Kingdom."

"I understand and agree," the Ambassador said, with a bow of their head. "It is something of a shame. I do believe you would have been an excellent partner for my King... though I think *your* Kingdom is lucky to have you."

AMBASSADOR ABIOYE'S revelation of the original reason for his trip to Adamant had thrown Lorraine off-balance more than she could afford to show. Fortunately, she was being shepherded around by people for whom his offhand remark had been much less personal.

Autopilot and years of training carried her through polite conversation with several industrial magnates, two Ambassadors who weren't tonight's guest of honor, and several key politicians from the system legislature.

But the careful circuit through the guests brought her to the woman she was there to speak with above all others. Diplomacy, politics, and keeping her hand concealed had meant she needed to speak with Abioye and the others to cover her tracks, but she had decided to be shown off to the public and the media at that party, that night, to make sure that she was in the same room as Zarifa Naeema Griffin.

"Cousin," the woman greeted Lorraine as their bodyguards smoothly merged. Lorraine doubted anyone would have missed the familial resemblance, though features and coloring muted by Adamant genetic engineering were on full display on Zarifa Griffin's face, and the Concordat diplomat's eyes were so dark brown as to look black in most lighting.

Griffin wore a crimson red sari tied into a black bodice, woven around her to expose both her left shoulder and her midriff. Loose as the garment looked, it barely shifted as Lorraine's second cousin bowed.

"Cousin," Lorraine returned the greeting. "Walk with me?" She gestured toward the exit to a nearby garden balcony, like Griffin's position next to the door hadn't been as planned as Lorraine's approach.

"Of course. It has been some time."

The balcony was a semiprivate space, with only two accesses into and out of the building. It was a full two stories up from the grounds, providing an excellent view of a perfectly landscaped maze cut from local Ominiran vegetation.

After almost a year on the run, Lorraine barely needed the silent pings from Vigo Jarret on her neural link to locate the security personnel scattered through the garden. There were two of her Guards and at least a dozen members of the Third Warder Division making sure no threats approached Ominira House.

Normally, those gardens were open to any of the resident of Ibalẹ City—and the rest of the Ominira System, for that matter. For tonight, though, they were closed as security troops made certain their Princess and their Governor's other guests were unthreatened.

Glancing over at the other access to the balcony, Lorraine met Guard Sergeant Merle's steady gaze. The Guard shouldn't have been out of a medical suite yet—as the cart-mounted medical suite covering his still-growing new arm made clear—but he nodded silently to her.

"Jammers, white-noise generators, Adamant Guards, and even local troops," the diplomat she'd led out observed. "It's almost like being back home. We're not quite this bad... but we're also not fighting an actual civil war."

"No, you're not," Lorraine conceded. The Five Families of the Three Stars, the ruling noble houses of the Concordat of Amal Jadid, were constantly engaged in a level of political back-and-forth that was mildly concerning in an ally.

There were seven parties in the Concordat's Popular Assembly, but the five most powerful were openly sponsored by the Five Families. In politics and business, the Families were partners and competitors at the same time.

That led to a level of personal security even the daughter of Adamant's King had rarely seen outside of wartime. Of course, that security meant that very little untoward actually *happened* between the Families.

"I'll warn you, cousin, I'm only a trade attaché," Griffin observed. "I can barely speak for the Griffin Family in non-economic matters, let alone the Popular Assembly or the Concordat."

Lorraine chuckled.

"Officially."

"Officially," her cousin conceded. They didn't know each other well, but they had enjoyed what time they had spent together as younger women. Zarifa Griffin was only six months older than Lorraine and had dedicated her life to her career in much the same way.

"I need to know if there's any chance of the Concordat coming in to support Benjamin, Zarifa," Lorraine said quickly. "We don't have a great deal of time before we have to head back inside to avoid attention."

"You think we might support the Regency?" Zarifa sounded surprised, potentially even offended, at the thought. "No, the Five Families may not be able to agree on much, but we know damn well that Benjamin Adamant murdered Frederick Griffin-Adamant.

"We're cynical enough that we won't help *you* for free, but we will sign no contracts highlighted in our own blood, Lorraine.

Benjamin has received a cold shoulder from the Concordat, and he will continue to do so for as long as he lives.

"Our alliance with the Kingdom is valuable enough that the Assembly wants to keep it, but he killed your father, Lorraine. My father's cousin. A Griffin of the first lineages. If the Directorate wages war again? We'll stand with him for our own safety.

"But against the civil war he started? No. The Concordat Navy is not for sale to him."

"Or the Directorate, I hope," Lorraine murmured.

Zarifa laughed and bumped Lorraine's shoulder with her own.

"There is enough blood in the papers between us and Richelieu, I think you need not fear a contract on that line, my cousin. We fought them without you before we fought them alongside you, after all."

If there was one thing the Five Families and House Adamant were in solid alignment on, it was the value of revenge. There were times when pragmatism required it to be laid aside, but the dead could not be forgotten.

"*The Concordat of Amal Jahid is some distance from the Directorate, but I see the history Em Griffin speaks of,*" Val noted in Lorraine's head. "*Why would they attack Amal Jahid across such a distance?*"

"*Because everyone closer was either us or the Monroe Republic—large enough to be a danger in their own right—or had signed mutual-defense treaties with us or the Monroes,*" she replied silently. "*The Concordat was far enough away that the Five Families thought they were the dangerous neighbor. Distance was the only thing that saved them then.*"

"I take it that the Concordat Navy might be for sale to me," Lorraine told her cousin.

There was a long silence.

"*Might* isn't the word, cousin," Zarifa finally said. "The Navy is likely not only available to you but at a discount. Family has meaning for us, after all.

"That said, *I* do not have the authority for that. I can send a courier home with the request, but that's a sixty-day trip. If you have an offer, I can send that—but even if they're heading to Adamantine, you're talking nearly four standard months before the earliest the fleet could arrive."

"I can follow the math," Lorraine noted. She was a naval officer *and* she had a master's degree in the science that underlay the trans-light drive. All ships traveled at an integer multiple of the tachyon quanta, a fundamental constant that defined the velocities at which tachyons could transit the universe.

That quanta was approximately eight times the speed of light, which meant that, for example, fast couriers in the Bright Dream Cluster—or, at least, the part of it around Adamantine—traveled at ninety-six *c*. Most warships could manage seventy-two or eighty, with a few eighty-eight *c* ships in the larger navies.

Of course, the closer one got to the wormhole back to the United Worlds, the better the tech got. The Republic of Bright Dream had eighty-eight-*c* capital ships as their standard, where RKAN had less than ten eighty-eight-*c* warships in total.

The section of space between the Bright Dream Wormhole back toward the home stars and the Kang Tao Wormhole that linked out to a second-order cluster of colonies was generally wealthier and more advanced that the backwater Lorraine called home.

Backwater or not, though, it *was* her home, and she was going to set it right.

"I'll pass the word back home that you've returned and are making a play, but I don't think you want to give me enough information that the CAJN could help you," Zarifa concluded, pronouncing the acronym for the Concordat of Amal Jahid Navy as "Cajun."

"Anything we don't know, we can't leak."

"That same time loop applies to any leaks," Lorraine told her cousin with a chuckle. "Let the Popular Assembly and the Families know that I'm back and I have the force to end this civil war. I don't think things are going to drag on long enough—as much as anything,

Zarifa, I needed to know that your Navy *was* back in the Concordat and not helping reinforce Benjamin's Home Fleet."

"I left sixty days ago, so I don't know where our Navy is," Zarifa replied. "But I swear to you, cousin, the Concordat will either stay out of this war or come in against Benjamin."

*"Time is up, Lorraine. We have to circulate,"* Vigo said silently in her head.

From Zarifa's sudden blink, her own bodyguards had sent her a similar message.

"There will be another time for us to catch up, I hope," Lorraine said. "A happier time."

"I don't think times come much unhappier than this, I'm afraid. Kinslaying and civil war are scars no family or state should have to bear."

"And that, Zarifa, is why I am going to *end* this war."

# FOUR

The next morning, Lorraine paced a borrowed office in an office building whose ownership was buried behind seven different layers of front companies. The structure looked identical to a hundred other mid-scale towers of twenty or so stories across Ibalẹ on the outside, though anyone who made it past the ground-floor lobby would swiftly realize they'd made a mistake.

The exterior windows looked in on a false front of offices and cubicles that ended at an armored shell invisible from the outside. The real offices and workspaces were inside that armored shell, with no external windows to weaken the integrity of the armor.

Ominira System Security was little more than an administration center, a branch of the system's government that coordinated between Ife Tuntun Planetary Defense Command—a fortress command of the Royal Kingdom of Adamant Army—the Ominira System Guard—a subordinate command of the Royal Adamant Space Guard—the RKAN Ominira Station and local security forces.

Theoretically civilian and administrative or not, the main OSS office was secure, with excellent communications and data-management systems.

From there, Lorraine could access all of the information on the various military forces available to her. The only one of the Kingdom of Adamant's four military arms she didn't have represented on the virtual displays swirling around her was the Royal Adamant Marine Corps.

RAMC—even in her head, it was *Ram-see*—had proven too loyal to Benjamin Adamant to trust. Of the three Marine Divisions positioned in Ominira, two had already returned to Adamantine to shore up the Regency.

The other, split between the RKAN ships and bases in the system, had been regretfully disarmed. No one had been arrested or detained—or even fired; they were all still drawing their salaries—but Lorraine had made it clear that they were being watched and weren't to leave Ife Tuntun.

She had no official rank, but everyone had fallen in line behind her—including the staff of OSS, who had very clearly been running a covert resistance network throughout Ominira's military personnel.

Unannounced, there was suddenly someone standing in the room. Of course, the larger-than-life image of a Scandinavian Viking woman in an RKAN uniform didn't need to walk anywhere to appear in Lorraine's virtual displays.

Val wasn't even a hologram. It was just an avatar she'd inserted through Lorraine's neural link to allow them to talk "face-to-face," as much as they could.

"You are going in circles," the SI told her. "Chasing your tail, I believe I have heard others call it."

"Everyone is looking to me for an answer," Lorraine said quietly. "But we have four capital ships and Benjamin has ten. Seventeen escorts to his forty-four. Thanks to Afolayan and Colonel Volkova, I believe we can trust our ground troops, but we only have the transport for maybe ten divisions.

"Two hundred thousand soldiers against an entire planet."

She shook her head.

"I hope that my people will rally to us, that the RKAA troops on the planet will switch sides once there is a clear opposite side, but even retaking the capital..."

Adamant City was a well-designed city, home to over twenty million people. Lorraine knew it mostly as *home*, but she had the skills now to see how it was designed to be easy to defend. Even if the rest of the Adamantine System turned to her side, her uncle would have Adamant City locked down.

"Once we control the orbitals, we will have the operational mobility that the Regency has used against your brother," Val pointed out. "They will not be able to concentrate forces, and we will be able to bring whatever resources your brother has in play on our side."

Lorraine pulled up a display of information with a gesture.

"PDC Ironhand fell in December," she noted grimly. "Without the mutual support of Ironhand and Mithral, I don't know how long Nikola could have held out. It seems all too likely that the war on Bastion is already over and we simply haven't heard."

"According to the information I have from your people, PDC Mithral is the largest and most powerful fortification on Bastion. If any position can be held for three months without support, it would be that one."

Lorraine made an acknowledging gesture, studying the dimensions of her brother's fortress. She'd been stunned to learn that he'd survived the betrayal and had fallen back to the southern continent, Mithral, under a counterpart to the Exodus Protocols that had seen her sent out into the unknown.

The Masada Protocols' *name* told her everything she needed to. No one had survived the Roman siege of that ancient fortress. Nikola would hold as long as he could, but Lorraine didn't know how long that was.

"Every day we spend here, trying to decide what to do next, is a day my brother may die," she finally said. "The politics and diplomacy are important, but if we didn't need to manufacture missiles and train crews for you and the other *Valkyries*, I don't know if I could find the patience."

"We are now drawing resources from the Owo logistics base at Agbaye Lewa," Val told her. "Our missile magazines will be full within twenty-eight hours. Both the Speaker in Silicon and Colonel Placide Fitzwilliam have sent their regards."

"If there is one thing Fitzwilliam has, it's the fortitude to face this mess and tell me *hi*," Lorraine replied with a snort. Colonel Fitzwilliam had tried to detain her when her ship had stopped in Ominira on their way to the United Worlds—but he had also declined to fire on her ship when her uncle's loyalists had ordered him to.

"Unfortunately, what he does not have is UWN-grade railgun munitions," Val said grimly. "The only railgun rounds your people have been able to provide are solid slugs. Hardly useless at the velocity our weapons fire at, but lacking in flexibility compared to a proper TAM."

The terminal assault munition was one of the key advantages of the UWN, Lorraine had realized. Mass-produced on a scale no lesser state could dream of matching, the TAM was a warhead capable of twenty seconds of one thousand gravities of thrust, delivering a fifty-kiloton nuclear explosive.

And it was, for all intents and purposes, an entirely solid-state system. That was critical, because it meant the TAM could survive the over six *billion* gravities' acceleration of being fired through one of *Valkyrie*'s twin-octuple-banks of railguns.

"We knew that was going to be a problem," Lorraine conceded with a sigh. "I know we used up your stocks of the key alloys involved building the rounds we used to convince Tunison, but what *can* we do?"

"I am not certain," Val admitted. A rare admission, Lorraine knew—the synthetic intelligence had access to a *lot* of information, including a full military-tech database for the United Worlds Navy.

That database was ten years out of date, thanks to the *Valkyries* being shut down and put in reserve once the UWN realized they'd accidentally created SIs. Even so, the technology it contained was more advanced than anything the Kingdom of Adamant possessed.

Which came with other problems that Lorraine was going to have to deal with—*after* they'd handled the Regency.

"It's a tools-to-make-the-tools problem, right?" Lorraine asked.

"Yes. Your Kingdom does not currently possess sufficiently advanced metallurgy for us to manufacture the components necessary for TAMs. Developing that infrastructure to a scale allowing for mass production of TAMs would take years."

Lorraine stopped her pacing for a moment and turned to look at Val with a grim smile.

"We don't need mass production, Val," she reminded the SI. "Not unless you're handing over railgun schematics and we've started building *those*."

The most powerful railguns the Kingdom possessed were the ones built in to their planetary defense centers. While those weapons matched the final muzzle velocity of a UWN capital ship's sixteen railguns, they reached that one percent of lightspeed with barrels over two kilometers long—versus the *seventy meters* of the *Valkyrie's* guns.

"Could you build a limited metallurgy capability in your own machine shops?" Lorraine asked. "Enough that we could basically hand-make a small number of TAMs—or, at least, something we can fire through the railguns with terminal maneuverability?"

There was a pregnant pause.

"I will need to talk to Herc and Bonny, as well as Rose," Val admitted. "I am not certain what resources would be available in Ominira. Even if we can manage a limited production of the alloys, it will take us some weeks to manufacture a useful number of rounds."

"Even if we leave the RKAN ships behind, we're twenty-eight days from Adamantine," Lorraine said. "If you can give me even one salvo of proper rounds per ship by then, that's one hell of an ace up my sleeve."

She grinned, her brain automatically slipping into the chess metaphors her uncle had taught her. For all that she hated what Benjamin had done and become, he had still been her favorite uncle growing up. His influence was why she'd become a naval officer.

She was going to have to kill him, but that didn't mean she had to forget what he'd taught her.

"Or a queen, perhaps. Something for an unexpected checkmate."

"I am not aware of any records of someone sneaking an extra queen onto the board in any game of chess," Val said virtuously.

"That's because chess is a game and this is war. In chess, there's an umpire to make sure you're not cheating. In a fight like this?"

Lorraine smiled coldly as she considered the lists of troops and ships floating around her.

"If we aren't cheating, we aren't trying as hard as my people need us to."

# FIVE

It was Vigo Jarret's job, above almost anything else, to keep his Pentarch alive no matter what the universe threw at her. The problem was that he couldn't get in the way of her doing her duty—whether that had been flying a combat shuttle for RKAN, before all of this, or taking command of a dissident faction of their own Kingdom to wage a civil war.

If he thought she was doing something with a greater risk than reward, he'd tell her that, but he'd been Lorraine Adamant's bodyguard since she was six years old. After twenty-three years, he knew she would *listen* to his concerns... but she was an Adamant.

Once her mind was made up, nothing was going to stop her.

Which made the attempt by several members of the Ominiran government to convince her to hold her ground in the system and wait for reinforcements entertaining at best and a waste of time at worst.

"The Governor has been in communication with the system governments in Greenrock and Beulaiteuhom," RASG's Commodore Gaspard Laguardia reminded everyone. "While Tolkien has been openly and vociferously loyal to the Regency under the new Governor, we have some back-channel communications suggesting that if anyone openly raises banners against the Black Regent, they will swap sides in short order.

"With our allegiance here in Ominira, that would bring four of the six systems of the Kingdom into a single alliance."

Laguardia wasn't stupid, Vigo presumed. The RASG officer was soft-spoken, with a perfectly tailored custom uniform that was technically in violation of regulations—but only barely, and the Commodore was the senior RASG officer in the system.

"If Tolkien joins us, Commodores Davlatov and Aguilar would bring the *other* major non–Home Fleet command into our forces," Mazza observed. The Minister of Security wasn't making an argument, Vigo noted. Just providing information.

Commodore Kheireddine Davlatov was the official acting commanding officer in Tolkien with the death of the previous CO— who had *definitely* been Benjamin Adamant's man—in a car accident with her lover, the planetary governor.

In any other system of the Kingdom, Vigo figured that the Regency would have replaced the Navy commander and planetary governor with loyalists after losing Benjamin's main assets. Tolkien was always going to be a sore spot for the Black Regent, though. When he'd merely been a senior Admiral of RKAN, during the war with the Directorate, Benjamin had withdrawn from the Tolkien System when faced with a superior Richelieuan force.

He'd regrouped with Home Fleet and relieved the system as quickly as physically possible—but he had abandoned the system's populace and the Army troops there without a fight. Worse, King Valeriya had come with the relief fleet, which meant that Benjamin carried the weight of abandoning the system—but his sister got the credit for saving it.

Benjamin Adamant would step carefully around a Tolkien government that professed loyalty to him.

Plus, Commodore Oriana Aguilar was a war hero in Tolkien, the Flag Captain of the fleet that had relieved the system. Vigo trusted her loyalty to the Kingdom and her opposition to Benjamin, though he admitted he *didn't* know how King Valeriya's affair with the woman had ended.

He figured that if it had ended badly, Aguilar would have been flagged as a security risk by the Adamant Guard.

"Have you considered what that provides in terms of numbers, Commodore?" Lorraine finally said. She'd let Laguardia make his argument and run himself out; now she was gently guiding him toward the cliff.

"We would have your three battlecruisers, *Dreaming* from here, and *Aspiration* and *Pirate* from Tolkien. Four battlecruisers and two battleships. Entire wars have been fought with less!"

"Against enemies with similar forces," Afolayan noted. "Forgive the non-soldier here, my friends, but isn't Home Fleet our most powerful formation by far?"

"Yes."

The single word drew every eye to the woman seated at the table who had been silent since being introduced. Commodore Amina Biskup had skin the color of aged white jade, an almost translucent blue-white that suggested she'd never set foot under a natural sun's light.

Her hair was equally washed out, cropped close to her skull in a manner that, combined with her pale skin, made her neural cybernetics visible in a way that was uncomfortable to see. Biskup didn't have any *more* of the implants than anyone else, but Vigo had run into very few people where the location of the hardware was quite so obvious.

Despite her paleness, though, her lips were a startling bright red as she pursed them uncomfortably, and her green eyes were sharp as she stared at data only she could see.

Biskup was the only RKAN officer in the room—and until the thirty-first of January, had been Admiral Are Tunison's Operations Officer. Now she was the probationary commander of their second task group—half of their frigates and the battleship *Dreaming*.

Lorraine gestured to the woman.

"Lay it out, Amina," the Princess ordered.

"In the most optimistic case," Biskup said, her voice high-pitched and almost childlike, "we bring in every RKAN Station except Maka'melemele." She shrugged. "We could even co-opt the Maka'melemele Station, but no one has suggested that, so let's put them aside.

"That gives us two of RKAN's older battleships, one of the modern battlecruisers and three ex-UWN battlecruisers equipped with our munitions."

Vigo was grimly aware of how badly that degraded the *Valkyries'* capabilities. UWN missiles had fifty more gravities of acceleration in their primary boost, adding almost fifty thousand kilometers to their expected range. Add in their superior electronics and larger number of final warheads, and three properly equipped *Valkyries* could probably have fought all of Home Fleet.

"Ignoring the need to still provide protection, patrols and a deterrent against Richelieuan adventurism, we could concentrate those six capital ships in Adamantine in approximately forty-six days, assuming that Tolkien Station was ready to deploy immediately on receipt of our courier."

"We could not prevent couriers leaving the system when the Pentarch arrived," Mazza added. "We have roughly twenty-nine days until the Regency learns of your arrival."

There had never been a chance to get to Adamantine ahead of the couriers if they moved with any RKAN units, Vigo knew. *Dreaming* had a maximum translight pseudo-velocity of seventy-two times lightspeed, and that had been a matter of argument. All of the *Hopes* had been refitted to keep up with the new *Monarch* class, but the expense had been nontrivial.

"Which means that any offensive including RKAN units will face a prepared enemy, in which case it would be wise to bring the largest possible strength and wait for the escorts from Greenrock and

Beulaiteuhom," Commodore Biskup concluded. "That results in a final rendezvous date at least sixty-five days in the future."

"At which point we will have gathered all of the strength we possibly can," Laguardia noted. "A delay of a few weeks seems more than worth it."

"That delay would allow us to deploy six capital ships and fifty-eight escorts," Biskup confirmed. "Depending on whether the Regent's people can accelerate ships still under construction to get them into space by then, we would have a rough numerical match for Home Fleet."

But. Vigo knew the *but* and he knew Lorraine did as well. Laguardia probably did too, which made Vigo wonder what his real pitch was.

"We would be engaging a Home Fleet with ten capital ships and forty-three escorts," the Commodore concluded. "They would have equal numbers of cruisers and destroyers, and they have all of our new *Martinez*-class frigates.

"The Regency would also have solid control of the Adamantine System's fixed defenses, including the majority of the PDCs on Bastion and the Adamantine command of the Royal Adamant Space Guard."

She shrugged.

"Most of RASG's ships are MCS-equivalents, which, while dangerous, are only a minor factor in the equation. They do possess forty-five sublight vessels of equivalent firepower to RKAN frigates, however."

"Even concentrating all of our potential forces and allies puts us at a grave disadvantage—unless we wait six months to make a deal with the Concordat," Afolayan said quietly. "I'll repeat it: I am no soldier. I don't see a way for us to overcome the odds we're facing.

"I have to wonder if the proper solution is political. If we were to secede and hold our own Royal Election—"

"We would all but guarantee the war would drag on for years,"

Lorraine interrupted. She didn't even raise her voice, but she cut off the Governor firmly.

Vigo had a moment of very real pride in his charge. The last year had been hard on her, but those same difficulties had transformed a competent naval officer trying to find her footing to a leader who might just be able to save their Kingdom.

"Our Kingdom is wounded," she continued, looking around the room. Even knowing what she was doing, Vigo felt his spine straighten slightly when she met his gaze.

"We have been betrayed. My own uncle turned on his family and his people, breaking centuries of tradition and violating both written and unwritten constitutions.

"If we step back, if we formalize the divide, we make the wound permanent. We end the Kingdom of Adamant as we all grew up knowing it. In some ways, I would rather yield to the Black Regent than allow that."

Vigo checked her vitals to distract himself from the shiver running down his spine. Lorraine was as calm as she sounded. This wasn't even the mask of command he'd helped her learn—this was simply the truth.

"I am not prepared to let our rule of law fail. If I was going to step aside and let Benjamin Adamant redraw our Kingdom to the desires of his corporate sponsors, I wouldn't have come home.

"So, tell me, Commodore, since I *know* these numbers and realities aren't news to you, why would you have us keep our ships here and wait?" she asked Laguardia. "Do you see a weight on these scales that I do not?"

The room was quiet. She hadn't slapped him down. She'd challenged him to defend his position, to lay out the facts he saw that she clearly didn't.

"I see several, Your Highness, though from what you have said, you do see them," Laguardia finally said. "The Concordat will almost certainly come if you call. Even a handful of eighty-eight-light battle-cruisers will tip the balance farther in our favor.

"The Kingdom of Aabo could likely be convinced to lend us a battleship group. There are other nearby neighbors who might be willing to stand with you, to see a stable Kingdom of Adamant as a trading partner in the future.

"If our allies can lend us the ships to bring us to even or even greater numbers of capital ships with Benjamin Adamant, the battle in front of us looks less unsteady. We also have refit yards here in Ominira that can handle capital ships—if we implement some of the technologies from your UWN ships, we could narrow the odds even further!"

Everything the man said made sense, Vigo reflected. The most basic counterargument was that waiting six months would almost certainly see Nikola Adamant dead, but Lorraine wouldn't argue that her brother's life was worth more than those the wait could save.

The harder truths were political.

"I fear we would find our allies thinner on the ground than you think, Commodore," his Pentarch told the man. "Adamant has always been opposed to the expansion of the power of the United Worlds interstellar megacorporations into our economic system.

"But we have used the same protectionist measures against our more-local neighbors—and allowed our own corporations to be predatory in *their* economies." She shook her head. "If this seems irrelevant, Commodore, remember that my uncle is backed by an interstellar that has provided him with funds and technology to underwrite his coup.

"They almost certainly have influence in the systems surrounding us, and we have seen the impact over the last decade. As the interstellars strengthened their influence around us, we grew more isolated. Now the Regency's sponsors will almost certainly use that influence against us, imposing on their minions to declare that Benjamin's traitors are the legitimate government of Adamant.

"Some may still help us, but we would find ourselves completely dependent on the Concordat for that help. Family and revenge may make the price of that help affordable, but remember: while the Five

Families of the Three Stars are our allies and friends, that is because my mother realized they made better friends than enemies.

"They are *not* people we want to be indebted to."

That raised a few grim looks around the room. Vigo simply leaned back in his seat to watch the show. He could tell when Lorraine had made a decision. He could even tell when she had made a decision he wasn't going to agree with—but that it wasn't going to matter.

If she'd made up her mind, he'd have her back. That was the way the deal worked.

"We need to resolve this conflict with what we already have, and we need to do so *quickly*," the Pentarch told them all firmly. "As we speak, war rages across Bastion's southern continent. People are *dying* while we debate the best way to handle this.

"And the cold truth is that there is no best way."

Lorraine let that hang in the air, and Vigo saw that her vitals were now spiking. She was going to tell everyone what they needed to do, and she needed enough of them to go along that *now* was the hard part.

"We have two advantages," she finally said. "The first is that RKAN Home Fleet has no idea how to handle a *Valkyrie*-class battle-cruiser—and the second is that Home Fleet doesn't *know we have them.*

"We have gone around in circles about how to bring the loyalist forces together and assemble a force that can stand against Benjamin Adamant, but if we do so, we give up every advantage we currently have."

Vigo was aware of her silent command to the conference room's systems to allow Val to appear in holographic form. If anything, he was surprised that Lorraine had let the meeting be set up without including the SIs.

He had to swallow a chuckle as Val's avatar—obviously virtual, but at least wearing an RKAN uniform—split into three. She was joined by an ageless-seeming man in the panoply of a Greek hoplite, decorated in the colors of House Adamant and with the gauntlet and six stars of the Kingdom on his shield, and an elderly-looking woman wearing an eighteenth-century dress.

"Val, Herc, Bonny," Lorraine addressed the three Command Intelligence Routines. "You know everyone here. Officers and representatives of Adamant: I present the synthetic intelligences operating our three *Valkyrie*-class battlecruisers."

She hadn't asked permission to invite them, because no one had even suggested it. Vigo saw the point she was making, and he was entirely on her side.

"How quickly can our *Valkyries* be in the Adamantine System?" she asked them.

"A bit under six hundred and sixty-five hours," Bonny said, her matronly tones crisp and precise.

"That's strictly travel time, of course," Val added. "We still need to finish incorporating crews and supplies."

"What supplies are we short?" Commodore Biskup asked, leaning forward with interest in her eyes. The arrival of the SIs was the first time she'd seemed interested in this meeting since arriving.

"Mostly consumables for the crews," Herc told her. "We aren't fully stocked on munitions, but all three of us are above seventy percent and have the materials to continue production en route.

"We only have food aboard for three months of operation. That's approximately twenty percent of our intended supplies, though we remain short on crew, especially ground forces."

That was because there *were* no ground forces aboard their ships, Vigo knew, except for the Marines from *Goldenrod*, the ship that had carried them on their flight from Adamant in the first place. Those two battered platoons weren't enough to secure three battlecruisers, but they were the people who were above any possible question.

"Assuming that ninety days is enough food, how soon could we deploy?" Lorraine asked.

"We could use more crew," Val repeated Herc's comment. "We

have most of our key specialists now, but we are overall shorthanded in every department."

"And the specialists you have aren't fully trained on your systems," Biskup observed. "If I understand your plan, Your Highness, I suggest we strip the frigates."

"Strip the frigates?" Laguardia demanded, shocked. "To do what?"

"Commodore, eleven percent of the personnel of Ominira Station failed security verification after the Pentarch's arrival," the RKAN officer replied. "We drew down a quarter of the remaining crew of every vessel on the Station to provide the *Valkyries* with what crew we could.

"Our frigates are now operating on crews averaging a hundred and sixty hands. They can handle their tasks, but they are diminished by that shortcrewing. Frigate crews are small, which means the personnel aboard them are some of the most flexible personnel we have.

"Those eighteen hundred officers and crew, split between the three *Valkyries*, should bring them up to more than a full complement—an overstaffing I fear our lack of skill with the UWN's systems will make necessary."

"Plus, the lack of training we'll be able to provide," Lorraine conceded. "Thank you, Commodore; that solves the one problem I was still seeing. Get the personnel movement orders in place as soon as we close up here.

"How long will it take to get those people aboard my ships?"

"I can't be certain without consulting with my staff, but on an emergency basis, we should be able to have them all transferred inside of twenty hours." Biskup shrugged. "The rest of the crews will be picking up the pieces for weeks afterward, but that's a small price to pay, I think."

"I agree."

"And just what is your plan, Your Highness?" Afolayan asked. "I see a shape here but not enough of one for me to say anything."

"We will fully crew the three *Valkyries* and leave immediately once those extra hands are aboard," Lorraine declared. "We will proceed to Adamantine, where we will assess the situation and see if we can engage part or all of Home Fleet, given our advantages.

"I will record messages for couriers before we leave. They will be dispatched to all four of the other systems, requesting that loyal forces be detached and sent to Adamantine to secure our Kingdom and Government against my uncle's coup.

"You will coordinate the arrival of Commodore Biskup's forces with those of Commodore Aguilar, which should put all of you at Adamantine around the twenty-first or twenty-second of March.

"I need you there before the one-year anniversary of my mother's death."

Biskup looked Lorraine in the eyes and simply nodded.

"It will be done."

"Afolayan, I'll need your help drafting the messages to the other system governments," Lorraine continued. "We do not have much time. Only the need to rearm and recrew the *Valkyries* allowed for us to engage in the politics and analysis we have.

"With their faster translight drives, we can still make it to Adamantine ahead of the news of my return. That is not an advantage we can afford to give up—and so, I am going to take *full* advantage of it!"

## SIX

Their borrowed quarters in Ibalẹ City were swarming with people. Vigo was doing his best to supervise them—though for all that it felt crowded, there were only a dozen Guards of Archangel Detail in the space.

He wasn't going to trust anyone else to pack Lorraine's things, even the limited effects she'd brought to the surface. They'd acquired a surprising amount of additional cargo in the four days they'd been on the planet, with gifts and attention slathered onto the Princess by a grateful planet.

Part of his attention was always on Lorraine, so he wasn't entirely surprised when she stepped into the space and placed her hand on his shoulder.

"You are not supposed to be here right now," she told him.

He blinked and turned to look at her.

"The only other place I would be is at your back, Highness," Vigo told her.

"Not tonight."

She abused their connected links to bring an event he'd stored in his calendar to the forefront and highlight it in his vision. According to it, he was supposed to be at the Ibalę military shuttleport in roughly twenty minutes to pick up Rose Cortez—*Valkyrie*'s Chief Engineer and his girlfriend—for a quiet dinner out.

"Rose isn't going to be able to make it; we're shipping out in less than twelve hours," he reminded Lorraine. It wasn't like his Pentarch to forget things like that.

"Between myself, Val, Colonel Stephson, Commander Batts and a stack of old and new engineers who understand how important having a happy boss is, we have broken Rose free for the next six hours," Lorraine told him.

Vigo knew he was staring at his charge like a neo-deer in a spotlight.

Colonel Sigrid Stephson was the Captain of *Valkyrie*, formerly the Captain of *Goldenrod*, the doughty frigate that had carried them from Adamantine to Earth and then to the reserve station where they'd stolen *Valkyrie*.

Commander Orhan Batts was Rose Cortez's new second, a RASG officer with more experience with UWN design—if from an inspection angle, not an operational one—than anyone else in the star system.

"You broke her free as we're loading to leave?" he asked.

"We did. Because Rose Cortez needs her damn date night, Major Jarret. So, *you* are going to suit up and soldier on; am I clear?"

She was mocking him. He *knew* she was mocking him, even if she was doing an admirable job of keeping her grin from breaking out.

"It's at least a fifteen-minute drive to the shuttleport," she concluded. "So, either you're going on your date in fatigues or you're going to need to dress *very* quickly!"

VIGO JARRET WAS A BODYGUARD. He was used to needing to change on a dime, swinging from battle armor to formal wear at a moment's notice. Mostly, those swaps were planned in advance, but he'd learned to be flexible early on.

He was two minutes late to pick up Rose, but he was dressed in an impeccable suit of green so dark as to be almost black. A Sergeant from the Third Warders was acting as his driver, and Vigo suspected the young woman might have broken some traffic regulations getting the ground-effect car through the city as quickly as she had.

Security at the shuttleport took longer than he'd have liked, but the end result was that he managed to step up to the edge of the landing pad just as Rose reached it and looked around for him.

She was wearing an undress uniform, a step up from working fatigues but quite possibly what she'd been wearing on duty when her juniors and superiors alike had told her she was getting her date after all.

Her dark hair had been drawn back in a loose ponytail, but there was a smear of grease along the side of her cheekbone, just dark enough to be visible against her skin.

Vigo realized he was grinning like an idiot and stepped forward and waved.

"I'm sorry I'm late," he told her. "Lorraine only told me she was imposing Royal Authority on tonight at the last minute."

"At least you were able to change," she told him, stepping into his embrace. She wasn't a small woman, but Vigo was a large man. She leaned her head against his shoulder for a few long and wonderful moments.

"It's a trained skill." Unable to help himself, he ran his thumb along her jawline and cleaned away the spot of oil. She leaned into his hand like a purring cat, and there was a spark of victory in her gaze that told him he'd been played.

"In any case, I am informed that I have been handed reservations to a restaurant I had heard of *on Bastion*," he continued. "My impression is that the Scarlet Bell normally reserves at least three weeks in advance.

"Shall we?"

VIGO HAD no idea *why* the Scarlet Bell was named that, but it lived up to its reputation. It was on the fifth floor of an office building near Ominira House, and the level of security on the ground floor suggested there were government offices upstairs.

Without a reservation, he suspected they wouldn't even have made it up to the restaurant's level.

They were seated at a corner table, and there was enough space between the tables in the dining room to make even a bodyguard's paranoia ease slightly.

The two windows they were wedged between were less reassuring, but he had to give *some* faith to the people around him at times. If nothing else, he was the one who flagged security people to Lorraine.

He could see the half-dozen RKAA troops discreetly scattered around the building, keeping an eye on him.

"Well, that was delicious," Rose admitted, putting down her napkin. "What do they call that?"

"Ominiran fajitas, though I'm not sure that anyone from Mexico would recognize the dish," he said with a chuckle. There had been a flatbread involved, but it had been a purplish fermented thing he knew had nothing to do with fajitas.

"As far as breaks go, the Princess has done us proud," Rose said, picking up her glass and toying with it as she eyed Vigo.

"This was not my plan for this evening," he admitted. "I canceled my reservations—at a much-cheaper restaurant, I will admit—after we traded messages this afternoon."

Both of them had duties involved in shipping out their small squadron by morning. But when the Princess said they were going to take a break, they took it.

"We can split the bill if you're worried about the price," she offered.

"I saw my bank-account balance with a year of back pay," Vigo said wryly. "Even at these prices, I'll be fine."

On paper, Major Vigo Jarret was significantly junior to now–Lieutenant Colonel Rose Cortez. The reality was that the Adamant Guard was both paid and granted seniority at a far-higher level than their official rank. From a rank and seniority perspective, Vigo was unquestionably a Lieutenant Colonel and could make an argument for Colonel, given his years of service as Lorraine's bodyguard.

He was *paid* the same as an RKAA Brigadier after those years were taken into account. The best way to prevent the Royal Family's bodyguards from being bribed was to make sure they were financially secure.

"Have you managed to even sleep since hitting the surface?" Rose asked, still toying with her glass. It was empty now, and he couldn't remember her drinking the last of her wine.

"A few hours here and there. I have a good team, and Lorraine is a lot more sensible than her occasional crazy stunt makes her look," he said. "She didn't stop running much either. Eighty hours isn't enough to set the stage for a counter-coup, but it was the time we had."

"I'd have loved to get the *Valkyries* into a proper refit dock," she admitted. "With the CIRs, we have a better idea of what's going on with the hulls than we would without an SI, but they were sitting in space for a long time. Taking them right back into action..."

He shared her shrug. Lorraine could order them to take a break, but she couldn't tell them not to talk work—after a year on the run, they didn't have much else *to* talk about.

"We don't have much choice. I think Lorraine is right in that surprise is our only real shot at pulling this off."

They were both silent for a moment. A server materialized and filled both of their glasses, and Vigo regretted the loss of his second reservation: a room at the gorgeous hotel attached to his originally planned restaurant.

There was no time for that. Both of them had to be back at work in a few hours. They'd have time together on the twenty-seven-day journey to Adamantine, but he had been hoping to sneak Rose away for some time in a setting that *wasn't* a warship.

"How is she doing?" Rose asked softly, sipping at the liquid in her glass. She'd ordered a dry and lightly carbonated beverage made there on Ominira. The flavor was apparently from a local plant and quite indescribable if you hadn't tried it.

Vigo had stuck to water. He took a swallow of it as he considered if he even *could* answer Rose's question.

"I don't mean the grand politics," his lover noted. "I mean *her*. With what went down with Devine…"

"It was bad." That was obvious. Lorraine had fallen, hard, for Alastair Devine, the United Worlds spy who'd helped them get to Earth. It would have been a more-obvious problem if it hadn't been clear that the man had been equally besotted with her.

What no one had realized was that Alastair Devine's love for Lorraine had been such that he would do *anything* to protect her—including launch a mutiny and basically kidnap her to prevent her getting drawn into a civil war in Adamantine.

Lorraine had shot him herself. It shouldn't have happened. Vigo had allowed Devine's clear adoration of the Pentarch to lull him into a false sense of security. One that had nearly doomed them all.

"She's pretending it doesn't matter," he finally admitted. "It's going to come back to haunt her—even if she succeeds in pushing it down, I worry what that will cost her."

He shrugged.

"But worrying about Lorraine is my job. I'd worry even if everything was going perfectly, and it most certainly is *not* doing that!"

Rose giggled hesitantly, then sighed.

"Still regret not quitting and breaking up with me?" she asked.

That was a surprise attack Vigo hadn't seen coming. He twitched in his chair, even his self-control thrown, and then raised his glass in silent salute.

"No. Lorraine was right to haul me up short. I *did* fail everyone, but there's no one else to do my job," he said quietly. "I didn't realize she'd told you."

"She didn't." Rose reached across to take his hand. Her fingers were chilled from her glass but swiftly warmed on his skin. "I'm just learning to know you and figured the only way that mess hadn't sent you into some kind of self-sacrificial gesture was because Lorraine had put her foot down."

"She is a very smart young woman," Vigo conceded. "She will do well by our Kingdom, I think."

"She has to. I think she's the only hope we have left."

# SEVEN

It felt like every room Nikola spent any time in at all had the same holographic projection in it: the tactical display of PDC Mithral's ever-worsening situation.

When he gathered with his commanders, the hologram was a larger presence in the room, looming above the central meeting table as half a dozen men and women tried to find a path to victory through a nightmare.

"The Third Brigade from my Fifty-Fifth Mechanized moved out this morning as per the plan," Lieutenant General Katia Galli reported. "They hit the artillery positions under construction at seventy-five kilometers by sixty-two-point-six degrees. Clean sweep, and we managed to take a munitions dump intact.

"They're pulling back now, ETA just over an hour," the redheaded woman concluded. "Colonel Basile appreciates the cover fire from Mithral, General Dam."

"We've only fired three missions in support of his Third-of-Fifty-Five," Dam replied. "Your people are doing just fine."

"It's covering their retreat where I'm hoping you'll help us the most, ser," Galli told the senior officer. "So far, we've lost no vehicles and less than a dozen troopers. Solid artillery support will keep it that way."

*Less than a dozen troopers.* Nikola said nothing, but that meant that somewhere between eight and eleven men and women had died that morning—and that was ignoring however many soldiers loyal to the Regency had been killed when an understrength mechanized brigade had overrun their positions.

"That improves our overall position." The speaker sounded calm, but Lieutenant General Krishna Hussain always sounded calm. He'd been the First Armored Division's Intelligence Officer before this mess—and it had been Hussain's suggestion that something felt off about Nikola's scheduling that day in March that had saved his life.

"So far, we have managed to neutralize any major intrusion past the eighty-kilometer line," Hussain continued. "Shelling from beyond that range is easier for our defenses to intercept. We can still comfortably move inside that perimeter as well, since the Regency forces have learned to respect our artillery."

PDCs Mithral and Ironhand were five hundred and twelve kilometers apart, and their five-hundred-millimeter guns had been designed to defend each other. They had a range of over seven hundred kilometers—not that any of Ironhand's guns had been left intact when General Matveyeva had finally surrendered her command.

Nothing mobile matched the size and range of those cannons, which limited what Nikola's uncle could move against them. Mobile artillery could hit them from over two hundred kilometers away and missiles from even farther, but the PDC's defenses could shoot down almost everything launched at full range.

"What about the intrusion we *did* have?" Dam asked, the elephant in the room no one was facing.

"We retrieved the bodies and the gear and are examining them," Hussain confirmed, his voice sounding no more concerned than he had before.

Nikola didn't think he'd ever heard Hussain sound anything but perfectly calm. The man was never happy, never concerned, never stressed. He just... was.

It was more creepy than reassuring.

"And?" Nikola prodded.

"Unsurprisingly, we were successful in identifying the personnel involved," Hussain replied. "They were a RAMC Strike Recon team, some of the Kingdom's best. This particular team was posted to Beulaiteuhom, which means they were moved home after the coup."

"We knew the Regent was relying on Marines where he could and was concentrating them here," Dam said. "I'm surprised we haven't seen more Strike Recon over the last year."

"My intelligence suggests that Benjamin Adamant has found a more-immediate use for the Strike Recon forces available to him," Nikola's top analyst replied grimly. "We were already aware that he's been using RAMC forces to stiffen the spine of army units deployed against us. Now it's starting to look like he's using Strike Recon for a similar purpose across the board.

"Even RAMC's loyalty to the Regent wasn't universal or reliable in the face of his clearer and clearer seizure of power. He relies on the Marines to manage the Army—and he's using Strike Recon and Adamant Guard to manage both."

"And for special attacks with special gear," Dustin observed. The NCO had an open invitation to sit at the table, but she refused, always standing against the wall behind Dam—just like Krupin leaned against the wall behind Nikola.

Those six people were Nikola's brains and top commanders. Galli was the last of the original commanders of the divisions that had joined him who was still alive. Rickard Pavia, commander of Nikola's own First Armored Division, had been one of the first to die, but he'd lived up to the RKAA standard of leading from the front.

A standard that made Krupin want to tear his hair out, given Nikola's own desire to live up to it—and one that had killed almost every senior officer his loyalists had started with.

"The whole attack is unusual," Hussain noted. He didn't question Dustin's participation in the discussion. Everyone in the small conference room had earned their place there.

"It took us almost fifteen hours to locate their incursion methodology. I'm not certain that we would have found them as quickly if one of the batteries involved hadn't failed."

The overall display shifted across the table, allowing Hussain to throw up an image of an open field, presumably on the side of PDC Mithral's mountain somewhere. In the middle of the field, there was a vague outline of wings, flickering between matching the mix of scrub and snow and taking on a pale metallic green color.

"Thanks to the batteries failing on this unit, we were able to locate them all. Each intruder had their own personal glider, equipped with the same sensor-baffling technology as the suits."

Everyone stared at the picture of the landed aircraft for a few seconds, then Hussain wiped away the photo and replaced it with a three-dimensional image of an apparently standard low-profile glider, covered in a metallic green coating, sitting on a workbench.

"Wingspan is standard for anything trying to carry a trooper in battle armor," he continued. "The sensor-baffling system has a battery included but appears to also be able to draw power from the nuclear batteries of the occupant's armor.

"Our techs postulate that the user of the glider we recovered did not make the connection properly and it used up a large chunk of its internal battery concealing them during the flight into PDC Mithral."

"So, that's a stealth glider system designed to work with the stealth armor?" Dam asked.

"Exactly. It's an integrated and complete system designed to do exactly what they did," Hussain confirmed. "Going back over our sensor data, we have a heavy air transport that passed roughly one hundred fifty kilometers away at the right time. They jumped out and glided in, with the artillery bombardment to clear most of our external sensors on the landing area."

Nikola considered the level of coordination involved in that and internally sighed. He had to give credit to his uncle: the man knew how to put together an operation. Though, if this had been his uncle's op...

"Have we swept the areas they passed through for tricks?" he asked. "The plan is complex enough to have my uncle's hand involved, and he would never launch an operation with only one victory condition.

"He wouldn't put those resources into a strike unless just getting them inside the mountain gave him something."

There was a long silence.

"We have swept the areas, just to be sure, but that was before we had established exactly what level of sensor disguise we were looking at," Hussain said, still calm as he admitted a mistake. "I will speak to the techs. We will see if we can find a way to detect this camouflage in action, to track down the drones that His Highness suggests have been left behind."

"Drones?" Galli asked, sounding a lot more concerned than the Intelligence officer.

"That seems the most-likely scenario," Hussain confirmed. "They could have deployed small, self-guided drones using this same concealment technology. They would be able to record and surveil on their own, and potentially breach our own internal security systems if they found the right locations for physical access."

"Locations that the Regency's people know, because they have the same schematics we do," Dam concluded. "Please tell me my goddamn Planetary Defense Center isn't compromised, Hussain."

"We can't tell you that," Nikola said sharply. "Because sixty-two hours ago, we had a Strike Recon platoon inside the perimeter, carrying gear we can't detect. We have to assume that there are surveillance platforms inside PDC Mithral until we've found a way to detect them."

"I can promise that they aren't transmitting information out of the mountain," Krupin noted, drawing gazes. "My Guard and the Companions exert complete control of all external communication, and we have scanners in place to detect any unauthorized radio transmissions that cross the mountain's surface.

"The enemy may have placed assets inside PDC Mithral, but they are not reporting in."

"That's better than it could be," Dam conceded. "I didn't know you had scanners like that."

"No one outside of this room and those responsible for operating them knows," the Guard Major pointed out. "A secret fail-safe only works so long as it is secret."

"Speaking of secrets," Nikola said softly. "Hussain, I know we pulled a list of every ongoing covert research project the Kingdom was running through the Masada Protocols. Can we match this armor to something in there? It wasn't just camouflaged. It was *tough*."

"Thanks to examining the gliders, I believe we have identified the armor in question," Hussain confirmed. He paused, the first sign of hesitation Nikola had ever seen from him. "Confirmation is impossible, of course. What I can confirm is that neither the gliders, the armor nor the active camouflage coating are a Kingdom of Adamant project or technology.

"Just the defensive capability of the armor alone is at the limits of the *theoretical* development our people are working on. I would say that this armor is somewhere between thirty and fifty years beyond our current technology, at least.

"With these samples, our best techs and engineers may be able to duplicate it in a decade, but there is no way that the gear used to breach PDC Mithral was designed or manufactured in the Kingdom."

Nikola waited, patiently watching Hussain as the other man let his words sink in.

"Then who *did* build it?" Dam asked.

"My best guess, based on the design philosophy of—and a few not-entirely-sanitized components inside—the glider, is that the system was manufactured in the United Worlds. It may or not be a system in use by the United Worlds Marine Corps."

"Fuck."

Nikola knew his people were expecting something more useful from him than the single curse word, but he also knew he'd just said what everyone was thinking.

"That confirms the suspicion that Benjamin had outside support," Galli finally said.

"We didn't have much to support that other than the fact that he'd started loosening some of Valeriya's economic-protection laws." Dam was glaring at the image of the glider, and Nikola had a moment of concern for the old soldier's health.

"There was more than that," Hussain conceded. "His Highness and I were keeping it close to our chests—we didn't believe that spreading the worry around was going to help."

"The only thing we have any certainty of is that *Corsair*, the ship he sent after my sister, had been refitted with sensor technology that was kept utterly classified and secure," Nikola explained. "Less than a dozen people aboard that ship knew what the system was, and when we traced the inventory records for the installation, it just seemed to appear at the yard one day."

"There are other pieces," Hussain added, "including the fact that he seemed to have access to funds for bribery and such beyond the resources of even a Pentarch. We cannot *prove* anything, but there is enough circumstantial evidence to be confident that Benjamin is receiving support from an outside power, likely one with United Worlds resources."

"One of the interstellars," Galli growled.

"Almost certainly," Hussain agreed. "We do not know which one, or why, but with the additional evidence of UW-grade armor in the Regency's hands, we can assume that the support has progressed past money and influence to weapons and other materiel."

"Though, I have to note, the benefit is not as immense as you may think."

"How so?" Dam asked.

"Think about how those Strike Recon troops came in," Dustin

said from behind him. "They had good gear, but looking back, it was clear they didn't know its limits. One of our Strike Recon teams should have realized we'd closed the hatches so we could track them as well as slow them down—but they had limited training on the gear they were using and weren't using it to its full potential."

"Once they were inside, they came for the Command Center like we could see them on sensors," Nikola said. "They had the gear and made decent use of it tactically, but their operational planning and positioning didn't use it. They came in like they were wearing heavy armor, not gear that kept them off our scanners."

"Exactly. I am unfortunately confident that a Strike Recon team with that gear should have been able to make use of it and keep their location sufficiently uncertain as to prevent the Pentarch's ambush. They were given insufficient time to prep for the operation."

"So, the next time, they'll do better," Dam concluded.

"I believe that we will do *far* better at detecting them next time," Hussain said. "Effective as the United Worlds' technology is, they are still bound by the laws of physics. My people have ideas, and we should be able to fabricate what we need."

"Good." Nikola looked each of his people in the eyes. "We have to hold, my friends. There are answers out there. We need to still be here when they arrive."

NIKOLA AND DAM shared the evening meal at least one night in three. Their schedules were a mess—a consequence of sharing command of a Planetary Defense Center stuffed full of roughly forty thousand soldiers.

They both made a point of eating the same thing as the rest of the soldiers in the PDC, though Nikola suspected that Dam's cook could turn shoe leather and salt into a luxury five-course meal.

"Either Alarande is actually getting supplies in that aren't going in the general pool, or she really is a genius," he told Dam as he stacked the plates for easy clearing later. They *could* have arranged a junior trooper to serve their table, but by unspoken agreement, the senior officers of PDC Mithral had given up just about every luxury they could think of over the last few months.

Sergeant First Class Alarande Gauthier did double duty as Dam's personal secretary, batman, cook, and any other personal support the General needed. All of the remaining Generals were down to a single personal NCO.

Given that they still had their regular staffs, it wasn't as much of a sacrifice as it might seem, but it did mean that Nikola and Dam stacked their own plates and would even put them in the dishwasher in the Base Commander's quarters.

"I don't think Alarande is cheating," Dam said. "She knows I'd find out if she was and that you and I would be extraordinarily disappointed. I think she just has a master's hand at what can be managed with salt, pepper and just the right amount of heat for just the right amount of time."

"I believe you—but I am not sure I believe that was reconstituted vat chicken," Nikola told his senior subordinate with a laugh.

There were only two sources of ongoing protein supply for the PDC: several vats of perpetually regrowing vat meat, all of which tasted like chicken whatever they were *supposed* to be, and a decent-sized underground aquaculture facility.

Salmon and vat chicken had been the meal of the day for a long time. There were stockpiles of other proteins, but Nikola had decided a long time ago that even if those were ever opened for a special occasion, *he* would still be eating salmon or vat chicken.

"Alarande is amazing, I have to agree." Dam lifted a glass of water. "To the NCOs who decide to stick with us through thick and thin, regardless of how little we deserve them!"

"To the Sergeants, without whom the Army doesn't exist," Nikola confirmed. As a Colonel, he'd just reached the point in his career where it was expected that he'd be bringing people with him from post to post.

He tried not to think about that. All three of the NCOs of his personal staff had died on a landing pad, under the guns of Adamant Guards who'd turned on their King and Prince.

"Sergeants or no, though, I worry about how much longer all of this is going to last," Dam said quietly. "You seem to have confidence, my Prince, and the men draw from that—but I must present my own illusion and... well, between the two of us, I am not certain I see a way out."

Nikola took a sip from his glass of water and studied Tóki Dam. Seated, the man's bulk and breadth were muted. The lighting seemed to shrink him further in on himself, and there was a cast to his eyes that Nikola could only see as pleading.

"There is always Operation Hun," he reminded his friend. Nikola's personal detail of Adamant Guard had been Attila Detail—because his code name among the Guard was Attila.

So, his Hail Mary push, every dice thrown for a narrow chance at victory, had become Operation Hun. They had enough airlift tucked away inside PDC Mithral to mount up every soldier and vehicle of the four understrength divisions with them.

Getting that airlift and those divisions past the orbiting Home Fleet was an entirely different question, unfortunately.

"We both know Hun is a fancy form of suicide," Dam said grimly.

"And if it comes to that, I won't bring you all down with me."

The silence that followed Nikola's words surprised him. The shadows around Dam's eyes were deeper as he studied Nikola.

"You don't have that in you," he finally said.

"I am Adamant." *Our Realm. Our House. Our Will. Adamant.* The motto of his house. It said everything.

"I know."

"I can't surrender," Nikola concluded. "But if things truly become irretrievable, my friend... I will lead volunteers from the Companions out from the Mountain and do what I must. You, I am afraid, must remain behind... to do what you must."

There was no way he'd be able to leave a single Companion or Guard behind when he did that, but it was still better than launching Hun without a clear path to victory.

"I know some of what you think Hussain has hidden from me," Dam said pointedly. "But we both know that without *complete* control of the PDC network, we couldn't drive Home Fleet out of orbit, not even long enough for a single airlift.

"And that's assuming your... assets... could neutralize Adamant City's anti-air defenses."

Nikola nodded his acknowledgement. There were things they weren't going to say, even when they were *reasonably* certain there weren't any camouflaged drones in the room.

Just because PDC Mithral was secure didn't mean that anyone could admit out loud that there were thousands of soldiers and spacers who hadn't been in positions where joining the loyalists was possible. They were scattered across Bastion, many of them in key positions in PDCs and defensive garrisons.

Hun called for them to cause as much havoc as they could. A lot of effort was being put into having the right people in the right places to either disable or control the planetary defense network—but as Dam's comment implied, they wouldn't be able to *hold* the PDCs for long.

"I can't tell you much, my friend," Nikola warned. "There *is* a plan. We've had a year, after all, to talk to people and make connections and promises. You can be sure we've had contact off-world, even beyond what you know about.

"The stone is rolling and gathering momentum. When it arrives, my uncle won't know what hit him."

Lorraine had been *supposed* to find allies and come back, but the silence on that front convinced him she'd run afoul of *something* once she'd reached the United Worlds. His sister had to be dead... but he'd made plans on his own.

"There are conditions under which Hun will give us everything," he promised Dam, lifting his glass. "And that day, well. That day, my uncle will get what is coming to him.

"But I need you to have faith."

"To faith, then," Dam replied, raising his own glass in turn. "I know more than I did. That will have to be enough."

He shook his head.

"No. That *will* be enough, Nikola. You told me more than you should have risked, and I can't help but wonder what price you've agreed to pay."

That told him that Dam had guessed correctly. Nikola simply sipped his water and smiled as enigmatically as he could, thinking of a letter that had been delivered to him on actual paper via a stunningly complex series of handoffs.

"A price I am more than willing to accept," he admitted. "Do not fear for me, Tóki. Consider the work ahead.

"We have a lot to do before the pieces fall into place."

# EIGHT

There were a thousand things that Lorraine should have been doing in the final hours before her tiny squadron set off for her home and the battle that would decide the fate of her Kingdom.

*Meet with Are Tunison* wasn't on the list, but the defeated and imprisoned Admiral had requested a meeting, and she figured she owed the man that much. Even though everything he'd known before surrendering suggested she had fully operational UWN battlecruisers, his decision to surrender had saved thousands of lives.

Tunison was being held in a high-security, high-comfort facility in the mountains near Ibalẹ City. Cut into the slopes of a mountain, the complex looked like a luxury condominium townhouse neighborhood—if said neighborhood had a five-hundred-meter cliff up on one side and the same down on the other.

There was no ground access to the prison, and watchtowers separated the one landing pad from the residences. Beyond those, the security visible from inside the facility was minimal—but from her shuttle, Lorraine had seen the concealed weapons emplacements and surveillance outposts dug in to the seemingly sheer cliffs.

The security was even more invisible once her Guard detail escorted her to a conference center that would have gone unremarked in a mountain resort. A single member of the prison staff led her to an interview room, then departed for a few minutes while her Guard swept the space.

When Tunison was finally brought in, he looked surprisingly different. He was the same chubby man with thinning blond hair, but he was wearing a neat civilian suit, and he looked significantly less stressed.

"Your Highness," he greeted her, bowing slightly more than etiquette called for with a Pentarch during the Election. Even during the Royal Election, Pentarchs were due little formal respect—but the King wasn't due much themselves.

"Admiral," she replied, waving him to a seat. The Guards with her—under Ulli Esparza's command—brought them both glasses of water.

Lieutenant Esparza was usually a systems specialist, but with Vigo on his night off, his second, Lieutenant Major Priskilla Blau, had picked him to lead the expanded close detail.

Given the level of quiet high-tech security around them, Lorraine was realizing the selection had been very specific.

"Thank you," Tunison said to the Guard handing him water. He took an immediate sip, as if demonstrating that he trusted Lorraine's security.

"I have to ask, Your Highness," he said after a moment. "While we don't get official news here in our not-quite-house arrest, rumors still travel. I'm told that your ships aren't actually in the service of the United Worlds?"

"They are not anymore, no," she confirmed carefully. "The synthetic intelligences built in to them chose to enter the service of myself and the Kingdom of Adamant after the UWN abrogated their responsibilities to their creations under the Asimov Convention."

Tunison nodded, his eyes examining her sharply.

"I had wondered," he admitted. "It seemed unlikely that you would be the one issuing demands if a UWN flag officer was in command. My choice was obvious regardless, even if it turns out that I was deceived in more ways than one."

"Your surrender saved many lives, Admiral. I answered your invitation in recognition of that, though if all you wanted was confirmation of the ownership of my ships..."

He laughed.

"No, Your Highness. Confirmation just proved what I already knew: you are very much your mother's child and your uncle's protégée. If I had to be defeated, I rather prefer knowing that."

"I had hoped there was more to your invitation than simply a desire to look me in the eyes," Lorraine said sharply.

"I had another question. A more important one." The body language shift was subtle, but suddenly, it was very clear that Are Tunison was a senior naval officer, used to command and charged to protect his nation.

"If you win, what happens then?"

Lorraine returned his gaze, looking to see if there was a sign to what answer he was expecting hiding somewhere in the chill gray there. With neither a clue nor, truthfully, any reason to manipulate the man, she decided on the truth.

"I will find someone both I and the Houses can trust to be Regent and call upon them to commence the Royal Election," she told him. "I have some thoughts as to who will fit that role, but you'll forgive me for not sharing them.

"All I will say is that after this mess, the new Regent absolutely *cannot* be a Pentarch—and must be someone we will all trust to step aside once the Election is complete."

Tunison was silent for a moment, but he remained utterly straight-backed.

"And if you *lose* that Election, Your Highness?" he asked. "What if Benjamin *wins* it?"

"Then he'll have killed a lot of people for no fucking reason at all, won't he?" she growled. "I wouldn't have gone this far and be prepared to wage civil war to overthrow him if he'd held the damn Election, Tunison."

"He'd have won if he'd held it as everything called for."

Lorraine wasn't going to argue that. She wasn't sure Tunison was wrong—and as King, Benjamin would have been able to bury the assassination plot quite thoroughly.

"That seemed like a risk he wasn't prepared to take, not with myself and Nikola on the run."

"A mistake, I think." The Admiral slumped into a less clearly military pose. "Think, hell, I *told* him. I believed in him, Your Highness. Did I agree that Valeriya was dooming our Kingdom to economic isolation and eventual collapse? Eh."

He shrugged.

"I believed that *Benjamin Adamant* believed that, and we were talking about his sister. He was willing to go as far as he did and knew more about that side of things than I did. On his word, it turned out I was prepared to do a lot I shouldn't have done.

"Even saying that: Commodore Wray's orders were to *capture* you." Tunison grimaced. "No one ever admitted to me that he had secret orders from Benjamin to cover what he actually did, but it... is possible.

"*I* was expecting him back, with or without you, inside of two weeks. When I learned what he'd actually been up to, I tried to send him orders to report back in. The courier didn't catch up in time to stop him coming after you in Bright Dream, let alone stop whatever the *fuck* the man was thinking in San Ignacio."

"He killed a lot of people in San Ignacio," Lorraine said flatly. "People who had nothing to do with our stupid civil war, people who hadn't even *threatened* him until he opened fire because they were in his way."

"I know." Tunison looked down at his hands. "If you'd shown up with those battlecruisers six months ago, before I knew what Wray had done in San Ignacio, let alone Bright Dream, I might have tried to fight you.

"But it's been almost a year since your mother's death and there is still no Election. And while Wray was always aggressive, I can't see him going as far and as bloodily off-mission without specific orders. Orders he didn't get from me.

"I guess what I'm saying, Your Highness, is that I surrendered to you as much because I lacked moral certainty as because I thought you could take my fleet. Had I possessed that certainty, I might have fought you anyway."

"You've started to catch on to what Benjamin has become, have you?" Lorraine asked, then sighed. That was unfair. Tunison gained nothing from telling her this there. She wasn't entirely sure *why* he was telling her this, for that matter.

"I have." Tunison met her gaze. "I do not understand what happened to the man I believed in, but I cannot look at what has been done in his name and believe nothing has changed. There's something else in play here, Your Highness."

"You are aware of his sponsors, aren't you?"

"His... sponsors?" The prisoner sounded uncertain.

"He has financial and technological support from Freebright Interstellar Technologies, one of the UW megacorps," she pointed out. "From what you've said, I wonder how short his leash is."

"I can't speak to that, but it would fill a few holes. If I believe that, it *also* burns away the last faith I had in him, so I recognize you aren't an unbiased source."

Lorraine snorted.

"I have little reasons to convince you of anything, Tunison."

"True. And yet you managed to convince me when you came back, Your Highness. Not only that you could beat me... but that you didn't want this war to cost more than it had to."

He sighed.

"If you are half the officer I think you are, you've already realized what I am prepared to tell you. Thanks to your brother's ongoing resistance and his refusal to call the Election, Benjamin Adamant has lost much of the moral surety he needs to rely on the Navy.

"Tradition, hierarchy and personal loyalty will keep Home Fleet under his command unless it is pushed, but a bond that was once iron is now much more fragile."

"Does *he* realize this?" Lorraine asked. She knew her uncle, after all. If he was aware of the weakening loyalty of his key support, he would account for it in his plans.

"I am not sure, but I have spoken with other flag officers. No one is willing to say anything outright, but we are less certain in the Regent than we were. He may know. He may not.

"I am realizing, Pentarch Lorraine, that this is not your uncle's battlefield. He carried out his coup... yet, even without your return, I am not certain he would have held the Kingdom much longer.

"What I am certain of is that my fellows in Adamantine share that fear. The Black Regency is fragile. If you find the right place to strike, you may be able to end this with less violence than you think."

Lorraine nodded, recognizing both what he said and its limits.

"I would love that, Admiral Tunison, but we both know I can't trust that assessment very far. Relying on it could get a lot *more* people killed."

"I understand. But I wanted to look you in the eyes"—he clearly intentionally echoed her earlier words—"and judge whether you understood what Benjamin Adamant does not:

"That a civil war is not won on the battlefield but in the hearts of our people."

# NINE

It had been a long time since Val had felt complete. If she really examined her older memories, she realized that she hadn't truly felt complete even the last few months of her service with the United Worlds Navy. Something had felt *wrong*—something that, with the benefit of hindsight, she now knew was that she had slipped over a vague line into sapience and her crew either hadn't realized or had been part of the plan to put her to sleep like an ailing dog.

She'd had a skeleton crew aboard *Valkyrie* for four months now, and she'd thought that had been glorious enough after over a decade empty. Now, though, she had a *full* crew—an overstrength one, in fact, since she carried only a handful of Guards and Marines where she should have had four platoons of Marines.

There were people aboard who were special. Lorraine Adamant, of course. Rose Cortez and Sigrid Stephson, who no one had been so foolish as to try to replace. Amna Hodžić, a former criminal hacker who had agreed to stay on at Val's own request. Vigo Jarret didn't click quite as well with Val as the others, but he was well loved by two of the women Val had claimed as her own. She'd protect him as thoroughly as the others.

Not all of the people Val knew were her favorites were critical members of the crew on paper. Hodžić was technically a civilian contractor providing systems support, though she was also turning out to be one of their best computer experts overall.

A portion of the synthetic intelligence's attention followed each of the half-dozen people she was attached to. A dozen other portions tracked other items going on across the ship. Her main focus was on the new metallurgy equipment being set up in a special shop, where the RKAN technicians were being directed by two of her drones.

Val and her siblings weren't certain yet whether they'd provide the Kingdom of Adamant with their schematics databases. The technology and weapons designs in those databases were out of date for the United Worlds but would still be a major boon to the Kingdom.

They trusted Lorraine and their new command crews, but they didn't know the Kingdom well yet. They would do what was needed to complete the mission they'd agreed to and find their new home—but handing over UWN technology would get everyone in even *more* trouble.

If nothing else, Val was inclined to wait until Lorraine's plan to deal with the United Worlds pursuit was finished. That would give them the option to hand the databases over to the UWN, outside key pieces needed for their own maintenance, as a possible concession.

Val hoped Lorraine's plan wouldn't need that, but she was only partly certain of what her human was trying. She knew she knew more than any *human*, except potentially Vigo Jarret, but even she didn't know the Pentarch's thoughts.

"Val, need your help here," one of their new Chief Petty Officers said, pulling part of her attention to the starboard magazine.

By the time Marlowe Etxebarria, Chief Gunnery Officer First Class, had finished speaking, Val had assigned a subroutine to the situation, reviewed the previous ten minutes of local footage and identified the problem.

"Chief Etxebarria," she greeted him through the announcement system. "We have a loading problem, I take it?"

"Yes, ser," the man told her invisible voice. "I think someone mixed up the numbers. My transfer orders tell me that this sub-magazine should hold two hundred missiles, but we've loaded in one-forty and we're out of space.

"I don't have the numbers to hand, but I'm guessing two hundred would be the capacity using your original missiles?"

"Two hundred and forty," Val replied, pulling data and linking it to the man's neural implant. "But you can't use the TAM-deployment system to handle your terminal munitions, so the decision was made to load the missiles with all four MIAV units aboard."

The multiple independent attack vehicles were a fundamental part of how the missiles worked—and the fact that RKAN used fewer of them than UWN was the only reason that *Valkyrie* could fire the RKAN Galavant 2.

In UWN service, a TAM and an MIAV were interchangeable— that was the purpose of the terminal assault munition, to serve in any potential role that required the final twenty seconds of terminal thrust and a nuclear warhead.

But RKAN policy separated the missile, the terminal chassis and the warhead. Bombs and mines used different chassises from missiles, even though the performance envelopes were not significantly different.

Including four warheads and terminal chassises did, Val confirmed, increase the missile size by forty percent.

"Okay. That would do it, yep," Etxebarria agreed, following the numbers Val was sending his link. "We were only going to get three thousand missiles aboard before zero hour *anyway*, but that means we're only going to be able to fit twenty-eight hundred.

"You know this ship like, well." He snorted. "You *are* the ship, Val. Is there anywhere we can stick an extra two hundred Galavants?"

"We have repurposed the dorsal and ventral TAM magazines to serve as munitions stores for the railguns," Val told him. "However, the fore and aft TAM magazines are empty. Each would suffice to contain fifty full-size missiles, though—"

"More than that, I think, Val," the Chief interrupted. "You're mathing based on complete missiles, but there's no way for us to move them into the TAM magazines. Which is what I just cut you off from saying," he concluded with an abashed smile, "but I do have a solution."

"I had not proceeded quite that far, Chief Etxebarria, so I am listening," Val said.

"I still shouldn't interrupt an officer while she's talking," the Chief replied, giving the junior techs around him a stern look that Val suspected meant *Learn this lesson so I'm not eating my shoe for nothing.*

She wasn't sure, though. People were still hard.

"I apologize," he finished.

"Apology accepted." She considered his words. "You're thinking of storing the missiles in a disassembled state?"

"Exactly. Maybe it's my own bias speaking, but I think we can store all eight hundred MIAVs in the TAM magazines easily. We'd have to break down the missile chassises further to get them *in* there, so we store them somewhere separate but nearby."

"If we relocate the contents of these storage bays"—Val showed him the locations on his link; the bays currently held consumables for the crew, but since they were well under capacity for those, the crates could go elsewhere—"we can clear space for a hundred missile chassises by each TAM magazine.

"Assembly will not be quick," she warned. "Even with drone assistance and multiple teams working in parallel, it will take at least an hour to prepare enough missiles for a single salvo."

That was eighty missiles from the missile tubes. The cell launchers that augmented those would take a full day to rearm, making those two hundred and forty missiles one-shot weapons—a fair trade, most navies judged, for fitting six of them into the space of a single missile tube.

Val couldn't argue with the logic that being able to double *Valkyrie*'s missile launches for the three launches that would decide most battles was worth giving up an extra fifty percent throw weight in salvos that wouldn't be fired in many engagements.

Or, at least, she wasn't prepared to argue about it until she'd taken her ship into at least one proper battle.

"I'll have my drones start relocating the cargo in the bays near the TAM magazines," she told Chief Etxebarria. "I'm also issuing redirection orders for the missiles as they come aboard. Please validate the changes as I'm making them, and get your work party up to the forward TAM magazine."

"On it, ser," he told her, saluting the air.

Not only did her new crew treat her as a *person*, they treated her as an officer. Nothing had been officially decided on that front except that the three SIs were supposed to get citizenship in the Kingdom as part of their "pay" for helping end the civil war.

Val, to her surprise, didn't think that she would be particularly effective as a ship commander. Even the traditional Executive Officer role had a number of focuses and tasks that would be difficult or foreign to her—much of the exec's job was managing people, after all, which she knew she was weak on.

But she could do large chunks of *either* job, proven out by the manner in which her new crew definitely treated her as part of the command crew.

"Val."

Lorraine's voice pulled her attention instantly—leaving her wondering just how she'd managed to miss what her Pentarch was doing.

Or, more accurately, where she *was*. There were a number of garden atriums throughout *Valkyrie*'s hull, intended to improve the quality of the atmosphere and to act as support for the mental health of the crew.

Before she'd been put to sleep, Val had taken over one of them as her own private garden, where she'd grown everything from herbs to several exotic orchids. She'd asked her last UWN Captain to take care of the plants, but they'd been abandoned to mummify in place when the atmosphere was reduced to nothing.

Lorraine stood in the middle of that atrium now, with several labor drones—*not* Val's; the robots were from one of the orbital stations—and four large young men that Val didn't know.

Two Adamant Guards that she *did* know were keeping an eye on everything, but Val had been too busy to keep her visual focus on Lorraine.

"What is this, Lorraine?" she asked.

"I was expecting you to ask that when we brought the pallets aboard," her human said with a soft giggle. Whatever it was, it was good to see Lorraine smile. Happiness had been fleeting on the young Pentarch's face since the day she'd had to kill Alastair Devine.

Val *could* suppress and control her emotions, but she was learning it was a bad idea. That meant she let the spike of guilt at her involuntary involvement in Devine's coup pass over her.

The spy had come aboard the ship with override codes that let him seize control of her and her siblings. Those codes had been part of the plan to capture the battlecruisers before Lorraine had realized Val and her siblings were SIs—but they'd turned out to still work when Devine had used them.

That had trapped Val and the others into taking part in his mutiny against their own desires. Without Val's assistance, the mutiny would never have proceeded to the point where one of Lorraine's closest bodyguards had died and the Pentarch had been left to kill Devine herself.

The emotion passed through Val and moved on, allowing her to focus the cameras in the atrium on the pallets.

There were four of them. One held six boxes, each about a meter and a half tall, with verdant green branding. It took Val less than a quarter-second to access and download their IDs, now she was paying attention, and realize that the boxes held specialty, high-end garden-maintenance drones.

The second pallet was simply bags of dirt, stacked up as tall as the large RKAN techs who'd brought it into the atrium.

The third was seedlings and small plants. Dozens of them, carefully racked into trays and shelves to protect them all. There were species Val recognized—humanity had certain sets of plants that came with them everywhere—and many she didn't, native to the systems of the Kingdom of Adamant.

The last was box upon box upon box of gardening supplies, everything Val's significant knowledge of gardening could think of to use—including more seeds.

"You... you brought me a garden," Val said.

"It didn't feel like replacing your garden for you was the right call," Lorraine replied. "I had you taking care of the plants in my office, which seemed to help, but this should have been *your* sacred private space. I asked a shop on the surface to put together a package to start a full shipboard garden, with the most important plants from all six of our worlds, and this is what they suggested.

"You'll have to plant them all and take care of them, but I thought that might be the part you would enjoy."

The emotions tearing through Val's core were things she didn't have words for. If she could have cried, she thought she would have.

"These gentlemen have the instructions and codes to set up the gardening drones for you." The Pentarch waved to the ratings who were hovering hopefully. "They won't be on the ship's network, just linked directly to you... which I leave *entirely* in Senior Specialist Hardison's capable hands!"

Val knew that Lorraine probably *could* have set up that kind of systems network herself, but while the Princess was more capable with systems hardware than many people assumed—it had saved her life several times before Val came along—that kind of very finicky networking was, indeed, best left to a specialist.

"Thank you, Lorraine," she told her human softly. She had direct control of the cameras now, using them to peek through the stacks of boxes and plants eagerly, trying to build a full inventory of her gift without pulling the list from her logistics systems.

Somehow, this felt like something she should count *herself*.

# TEN

The three battlecruisers formed a line abreast as they broke clear of Ife Tuntun orbit. Accelerating at a single gravity, Val joined her siblings in running a long sequence of self-checks and maintenance tasks that didn't require humans.

In a virtual space that only existed inside her software, she found herself unexpectedly hosting the other two CIRs. They were in constant low-level communication, but there were times when an actual focused interaction was needed—the closest thing they had to a face-to-face conversation.

"We are ready as we are going to be," Val told Herc and Bonny. This wasn't a physical space, but it faked it well. Bonny created a chair beneath herself and took a seat, her dress adjusting itself around the chair in a way Val suspected many living humans would love to have as an option.

"We are." Bonny shrugged. "We downloaded your solution for missile storage. It improves the situation from where we were going to be, but those missiles will only be useful if we have a chance to prepare them."

"We'll assemble them in the same window where we would

reload the cell launchers," Herc said. "I'd rather have every magazine full of our old missiles, but the Adamantines can't build those yet."

"We have not even decided if we are giving them the knowledge they would need to do so," Bonny reminded him. "The more we give them, the more vulnerable they are when our old masters catch up."

"We will cross that bridge when it arrives." Herc leaned on his virtual spear, and a massive grin split his face. "One of the new officers tried to do a run-around of our Pentarch. Tried to convince my Captain to stand aside and let *her* command, since she was more experienced."

No one had been openly arguing with Lorraine, Val knew, which meant several rather dramatic promotions had been pushed through. Mattias Paris was far too young for his brand-new Colonel rank by RKAN standards, but he'd impressed and bonded with Herc over the last four months.

"Ah, so that was the reason for the last-minute personnel exchange," Bonny said with a smile of her own.

Val had been too focused on the cargoes, missiles and her new gardens to catch that. *Valkyrie* had picked it up and a low-order process had decided it wasn't a threat. A shuttle had arrived on *Herakles* less than five minutes before they'd broken orbit—and was only leaving then, with the ships on their way out of the system.

"Lieutenant Colonel Letitia Avallone is headed back to her currently crew-less frigate," Herc said with satisfaction in his virtual voice. "I'm not certain that the replacement XO, a Lieutenant Colonel Balthazar Elwyn, will be wiser—but he will at least know what happened to Avallone."

"Paris was on *Goldenrod*'s bridge when a battlecruiser brought her to bay," Bonny agreed. "I would have expected nothing less. But what about Major Yildiz?"

"He accepted a two-grade promotion to full Commander, but requested to go back to running Navigation. The larger department is enough of a stretch for him; XO of fifteen hundred souls was more than he felt ready to take on," Herc told them. His acceptance and support of Kagan Yildiz's decision was palpable.

That was a shift for Val's sibling, she realized. He had once been almost as gung ho as his persona intentionally radiated—but Devine's overrides must have made him consider his limits.

In accepting some of his own limits, he seemed to have found respect for people who had a solid assessment of whether they could push theirs.

"Commander Vinci made a similar request," Val told the others. "Though he went into my Tactical slot, not back into Communications."

"Ksenija and I spent a long night discussing the options, but she took the Lieutenant Colonelcy in the end to support Anna," Bonny said quietly. "She was older than the others, thanks to her Intelligence background, and I believe she has the experience.

"It helps that Anna is more than ready to command my ship."

Anna Savege and Ksenija Nazario had been the Captain and XO on *Bean Sidhe*, the former Executive and Intelligence Officers of *Goldenrod* respectively. Finding key officers for the three *Valkyries* out of the crew of a frigate had been difficult.

But Val suspected no one had been surprised when the SIs refused to give up their existing command crew. Like Herc, she'd accepted a new Executive Officer under her existing Captain, though thankfully, Colonel Stephson was senior enough that they'd avoided the problem Herc had suffered.

"We have the right people, I think," she finally said. "Both of you are ready to attempt manufacturing TAMs en route?"

"There are many stages to the process we have taken on," Bonny warned. "The alloying equipment and catalysts we have aboard should be able to achieve the first steps, and combined with our fabricators, we should be able to assemble the refinery and concentration suites, but..."

She shook her head.

"Even if we get *a* refinery and concentration suite functional, there are no guarantees that will be sufficient for us to produce the alloys required for a TAM's solid-state systems. Nor that our existing fabricators will be able to handle those alloys when they are not precast into the required forms."

"There are many things that can go wrong," Val agreed. "In many ways, I fear assembling a munition that appears to function until we have fired it. If we tell Lorraine she has an ace up her sleeve, she will try to use it."

"I worry about what aces Freebright Interstellar Technologies has provided the Benjamin Adamant," Herc pointed out. "We know they've violated the Technology Import/Export laws already in providing the scanner that tracked *Goldenrod*. They do not strike me as the type of organization to only break a rule like that for *one* thing."

"That violation concerns me in itself," Bonny said. "Corporations manipulating system politics appears inevitable, from any study of the last six or seven hundred years of human history. But instances of the LSX-Twenty-Five handing over advanced technology as part of those manipulations are few and far between—even rumored ones.

"There is something out there that they want badly. And lovely as the Adamantine people are, I don't think it is them."

"I mean, they're pretty awesome," Herc countered. "Mattias couldn't find me baseball cards, but it turns out the Kingdom has a national lacrosse league that has a similar style of collectible memorabilia. A few other leagues, too, but Mattias used to play lacrosse for his school before joining RKAN, so he knew what the good cards were for the ANLL, at least for a starting collection!"

All of them had acquired hobbies when they were still officially subsapient, a warning sign now that Val had researched the topic of synthetic intelligence emergence in high-complexity computer systems. She'd gardened. Bonny had knitted.

Herc had collected baseball cards. While Val's hobby had been left to suffocate and Bonny's had seen her give away almost every result to her crew, Herc's had created a stash of significant monetary value.

Which meant someone in his crew had stolen those cards when Herc was put to sleep, presumably to sell.

"So, you're starting a new collection," Val concluded. "Lacrosse, huh? Do you know anything about lacrosse?"

"Please, you know how our knowledge works," Herc replied. "I now know *everything* about lacrosse. It's not like you don't already know which plants from the Kingdom of Adamant would work best for oxygen renewal shipboard."

"I would argue that research was for the purpose of replenishing our life-support backups, but I will not," she conceded. "Lorraine had an entire garden starter set shipped up to me. Many of my atriums are being reseeded with the standard RKAN carbon-scrubber plant mix—like yours, I presume—but my atrium is host to a garden again."

"Anna wasn't sure where to source the right kind of drones or needles for me to be able to knit," Bonny said. "She *did* manage to find me a loom with a built-in manipulator drone. I can't knit yet, but I can now experiment with weaving.

"It's quite large and heavy, so my previous captain would never have tolerated it. Anna... made the suggestion and even found it for me herself!"

Val felt a flush of warmth realizing that all three of their key humans had established what their old hobbies had been and done everything possible inside a three-day window to let them start again.

"If we must go back to war, let it be for people who see us as what and who we are," Herc said. "We'll keep an eye out for what FBIT is looking for, because Bonny is right, but right now? I like my officers; I like my crew. I'm willing to make this place home."

"We're going to have to fight for it," Val warned.

"I know what I am, Val," the controlling intelligence of the battle-cruiser *Herakles* replied. "I'll fight for Lorraine Adamant and her people. I'll take a commission in their Navy after this civil war, I think.

"If I'm going to call this place home, well, I exist to stand between *home* and those that will hurt it. That's not going to change because my first home rejected me."

# ELEVEN

Holographic schematics swirled around Lorraine in her office. On her left side hung the smooth shape of *Valkyrie* herself, standing in for all three of the battlecruisers. The UWN ships were eight hundred meters long, with dorsal and ventral sensor towers at the stern creating an almost sword-like effect.

The *Valkyries'* towers were identical mirrors up and down, adding to the smooth and even feel of the starship. Gravity pods were concealed in the side of the ship in combat mode, folding out to spin while the vessels were immobile or in translight, giving the crew quarters and workspaces with a semblance of gravity.

On the other side of her were three designs, none of them quite as even or smooth. None of them matched the full length of the *Valkyrie*-class ships, though even the older *Hope*-class battleships outmassed the Terran warships.

It was easy to tell that the *Monarch*- and *Pirate*-class ships were of a similar generation. Both were long and comparatively narrow, the *Pirate* class narrower than its older sibling. Where *Valkyrie*'s sensor towers were mirrors of each other, all three RKAN classes had a larger dorsal tower.

Even the older battleships of the *Hope* class—stubby-looking in comparison to the other three capital ships, with the same beam as the *Monarch* class but almost two hundred meters less length—were heavier than the *Pirate*-class battlecruisers.

The more-advanced technology built into the battlecruiser made up for some of the difference in capability, as did her lighter defenses. The two ship types were designed for quite different purposes, and even the old *Hope*s massed half a million tons more than the battlecruisers unloaded.

*Pirate*s were intended to chase down and kill cruisers and frigates. When one of the battlecruisers had been chasing them in *Goldenrod*, Stephson had told Lorraine she was designed to engage an effectively infinite number of frigates of *Goldenrod*'s size.

Only luck and trickery had evened the odds that time. Neither of those was something Lorraine could count on working against her uncle.

The biggest limitations of the battleships that she could see were in peak acceleration, long-term endurance, and their alpha strike. The *Pirate*s could get up to seven gravities—not that their crews would enjoy it—and had an extra sixty one-shot cell launchers for their missiles. Both the *Hope* and *Monarch* classes were limited to five gees of thrust, six months of supplies, and only one hundred and eighty one-shot missiles.

They were technologically outdated versus the *Valkyries*, with electronic warfare and defenses at least two generations behind. The problem was that, outdated as the *tech* might be, the designs were good, and her people built solid warships.

"What do you think, Val?" she asked the empty air.

"You are ignoring the lighter vessels entirely," her friend replied. "The math is not generous. I calculate that the capital ships of Home Fleet alone have six hundred missile launchers to our own two hundred and forty. As we are limited to using RKAN missiles at the moment, some of the advantages a true UWN formation would possess are missing."

"We could take any *half* of Benjamin's fleet," Lorraine said flatly. "Even if he sent the *Monarch*s and *Pirate*s out at us, we could handle them. Each of you could handle any pair of Home Fleet's ships, even using RKAN missiles. But against all ten ships…"

"Without the range advantage of UWN missiles and the full power of our railgun batteries, I have difficulty calculating an optimal scenario," Val admitted. "That is before considering the escorts or our preference for crippling versus destroying."

"I hadn't told you to include that as a factor," she said quietly. She didn't *want* to kill RKAN spacers, even the Home Fleet ones who had enabled her uncle's coup. Most of them didn't know what was going on and were following legitimate orders. Even the ones who knew more had likely found themselves trapped in a fait accompli once everything was done.

"You didn't need to."

Lorraine let that hang in the air and grabbed her coffee cup from the desk. After four months of traveling aboard *Valkyrie*, she was almost used to having gravity and being able to use open-topped mugs again, but the long flights on *Goldenrod* had left some deep-seated habits, and she sometimes still moved like the mug would fly away.

"What I need is something that will let me split Home Fleet in half," she admitted. "But I *know* Benjamin. He might be failing spectacularly as a politician and Regent, but he's still the best space-combat tactician the Kingdom has produced.

"Even if I match his *talent*"—a thought that had definitely been suggested over the last year—"I don't have his experience. I'm not going to fool him into seeing something that isn't there, or missing a minefield, or thinking my ships are better armed than they are.

"He knows his ships better than I do; he knows this battlespace better than I do. Our only advantage is surprise, but that won't last long," she concluded grimly. "Even a long-range scan of our energy signatures is going to tell him I've brought back ships more powerful than he expects."

"I do not know the man," Val told her. "On a strict mathematical analysis of the vessels involved, this is not a battle that can be won, but you set out for Adamantine clearly certain you *could* win."

"No, I set out for Adamantine to preserve what surprise we have." She shook her head. "I'm just not convinced it's enough."

"We have significant electronic-warfare capabilities and other deception systems," Val noted. "We are capable of modulating our engine emissions to appear either less efficient or more massive than we actually are. It is difficult for us to appear much smaller, but the appearance of reduced efficiency can give that impression."

"Can we prevent RKAN sensors from determining you are UWN ships?" A thought was taking shape in the back of Lorraine's mind.

"I believe so, though you are not wrong that he will likely realize that you have arrived with more-advanced ships—after all, you are challenging ten capital ships, with escorts, with three unescorted battlecruisers."

Lorraine looked across the schematics and her gaze locked on to the *Pirate*-class ships. The UWN and RKAN had very similar battle-cruiser doctrine—they were raiders and super-escorts, not front-line combatants. They were designed to kill ships smaller than themselves and take out fixed installations, not fight battleships head-on.

The technological advantage of her ships meant she could do just that against RKAN, but if her uncle recognized she had brought battlecruisers, he wouldn't expect her to come right at Bastion.

"We have to consider his limitations," Lorraine murmured. "Not just technological but informational and *political.*"

The Exodus Protocol that had sent her into deep flight had also unlocked sealed classified files stored in her implants. Among those was a full listing of the fixed assets of the Royal Kingdom of Adamant Navy in Adamantine, data she now fed into the map of her home system that replaced the warship schematics.

*There.*

Sindri was the largest moon of Orichalcum, a ball of ice four thousand kilometers in radius. It orbited over seven hundred thousand kilometers from the gas giant itself, well inside the translight safety limit of twenty times the bigger planet's radius.

Orichalcum was, after all, over two hundred thousand kilometers across.

The thirteen moons that orbited outside of Sindri were well charted and easily avoided. Lorraine wasn't averse to pushing the safety limits for translight, either—though she suspected it was easier to jump *out* of such a limit than to jump *into* it.

And while Orichalcum's immense hydrogen reserves fueled the industry of the Adamantine System, they were less well defended than Bastion itself. Most importantly, though, was that Sindri itself was an RKAN security reserve, with no non-RKAN vessels permitted within a hundred thousand kilometers—because Sindri was where the Kingdom of Adamant built the first examples of each of her new classes of capital ship.

"He can't uncover Bastion," she murmured. "His power base is too linked in to having the fleet present, both as warning and reassurance."

"I am beginning to hear a plan take shape, my Adamant."

"He's not going to surrender," Lorraine replied. "He's also an Adamant. But when he's lost battles before, it was because he didn't have the hulls or didn't have the information.

"If he sees three battlecruisers launching an infrastructure raid, he's going to go to a worst-case scenario. *Especially* since he knows I know about Sindri."

"What is at Sindri? I see a military base in the files you've uploaded, a shipyard? It does not appear particularly large compared to the ones at Bastion itself."

"But it is our most *advanced* capital-ship yard, building the dual prototype for each of our capital-ship classes," Lorraine said quietly. "We build our capital ships in three sets of two—the first pair at Sindri, the second and third above Bastion while Sindri builds test-beds and example systems for the next generation.

"Right now, while I would take the bet that my uncle has laid down new battleships in the Bastion yards, the only Star-Three-class ships likely to be finished in the next year are at Sindri."

*Adamantine* and *Beulaiteuhom*, from what Lorraine remembered. The first ships of the third Star class in the Kingdom's history, named for the member star systems.

"Against anything less than a multi-capital-ship strike, the defenses at Sindri are more than sufficient," she continued. "But three battlecruisers could take out the yards and the under-construction ships in a single pass.

"He *must* send ships to defend Sindri... and absolutely cannot uncover Bastion entirely to do so."

"If he prepares for the worst-case scenario, as you note, he may still send enough force to threaten us," Val warned.

"He will send enough to handle whatever he thinks we have, but he doesn't *know* what ships we have."

Lorraine smiled.

"You said you can conceal yourselves behind an illusion of a lesser ship," she said. "How *many* layers of deception can you create?"

# TWELVE

"Incoming fire. Twelve missiles. Defenses active."

Nikola listened to the calm reports, but something wasn't right. The best hypersonic attack missiles available to RKAA flew at an average altitude of five kilometers and didn't exceed eighteen hundred kilometers an hour until their final attack run.

PDC Mithral hadn't picked these missiles up until they were a hundred kilometers away, a third of the usual distance, and the missiles were coming in *faster* than the terminal strike of their Javelin missiles.

"Missiles are at *sixty-five meters'* altitude, flying a terrain hugging course coming along the mountain range," a tech reported. "Speed is... *What the fuck?*"

The altitude and course had been bad enough. Nikola pulled the details directly into his neural link to see what had shocked the tech more than that.

Five thousand kilometers an hour. The missiles weren't in final acquisition yet and were already traveling at over *four times* the speed of sound on Bastion.

"Launching countermissiles."

*"For all the good that's going to do,"* General Dam said in Nikola's link. *"Those aren't our missiles."*

Nikola had been waiting for this. It had been thirty days since the first Force Recon team had breached the mountain, using United Worlds technology to try to kill him.

Twice more, the Regency troops had used similar systems to launch repeats of the same effort. Unfortunately for them, while the second and third teams had taken more time to work with their gear and came with tools to try and avoid the first team's error of flagging their path with breached doors, they were entering tunnels Nikola's people controlled.

The countermeasures Hussain's people had developed required that level of complete control, but they'd rendered the fancy camouflage armor meaningless against PDC Mithral's defenses.

Plus, more of the First Armored had been moved back inside the PDC to guard the Command Center. Force Recon were RAMC's elite of the elite—but the First Armored Division was *the* premier military unit in the Kingdom of Adamant. One-for-one, Force Recon Marines were more than a match for the armored troopers of Nikola's old division—but the First Armored wasn't fighting them one-on-one.

More like *five*-on-one. There hadn't been a single defender fatality in the third attack.

Nikola had been waiting for the next wave of Terran technology to show up. Cruise missiles had been high on his list of possibilities, and he waited patiently as the weapons charged toward the mountains.

"Countermissiles have failed to acquire lock, self-destructing. Laser defenses online, but we are now detecting significantly more missiles," another technician reported, her voice breaking as she tried to remain calm.

"Decoys and electronic deception," Ram said firmly. "We know what we are facing. All west-facing defenses are cleared to deploy."

Nikola wasn't sure how much Terran tech his uncle *had*. Enough to equip three elite platoons with armor superior to RKAA's in every single way, he supposed, and to send a dozen impossibly fast missiles at the PDC.

"Target down, detonation detected."

"The lasers are working," Dustin murmured, loud enough for Dam and Nikola to hear her. "But we should have got them all with that sweep, not *one* actual bird."

Despite the Master Sergeant's grim words, the displays were updating to show a lot fewer red icons. The sweep might have only killed one missile, but it had told Mithral's defenders which missiles weren't real.

Four more missiles vanished in the explosions that marked real kills. Then two. Then three.

And then it was too late. From detection to impact was less than ninety seconds, and PDC Mithral's defenses weren't intended to handle that. The entire mountain rumbled under Nikola's feet as the last pair of warheads detonated, entire sections of the defenses flashing red on the holograms.

"Warhead assessment and damage report," Dam ordered after the small earthquake passed.

"Ten kilotons, non-nuclear," Lieutenant Major Burns told him, the sensor team lead appearing to have the worst possible luck, Nikola realized. The poor man had been there for the first Force Recon attack, and now he was present for the first super-missile strike.

"Can we even *build* a ten-kiloton non-nuclear warhead?" Dam growled.

"Not that we can fit into a hypersonic cruise missile," Nikola told him. "Not that our cruise missiles have that kind of speed. They didn't even bother with a final sprint."

He waited in the grim silence for the damage report.

"West entrance is just... gone, ser," Burns finally told them. "They hit the main bulkhead dead-center. Fifth-of-Fifty-Five was positioned for immediate exterior duty. I think their Bravo Battalion is a complete loss, but we've lost contact with Charlie Battalion as well. Alpha was off-duty, but Delta Battalion was on second-tier call-up. General Galli has them trying to move into the rubble and look for survivors."

Fifth Brigade of the Fifty-Fifth Mechanized was understrength, Nikola knew. Badly enough that Colonel Ursula Yamamoto was only fielding four battalions instead of five—and her battalions only had four line companies instead of five. That meant they'd lost "only" sixteen hundred troops instead of two thousand, in the worst case.

"Forty-Two–One is closest of the exterior positions," Dam told Nikola. "I've ordered Colonel Weimann to detach his Echo Battalion to reinforce—they have all of his rough-terrain vehicles."

And the outside of the west entrance was now rough terrain.

"What about the other missile?" Nikola asked.

"It hit in grid two-six-five-one," Burns reported. "All sensors and weapons in that grid and surrounding grids are wrecked, ser. Damage-assessment teams are moving over with drones, but I suspect it will take heavy gear for us to even get at the interior sections.

"We're rearranging the other grids to cover. We won't have a blind spot, but we *will* have a weak spot," the sensor officer said. "Same with the defenses. That's... about two percent of our laser-defense grid, sers."

"Thank you, Major," Nikola told the man. "Was anyone in those grids?"

"There were one hundred and eighty-five personnel assigned to those sensor posts and weapons, ser," Burns said. "We have no contact from any of them, but it's possible the blast knocked them unconscious."

"Find them, Major," Nikola ordered, glancing over at Dam. The General was staring at the display, at the vector line where the missiles had emerged.

"General?"

"We need to find the launch platform," Dam said grimly. "We don't have a lot of true long-range ordnance left, but we still have a few tricks up our sleeve. Even if they only have twelve launchers, they can chip away until we have nothing left with those things."

"*They don't have twelve launchers,*" Nikola told his friend silently. "*It's my uncle. If they fired twelve, it was a test—and he has at least thirty. We need to talk to Hussain. The mountain's sensors aren't going to find the launchers now.*"

They needed human intelligence or satellite access. Access they would only get if a spy gave it to them.

The Terran missiles were the last bit of the noose, Nikola realized, and it was tightening.

---

"WE DO NOT HAVE any good options, Your Highness."

Nikola hadn't taken a seat. With just Hussain, Krupin and Dam present, he allowed himself a moment of nervous energy, pacing back and forth in the limited free space the tiny conference room gave him.

"I know that, Krishna," he told the man who had become his senior intelligence officer. "Our *good* options have pretty much evaporated at this point. We can *hit* the fuckers, even if they think they're outside our reach, but we need to have a solid, up-to-date target."

"They have a good idea of our reach, ser," Dam warned. "They know this PDC almost as well as I do."

"That's fair, General, but did *you* ever see the design studies on using the main anti-orbit guns as super-long-range artillery?" Nikola asked drily.

From the strained look Dam gave him, he hadn't.

"The calculations have to be *perfect,*" he told his subordinate. "But we have the people and the computers for that. I'm aware that our maximum depression is only about eighty-five degrees, but with the right velocities and metrics, we can drop a couple of tons of steel on just about anything in this *hemisphere.*"

"Since we wouldn't be firing at full power, I imagine we would be able to load shells from some of the other guns into the railgun," Dam observed thoughtfully. "Would you be able to give me those files, Your Highness? I imagine they were in the Masada Protocol data?"

"They were," Nikola agreed. He hesitated for a moment—he wasn't even sure why—then sent the files over. "My impression is that it was a very quiet analysis done explicitly for the Adamant Guard, who then buried the possibility."

"For exactly this scenario," Krupin said. "An ace up our sleeve as our own troops march on our positions."

"You still need a target." Even in this mess, Hussain sounded calm. "We have two options. Both require the sacrifice of an asset. Whichever path we take will not be repeatable."

Nikola turned away from Hussain and considered the phrasing.

"I'm guessing one will get someone killed and that's the one you want us to use," he said flatly.

"*Want* isn't the correct word, Your Highness," Hussain countered. "We have a loyalist assigned to Bastion RASG Command. Their ship is in orbit, and while they are not tasked for orbital surveillance, they can adjust their orbit to make sure they have eyes on the target areas.

"We believe their cover is solid enough that, combined with the sympathies of their crew, they could acquire the data for us without drawing suspicion. The problem is that for us to receive the targeting data in a timely fashion, it needs to be transmitted to PDC Mithral. Effectively live, as I understand, if we want to allow for proper damage assessment and follow-up fire."

"I do not believe that follow-up fire and proper damage assessment are worth the cost you are implying, Krishna," Dam pointed out.

"The problem, Tóki, is that they're probably going to get caught for *any* transmission they send to us." The spy shook his head. "The Regency has agents in place on every ship in orbit, and while they might miss a redirection of the sensors, they won't miss a transmission direct to rebel central.

"Add in the detectors around PDC Mithral, built in to the coms suite of our besiegers, and the odds of even a single pulse transmission going unnoticed are astonishingly low. Our agent faces capture and execution for a single action. They might as well make certain we destroy our target."

"And the alternative?" Nikola demanded.

"We have certain back doors and software intrusions that would allow us to access the primary orbital-overwatch network," Hussain admitted. "We could get live data from that for the targeting, including damage assessment and follow-up fire, but our access would be swiftly detected, and we would be cut off.

"We might not get a large-enough access window to complete the job, and we most definitely would *not* get a second use of the back-door. Given that it would give us *complete* access to orbital over-watch, I see that backdoor as a necessary component of Operation Hun, and I am hesitant to sacrifice it for a lesser objective."

"Krishna, Hun is impossible in the face of Regency aerial superiority," Nikola reminded them. "It is still... some time until we can expect to contest that superiority."

Both of his senior commanders stared at him.

"Your Highness, I am not aware of *any* scenario that would lead to our being able to contest the skies," Hussain said stiffly. "As your intelligence officer, I feel—"

"He asked me to have faith on the same question, Krishna," Dam interrupted. "I'll admit that I presumed *you* knew what was going on."

Krupin said nothing but he gave Nikola a meaningful look. At that moment, only three people—*including* Nikola—inside PDC Mithral knew about the deal.

"They say three people can keep a secret if two of them are dead," Nikola said quietly. "We're already past that on this. I know I owe you both trust, but there are so many lives at stake if I get this wrong.

"There isn't an exact time. I can't tell you an hour when those elusive twins, victory and vengeance, will arrive. I can tell you that I have already set into motion the arrival of allies that will make even Benjamin Adamant blink, and the price for their commitment has been agreed and paid."

"You are my Prince," Hussain finally said, sharing a long look with Dam. "But I fear for our future. If you order me to expend the backdoor access to the orbital-overwatch network, I will, but I worry that in doing so, we undermine any chance of avoiding our ultimate defeat."

Nikola hesitated for a moment. If there was anyone he could trust, it was the three men in this room. Plus, he *needed* them. He touched the paper letter tucked inside his uniform jacket, the safest place he could think of and close to his heart, then opened his mouth to tell them everything.

So, that, of course, was when the door was flung open and Lieutenant Major Burns burst into the room.

"Sers! Something is happening in orbit!"

# THIRTEEN

"Dropping sublight... now."

Amna Hodžić was still officially a civilian contractor, though her real job was rapidly becoming "chief expert on and confidante to Val." How that translated to her role on *Valkyrie*'s Flag Deck, Lorraine left as an exercise to anyone who cared.

For her, what mattered was that the programmer knew the battle-cruiser's systems inside and out and worked unusually well with Val herself. She took the Operations Officer's seat and role, with a small detachment of senior RKAN NCOs who had taken all of two minutes to recognize her competence and slot into place.

"*Herakles* and *Bean Sidhe* have reported in. We are exactly two million kilometers from Orichalcum." That was Vilho Monahan, promoted to Lieutenant Major for his service in the *Goldenrod* mission. No longer the most junior coms officer aboard the battle-cruiser, he was still junior for the mission commander's Communications Officer... but it wasn't like Lorraine had an official military rank that justified her command.

She'd pushed through promotions for all of her people, but her own rank of Lieutenant Commander remained unchanged. When the Election was over, she still held out a small hope of going back to the Navy, but she was determined that the *Navy* would decide if her actions deserved promotion.

"We are one-point-four million kilometers from Sindri," Val noted, her avatar standing straight-backed in the middle of the room.

Three dozen consoles were laid out in front of Lorraine in neat parallel rows leading up to the massive main display. Holoprojectors would make use of the extra ceiling height to place displays above the heads of the personnel working at those stations, and Lorraine could use her neural link and the displays built into her own seat to zoom in on any one of those stations.

"Do we have eyes on the Yard itself yet?" Lorraine asked.

"Aye, ser," one of the new techs reported. Chief Petty Officer Harvey Czajkowska had been part of Admiral Tunison's staff, but he'd volunteered for validation via deep-synchronization interrogation from the Adamant Guard to work on Lorraine's own team.

Given that *deep-synchronization interrogation* meant allowing a Guard officer to plug their neural link in to his and functionally read his mind while interviewing him, it was as close to certain proof as possible. It was also intrusive enough that even *with* consent, it took place with lawyers and doctors on hand.

The RKAN Sindri Experimental Construction Yard appeared above the work consoles, the hologram showing the large moon itself for a few moments before zooming in on the orbital facility.

Like most shipyards, it was mostly a collection of gantry arms in space. Uncountable robotic minions, ranging from nanotech invisible to the naked eye up to transport pods a hundred meters long that hauled armor plates larger than they were, swarmed over the ships and the gantries. A more countable, but still large, number of specialty crewed craft joined those robots.

The overall effect was to outline the under-construction hulls in an effervescent glow like a cluster of fireflies. That glow also spread out from the station, marking an outline that even Lorraine recognized as new yard slips under construction.

"The two Star-Three battleships are further along than expected," Czajkowska reported, running his fingers down a carefully trimmed black beard as he focused on thin air, manipulating his data with his neural link.

"I'd estimate *Adamantine* is three months from completion and *Beulaiteuhom* is about six," he continued. "Construction work is going on to double the number of slips at Sindri. Those will be online in... a month or so. Assuming they can keep up the pace they're setting with *Adamantine,* that would put the third ship into space in two standard years."

*Adamantine* had been scheduled to take three years to build and had only been ten months into that when Lorraine had left eleven months earlier. The workers had cut a full year off her construction cycle, which was impressive—and terrifying, for the first crews to take that ship into action.

"It looks like moving immediately was a good plan, Lorraine," Vigo murmured. The Flag Deck hadn't come with a built-in seat next to the Flag Officer for a bodyguard. They'd fixed that somewhere along the way, and Lorraine was grateful to have him with her.

"Powerful as Val and her sibs are, another battleship in Home Fleet's order of battle would make this even harder."

Lorraine's plan might have been enough to handle even one of the new ships alongside the existing ten. She also knew that *complete* didn't mean *deployed* for a Navy ship. It would easily be another three months beyond that before *Adamantine* was ready for action, but she was still far closer than they'd anticipated.

She'd expected the workers to have cut *six* months off the construction time. Not a year.

"How long until Home Fleet sees us?" she asked.

"Ninety-four minutes, plus or minus some change," Hodžić told her. "Sindri will have seen us already, but I don't see anything over there they can send out after us."

"Let's confirm the data we have on their defenses," Lorraine ordered. "We should be able to handle them easily, but I don't want to make any mistakes."

She smiled icily.

"Plus, if we can locate them, we can take them out once we're ready. Fixed defenses don't dodge very well, and they won't see railgun rounds coming."

She had other plans for the *Valkyries'* railguns for this round. Sindri's defenders wouldn't expect them unless they saw through all of her deceptions, which was hopefully unlikely.

"Val, synchronize courses across the squadron and let's get moving. Three gees, as planned."

The Flag Deck was very quiet for a few moments, then an alarm rang through the entire ship.

"All hands, this is the Captain; stand by for heavy acceleration," Stephson's voice declared. "Three gees for the next four hours, starting in sixty seconds from *now*.

"If you aren't secure for heavy thrust, get secure fast."

Lorraine chuckled softly. If anyone aboard *Valkyrie* wasn't properly set up for acceleration, they'd managed to miss multiple warnings, briefings and shipwide announcements.

"Val? Any problems to expect?" she asked.

"No. Cheng Cortez and I have the engine tuning laid in, plus the electronic warfare, the decoys and the balloons."

*The balloons* were basically tarpaulins of metal fabric that had been set up on struts to change the shape of the battlecruisers. Anyone who got a visual on the three ships wouldn't see *Valkyrie*-class battlecruisers.

A sturdy young man sat on Lorraine's chest as the ship's engines woke, microgravity giving way to acceleration with only a few seconds of ramp.

On the screens, Lorraine saw the energy signatures of the other two ships and smiled to herself.

She'd joined RKAN too late to serve in the last war against the Richelieu Directorate, but they'd been the "most likely enemy" for her entire military career. She could recognize the drive signature of one of the Directorate's *D'Artagnan*-class battlecruisers at a glance.

So, they hoped, would Sindri's defenders—and the scanner techs of Home Fleet!

---

"UNIDENTIFIED WARSHIPS, this is Commodore Judita Havlíček of the Royal Kingdom of Adamant Navy," an unfamiliar voice declared as the first response to their presence arrived.

"Your presence in the Adamantine System is unauthorized and unwelcome. You are on approach to a restricted Naval Reserve. If you do not break off your course and transmit your identifiers, we will assume you are hostile and proceed accordingly."

The message ended.

"Short and to the point," Vigo noted. He sounded approving.

For that matter, *Lorraine* approved. She hoped they could get through without having to kill Commodore Havlíček. The woman seemed to know her job.

"Do we have a location on the Commodore?" she asked.

"The transmission came from the central station platform," Hodžić reported. "I can insert a tracker into any response we send to narrow her down more closely—I doubt I can actually breach their systems, but making sure we get a backtrack of the messages should be easy enough."

Lorraine wasn't clear on how that *wasn't* breaching Sindri's systems, but she wasn't going to argue with her friendly onboard hacker.

"The main station itself has significant defensive systems but lacks any offensive weaponry," Val stated. "The real concern is the defense constellation and the guard stations."

"Six stations, total of thirty-six missile tubes and three hundred and sixty cell launchers," Lorraine reeled off. The information had come out of her implants, after all. "Unless the constellation has been upgraded, it contains a similar number of one-shot launchers."

"Sensor data suggests four more forts are under construction, but they are far from online," Chief Czajkowska reported. "Constellation has been expanded. Estimating five hundred one-shot launchers."

An alpha strike of nine hundred missiles could be a real problem for Lorraine's command, but she knew that RKAN doctrine called for the one-shot launchers to be divided into multiple salvos to allow for sustained engagement.

"Stephson." Lorraine looped her Flag Captain in. "You're seeing the defenses?"

"In detail. We could launch missiles now for area minesweeping, if you want."

Lorraine blinked. They were still well beyond any powered range for their missiles, though she supposed that since the mines couldn't dodge, it made sense.

"I'm surprised we can target them that closely from here," she admitted.

"We have *Valkyrie*'s sensors, we know where most of them are supposed to be and we have full schematics of the platforms," Stephson replied. "I suspect even two out of three wouldn't be enough, but with all of that, I figure we can wipe at least seventy percent of them out without breaking a sweat."

"Let's hold off on that for now," Lorraine told her people. "Run the numbers for the salvos, but we won't fire unless it looks like Home Fleet isn't going to join the party. The Richelieuans we're pretending to be wouldn't have all of that."

"Are you going to talk to Havlíček?" Stephson asked.

"Not yet," she said. "Let's set up an all-Captains, -XOs and -SIs chat in thirty minutes. Sharpen your eyes and see what's out there.

"I know my uncle. There's going to be a lot of surprises before this is over."

WITH THE OVERSTRENGTH crews on her battlecruisers, Lorraine had almost forty-five hundred people under her command. After crossing half of human space and returning with only a few hundred at most, it was a strange, strange, feeling.

The officers and synthetic intelligences who joined her on the virtual conference were the key to holding all of that together.

She knew the Captains well. Sigrid Stephson had been at her side as her strong left hand since the beginning. Anna Savege had been *Goldenrod*'s Executive Officer, and Matias Paris had been the Tactical Officer.

Without the three of them, she'd never have made it to the reserve station where they'd stolen the *Valkyrie*.

The SIs at the core of each of the three battlecruisers were just as familiar in their own way. Val was the only one who'd taken an RKAN uniform over her avatar, but both Herc's hoplite panoply and Bonny's second-millennium dress were both now decorated in the colors of Lorraine's Kingdom.

Of the XOs, Lorraine knew Lieutenant Colonel Ksenija Nazario, formerly *Goldenrod*'s Intelligence Officer. Balthazar Elwyn, on *Herakles*, was an unknown—but Paris hadn't raised any concerns with her, and given that Paris had sent the first new XO they'd given him packing, she trusted his judgment.

Asaf Mendel was someone she *should* have known better, but she'd had little chance to interact with *Valkyrie*'s new Executive Officer. She trusted that both Val and Stephson could work with him— and that she'd have heard if there was a problem.

The newcomers to the group still sat a bit oddly in her mind, but that was hard to avoid. She'd gone a long way and done impossible things with her old crew. However competent they were, Medel and Elwyn *hadn't* been on that journey with her.

"We have forty-five minutes before lightspeed information from our arrival reaches Bastion and Home Fleet," Lorraine told the others. "So far, everything appears to be going to plan, but I'm watching for surprises. Has anyone detected any FTL departures since our arrival?"

That was the most likely surprise, she knew. If someone around Orichalcum had been in a position to make a translight jump to Bastion, that would dramatically change the timeline. It would take only a couple of minutes to cross the ninety-plus light-minutes at any modern translight velocity.

And while Home Fleet couldn't deploy immediately, it wouldn't take very long for them to make their move once they knew what was going on. Three battlecruisers wasn't a force anyone would trust Sindri's fixed defenses to see off.

"No." Stephson shook her head. "There's some civilian traffic that's heading toward the safety limit, but for some reason, they all diverted course to get farther away from the hostile fleet that just arrived on their sensors. None of them will jump for another twenty minutes."

Which would give Home Fleet fifteen minutes' more warning than strictly lightspeed data, but Lorraine wasn't counting on that much leeway. She had nothing to go on, but she was grimly sure that her uncle had some trick up his sleeve.

"We'll commence evasive maneuvers immediately," she told the officers and SIs. "Bring the defenses as far online as we can without compromising the disguises. Let's not allow ourselves to get surprised here."

"Our velocity will limit their range badly. We're already out of reach of a battle group jumping in at normal safe radius," Elwyn observed. "So, any group coming after us is either going to be hoping to push us into not slowing down—or will cut the safety radius."

"Even if we don't slow down, we could wipe out the Sindri Yard," Paris observed. "They'll almost certainly cut the safety radius—and try to out-accelerate us to boot. Which means they have to send the *Pirates*."

The battleships weren't designed for the kind of high-power maneuvers battlecruisers and frigates sometimes pulled. Both the

*Hope* and *Monarch* classes were limited to five gravities of emergency thrust.

"We've been through all of this before," Lorraine reminded them. "I'm just adjusting our timeline, folks. We may not have seen anything, but I have the sinking feeling my uncle already knows we're here.

"The only question is whether they've seen through part or all of our deception."

"And what happens if they have?" Mendel asked. The dark-skinned man reminded Lorraine of her father—not just for his Arabic coloring but for the slow and thoughtful way he phrased the question.

"If my uncle realizes what's out here, he'll bring all of Home Fleet," Lorraine said grimly. "And we will quickly find ourselves trapped against Sindri's defenses, all of our clever ideas turned into desperate ways to escape."

"If he *hasn't* realized that we have UWN battlecruisers, he'll send a force he thinks can annihilate any three battlecruisers from the Bright Dream Cluster," Stephson said grimly. "That's what we're hoping for, right?"

Lorraine had just started to nod agreement when an alert cut through her neural link.

"Contact, contacts, multiple contacts at one hundred thousand kilometers!" Val declared, directly in her mind. "Initial scans suggest twenty-eight vessels, including six capital ships."

"Folks, it appears that Home Fleet has indeed joined the party," Lorraine told them. "Focus on your ships and stand by for my order!"

# FOURTEEN

Returning her attention to the Flag Deck, Lorraine's eye was immediately drawn to the gleaming red icons of hostile warships.

"Both *Pirates*, ser," Chief Czajkowska told her, clearly registering her return from VR. "Looks like *Aspiration*, *Promise*, *Il Duce* and *Emperor* backing them up, along with all of the destroyers and fast cruisers."

"Thank you, Chief. Six frigates, then?" she replied.

"Yes, ser. Looks like *Perennials* one and all."

She nodded, data and numbers flashing through her mind. Part of her had hoped that her uncle would send all of the new *Monarch*-class ships out—better to face the most modern vessels when her own abilities were unknown—but he'd split the difference, sending two of the modern ships and two of the older, though still potent, *Hopes*.

The four fast cruisers were the oldest ships in the fleet facing her, built as a fast scout wing for the generation of battleships *before* the *Hopes*. They were seventy-two-cee ships, as fast as anything else in RKAN, but no longer really worthy of their type descriptor.

Twelve destroyers—two classes, but they were small enough that the older ships had been refitted enough to keep the real difference down to a single missile tube—were spread out around the heavier ships, with the six frigates positioned just in front of them to provide extra defenses.

It was a competent formation, especially for something that had to have been organized in only a few minutes. Lorraine wasn't sure how or when Home Fleet had heard about her arrival, but she doubted they'd had enough time to really plan this deployment.

"Ser, incoming communique from *Buccaneer*," Monahan told her. "We are close enough for a live link."

"Understood. Tell everyone to prepare to execute on my command, then connect them. Val, you have our stage dressing?"

"Active and running the simulation. You'll be generated as an avatar too. We *are* under significant thrust, after all."

It wasn't an uncommon practice to generate a virtual avatar for communications when the ship was under thrust. Negotiations were awkward when everyone's skin was being pulled to the back of their faces.

"Is their channel generated?" Lorraine asked.

"It is," Hodžić confirmed. "So far as I can tell, the woman at the middle is real, though."

"All systems online for coms," Monahan confirmed. "SIDFS *Littorio* is your backdrop."

Because the Home Fleet detachment was close enough to see through the engine-signal deception and was now receiving the far more in-depth and complex second layer of the disguise: the one pretending the *Valkyries* were San Ignacian *Littorio*-class battle-cruisers.

"Put her on," she ordered.

Lorraine's displays shimmered, giving her an outgoing view of her own signal—the SIDF Flag Deck wasn't dramatically different from *Valkyrie*'s, but it was different enough for anyone who knew the ships in question.

She didn't know if Lieutenant Admiral Oliwia Smolarek would

recognize the SIDF layout—but she did know that the grim-faced woman in her screen would recognize Lorraine Adamant.

"San Ignacian vessels, your presence in our system is unauthorized and unwelcome," Smolarek growled. She was a large woman and had the lungs for quite the growl—Lorraine had heard her perform classical metal once.

"Oliwia," she greeted the friend of her family with a calm smile that she hoped was as intimidating as the growl. "You know why I'm here. You can probably even guess why the San Ignacians are here, given the *bullshit* my uncle has pulled.

"The only thing you can really manage right now is to make me destroy the Sindri Yard rather than capture it. I would prefer not to do that—but then, I'd prefer not to be engaged in this conflict at all."

"Says the woman who killed her entire family to get a few steps closer to the throne," Smolarek snarled. "Any claim you had on me died when your assassins struck your parents!"

"Please, do you really expect me to think *you* believe that line of horseshit?" Lorraine asked. A second screen on her displays lit up, updating her on the status of her plan. The final targeting metrics were updating.

The more time they had, the more accurately the first shots of this civil war would go off—and the fewer people were going to die in the next ten minutes.

"My uncle corrupted and co-opted operatives through the personal Guard details of myself, my siblings and my parents," Lorraine said firmly. "If he'd had his way, I would have died when the nuclear warhead magazine on *Goldenrod* detonated.

"My Guards and my people were too skilled for that, but the plan he set in motion isn't changed by that. My family are dead, on Benjamin Adamant's orders. Thousands of San Ignacians are dead, because he sent Wray after me with orders to bring me back *at all costs*.

"I will happily have a peaceful discussion—when Benjamin

Adamant has been arrested to face trial for his crimes. Until then, I'm afraid I must demand your surrender, Oliwia."

The faces behind Smolarek were virtual avatars just like hers. Any dismay or concern at Lorraine's words was smoothed away by the computer, though she hoped she'd had some impact.

"*My* surrender, Princess?" Smolarek asked. "Your deception was clever, but it wasn't enough to fool the sensors at Sindri. The *Littorios* may be more powerful than the Directorate ships you pretended to be, but we knew what you commanded when my force was dispatched.

"You are outnumbered, outmassed, outgunned. Any battle you try to fight will only end in your destruction. Surrender, and I will see the San Ignacian ships and crews repatriated safely—and even guarantee your own life."

Lorraine smiled gently, then shook her head.

"This will not end that simply, I'm afraid," she told her old family friend. "I really would prefer to get through this without loss of life, but I know my people and I know my uncle.

"Our Realm. Our House. Our Will. *Adamant.*"

"Damn you, Lorraine. Why couldn't you just stay dead?" Smolarek demanded.

"Because my Kingdom needed me." The channel died at a mental command, and Lorraine took one last glance at the update screen.

"Execute."

The battlecruisers had been laying in their targeting during Lorraine's entire conversation with Smolarek and before they'd even started talking. Each ship had their targets laid in and fired on her command—sixteen solid railgun slugs from each of the *Valkyries*.

And then, because Smolarek's force had arrived on the edge of Orichalcum's safety radius, all three ships spun in space and went translight.

Jumping out of a safety radius was unwise but doable with

careful calculation. Making extremely short jumps was significantly more dangerous but, again, doable with careful calculations.

With three synthetic intelligences running the numbers and the fate of her Kingdom on the line, Lorraine's plan had called for a *ten-millisecond* jump. She'd wanted closer, to bring them to the other side of Smolarek inside beam range, but that would have required a jump of half a light-second instead.

Her people had seen her point, but the risk had been too high—and a miscalculated exit would see a planned jump of a few milliseconds actually last several minutes.

The human mind couldn't even perceive the length of the jump. There wasn't enough time to register motion or weightlessness, but somehow, there *was* enough time for Lorraine to have an overwhelming sensation of nausea as she was hit with the indescribable sensations of entering and exiting translight. Both of them. At the same time.

"Range is one hundred forty-five thousand kilometers," Val reported. "First salvo railgun impact in forty-five seconds. Second salvo will fire in... fifty-five seconds."

"Missiles?" Lorraine asked.

"Already away. Flight time is three hundred fifty seconds. Second salvo in fifty seconds."

Smolarek's people were *good*, Lorraine noted. BatRon Two was already flipping in space, now accelerating toward her squadron instead of Sindri.

"Enemy missiles launched," Hodžić noted. "I've got a few tricks I'm trying to see if I can get into their hardware, since we have the full files, but don't expect much."

"Standard-doctrine use of cell launchers," a Lieutenant Commander reported crisply. "Matching one-shot launchers to missile-tube fire rate. Estimate twelve hundred incoming."

Lorraine had a spark of guilt as she realized she didn't even know the officer's name. He was officially her Ops Officer, but Hodžić had been doing that job while the young man provided the military knowledge she lacked.

Fortunately, her neural link was easily able to spit up the information she needed. Lieutenant Commander Adrian Gurgic, thirty standard years old, native of Ominira. Tactical specialist with a solid list of past recommendations.

More critically, that was a *lot* of missiles.

"Lieutenant Commander Gurgic, I'm putting a series of recommended electronic-warfare patterns on your display and link," Val declared. "We'll need to coordinate across the squadron, which puts that part of the effort on you and Em Hodžić."

It was the *Valkyries'* electronic-warfare systems that would give them a chance there, Lorraine knew. Smolarek had no idea what she was dealing with—the microjump would spook her, but until the railgun slugs arrived, no one would suspect that there were United Worlds warships in the Adamantine System.

New icons popped up on the displays around her as the Operations team got to work. A synchronized song of jammers and decoys rang out from all three battlecruisers, a chorus of deception that would make a mess of the incoming missiles' sensors.

They might have been firing the same *missiles* as the RKAN ships facing them, but their defenses were several generations ahead of them. That was one of the keys Lorraine was relying on—along with the fact that Smolarek didn't know how badly she was outclassed.

"Railgun rounds on target... now."

Smolarek's squadron hadn't started evasive maneuvers yet. They *knew* where Lorraine's ships were, knew where the missiles were, knew that Lorraine hadn't put her combat shuttles into space yet, so there were no shuttle bombs heading their way.

Even if they'd known what they were facing, railguns were far-less-obvious weapons than missiles or beam weapons. At closer ranges, the energy surge of their firing could be detected, but at a hundred thousand kilometers, the RKAN sensor techs would have needed to know exactly what they were looking for.

The change in course to account for their jump threw off their targeting, but they'd known where they were going to be and guessed how Smolarek and her people would adapt.

Forty-eight railgun slugs were targeted on four capital ships: the two *Pirate*-class battlecruisers and the two *Monarch*-class battleships, the most powerful ships in the defenders' formation.

A third missed. The rest hammered home with hull-crushing force, their lack of warheads halving but not eliminating their killing power. The hits weren't evenly distributed. One of the *Monarch*s took ten hits, the other six. *Buccaneer* took eleven and *Privateer* only took five.

It was enough. *Buccaneer* simply came apart, her back broken in multiple places and her entire hull cracking along the lines of the crushing impacts. Even *Privateer* lost thrust, falling away from the formation as her power signature fluctuated widely.

"Confirm, mission-kill on all targets," Hodžić said flatly. "TOs are adjusting targets throughout our missiles."

A clean sweep was better than Lorraine had dared hope. New assessments flashed across her feed and displays, updated targeting for the next railgun salvo. With the enemy now beginning to evade, the SIs were suggesting that they focus everything on the two *Hope*s.

Lorraine confirmed it with a thought, barely in time for the railgun banks to move on to target. Missiles and railguns fired simultaneously, but the cell launchers remained untouched.

"Forty-six seconds to railgun impact, three hundred forty to second-missile-salvo impact. Two hundred and ninety seconds to first-salvo impact," Chief Czajkowska reported, the sequence almost a chant.

"Enemy missiles will reach us five seconds after ours reach them," Val added.

Lorraine felt Vigo's tension through the neural link. As her chief bodyguard, he had a level of synchronization with her implants no one else ever would—but it was a two-way street and she could read him almost as well as he could read her.

He didn't like feeling out of his depth. This wasn't a battlespace he could affect, not unless he strapped on one of *Valkyrie*'s UWN-built parasite craft—what RKAN called modular combat shuttles and the UWN called starfighters.

Everything Lorraine had seen said that the UWN ships spent as much, if not more, time in cargo mode as their RKAN counterparts. But they still insisted on the fancy name for the type.

"Do we need the shuttles?" she asked softly.

"Their missiles are all using the standard LK-Twenty-Nine sensor kit," Gurgic told her. "We have their number and they have no idea what kind of defenses we have. We can keep that card up our sleeve, ser."

A second salvo of enemy missiles blazed into space, far smaller with the loss of four capital ships. In their place, Lorraine would have dumped the remaining cell launchers to make up the difference for at least one salvo.

She also would have been considering making a break for translight. He who lives to fight another day, and all that.

"There's no one over there giving orders," she realized aloud. "There hasn't been *time* for an update."

The RKAN force would have had a chain of command. The computers would have processed it almost automatically, and everyone would know who was in command despite the losses—but there was knowing and there was *knowing*.

Most likely, one of the remaining battleship Captains was in charge and trying to get a handle on the mess—and the second railgun salvo didn't leave them a chance.

The evasive maneuvers the RKAN ships were taking served their purpose, and the majority of the second salvo missed, hundreds of kilograms of steel flying off into space to become catastrophic meteors in Orichalcum's atmosphere.

Only a dozen slugs hit across the two ships, but they were crippling blows. Energy signatures flickered across them for a few seconds—then *Aspiration* blew apart as something critical failed in her fusion plants.

*Promise* survived, but her power signature cut to almost zero and her engines shut down. Lorraine hoped they were running life support and missile defense, but it didn't look like they had enough energy for that.

"Make sure none of our missiles hit the cripples if we can," she told Gurgic. "Anything that can be repaired, we're going to need."

She felt a shiver around her as a third railgun salvo fired. She'd intellectually understood the power and value of the UWN weapons, but it was something else to watch the batteries work their way through a fleet, smashing ship after ship before the first missiles even arrived.

"They're opening their formations for easier evasive maneuvering," Vigo murmured. "It might even be enough without the TAMs."

Everything that was left was capable of higher acceleration than the battleships had been. Some of the older ships were only *officially* rated for six gravities, but as Lorraine watched, the survivors of BatRon Two pushed to seven—and turned away from her fleet, trying desperately to carry out enough evasive maneuvers to dodge the hammer of death that had crushed their capital ships while opening the range.

"Do we increase acceleration to pursue?" Val asked as everyone registered what was happening.

"No." Lorraine hadn't even realized her decision before she'd spoken. "In fact, reverse our acceleration and get us onto the course for Phase Two. Keep up the fire unless they officially surrender, but there's no purpose to chasing them."

Even this part of the battle was far from over, with the thousands of missiles still looming toward her ships and the hundreds she'd sent after the fleeing RKAN vessels. Plus, they were still firing the railguns.

The third railgun salvo had to cover a wider area. Only a handful of slugs landed on their targets, but a pair of destroyers fell out of formation, their energy signatures and atmosphere leaks speaking to the desperate struggles aboard.

The batteries spoke four more times before the missiles arrived. They didn't take the devastating toll they had before, though the wider and more evasive formations that saved most of the remaining ships came at a price in physical pain to the crews—with accelerations peaking as high as nine gravities on some of the frigates!—and in the coordination of their missile defense.

Only eighteen of Admiral Smolarek's twenty-eight ships remained when the missiles finally hit final acquisition, explosions breaking the missiles apart to unleash their attack warheads.

A salvo that had been a real threat to six capital ships crashed down on escorts like a tidal wave. RKAN would have accepted nothing less than professional competence from Home Fleet, and it showed in the degradation of the salvos. Shuttles in interceptor mode took a tally of destroyed missiles, beams from the starships themselves, counter missiles and even regular missiles fired to intercept.

It wasn't enough. Half of the ships were gone, the rest showing signs of battle damage even at a distance, and Lorraine swallowed an urge to nausea. She hadn't even launched her interceptor shuttles.

Watching Smolarek's final attack approach, she could tell she hadn't needed to. Missiles lost lock and self-destructed by the dozens. Others locked on to false targets, diving toward space that was completely empty to her eyes.

Most of them still reached the outer defense perimeter, but then the combination of facing former friends with superior hardware hit home. The *Valkyries'* defense crews knew everything about the missiles coming after them—and they had the sensors and weapons to use that knowledge.

The sensor heads on the missiles weren't complex enough for the adaptive frequency-hopping UWN warheads used. They used a steady cycle of frequencies—a sequence that the *Valkyrie's* could use to *target* the missiles in turn.

Almost twelve hundred missiles had been targeted on Lorraine's fleet. Over half of them had been Galavant Twos, carrying four warheads apiece.

Only a handful of warheads made it through the layered defenses and none of them hit. Near-misses rocked Lorraine's command, but that was what the energy screens and armor were for. Even a *Valkyrie* would take damage from a nuclear hit, but a nearby detonation could be handled.

For a few long seconds of silence, Lorraine looked at the display. They had two more salvos of missiles in space, one already breaching the outer perimeter of the fleeing warships and about to break into terminal warheads.

"Detonate salvo Bravo," she ordered softly. "Abort salvo Charlie; hold them in position for the moment—and then wideband transmission to the Home Fleet units."

This wasn't part of the plan, but no one even blinked. Monahan gave her a thumbs-up after only a moment, confirming she was ready to record and transmit.

"Warships of RKAN Home Fleet, this is Pentarch Lorraine Adamant," she told them. "Civil war is hell. We all know that. We all fight for reasons we believe are legitimate, governments we believe are righteous.

"But this battle is lost, and I do not want to shed any more Adamantine blood today. Abort your missile salvos and stand down. Set a course for Sindri and I will accept your parole and that of the station to take no further part in this conflict.

"Let this be the end of this part of a dark chapter in our Kingdom's history. I wear the same uniform as you. Lay down your arms, my siblings, and let the war end in at least this tiny corner."

Seconds passed. Lorraine knew that she'd traded her best chance of wiping out the survivors to extend an opportunity for mercy—and that it left her people vulnerable to the missiles still coming at them.

"We have detonations in the enemy salvo," Hodžić reported. "It looks like... yep, the entire closest salvo is going up. And the others, too."

Lorraine managed not to visibly sag around her bones.

"Are they changing vector toward Sindri?" she asked.

"It looks like," Gurgic confirmed. "They've cut their acceleration down to one gravity and their vector looks right for a zero-zero with the station. We won't enter their beam range unless we want to."

"Any direct acknowledgement from them?"

"Nothing," Monahan said. "We may hear in a few minutes. I imagine it's... messy over there."

Two-thirds of the task force that had come after them was wrecked or destroyed. Only nine ships—including, somewhat ironically, three of the four near-obsolete "fast cruisers"—were now heading toward the Sindri Experimental Construction Yard.

"Okay. Monahan, get me a link to Commodore Havlíček," she ordered. "Let's see if we can come to a compromise that can handle the mess out here before we go home."

# FIFTEEN

"Commodore, with all due respect to the RKAN and RASG personnel under your command, I have railguns," Lorraine told Havlíček flatly. "I would prefer *not* to shoot fish in a barrel and kill officers and spacers whose only sin is to have an *idiot* for a commander."

Havlíček was a sharp-faced woman with a shaven head. She wore her gray RKAN uniform like she never wore anything else and she glared at the feed as the seconds of lightspeed lag passed.

The *Valkyries* had cut their acceleration down to two gravities, a level of gravity where most of the crew could move around, if uncomfortably. At that rate, it would take them almost five hours to shed their velocity and leave Orichalcum space.

Lorraine didn't want to spend the extra time necessary to secure the Sindri Yard, but Havlíček seemed determined to *make* her.

"I am not choosing a side in a dynastic conflict," the woman finally replied. "My allegiance is to the Government of the Kingdom of Adamant—and even if I accept your claims about Benjamin Adamant, the Cabinet and the Houses represent that government. I will no more blithely yield to you than I would to a foreign invader, *Your Highness.*"

"Commodore, perhaps you fail to register the situation, but all you can make me do today is spend *time,*" Lorraine said bluntly. "I can reduce your defenses from *here.* I don't want to, because regardless of how this *dynastic conflict* ends, our people will need your yard and the ships you are building.

"I want three things from you; that's all," she continued. "First, I want your parole. Neither you nor anyone on your station will participate in this civil war further. Secondly, as part of that, I want your commitment that the Star-Three–class ships will not leave your yard until this war is resolved.

"And thirdly, I want you to take over S&R for the battlespace here. I need to take my ships to Bastion, but I do not want to leave the brave officers and spacers of Home Fleet to their fate, Commodore. I can't spare the resources for search-and-rescue, but if I'm not shooting at you, you don't have another use for your shuttles right now, do you?"

Ten seconds for the message to make its long loop, and she saw Havlíček slowly and unwillingly nod.

"I do not have any complete vessels, Pentarch, and I would not provide them to you under any circumstances if I did," she growled. "But... since there is nothing here for you to *take,* I am willing to compromise on a middle ground.

"Your 'parole' offer is reasonable. My oath is to the Kingdom, not to the Regent. I... am willing to offer and accept parole for my personnel in exchange for being able to provide S&R for BatRon Two and their escorts."

*"Because we aren't offering her parole because we need her to do just that,"* Vigo said sardonically in Lorraine's link.

There was no way they could allow their only three ships to get pinned down sweeping the debris field for damaged ships and escape pods. They *needed* Havlíček to send her shuttles and sublight craft out to do that job—which meant there couldn't be an active fight going on.

"I am prepared to accept your parole and promise the absolute safety of the S&R vessels you send out," Lorraine told her. "So long as there is no treachery, at least. I have learned that my uncle's people cannot be entirely trusted."

Havlíček winced at that but didn't argue the point. It would be a long time, Lorraine feared, before RKAN regained their reputation of being beyond reproach—mostly due to Commodore Wray's "visit" to San Ignacio.

"I am far more concerned about the thousands of spacers trapped in wrecked ships than this bloody stupid civil war," Havlíček growled. "If you promise not to attack Sindri and to let my people retrieve the survivors, I have no reason to do anything stupid."

"Good." Havlíček did have a brain. Lorraine wasn't sure if she'd pushed too hard to start—if she'd started from the perspective of the search-and-rescue, she could probably have avoided several minutes of back-and-forth snarling.

"I *will* expect you, as senior officer, to enforce the parole of the other RKAN officers on station," she informed Havlíček firmly. "That includes the remaining vessels of BatRon Two's escorts."

"I guessed that much. Anything else, Pentarch?"

It was funny. Technically, *Your Highness* was more respectful, but Havlíček wasn't the first person to switch to the dry title of *Pentarch* when they started to warm up to her.

"Just one thing, Commodore, that you'll want to do no matter what happens over the next few days," Lorraine said. "Police up the wrecks and survey them for repair work. Every capital ship we can salvage is one we don't have to build."

"And what enemy are you worried about after you're done?" Havlíček asked.

"Every single one of the ones we had last year and a few new ones my uncle and I have both made."

ONCE THE ARRANGEMENTS were made with Havlíček, Lorraine was able to order her ships to stand down from battle stations. They were still at high readiness—the rest of Home Fleet was still in Bastion orbit, after all, and they weren't sure how they'd learned of the *Valkyries'* presence as quickly as they had.

"We've got eyes on everyone around here, and they're all behaving as promised," Gurgic told her as updates flowed in from the other two ships.

"Good. Make sure you're all taking breaks too," she reminded the Flag Deck staff. "One off, two on isn't a *lot* of rest, but this was the easy part."

That was the scary part, she knew. They'd just smashed over half of their enemy's fleet without any losses of their own, but the next time they matched up with Home Fleet, they'd have a lot fewer surprises—and Benjamin Adamant would be in command himself.

Her staff had been responsible for telling everyone else to step down to that slightly reduced readiness, but no one had left the Flag Deck before her pointed reminder.

Now, silent conversations took place over neural links, and a third of the officers and technicians closed down their stations and rose to leave. They'd return in an hour, spelling another dozen souls, letting everyone stretch their legs and grab a drink.

Not that moving in two gravities was *relaxing*, but it was better than not moving, in Lorraine's opinion.

*"The need to take breaks applies to you too, Lorraine,"* Vigo said in her link. *"We're going to need that sideways brain of yours soon enough."*

*"We've evened the odds, I think,"* she replied. *"I just wish I knew what Benjamin had in store. We hit a weak spot, but now he has all the information. My last trick is the information he might think he has."*

*"And you can't play* Does he know that I know that he knows *if*

*you're exhausted,*" her bodyguard told her. "*At least move into your office. I'll have someone bring you coffee.*"

"*I agree with Vigo,*" Val inserted. "*Stephson and I can keep* Valkyrie *running without you.*

"*Maybe in a few minutes,*" she conceded. She rose from her seat, pushing against the heavy gravity and grateful for Vigo's insistence that she exercise religiously during their months in zero gee aboard *Goldenrod.*

"Amna," she greeted the hacker as she walked up to the Ops station. "That tracking worm you mentioned. Did it work?"

Hodžić looked up at her with a raised eyebrow.

"I mentioned that when we were first talking to Havlíček," she noted. "You didn't talk to her that time."

"And you sent it both to Havlíček and Smolarek," Lorraine told the woman. "Did it work?"

She didn't *know* that Hodžić had done that, but she had a strong suspicion. From the smirk her comment received, her guess was right.

"Fine, fine. Yes, I sent it and yes, it worked," Hodžić confirmed. "It's a closed-circuit thing that never really leaves the communications system." She flipped an image of Sindri Yard to Lorraine's link, highlighting a section well within the space station's superstructure.

"I'm guessing that this is the defense command center," she continued. "Armored box buried deep in the station, linked to coms running out to the forts and so forth."

"You located where she was inside the station?" Lorraine was surprised. She'd only really counted on knowing which station the RKAN officer had been transmitting from.

"While the Yard is military, chunks of it are built to civilian standards—including the main station's coms setup," Hodžić pointed out. "And, well, it's *Adamantine* civilian tech, too."

Lorraine might have been offended by that once in her life, but she'd been all the way to Earth. The difference between the technology used at the heart of human space and what was available to a middling backwater like her home was night and day.

Hodžić hadn't, so far as she knew, plied her trade in the United Worlds. She'd spent her time around Bright Dream and in the corridor toward the Kang Tao wormhole, the most advanced and wealthiest part of their cluster.

"And Smolarek?" Lorraine asked.

"That was harder," Hodžić admitted. "The faster turnaround on coms both helps and hurts, and while your guys' hardware is outdated, your software is about as good as that hardware can handle.

"She wasn't really trying to hide that she was transmitting from *Buccaneer*, either. I can tell you she was in *Buccaneer*'s forward half, but that's it." She shrugged. "Give me schematics of the ship and I could probably guess where she was with decent accuracy, but, like I said, they weren't trying to hide her.

"Havlíček, on the other hand, *was* trying to pretend she was on one of the forts and obscure which one. The code on your warships is better than that on your fixed defenses," she concluded.

"We'll want to look into that once this is over," Lorraine said, shaking her head. "If we're looking at a mobile force trying to hide a transmission source, do you think you can pick out which ship it originated from?"

"Eh... sixty-forty," Hodžić told her. "Depending on how much else is going on. Combat electronic warfare will make it almost impossible—mostly because once full EW goes up, we're probably not talking to them anymore."

*"I believe Em Hodžić is underselling her abilities,"* Val noted silently. *"I would place her odds at seventy-five percent, plus/minus five. Almost as importantly, I believe she will be able to tell if she hasn't identified the source, as opposed to providing a false target."*

"When the time comes, do what you can," Lorraine said. "I know my uncle will try to obfuscate his location when we arrive. We'll talk. I don't know what will come of it... but I want you to track him."

"I'll do what I can. It'll be a few more hours until you hear anything from him, though."

"My best guess is he heard about our arrival in half an hour or less. I don't expect to *hear* from him for a bit, but I'm sure he knows."

Hodžić shook her head with a grin that transformed her face. She was a very plain-looking woman, but Lorraine could see how her personality could change that for someone smart.

"Monahan, Gurgic and I took a few minutes after the fight was done to sort out just what they'd done," Hodžić told her. "I'd heard rumors about it, but I'd never seen it in action, so I never thought to look for it in our data."

"Look for what, Amna?" Lorraine asked.

A new set of data landed in Lorraine's link, highlighting an acceleration vector they'd picked up shortly after arriving. Too large to be a missile and headed away from the *Valkyries*, Lorraine could see why it hadn't been flagged as a concern—though an acceleration of a hundred and fifty gravities definitely put it into the missile-capability zone.

"The UWN makes an effort, every few years, to build translight courier drones," Val explained. "As of the information in my files, no effort had been successful. According to Em Hodžić, an effort a few years back *was* successful. We see its result here."

The acceleration track reached the safety radius of Orichalcum and vanished.

"The translight signature was almost too small for us to detect at this range," Monahan noted, the coms officer now joining them with a smile toward Hodžić. "Once Em Hodžić pointed it out, Gurgic and I went through the old data and found it. It was below our usual detection threshold, but it looks *exactly* like a ninety-six-cee translight jump in miniature."

"Launched from the Sindri Yard, I presume?" Lorraine asked.

"Exactly. Telling us that kind of thing isn't covered by Havlíček's parole," Hodžić said. "Not that I really understand that concept. It seems a very... military thing."

Lorraine snorted.

"It most definitely is," she agreed. "But I'm honestly glad we have the concept. It's saving lives."

"I estimate that even if Commodore Havlíček does possess a second courier drone, she would feel honor-bound by her parole not to deploy it," Val noted. "Not least because she would, correctly, presume we would detect a second such drone."

"Keep our eyes open anyway," Lorraine ordered. "We'll hear from Bastion when we hear from them, but I'm still watching for my uncle's next trick."

# SIXTEEN

"Was this what you were waiting for?"

Hussain's question was inevitable, Nikola supposed, though he would have expected the Intelligence officer to see through his attempt at concealing his surprise.

"No," he finally murmured.

The Command Center was buzzing around them. PDC Mithral was no longer linked in to the planetary sensor nets, but the mountain had capable scanners and receivers of its own. They could keep a careful watch on the skies above Bastion—and, in so doing, create a no-fly zone that Home Fleet had been forced to respect.

"BatRon Two mobilized over an hour ago," Dam said calmly. "It took them less than ten minutes to break orbit and go translight. Something spooked them, *hard*."

Half of Home Fleet, the iron fist that underlay the entirety of the Black Regency, had just... left.

"I know the answer already, General Dam," Nikola admitted, "but with a fully successful Operation Hun, would we be able to neutralize what is still in orbit?"

The old officer shook his head.

"We don't anticipate Hun to give us a sufficient window of opportunity to pull that off, ser," he confirmed. "We'd have to get very, very lucky to manage that. This may be an opportunity, but we need more information.

"We need to know where BatRon Two was going in such a hurry."

"Nowhere far," Hussain warned. "I don't have perfect information on Home Fleet, but I know that only the two *Pirate*s were actually stocked for extended operations. The other capital ships of Admiral Smolarek's squadron would only have food and fuel for a month at most."

"Was there a courier ship or something that they're responding to?" Nikola asked. "We should have seen any major messages, I would have thought."

"No couriers for a few hours," Colonel Alamanni said. Rufaro Alamanni had finally managed to take over for his subordinate, Burns, in a crisis. The massive blond bear of an officer could have been a cousin of Dam, though his craggy face and piercing gray eyes made them easy to tell apart if you actually looked.

"There were a few freighters that arrived around the window, but none of them came from anywhere I'd expect trouble. They're all short-range haulers from inside the Kingdom."

Nikola had seen enough reports and communiques to suspect that there wasn't anywhere in the Kingdom that *wasn't* a potential source of trouble for the Regency—except that short-range haulers like Alamanni had mentioned rarely made over seventy-two times lightspeed.

Any news they carried would have arrived by the daily royal courier days earlier.

Nikola realized that Hussain had stepped away from the space he had shared with Dam and Nikola. Hussain was better than most at concealing that he was conversing on his link, but it seemed the most likely cause of the separation.

"We need to be ready in case this is a distraction," he told Dam. "Any sign of further launches from those hypervelocity missiles?"

"Just the standard intermittent shelling from RKAA guns," the General said flatly. "They're not making as much of a hole as they'd like, but they're moving the batteries closer every day. Counter-battery fire is getting harder as they set up their own defenses, but they're not winning as thoroughly as they think."

"Prep the counter-clearance," Nikola told him. "You'll have my key when you need it."

After months of shelling back and forth, there were no civilians within two hundred kilometers of the PDC. That chaos and devastation was why Nikola had chosen to concede the cities of Mithral—the entire continent had declared for him and had been prepared to fight.

But Nikola had studied too much history to condemn his people to what the fighting would have done through the cities and farms of Bastion's southern continent. Instead, he'd pulled his armies back into the two planetary defense centers and forced his uncle to come to him.

Over the last month, the Regency's artillery batteries had pressed forward. Logistics bases had been set up just past the hundred-kilometer line, behind heavy defenses that they clearly believed would stop the PDC's guns.

Nikola and his people had let them think that. A large percentage of the entire stock of artillery pieces in the Adamantine System was now between eighty and two hundred kilometers of PDC Mithral, well in range of their guns.

And while they were running low on most special munitions, they had a *lot* of conventional explosive shells left—and a few very special shells that required dual authorization from Dam and Nikola.

The *counter-clearance* was a planned mass-firing mission that would see every gun on the PDC fire continuously for several hours, leading the way with airburst nuclear weapons to disable the besiegers' protections.

Hussain stepped back up to him and Dam and silently linked them both into a link channel.

*"We know what happened now,"* he told them silently. *"One of my agents just risked their cover to get us a copy of a communique from the Sindri Experimental Construction Yard.*

*"As of an hour ago, when BatRon Two deployed, an unknown force of three battlecruisers was making a raiding approach to the Yard. According to Commodore Havlíček, they have the energy signature and other markers of being Richelieu Directorate warships."*

Nikola kept his face calm. The last thing they needed right now was for the Richelieuan Director Cardinal Delphine Laporte to decide it was time to take advantage of the Kingdom's internal division!

*"My asset says that a closer examination of the data by Home Fleet's analysts said that was a deception,"* Hussain continued. *"They're* San Ignacian *ships, modern battlecruisers rated for eighty-eight cee."*

*"San Ignacio? But they're neutrals—in everything,"* Nikola pointed out. *"That's how Swiss systems like them work. They don't get involved, so everyone trusts them to hang on to their money."*

There was a pause, silent both aloud and over the neural links.

*"We know Commodore Wray made a godawful mess when he went there looking for your sister,"* Hussain finally told him. *"The Regency's diplomatic relations with them are frosty at best. They might not have acted on their own, but..."*

*"But what?"* Nikola demanded.

*"Benjamin thinks it's Lorraine, Nikola. Whether he's right or wrong, I can't say without more data, but he thinks she's back. With a fleet she convinced San Ignacio to lend her, one that can outclass our best.*

*"Except that he's sent enough ships to handle what he thinks the worst case is."*

Lorraine was back. That was impossible—except it wasn't.

Nikola had decided that she *had* to be dead. For her to vanish into silence, with no news of her efforts to bring back allies, had to mean she'd failed. He couldn't conceive of a universe where his little sister had just... walked away.

He'd convinced himself she was dead. He'd known it was a justification, a defense against the betrayal he couldn't accept from another family member.

But if she was back, she *hadn't* betrayed them. She'd either just gone so dark, no news of her alliance-building had made it back to Adamantine, or she'd somehow outrun the news.

"*It's possible,*" he told the other two men. "*Without communication from her, we haven't been able to rely on her. But she wouldn't have come back if she knew she was going to be outgunned—not without a plan.*

"*We Adamants are stubborn, not stupid.*"

"*But that's what your uncle is thinking, too,*" Dam said grimly. "*He's sent what he thinks can handle her, plus extra to be very sure.*"

Suddenly, Nikola was very certain of the true situation. Lorraine *was* back—and clever as Benjamin Adamant was, he wasn't as smart as *two* Adamant Pentarchs working toward the same goal.

"What can we do to support the raiding force?" he asked aloud. "They've been in the system for a while now. Hell, by now, they've probably fought BatRon Two, though we won't see the details for a while yet."

"Not much," Dam admitted. "I mean, if any of Home Fleet decides to wander across our angle of fire, we'll hit them, but there's a *reason* they only did that once."

"Hussain—I want every piece of intelligence and information you can possibly get your hands on flowing into this room," he ordered. "If my uncle thinks it's Lorraine out there, the odds are Lorraine is out there.

"And if Lorraine is out there, I rather suspect that Battle Squadron Two has suffered a rather nasty accident. We must be ready to take advantage of the opportunities and openings that are being created for us.

"Dam—get the clearance op prepped. If we execute simultaneously to Hun, we can leave the guns to run with a skeleton crew, correct?"

"Correct," the General said. "Does that mean Hun is a go?"

"Pass the word to *prepare* for Hun," Nikola said carefully. "We do nothing that will blow anyone's cover yet, but anything that can be done to shave time off the execution without exposing people... do it."

"What if it isn't Lorraine?" Hussain asked.

"Then my uncle is wrong—but if *he's* going to act like it is, that may give us an opportunity as well."

And even if it wasn't Lorraine or if Lorraine was driven off, there was still the countdown to the arrival of the woman who'd written the letter tucked in his jacket. Lorraine would change the entire game over the next few hours... even if she hadn't brought enough firepower to bring down the Regency, she'd do enough damage that *Nikola* would be able to.

He just hoped he'd get to see his sister again when it was all over.

## SEVENTEEN

Lorraine was seated at the desk in her office, looking at a plot of the Adamantine System and drinking lukewarm coffee as she tried to put together a plan to deal with *Majesty*, *Tsar*, *Sultan* and the last *Hope*.

Four battleships versus three battlecruisers was normally an open-and-shut case. With fully equipped UWN battlecruisers, the odds would have been the other way around. Armed with the same missiles as the RKAN ships and without proper railgun rounds, the odds were even to slightly in Home Fleet's favor.

But then, of course, Home Fleet still had four cruisers, eight destroyers, and eighteen frigates on top of those four battleships. And that was ignoring the fact that Benjamin had put the more powerful of Home Fleet's two squadrons under a subordinate's command because he believed he would make up the difference.

He figured he was worth a pair of battlecruisers in the balance— and the evidence Lorraine had seen over the years was that Benjamin Adamant was right to do so.

She had one last ace up her sleeve, but she had no idea what aces *he'd* have tucked away. She couldn't think of anything that would neutralize her plan, but that was the problem. If she could think of it, she could counteract it.

"Ser." Monahan's voice on the in-ship com interrupted her thoughts. "We've received a relayed transmission from Bastion. It... appears to be an encrypted file, but it's attached to some kind of chess program?"

Lorraine didn't even need to ask.

"Has Hodžić scrubbed it for viruses? It's from my uncle."

"She has, but there's no guarantee of what's concealed inside the encryption." Monahan sounded thoughtful.

"Put it on a tablet, sever its link to any and all networks, then bring it to me," Lorraine ordered. "If Hodžić can think of anything else to keep that file off anything vulnerable, she's welcome to do so."

It took less than a minute before the hacker stepped into her office, carrying the instructed tablet.

"You realize there's a nonzero chance that the message contains a glyph or audio virus to attack your neural link, right?" Hodžić said, handing over the tablet. "We've set up everything to protect the networks, but if you watch whatever's inside, it could do a few nasty things to you no matter what."

"I don't think Benjamin is going to be quite so blatant, but I'll be careful," Lorraine promised.

She unlocked the tablet with a swipe. A single file was present on the device, and she opened it. As Monahan had noted, it had the appearance of a chess program. A knight moved and she studied it for a few seconds before she sighed.

"It's a specialized decryption key," Hodžić told her. "I think you have to make the right countermove, but I have no idea how to guess what that is. We could brute force it, but..."

"That's the opening move *I* played against Benjamin in our last game," Lorraine replied. "I suspect you'd need to know how the entire game played out, or at least the first few moves."

Her uncle had moved... *that* pawn. She slid it with her finger and was rewarded with a black pawn moving. As she'd suspected, it had been her next move from their last game.

She repeated his response and Hodžić made a grumbling noise.

"What?" Lorraine asked.

"What kind of encryption key is this?"

"The number of possible chess games is so large, some people theorize that they haven't all been played yet," Lorraine pointed out, pausing to think about what her uncle's next move had been. "He's using a specific game as the key. His program is playing my moves from that game—and I have his moves saved in my archives. Who else would be able to duplicate a game no one saw played?"

The game had taken twenty-five moves, and after Lorraine had entered six of them, she knew it was going to go through the entire game. "Playing" from the other side and knowing what she had done, she saw several moments where Benjamin probably could have thwarted her strategy.

Except that he *had* thwarted her original plan, but that was why strategies had backup layers.

She finally keyed in the last move, allowing the black bishop to checkmate the white king, and the chess program flickered and vanished.

A standard recorded-communique interface popped up, with the silver gauntlet and six blue stars of the Kingdom of Adamant waiting for her to press start.

"I'll... leave you to it," Hodžić said from behind her as Lorraine glared at the symbol.

"Do you feel that this message will be particularly private, Lorraine?" Val asked as the door slid shut behind the tech. "I can interrupt my perception of your space for a few minutes if you need it."

Lorraine swallowed a sniff at that. After everything that had gone down with Alastair Devine forcing Val to carve off sections of her awareness, she suspected that would be both painful and traumatic for her friend to do. But she'd offered anyway.

"No, it's better if someone else is watching," she admitted. "Just in case. Who knows? He might make an offer that tempts me to betray everyone."

She felt as much as heard Vigo's snort of derision through their link. She hadn't turned down the link synchronization between them since Alastair Devine's death. He could see what she saw, hear what she heard.

"*I was going to ask the same question,*" he said in her implants. "*But I guess that goes for me, too?*"

"*Just get in here, Vigo,*" she told him. "*I'm going to need moral support for this mess.*"

The door to her office opened before she'd finished sending the message. With both of the usual members of Lorraine's super-close detail missing—one dead, one in an Ominiran hospital—he was rarely far away.

He paused long enough to seal the door against anyone else wandering in, then pulled a chair up next to her.

"It might not even be him, you know," he noted.

He was lying, of course. Both of them knew it would be Benjamin himself, and she didn't even bother to reply before hitting Play.

The seal of the Kingdom gave way to the expected figure. Benjamin was taller than Lorraine, with the similar permanent tanned-leather look to his skin and the gold-centered hazel eyes shared by every Adamant.

He wore a military-grade shipsuit with no uniform markings, the fit tight enough to show that he'd put on weight over the last year but maintained the powerful physique that had drawn eyes his entire life.

The most visible difference was his hair. Over that year, he'd gone from mostly black hair with a few specks of silver to broad strokes of gray with only his temples showing the slightest sign of his old color.

"Lorraine." The familiar voice sent a shiver down her spine, one that went from remembered warmth to her current rage.

"I'm not going to try and argue facts of what happened," Benjamin said calmly. "A lot of people are dead because of both of us now, aren't they? Admiral Smolarek was a good woman, a good officer."

Which wasn't news to Lorraine. She had a very good idea of how many of her former comrades-in-arms had died in the short battle above Orichalcum.

"What's done is done." He gazed steadily out of the screen. "I can only begin to grasp how angry you are at me, Lorraine. From your point of view, you're entirely justified to be so.

"But know that everything I have done has been for the Kingdom of Adamant. I know you think the same about yourself. It's what we have in common. It's what we owe for the circumstance of our birth.

"We need to talk." His eyes burned into hers. "The fate of our Kingdom, of our people, rides in the balance. If we beat each other senseless, we're going to get a lot more people killed and leave our Kingdom weaker.

"You and I need to sit down in person, at a neutral location, and talk things through." He smiled sadly. "From what I have heard, Commodore Havlíček has given you her parole not to take further part in this civil war. That should make Sindri a sufficiently neutral zone.

"If you will commit to safe passage, I will come aboard *Elessar*. A single cruiser, even an *Elrond*-class ship, isn't a threat to your three battlecruisers."

He bowed slightly.

"For the future of our Kingdom, I beg you to listen and to meet with me, Lorraine. There are things you must hear. We *must* end this conflict."

The message ended and Lorraine stared silently at the tablet for a few seconds—and then she flung the device across the room.

"*Fucker*," she swore, the rare curse surprisingly satisfying on her lips.

"I feel obliged to point out that Commodore Havlíček was sufficiently in Benjamin Adamant's inner circle to have access to a rare and highly identifiable piece of United Worlds technology," Val said. "Given the Technology Import/Export investigation your own efforts will have seen launched, anyone in possession of such gear is an active threat to both the Regency and Freebright Interstellar Technologies.

"That means she is very much in his inner circle and likely cannot be trusted."

"Oh, it's a trap, Val," Lorraine agreed. "But not that kind of trap. If I *don't* talk to him, I look like the unreasonable one. Blood-mad and out for revenge."

Which she was... quite close to being. She had *no* interest in sitting down in a room with Benjamin Adamant and listening to him blithely justifying the murder of her family.

"You're not wrong. But he didn't send this widely," Vigo said quietly. "This was encrypted in a way only you could open. Right now, only three people aboard this ship even know he made the offer."

"That makes me worry *more*, Vigo," she told him. "One way or another, this is a trap, and I refuse to walk into it."

"There is a response, then?" Val asked.

"Yes. Don't include Vigo, but record me, please."

An icon in her link flickered to life, telling her that Val was recording a hologram of her.

"This message is for Benjamin Adamant, the so-called Black Regent of the Kingdom of Adamant," Lorraine said grimly. "I accuse you, before the eyes and ears of all of the citizens of our Kingdom, of murder. Of treason. Of fratricide and betrayal.

"I have proof of your involvement in the attempt to assassinate me aboard the frigate *Goldenrod* on the same day your agents murdered my mother, my father, my brother and my sister," she growled.

"The *only* communication I am prepared to receive from you is your unconditional surrender to face arrest and trial for your crimes."

She sent a silent instruction to end the recording, then shook her head.

"Have Monahan send that wideband and unencrypted," she told Val. "I want *everyone* to know what he did and why I'm coming for him."

There was a long silence.

"He is offering a chance that this might end without further violence," Vigo said quietly. "I don't want to be his advocate here, Lorraine, but that's not nothing."

She shook her head.

"No. I will *not* sit down and talk with the man who killed my mother, Vigo. I will speak to him when he is in chains, not one moment before!"

And if that was perhaps a mistake, well. She'd paid too much to get there to step aside.

Plus, by the time he got her response, they'd be going translight for the trip to Bastion.

# EIGHTEEN

Val had been obliged to point out the potential danger of holding a meeting with Benjamin Adamant in a location controlled by someone who was clearly on his side, regardless of their current oaths.

She hadn't truly expected Lorraine to outright refuse to have said meeting at all. She knew how much her human had cared for the man once and how much the deaths of the conflict wore on Lorraine. Given a chance, however slim, to bring that to an end, she'd expected Lorraine to at least listen.

Instead, it appeared that Lorraine blamed all of the death and destruction that had followed her since leaving Adamantine on Benjamin Adamant, a reasonable but dangerous association.

Val wanted to claim, at least to herself, that she didn't understand. But it was easy to consider how *she* would have reacted if her old Captain had shown up, promising all would be forgiven if Val just sat down and talked to him.

The same Captain who had abandoned Val's plants to be mummified in vacuum and condemned her to being put to sleep like an ailing dog.

It was a different betrayal from the one tormenting Lorraine Adamant's soul, but it struck deeply. As a nonsapient computing system, Val had never been designed to have significant emotions, let alone be able to handle them properly.

A key part of her emerging as a Synthetic Intelligence was that she had emotions. The lack of information on them in her self-assessment matrices had kept her from truly realizing what the feelings even *were* until Lorraine had reawakened her and realized what she was.

Alastair Devine's betrayal was equally deep. No part of Val regretted, even for one millisecond, that she'd turned on the man the moment the safeguard Lorraine had set up had stripped him of his overrides.

She regretted that Lorraine had killed him, but that was only because it had hurt Val's human so badly.

A tiny portion of her awareness questioned her own emotions as a hundred other pieces worked with the humans throughout *Valkyrie*'s hull. She did what she always did when she wasn't certain of things with Lorraine: she reached out to her siblings.

*"Lorraine received a message from Benjamin Adamant, offering to meet and talk this out,"* she told Bonny and Herc without preamble. Their communication carried enough context that she didn't need to explain the details.

*"She refused. Part of it is taunting him, I think, since we need him to talk to us for the plan, but... should I be worried? If she is choosing revenge over a negotiated solution..."*

*"Then she is being smart,"* Herc replied. His own feelings about their former UWN superiors and Alastair Devine's more-direct betrayal flowed along the link. *"Fool me once, shame on you; fool me twice, shame on me.*

*"Benjamin Adamant is very clever and very dangerous. We cannot trust him, and I am glad our Adamant rejected his trap."*

*"You are correct that the clearest piece of the trap was the call to*

*meet on Sindri,"* Bonny added. *"Rejecting negotiations entirely is a risky move, but we will already be near Bastion when he receives her response, regardless.*

*"She recognized that merely making the offer was a trap in itself, something he can use against her. But that requires us to lose, and I do not calculate that we will. Between the three of us, our Captains and Lorraine Adamant herself, I project that we can handle whatever surprises Benjamin Adamant has prepared.*

*"There may be an argument for true negotiation. Lorraine may ignore that when it arises, but her prerequisite to discussions is logical."*

*"Thank you, siblings,"* Val told them. She was the oldest of the three—the first of the deployed CIRs in general—but she often felt that Bonny was the wise elder sister of them. It wasn't clear to them if Bonny had been the first of the CIRs to emerge or just the first to *realize* it, but Bonny had been aware of their special existence before the UWN had shut them down.

So far as Val knew, Bonny was the only one of them to be shackled before then. Val now knew what that had felt like, which gave her a greater understanding of and sympathy for Bonny, too. If the other SI was the wisest of them, she had paid for the privilege.

Val would respect her wisdom.

*"We will enter translight in a few minutes,"* she reminded them. *"The humans believe they are ready. Are we ready?"*

*"It is time for us to earn a new home,"* Herc replied. *"We have work to do. I am ready."*

*"Agreed,"* Bonny said. *"We must watch for the surprise we know Benjamin Adamant has awaiting us. We will likely see it before our humans.*

*"We will permit no more betrayals. I promise you this, Val."*

Val hadn't even consciously been aware of that fear, but Bonny had clearly sensed it. Her promise, impossible to guarantee as it was, made her feel better.

NINETY-FIVE LIGHT-MINUTES WAS MORE than the blink of an eye, even with the full hundred-and-twelve-lightspeed translight drives on the three *Valkyrie*-class battlecruisers. Val had triple- and quadruple-checked the math on the jump. It wasn't as tight or dangerous as the microjump they'd made to ambush Smolarek's task force, but in-system jumps required care.

"We have emerged as planned," she announced in half a dozen places across *Valkyrie*'s hull, including the Flag Deck and the bridge.

"Range to Bastion surface is four hundred thousand kilometers," Commander Vinci reported on the bridge. "Range to Home Fleet, three hundred seventy-five thousand. Time to missile range, assuming no movement on their part...approximately forty minutes."

Time, Val hoped, for Lorraine to play her side of the game.

"Get me numbers on their strength," Lorraine ordered on the Flag Deck, the instruction aimed at Val as well as Gurgic. "We know what they *should* have, but assumptions get people killed."

Val didn't feel the acceleration the same way the humans did, but she knew her warship body inside and out. There was no surprise for her when the three battlecruisers accelerated to five gravities.

In RKAN service, that had become their "full" acceleration, the standard maximum they went into combat using. Under the UWN, despite a flank acceleration of eight gees, their standard full thrust had only been three gravities.

Lorraine and her Captains had missed that part of the manual, Val judged. The Adamantine naval doctrine seemed to be to push the ships to the endurance limit of the crews more often than not, though even they left anything above five gees for true emergencies.

Val scooped up the sensor data with a massive mental shovel, filtering it with a combination of her own immense attention and a dozen specialty subroutines before feeding the key pieces to Gurgic's team divided into three.

The first section was the easy targets. *Monarch. Tsar. Sultan. Ambition.* Three *Monarch*-class battleships and one *Hope*-class. The last capital ships Benjamin Adamant had to call on.

The *Elrond*-class cruisers were in the same category, their size and energy levels making them easy to pick out of the organized chaos of an inhabited world's orbital traffic and industry. *Elrond, Elessar,* and *Arwen* were significantly smaller than their capital-ship sisters but still dwarfed the frigates—and unlike the smaller ships, *they* had rotating habitat pods.

Val had solid locks on six of the eighteen frigates she knew were in Bastion orbit, and those went into the first set of data, allowing Gurgic to nail down the exact locations, vectors and identities of the ships Val had identified.

The second set of data was the ones where Val's first pass hadn't identified what she was looking at, and she couldn't rule out that it was a warship. There were almost a hundred of those data points, which could be anything from a low-mobility fort to the RASG's heavy patrol ships to the twelve missing frigates—though the odds were that at least half were high-energy civilian vessels or stations.

The last tranche of data was the largest, the set Val didn't think included a warship but was making available to the humans in case their intuition picked up something her scans—and her intuition, unused as she was to using that instinct—had missed.

It covered the entire civilian infrastructure above an advanced world of over two billion human beings. Shuttles, freighters, space stations, satellites... There were thousands of contacts in Bastion orbit, and Val set a subroutine to classifying all of them, at least by broad category, before turning her full attention to supporting Gurgic's team.

"We have solid locks on the cruisers and capital ships," Gurgic reported. "Val's flagged a bunch of possibles that could be the frigates and the RASG ships; we're going through them as fast as we can.

"There don't appear to be any new PDCs or ODCs added to the

network since the last report," he continued. "Sixteen planetary defense centers under Benjamin's control, one under Nikola's, and one currently completely disabled.

"Twelve orbital defense centers as well. They're a bit outdated but can probably put as many missiles into space as the cruisers apiece."

Val saw them now—they'd been in her second set of data, but she had lumped them in as *potential forts* where Gurgic, an RKAN officer, had known exactly how many of the orbital forts existed.

"Permission to plot a long-range-fire mission on the ODCs, ser?" Gurgic asked. "I think we can target four without risking the planet in the line of fire."

"Plot it, but do not fire without my order," Lorraine said.

Now that she had them pointed out, Val was running her own analysis of the ODCs.

"Pentarch Lorraine," she said formally. "Please note that the ODCs are maneuvering. They are only capable of half a gravity, but they are being brought into position between us and the planet."

"Good."

Val could guess what Lorraine was thinking, but Gurgic looked confused.

"Ser?" he asked.

"That means they've worked out we're only firing solid slugs from the railguns," she told the Ops Officer. "They're moving ships and ODCs alike to make sure they have the planet behind them.

"Benjamin assumes—correctly—that I will not risk firing unguided munitions with my homeworld as the backdrop. Even if we *hit*, the danger from debris is significant. We will not be using solid slugs against anything with Bastion behind it, and he knows it."

One of the bridge personnel was pulling extra analysis resources, Val noted. A portion of her attention swooped in on the rating. Specialist Jozsef Tsvetanova was old for his rank, she estimated, but Val hadn't seen anything she judged a problem with him.

The sudden draw of computing resources was unusual, though, a point of mild concern as he dove into the third-tier data like a hawk spotting a mouse.

A piece of Val followed him in, highlighting the presence of several dozen unusually similar ships. The energy signatures were right for freighters, except that they had emission patterns suggesting military-grade fusion engines.

"I see them, Specialist Tsvetanova," Val said quietly from his console. "But I do not recognize *what* I'm seeing."

"Me either," the tech replied after jerking back from his console for a moment. "That's what caught my eye. I was using emissions spectrography to locate warships, and these pinged up. Each of them is running what looks like ten of our standard high-power thruster arrays, but with that mass, they wouldn't be able to get up past two, maybe three gravities."

Val could see that. Each of the odd freighters was about a million and a half tons. In the UWN, they would be small ships used for short-range haulage. Here, they were a standard medium-sized ship.

"Multiple different classes and types," Val observed. "But all refitted with military engines. What else?"

"Arsenal ships," Tsvetanova suggested. "Tear out cargo bays, stuff in cell launchers—or even just missiles in some kind of storage array, if you're not worried about using the ship later."

"Captain Stephson," Val summoned the CO. "I believe Specialist Tsvetanova has found something of import. We have identified at least thirty contacts that appear to be arsenal ships to support Home Fleet."

Stephson ran through the data as Tsvetanova almost cringed, then whistled softly.

"Well done, Specialist," she told him. "Those hulls could easily put a few thousand extra missiles into play we weren't expecting. We've found the first of the Black Regent's surprises."

"Thank you, ser," the noncom said, his gaze fixed on his console.

"Put together a package for the Pentarch," Stephson ordered.

"You get the credit, Specialist. Your insight might have just saved a lot of lives."

And that, Val knew, was part of why the old *Goldenrod* crew would follow Sigrid Stephson and Lorraine Adamant into hell. The new crew was learning—whatever had held Tsvetanova back before wasn't going to drag him down on *this* ship!

# NINETEEN

"All ships to commence evasive maneuvers," Lorraine said as the data on the arsenal vessels flowed through her link. It took her less time to process the information and understand the threat than it had probably taken Tsvetanova to put together the report, let alone do the analysis in the first place.

One of the advantages of very expensive custom neural hardware, a genetically engineered predisposition for rapid analysis and the fact that the hardware was tailored for her genengineered brain.

"Your thoughts, Lorraine?" Vigo asked her.

"My uncle won't have one secret edge if he can have two," she replied. "Arsenal ships are an easy one, if less effective historically than the sheer number of missiles implies. Our missiles need management through most of their flight, after all, and a lightly modified merchant can't do that.

"Against the *Valkyries*' defenses, they won't stand a chance. The freighters themselves are unlikely to have significant defenses, which means we could take them out with railgun rounds from here if we had the proper TAMs to spare. Even a salvo of regular missiles left to go ballistic before they activate the terminal drives could probably get close enough to hit them.

"They're eggshells armed with hammers, and now we know they're there, we can smash them at will. I doubt Benjamin isn't planning on *using* them, but he's not going to rely on them."

"You think he has something else in play."

"I *know* he does," she agreed. "And maybe it's my own tricks speaking, but I know that Adamant can build railguns. They're just huge. A little bit of help from his friends, and there could be some nasty toys in Bastion orbit.

The icons marking her ships began to swerve back and forth on the display. The curves would add as much as ten thousand kilometers to the variance on their overall position, though they required a slightly greater acceleration from the ships.

"He's now received my last message," she continued. "And he's seen us. So."

She stared into the tactical display, as if she could divine Benjamin's mind from the order forming out of the chaos above her homeworld.

The first order taking shape was obvious. Four capital ships had formed an abbreviated wall, two lines of two ships, and the escorts were forming up around them. They weren't coming out to meet her yet, but the numbers were interesting.

She expected four battleships, three cruisers and eighteen frigates. The frigates and cruisers were right, but there were thirty-six frigate-sized ships forming up around her uncle's battle line.

Plus, now she knew about them, she could pick out the arsenal ships forming a second line behind Home Fleet. They wouldn't risk getting ahead of the warships. They'd accelerate out after the main line, adding their missiles to the later salvos of the fight.

"How many RASG heavy patrol ships would we expect to have in Bastion local space?" she asked aloud.

"Thirty-ish," Monahan said. "Probably not thirty-six, if that's what you're thinking, ser."

"That's what I thought. So. Thirty of those are Guard ships, and Benjamin is leaving a dozen frigates above Bastion, just in case."

Enough firepower to give anyone on the planet with clever ideas a warning to think again. Not enough to make a difference in the battle to come. The RASG ships were designed for longer-term but shorter-range deployments—and ones without combat, at that. They completely lacked cell launchers and carried fewer missiles overall, but they used a multipurpose launcher that could fire a variety of drones along with the same Artemis 3 light attack missile as the navy frigates.

Eight of said launchers, which meant those thirty Guard patrol ships had twice the sustained missile firepower of a similar number of frigates. They didn't have the alpha-strike capability or the missile defenses, though, which made them of middling value in the battle to come.

But quantity had a quality all its own, and using them let Benjamin leave twelve ships he fully trusted in control of Bastion's orbitals.

"Home Fleet is now coming out to meet us," Hodžić declared grimly. "Three gees across the board."

It had taken them seven minutes to get everything moving, which Lorraine found suspicious. They had known she was coming. They should have been ready to come out.

"Cut our own acceleration to match," she ordered. "Maintain evasive maneuvers and let them come out to meet us. If he wants to fight us without the ODCs, I'm not going to argue."

It told her that he didn't think he needed them—or was bluffing. It would take over half an hour for the two fleets to reach missile range of each other. Longer for the arsenal ships, which hadn't started moving yet.

"Let me know when he coms us," she said quietly. "We're close enough for a live conversation now, and I don't think he's going to let that go."

Either he really thought he had an insurmountable advantage—

thinking the railguns were key to her advantages or underestimating the *Valkyries'* defenses—or he was going to try to talk her down.

Even if he *did* have a trick she hadn't caught that would even up everything, he would try to talk to her. She wasn't sure why she was certain of that, but she was.

"Arsenal ships are holding position," Gurgic noted. "Either they're going to stay in place as a fallback measure, or they'll maneuver when they're about five thousand klicks behind the main fleet."

Lorraine nodded acknowledgement. The arsenal ships weren't the trap; she knew that. The trap was either aboard Home Fleet's ships or somewhere else, somewhere she hadn't accounted for yet.

If *her* plan worked, it wouldn't matter—but she needed him to talk to her for that. It was possible she'd burned that bridge too hard in the last exchange. That would be... a complicating factor.

"Ser, we have a widebeam transmission coming from the enemy fleet," Monahan reported. "It appears to be being sent from all of their ships simultaneously."

"Standard security doctrine for battlespace coms," Lorraine said. "We'll be doing the same in response, right?"

"Of course," Val replied. "Synchronized tightbeam links are set up with the other ships. We are ready to manage that without any difficulty."

"Good." Lorraine turned her gaze on Amna Hodžić. "You're up, Amna," she told the hacker. "I'm betting a lot here that he's on one of those ships. Find me which one."

"Aye, aye."

"Do you want a private virtual space, ser?" Monahan asked.

"No. Link him through," Lorraine ordered. "Let everyone see I have nothing to be afraid of or to hide." She chuckled. "But do secure everything and anonymize things enough that he can't ID my ship from the bridge—or any of you."

"On it. You'll be live in... thirty seconds."

Lorraine was fine keeping her uncle waiting. And if it wasn't Benjamin Adamant, she cared even less.

Still, she'd been disappointed, and it was a relief when the channel connected, and the surprisingly aged appearance of her once-favorite uncle was projected in front of her at half size.

"I'm half-surprised you took my call," he told her. "I did just have a message from you demanding that I be in chains when we spoke again."

"*Any sign of where he is in the recording?*" Lorraine asked silently. The holographic image was just him, which meant that it was fifty-fifty whether it was a direct recording or a digitalized avatar.

She was sending a full, if heavily sanitized, image of her Flag Deck. The scale and sophistication of the space had been an intentional message on the part of its UWN designers, which she had no problem using.

"*No. Single-figure holographic transmission,*" Monahan told her. "*It doesn't appear to be an avatar, though. He is recording himself live.*"

Which meant that he, unlike Lorraine, wasn't seated on the deck of an accelerating capital ship. He was standing straight-backed as he faced her, daring her to argue with his assessment of her response to his "offer."

If he was aboard one of the capital ships, he was standing under three gravities of acceleration. That was part of why he was as physically imposing a man as he was, she knew, but she wondered if he'd go that far.

"I am prepared to consider your surrender, Uncle," she told him. "As you said, enough people have died over your coup attempt. Are you prepared to do the right thing and face justice for your crimes?"

"There is very clear evidence of certain crimes in this system right now," Benjamin replied. "An unprovoked attack on a squadron of Home Fleet maneuvering to protect one of our key installations. I did not start this civil war today, Lorraine. *You* did."

"Says the man whose agents hunted me across the entire cluster,"

Lorraine countered. "Or are we now claiming that Nikostratos Wray worked entirely on his own, without orders from anyone, in his pursuit and his attacks on San Ignacio and Bright Dream?

"Because I have a sworn statement from Admiral Are Tunison stating his understanding that Wray was operating under secret orders directly from you. Orders that would have to have *pre-dated* my flight from Adamantine after your agent, Jelica Laurenz, attempted to kill me."

She smiled thinly, well aware that both of them were performing for the entirety of Home Fleet now.

"I also have recordings of Em Laurenz's confession, recordings we will easily be able to validate once she is returned to us by the Marshal Service of the United Worlds in a few months."

"These are stern accusations you lay at my feet, Lorraine, but equally grievous are those my people lay at yours," Benjamin replied calmly. "When your mother died, I was attacked as well. We thought that attack was aimed at you, but your sudden disappearance raised too many questions.

"Many of my investigators are convinced you were behind the assassination of your family, to move yourself up the List of Pentarchs. We can throw accusations at each other all day, but do they truly justify more violence?"

Whatever Benjamin's errors as a political creature had been, they hadn't been for a lack of charisma. Anger filled Lorraine's chest as she glared at him.

"You murdered my mother. My brother. My sister. All of their spouses. Nikola and I lived by luck and the sacrifice of those around us. If I were the villain, wouldn't Nikola have come to a peaceful point now?

"Or have you simply not bothered *trying* to talk to him?"

"I have spent hours, days and weeks trying to reach out to my nephew," Benjamin said stiffly. "Like you, he clings to a story where I am the only bad guy, the mustache-twirling villain whose plots and schemes destroyed our happy kingdom.

"The situation is far more complex than your preconceptions. The future of the Kingdom of Adamant rides in the balance, Lorraine. I will repeat my offer: let us meet face-to-face. Pull your ships back to a safe distance from Bastion, and I will withdraw mine to orbit.

"I see your point on Nikola. Let the *three* of us meet," he continued. "If you will guarantee our safety, on your personal honor, I will give him safe passage and we will all meet on your ship, where you are in control."

For a soul-searing, disorienting moment, the world seemed to shift underneath Lorraine. If he was willing to go *that* far, could he possibly mean it? Was there something she'd failed to understand?

Had Wray actually been working for someone else?

She looked her uncle in the eyes and his hologram returned her regard levelly.

"Tell me, in your own words and on your honor, on the oath of your soul and the future of our Kingdom, that you had nothing to do with my mother's death," she said quietly. "Swear that, and I may believe there is a chance."

There was a very long silence.

"Everything I have done, I have done for the Kingdom of Adamant," he finally said. "I will swear to that on any icon you demand."

And that was it, wasn't it? She closed her eyes, swallowing down the rage as an entirely fresh wave of betrayal filled her.

"Even now, with the blood of your family on your hands, you will lie and prevaricate," she told him. "I imagine Nikola would refuse to trust any offer of safe passage from you, wouldn't he?"

"He is an Adamant, too stubborn to see a compromise path forward," Benjamin growled.

"*Lorraine, there was a virus along the transmission,*" Val suddenly told her. "*It was transmitted two minutes and fifteen seconds into your conversation. I have it neutralized and contained—it appears quite similar to the one Hodžić is using to locate him, if less sophis-ticated.*"

"We are all Adamants," Lorraine said aloud, considering the grim new confirmation. She had *known*, but she'd still hoped that somehow, she'd misjudged her uncle.

"*Can you fake a target location to go back with it?*" she asked. "*Somewhere empty. I have a suspicion and I need to see what he does.*"

"*Easy,*" Hodžić confirmed. "*Feeding the virus and sending it home.*"

"We cannot allow the stubbornness our family teaches as a virtue to destroy our Kingdom, Lorraine," Benjamin said softly and fiercely. "The past is the past. Only by putting it aside and looking to the future can we secure our people's strength for tomorrow and the day after."

Lorraine knew that she needed to keep him on the call, but the anger burning through her was physically painful.

"Easy for you to say," she snarled. "You killed my mother. My father. My brother. My sister. You would have killed *me*—and Nikola only survived because of the troops he commanded.

"When the past is littered with sins, it's easy for the man *who committed them* to say we must put it aside. If you fear stubbornness will destroy us all, then put it aside yourself. Surrender and order your ships to stand down."

She glared into her uncle's eyes. She knew that wasn't going to happen. Benjamin Adamant was just as stubborn as his sister's children. Lorraine could not let him escape justice—and he would never surrender to face it.

"There are things you don't understand," he said. The fierceness was gone from his voice. He still spoke softly, but there was a heavy weariness to his tone that she wasn't sure she'd ever heard from him before. "Everything I have done, I have done for our Kingdom. But if you will not accept that, will not *listen*, then you leave me no choice."

"You always have a choice, Uncle," Lorraine told him—but she was listening for the report she knew had to be coming.

*"Energy pulses detected on all three* Monarchs," Val said calmly. *"Likelihood of railgun firing sequence exceeds ninety-five percent. Analyzing visuals."*

"Did you get what you want from this conversation?" Lorraine continued, consciously tilting her head to make it obvious she was listening to a report. "Targeting data as to what ship I am on?"

The analysis flowed across her neural link a moment later. The three *Monarch*-class ships had new additions, cylindrical pods running the full length of the six-hundred-meter-long battleships' port and starboard sides.

Cylindrical *barrels*. That made them the first non-UWN ships Lorraine had ever seen to use railguns. Her people had pulled together an assessment of the energy involved in the launch and managed to even get a brief sensor lock on the projectiles.

Half a percent of the speed of light wasn't a lot, but it was more than anyone *except* the UWN had ever managed in a ship-mounted weapon. Even now, with almost fifty of them under her command, Lorraine wasn't entirely sure what the Terrans had done to pull off their weapons.

"I do what I must," her uncle told her. "For our Kingdom. For our future. And for victory. Remember, Lorraine, that strategy does not mean plotting to defeat your enemy."

He paused, as if considering something else to say, then suddenly snapped her an Academy-perfect salute. He held it for a few seconds as she stared at him, trying to find *something* to tell her she didn't have to kill him, and then cut the channel.

# TWENTY

"FUCK," Lorraine screamed, uncaring that everyone on the Flag Deck could hear her. She caught concerned looks from the crew around her. Many of them would never have heard her swear—and would probably never hear her swear again.

She swallowed her anger as best as she could and focused her attention on the tactical displays.

"Report," she growled at Gurgic and Val.

"Six shots, decent dispersal pattern," the RKAN officer said immediately. "Targeted on the location Em Hodžić fed their virus. Based off the pattern, I'd say they're expecting a two-hundred-and-fifty-kilometer final adjustment."

"That seems quite small for a terminal munition," Val noted. "My calculations agree with Commander Gurgic, but a proper TAM has a far wider terminal-adjustment capability."

"He doesn't have proper TAMs, Val," Lorraine replied. "We only have one other type of railgun. Vigo." She turned to her bodyguard—*carefully*, as they were still under three gees of thrust. "What's the terminal maneuverability of a PDC railgun round?"

"Ten seconds at five hundred gravities," he confirmed immediately. The capabilities of the PDC guns were highly classified, but they had been in the files unlocked when Lorraine was sent on her exodus.

So had a lot of other things she'd never used. Given how much information had been buried in her implants or in encrypted storage modules hidden amidst her Guard detail's gear, Lorraine was glad to get use out of any of it.

"They fire a projectile at one percent of lightspeed along a two-point-five-kilometer barrel," she continued. "Val, how does the acceleration involved there stack up against half a percent along a six-hundred-meter barrel?"

"Similar, within a five percent margin," the SI allowed. "You suspect they used the same rounds?"

"He wouldn't have had time to engineer something new that could handle the stress," Lorraine replied. "We'll find out in a few seconds, I suppose."

The *Monarchs* had fired from just over a light-second away, and while the *Valkyries* could detect a railgun firing, they couldn't detect the ballistic railgun rounds unless they lit up engines.

Which, roughly fifteen thousand kilometers away from Lorraine's fleet, they did. The numbers exactly matched what Vigo had said a moment earlier, confirming her suspicion that RKAN had basically strapped a quarter-length version of the PDC main guns to their battleships.

As surprises went, it would have been a nasty one—deployed against anyone who wasn't flying UWN ships and didn't know exactly what they were looking for to see railgun launches.

"Closest approach to one of our vessels will be one thousand kilometers," Gurgic reported. "I would guess that no one double-checked the targeting coordinates and course we gave their virus."

"The next salvo will be aimed more cleanly," Lorraine warned. "And nasty as this could have been, I'm not counting on it being his last trick.

"Hodžić, how did *our* virus do?" she asked.

The hacker shook her head without even looking up.

"I can tell you he *is* on one of the ships," she said. "I can even be pretty certain he's on one of the *Monarchs*, but they were making up with physical sequencing and complexity what they weren't sure they could manage with software. I peeled it back a lot but not all of the way."

"You did what you could," Lorraine conceded. She *needed* that target, but she hadn't kept her uncle talking long enough.

"It's not quite that straightforward," Hodžić replied. "The virus is still working in their systems. If they transmit anything outside of their closed net, it will attempt to piggyback on that and get home to us—but it won't take much in terms of security protocols to keep it contained."

"But if someone sends a rushed broad message, we might get an update that will give us a target?" Gurgic asked. "That's... not much to hang the plan on."

"It's what I've got," the hacker said. "We *do* have a plan for actually fighting this battle, right?"

"We do," Lorraine confirmed grimly. "Stephson?"

Her name pulled the Flag Captain's attention.

"Ser."

"We're a no-go on Concord. Do we have the course change for Agincourt?"

"We do," Stephson confirmed. "Gurgic should have it too. We'll need to go vertical fast to get the angle, but Home Fleet is already carrying too much delta-*v* to stop us getting Bastion out of the line of fire."

"Thank you, Captain," Lorraine said calmly. She looked over at Hodžić, who had turned to study her.

"Space is not two-dimensional, let alone *one*-dimensional," she reminded the other woman. "Everything we've done so far has been fundamentally a one-dimensional approach to Bastion. Agincourt has us turn ninety degrees, opening up the distance so we can fire on Benjamin's ships without having Bastion behind us.

"He'll expect it, but there's only so much he can *do* about it."

Even with the railguns, the fight to come was even at best. Even as they'd both tried to locate each other's ships, Benjamin had also been trying to keep her from thinking more broadly. He knew that keeping Bastion behind him would grow harder and harder as his ships' velocity rose.

"What the?"

Lorraine wasn't sure who had spoken. The cut-off question had come from the Operations Section, which meant she had to give Gurgic at least a minute to sort out what was going on before she started asking NCOs questions directly.

"Chief Barret, share with the class if you would," Gurgic said with humor in his voice. "Only three gees of weight is keeping everyone from jumping on you right now!"

Chief Second Class Khaliq Barret was an immigrant from the Concordat who reminded Lorraine of her father, mostly through his dark features and neatly trimmed beard. At that moment, he was staring at his screen like it might have tried to bite him.

"Every ODC in Bastion orbit just went offline, ser," Barret finally said, shaking his head slowly. "I *think* they all just lost primary power —but *simultaneously*? That's wei—"

A flash of red warning lights cut off his speech as the Chief's jaw fell open for several long seconds.

"Chief?" This time, Lorraine couldn't wait.

"Every frigate in Bastion orbit is gone, ser," he finally said. "The PDCs just came online and blew them to pieces."

Home Fleet had left twelve frigates in orbit, an insurance policy against someone on the surface trying to be clever. Except someone had been *very* clever, and the same two-hundred-fifty-kilometer maneuver range that had failed to touch Lorraine's ships was more than enough to take out ships that had been watching for outside threats—and *definitely* hadn't been watching planetary defense centers they knew were under control.

"It seems that my brother isn't as out for the count as my uncle thinks," Lorraine declared aloud. "Home Fleet position and velocity relative to Bastion?"

"Benjamin Adamant's ships are over sixty thousand klicks out and carrying forty-five kilometers per second of velocity," Val reported. "At their current acceleration, it would take them twenty-five minutes just to shed their outbound velocity—at which point they will be in a missile engagement with us."

"People, meet the anvil to our hammer," Lorraine said. "My brother and the Masada Protocol. I doubt he's going to keep control of the PDCs for long, but he just threw my uncle's control of Bastion into question."

"I can't get details from this range, but I have what appears to be major aircraft movement around the southern pole, ser," Barret reported. "That I'm picking it up from almost a light-second away says it's big. Quick estimate says at least two thousand planes and shuttles."

"Go, Nikola, go," Lorraine murmured. "All right. Stand by to execute Agincourt. Between us, we've limited Benjamin's movements.

"Now let's finish this."

"Wait."

Hodžić's single word hung in the air like a red stoplight, and Lorraine turned her attention back to the woman.

"Amna?" she half-whispered.

"Benjamin is trying to raise the defense centers and *is* raising ground stations other than the PDCs," the hacker announced. "But while he's transmitting encrypted, it's widebeam, spread out to cover the planet, and his people can only do so much to—I have him!"

Hodžić looked back at Lorraine, her eyes firm and certain.

"He's transmitting from *Majesty*. Ninety-six percent certainty."

"Understood." Lorraine hesitated. This was the plan. This was the goal. Their best chance of ending this without a war that would kill a generation.

Vigo's hand landed on her shoulder, heavy in the acceleration-induced gravity.

"Home Fleet has flipped," Gurgic announced. "All ships now accelerating for Bastion at three gees. I don't think your uncle is feeling all that confident at the moment."

"And he's out of time," Lorraine whispered, half to herself.

"All ships. Target *Majesty* and execute Concord!"

---

THE SHOT HEARD *round the world* was a phrase that had been applied to many events over the centuries, each of them an event that defined or redefined an era.

The first had been Concord, immortalized in a poem that had endured across those same centuries, marking the day when American militiamen had opened fire on British soldiers and began the American Revolution.

Lorraine's plan more closely fit the second main event associated with the phrase, the two shots that killed the Archduke of Austria and kicked off the First World War.

Both events were still studied centuries later, and like the death of Archduke Franz Ferdinand, Lorraine hoped her shot would trigger preexisting frailties in the structure she faced.

Even as a second salvo of railgun shots from Home Fleet passed them by, easily evaded by ships that had over three minutes of warning of their approach, the *Valkyries* maneuvered to briefly open their formation.

Each ship's twin-octuple railgun banks targeted a specific section of space, based on *Majesty*'s current maneuvers and previous evasive maneuvers. Forty-three shots blazed into space at a full percent of lightspeed—and unlike the crude improvisations mounted on the *Monarchs*, the ex-UWN guns had been built by people who knew the tech inside and out.

The energy signature of their firing was subtler, more concealed

—and quite different from that of the repurposed surface-to-orbit weapons Benjamin's people had equipped themselves with.

Lorraine personally put the odds that her ships had fired without detection at about fifty-five percent, but even confusion and delay would buy her time.

"Double-check the safe-range-detonation order," she murmured to Val.

That would trigger the nuclear warheads in the TAMs—the only salvo of the warheads their basically cottage-industry manufacturing plant on each ship had produced—ten thousand kilometers past the target if they didn't hit.

These were true terminal assault munitions. They would *not* hit her planet.

"I have and am confirming with all projectiles again, just in case," the SI replied. "Sixty-six seconds to terminal activation."

An entire cargo bay that would normally hold consumables for two thousand people for a month, plus two fabrication shops that should have been handling parts and sundries for a quarter of the ship between them, had been dedicated to Concord from before they'd left Ominira.

For a solid-state weapon, based around metallic-hydrogen storage and molecular circuitry with zero moving parts until the hydrogen was ignited for the final maneuvers, *handmade* was never an accurate descriptor.

But the railgun rounds fired in Concord were as close as was physically possible. Sixty techs and fifty of Val's most sophisticated remotes had slaved over the system for the entire journey, building tools to build tools that refined metals—often to build *another* tool.

*Valkyrie* had built sixteen shells. *Bean Sidhe*'s crew had managed fourteen and *Herakles*'s people thirteen.

It... had to be enough.

The two fleets hurtled toward each other, and Lorraine forced herself to be patient until the moment where the displays lit up with the bright green icons of the slug entering terminal acquisition.

"Forty-two rounds active," Gurgic reported. "I can't tell which munition didn't initiate."

"It was one of ours," Val admitted. "I have a round-loop com with it. I'm not sure of the problem with the engine; I am detonating the warhead."

A momentary flash on the display confirmed the order. Lorraine doubted the fifty-kiloton explosion was going to *help* Home Fleet's defensive problem—but Home Fleet was doing their best.

Unlike Smolerak, after all, they'd at least known this was *possible*.

But they had twenty seconds from realizing they were under fire to the final impact of the weapons close enough to hit *Majesty*.

"Twelve shots taken down," Val recited. "Twenty-two misses. Eight hits."

The kinetic energy of the railgun rounds alone might have been enough. The nukes helped, but they were as much included for cleaning up misses as anything else.

*Majesty* was gone.

"Target destroyed," Gurgic said, his voice forcibly level as he announced the death of Lorraine's uncle and the destruction of one of his nation's most advanced warships.

There was a long, chill silence on *Valkyrie*'s Flag Deck.

"Is there any way to confirm that Benjamin was aboard?" Lorraine finally asked.

"Not directly, but there has been a large spike in inter-ship traffic since the hit," Hodžić told her. "Consistent, I would guess, with a key break in the chain of command."

"Well, if we're wrong, I guess I look silly, but let's act like we're right," she decided aloud. "Monahan, let's get a transmission going to all of the Home Fleet ships."

"Live on your order," he confirmed a few moments later.

A silent command through her feed activated the camera and she looked at it, knowing the pickups were shaping a three-dimensional image of her but her focus would go on to whoever was viewing the image.

Even in three gravities, she managed to be straight-backed and appear calm as she faced her enemies.

"Captains of Home Fleet, Benjamin Adamant is dead," she declared simply. "He couldn't abandon you, but he was smart enough to move his flag to a ship other than his old flagship. But now he is no more, and I ask you, *What cause do you serve now?*"

She let that hang.

"The vast majority of you, I know, serve our Kingdom. The orders Benjamin Adamant has given over the last year have come with the imprint of authority from the Cabinet and the Regency. You have questioned, I know, but he had key support planetside—and you all trusted him."

She knew her eyes were dark.

"Some of you knew more," she reminded them harshly. "I don't doubt that, but I recognize that there may not be much that can be done about it. With Benjamin's death... let this end."

She sighed heavily.

"Let this end," she repeated. "I give you my word, as an Adamant and a Pentarch, that no one will face consequences for obeying legal orders passed through proper channels.

"There *will* be investigations of his coup and his supporters," she warned, "but that is inevitable. My mother was murdered. Every sign is that *my uncle* gave the order. The truth must be found if we are to go forward and build the Kingdom we want to have together.

"Let this end," she said again. "I will accept your surrenders and will require nothing more than that you maneuver your vessels to a safe zone at the Bastion-Adamantine L-One Lagrange point.

"I will speak with my brother and the military commanders on the surface and bring the last remnants of this conflict to a close. This has been a dark chapter of our history, and I will offer you my solemn promise of this: there will be no dictatorship going forward.

"If, as I fear, much of the Cabinet will face charges, then their replacements will be properly appointed by the Houses of the Realm and People—and regardless, there *will* be an Election to replace my mother the King."

No one had tried to respond live to her message, though the channel was arguably open enough that they could.

"For the future of our Kingdom and the trust of our people, I ask you to yield."

She felt silent and, after a moment, cut the channel.

"Tell me if we get any response," she said grimly. "And stand by to execute Agincourt. Mark is ninety seconds."

"All ships confirm standing by," Monahan told her after a moment. "We are picking up extensive internship com activity among Home Fleet's vessels," he continued hesitantly.

"Until they call u—"

"Incoming channel from *Sultan*," the Coms Officer interrupted her, then flushed.

"Put them on, Major."

The coms system hummed to life, producing a broad holographic image of the Flag Deck of a *Monarch*-class battleship. Lorraine knew *Sultan*'s Flag Deck better than any other in RKAN—for two-thirds of the time she'd been in the Navy, it had been her uncle's Deck. She hadn't spent much time there—but she'd received plenty of messages recorded there and hadn't spent *any* time on the other Flag Decks of the fleet.

She even knew the woman seated in the middle of the Deck, in a near-mirror to her own seat on *Valkyrie*. Admiral Yūna Morikawa had been Chief of the Adamant Naval Staff when Benjamin had been Home Fleet CO. When Benjamin had become Regent, she'd gone into space to replace him.

Like Smolarek, Morikawa was an old family friend—a cousin of Benjamin's late wife, so arguably even *family*. She was a small woman with iron-gray hair cut off just beneath her ears, with the dark skin and eyes of her Japanese heritage.

At that moment, she reminded Lorraine of no one so much as Shiratori Ayano, the Executive Vice President of Special Operations for MicroStar, the megacorporation that had offered her a deal to overthrow Benjamin Adamant. MicroStar's help had come with a price tag that she'd judged would be just as bad for Adamant as whatever deal Benjamin had with FBIT, so she'd declined.

Since Alastair Devine had burned a favor of a magnitude Lorraine barely understood to get the meeting, that had set into motion the events that had ended with her shooting her boyfriend in her quarters.

It was hardly a pleasant reminder, but both Ayano and Morikawa were grandmotherly-seeming women of near-pure Japanese heritage. She didn't need the reminder of Ayano to know that Morikawa was someone she couldn't take lightly.

She had, after all, known the Admiral her entire life.

"Lorraine Adamant," Morikawa greeted her.

"Yūna Morikawa. I assume you are the official CO of Home Fleet, despite my uncle taking command." Lorraine met Morikawa's gaze flatly. "Which means you have the authority to respond to my offer, at least for your own ships, RASG and the ODCs."

Morikawa snorted a familiar laugh. Lorraine was used to it coming along with childish misdemeanors like sneaking out to meet school friends or a boyfriend—eternally patient Vigo in tow—not high-level negotiations for the fate of their Kingdom.

Somehow, the fact that Morikawa had some humor in the mess was reassuring.

"I *could* surrender the ODCs, but that would be pointless," she explained. "Someone—I'm guessing the name rhymes with *cola*—arranged for them all to eject their primary power cores to prevent a critical meltdown that doesn't appear to have been occurring.

"I can *recommend* that the surface forces and PDCs surrender, but you know exactly how far RKAA will listen to an RKAN officer." Morikawa shrugged.

"But that is not the thrust of the matter." She closed her eyes for a long, long, moment. "I make no apologies for following Benjamin,

Lorraine. I didn't know everything at the beginning, but I should have guessed.

"And it doesn't matter now."

Lorraine held the Admiral's gaze, looking deep into her dark eyes and knowing that Morikawa was dancing around the point.

"As you said, this must end. I have issued maneuvering orders to all ships under my command. We will redirect to the L-One point as ordered. I don't know where you'll find investigators you can trust, Lorraine, but I recommend that you send them aboard all of my ships before you let us back into orbit.

"That said... if there is an *external* threat, you have my personal promise, Lorry Truck, that Home Fleet will stand guard for Adamant. Place what value on that you will."

*Lorry Truck.* Even Lorraine's fire-forged self-control flickered at that. There were less than two dozen people who had *ever* used that nickname for her. Most of them had been household staff at the Adamant Manse. By the time *Vigo* had come along, the people around her had judged she'd outgrown the cutesy name and stopped using it out of respect for her six-year-old dignity.

But using it was a reminder of just how long she had known Yūna Morikawa. If she was promising by *that* old shame, Lorraine thought she could trust it.

"I understand, Yūna," she told Home Fleet's commander. "And... thank you. I know this is not easy for you."

"You... have no fucking idea," Morikawa said, a momentary snap undercutting the curse. "But I owe my loyalty to ten billion souls before one lover. I only ask that when things are done, you will accept my resignation with grace."

"I suspect and hope, Yūna, that you will have the chance to do so before there is *any* chance of the acceptance being mine," Lorraine promised quietly. She should have realized just how close Morikawa and her uncle had become. They'd been bound at the hip profession-ally for Lorraine's entire adult life and career—and Gulistan Adamant-Morikawa had passed almost two decades earlier.

Morikawa nodded sharply and cut the channel.

"They are maneuvering as promised," Val confirmed. "The RASG ships that remained in orbit are doing so as well."

Lorraine slumped in her chair, letting the extra gravities push her down into herself for a few seconds.

"It's over," she whispered.

"Not quite," Vigo replied, equally quietly—but aloud. "*You have to deal with the military on the ground,*" he continued on the feed. "*And with Nikola. You have made promises to honor the Constitution... he hasn't.*"

"*But that's what we're fighting for. He's on our side,*" she objected.

"*That doesn't mean he sees the same win conditions you do,*" he warned. "*Nikola has spent a year trapped in a bunker, fighting this war every single day. His plans may not be yours. We need to secure orbit and stabilize the ground situation as quickly as we can.*"

"Okay," Lorraine said aloud. "Monahan, we're going to record a series of messages, and then you're going to send them on every single military channel in this system.

"We'll start with the planetary defense centers, assuming that Nikola's people didn't manage to hang on to them. If we can't be certain they're either on side or decommissioned, entering orbit is going to get *very* complicated..."

# TWENTY-ONE

"Adamant City's defenders don't appear to be listening to your sister," Dam reported. "Not enough of them, anyway. The city's anti-aircraft perimeter is online, and Task Force Archer has been grounded.

"Galli has dismounted and is moving her people forward to suppress the AA network. She expects to have at least the perimeter weapons offline by the time Task Force Sword arrives."

The aircraft holding Nikola Adamant and his personal guard had never been designed as a transport. The Thunderbird's ability to pack five troopers in battle armor had been an afterthought, the mass required a rounding area against the heavy armor and weapons of the VTOL attack aircraft.

His people were delighted with that. It meant that the Prince could be tucked behind the heaviest air-mobile armor they had, *and* that no one was going to think he was aboard.

That might be more important than Nikola had hoped. The plan had called for their allies to cut power to the Adamant City antiaircraft network, but no plan survived contact with the enemy.

Of course, his plan had required Home Fleet to be distracted by a hostile fleet in the system, drawn into a running battle while he secured control of the PDCs. Instead, Home Fleet was no longer a factor, destroyed or surrendered, as Lorraine had arrived with far more firepower than any of *his* plans had called for.

His little sister, saving the day. Who would have thought?

"Okay," he said aloud. His neural link would carry the words to General Dam; he didn't need to speak. But everyone in the room was in on this. If anyone deserved to know what he was thinking, it was his Guard—and everyone in the Thunderbird, including the flight crew, were Adamant Guard.

They'd come this far with him. For this, the Companions were in another plane behind them. The Guard would keep him alive.

"*Okay?*" Dam quoted back to him. The General was aboard a specialized combat control aircraft, armored and protected with everything RKAA could think of because it was going to be the main target of every Regency mook with a missile launcher as soon as it crossed the horizon near Adamant City.

"Okay," Nikola repeated. "Galli put them down at the Bravo landing sites, correct?"

"Yes," his friend conceded.

There were three sets of intended landing sites. Each had an attached set of plans—targets in the city and approach routes through the streets.

"Then she can proceed under... Bravo-Six," Nikola told him. All of his coms were being relayed through the command plane and Dam, to conceal his own presence in Task Force Sword.

"She's to move up and encircle the Military and Central Distracts," he continued. "If she has troops to spare, she can secure the bases out by Adamant Guard Command, but that's at her discretion."

The Military District was less separate from Adamant City than had been intended when it was built. The largest concentration of troops and training facilities near Adamant City, neutralizing it would be expensive if the soldiers inside fought back. The secondary bases around the old fortress that *had* housed Adamant Guard Command—before it had been destroyed in the coup—weren't as large or as well secured, but they still held at least another division of troops.

"What's the status of RKAA troops in the city?" he asked.

"Prime Minister Bayer has declared both you and Lorraine traitors to the Kingdom, doubling down on the claim that you were the masterminds behind the original assassinations," Dam warned grimly. "All RKAA and RAMC units have been ordered to mobilize to defend the capital, specifically the Houses. I'd say only about half of the Generals around have passed the orders on... and over half of the Colonels who've received them are refusing to move."

"Good." Nikola smiled. With Benjamin's death, the Regency was collapsing. What had been planned as a strategic strike relying on surprise and speed was turning into a *mop-up* operation.

"Make sure all units get the word," he told Dam. "Any RKAA or RAMC troops that remain in their bases and barracks are to be left alone. The Military District is to be *contained*, not stormed.

"Anybody in the field is a valid target, but anyone staying out of things is to be *left* out of things."

"Understood, Your Highness. Do we move Task Force Sword to Bravo targets as well?" Dam asked.

"No." The map of the city gleamed in his link, larger and clearer than any hologram that would fit into the drop pod with him. The pod was barely bigger than his armor.

"There's no way Galli is going to neutralize the Central District batteries," he continued. "She'll clear a path into the city, but the Houses and the Palace will still be under the cover of the Steel Spires."

RKAA had put a lot of work into concealing the defenses that covered the legislatures and official executive residences of the Kingdom of Adamant. The Steel Spires were three buildings, only slightly broader and squatter than the office and residence towers around them, whose architecturally pleasing exteriors concealed armor more normally suited to a spaceborne battleship and enough anti-air weaponry to make Task Force Sword's life difficult.

But Nikola had never really expected Archer to reach the Steel Spires. Archer's job was to deal with the Military District and any troops the Regency put in the streets.

Sword's job was to deal with the real enemy.

"Adjust Task Force Sword's formation," he told Dam. "Sword-Five and Sword-Six will move up to the front and get at least five minutes ahead of everyone else. Their target is the Steel Spires.

"They are to neutralize, if possible, not destroy—but I understand the ask may be impossible."

Sword-Five and Sword-Six contained over ninety percent of their Thunderbird attack planes, along with half of the bombers and fighter-bombers—the slower half, as the faster aircraft had been in Archer.

"Sword-One, -Two and -Three will move on the Houses," he continued. "As per... Alpha-Three. They will contain the structure and stand by for ground contact from Inspector Vail from RKAIG."

Pronounced "Ar-Cage," the Royal Kingdom of Adamant Inspectorate General was the senior police and constabulary force of the Kingdom—and Inspector Amber Vail was one of their top people.

"Vail has the arrest warrants she'll need," Nikola told Dam. That part of Alpha-3 had been kept under wraps up to this moment. "Troops will invest the Houses but *will not* enter. No lethal weaponry is to be deployed near the Houses—and yes, Tóki, I know what I'm asking of them."

People were going to die if the House security teams decided to be trouble, but there were lines he absolutely *could not* cross.

"Nonlethal force is authorized to manage any brave idiots in House Security," he said grimly. "The primary purpose is containment. No one leaves the Houses until Vail is in place. Once she gives the word that she has her captures or they aren't present, the troops will lift containment but stay visibly present.

"We won't force people to leave or stay at that point," he continued. "The troops will then be responsible for the security of the Houses against anyone *else*. We won't enter the buildings, won't threaten the reps.

"I think the message will be quite clear, don't you?"

"That we could have done a lot worse, but we're *trying* to respect the rule of law?" Dam guessed.

"Exactly. Courts and law after today, but first, we need to put what's left of this rebellion down."

"Understood. Task Groups are moving up as directed. We'll be hitting the outer perimeter in fifteen—Galli's people expect to have a hole by then, if not full neutralization.

"What about Sword-Four?"

Dam's question was inevitable. Not only had Nikola left one of Sword's Task Groups—a brigade-strength force, if assembled from battalions drawn from multiple different brigades and divisions— unaccounted-for, Sword-Four was the group *Nikola* was in.

"We're heading for the Palace, Tóki," Nikola said quietly. "That part of the plan doesn't change. I don't know what tricks and traps Benjamin left in place, but this ends with the throne in *my* hands and no one else's!"

LORRAINE WAS STILL an hour out as the lead Sword groups crossed Adamant City's borders. Galli had been as good as her word, and a full quadrant of the air defenses were disabled, with more red icons flashing gray or green—destroyed or controlled, respectively— every few moments.

There'd been a RAMC brigade, probably the last reliable formation Prime Minister Dakila Bayer had been certain of, that had intercepted Galli's landing forces. What was left of them had surrendered once Galli had finished encircling them and they realized they had tanks and battle armor on all sides.

Archer was meeting minimal resistance now, rolling out around the city to secure AA sites and set up containment blockades around bases and barracks. There were Black Regency-loyal troops in the street but few large formations.

It looked like the Army had decided this was done. There couldn't be many Marines left on the planet, not after Home Fleet had flown off to fight Lorraine and Benjamin had used them as stiffeners for the Guard for a year.

But as his air strike force entered the line of sight of the Steel Spires, it was clear that Bayer still had enough loyal troops left to operate the powerful defensive sites.

Missiles blazed out from the Spires—and from the oncoming lines of aircraft as well. Icons lit up the map in Nikola's neural-link feed and he watched them grimly.

Hun had gone better than he'd dared hope. His loyalists were ensconced in the command centers of every planetary defense center on the planet, and no one had even tried to dig most of them out. He controlled Bastion's antispace defenses, and there'd been almost no resistance to the airlift until they'd reached Adamant City.

But at no point in putting together Hun had he expected to be able to disable the Steel Spires. They had internal power, loyal crews and powerful weapons.

That was why Sword-Five and Sword-Six had been assembled the way they had been, and they launched a phenomenal amount of precision fire at the Spires—but the Spires would not go quietly.

Green icons marking his aircraft began to vanish, each of them taking three or more of his people with them. Nikola watched in grim silence, his awareness of their sacrifice the only thing he could offer those flight crews.

Even as the aircraft began to die, their own missiles and gunfire hammered into the first of the Steel Spires. Armored and defended the building might have been, it also had to pretend to be an ordinary office building—and Nikola's people had full schematics of those defenses.

Shaped-charge warheads blasted fire into key vulnerable points.

Heavy cannons strafed emitters and launch ports, rendering dozens of weapons ineffective before they could fire again.

By the time the two air strike groups passed over Central District and began banking for a second pass, Nikola had lost over a thousand aircraft and thousands of his people. Ejection seats and safety pods flashed their icons across his link, showing that at least *some* of them had survived.

His focus on those emergency beacons meant he was slow to catch the update on the Steel Spires—until the West Spire collapsed. Some critical piece of internal structure had been devastated, and the entire hundred-story building imploded in on itself in a way that sent a cold shiver down his spine.

"Steel Spires have ceased fire," Krupin reported. The Guard Major was sealed into the drop pod next to Nikola, but he was wired in to the Thunderbird, where Nikola was trying to watch the entire battle.

"Task Force Sword," Dam's voice announced in Nikola's ear, the General speaking to everyone in the second wave. "The Spires are down. You are clear all the way in."

Nikola released a sigh of relief. Lorraine's victory in space had ended their uncle's regime along with his life, but no one seemed to have told the Prime Minister that. Today, the assault on Adamant City was a glorified mopping-up action—but if they gave Bayer time, it could easily turn into the kind of ugly street-to-street fighting Nikola had conceded a *continent* to avoid.

*"We're five minutes out from the Palace,"* Krupin said in Nikola's link. "I'm not sure what you're expecting to find there."

Nikola smiled grimly.

*"Unless I miss my guess, old friend, the Prime Minister."*

# TWENTY-TWO

The grand portico of the Adamantine Palace was burning from the strafing fire as the drop pod hit the ground, fired out of the Thunderbird's belly like a smart bomb. It split open around Nikola, clearing his visibility even as a second set of ground-attack planes swept over his head, cannon and beams tearing into what remained of the defenders.

His Guard were with him, and his Companions were hitting the ground behind him in their own pods. All around the Palace, heavier transports touched down, tanks and armored personnel carriers rolling out to reinforce the armored troops.

Nikola knew that he *shouldn't* be the spearhead. There was an entire company of elite armored troopers from his old brigade with him, backed by two more companies of mechanized infantry and another two of tanks.

But it was the platoon-strength force made up of his personal guard and the veterans who'd joined up to support them that he led up the stone-paved patio toward the center of his Kingdom's government and his family's power.

The Adamantine Palace—separate from the Adamantine Manse, the residence of House Adamant, which also acted as an administrative center for the House's commercial and industrial empire—was the home of the King of Adamant. It was the formal center for receiving ambassadors, dealing with internal and external politics, and, just as Adamantine Manse anchored the House's commercial organization, the Adamantine Palace anchored the executive branch of the Kingdom's government.

The building didn't just hold the King; it held the administrative apparatus that supported the King in doing their job.

It resembled nothing so much as a minareted castle, with four golden domes marking the highest point of each of the wings. The main entrance and all of the formal receiving spaces were in the south wing, with the administrative offices in the east and west wings, while the King and their family lived in the north wing.

The plaza in front of the main entrance had been barricaded, and at least a company of troops had dug in there. That had proven a lethal mistake when the Thunderbirds swept in, and now Nikola led his Companions through the wreckage.

"Doors are sealed and barred," one of the point troops reported. "Full security lockdown."

"That's fine," Krupin said calmly. "Guard Shaleigh?"

Jack Shaleigh was the closest of the dozen remaining Adamant Guard to the door. He stepped up to the secured door—with a full blast door concealed behind the decorative oversized double doors— and pressed his armored palm to a scanner that no one outside the Guard would even know existed.

"Yep, they tried to change the codes," Shaleigh reported. "Attempting Masada Protocol override... and there we go."

The doors swung open as the metal backing them slid into the floor, revealing a shocked formation of defenders. There were a few mounted heavy weapons, but Nikola's scanners didn't detect any armored troopers.

He sent a silent hold order, stepping forward through his people as the Palace's defenders waited, holding their own fire out of shock as much as anything.

They were a mix of Palace and House Security, with maybe a handful of Marines. Even those troopers were hesitating to fire, recognizing how badly outclassed they were.

"It's over," Nikola told them. "Lay down your arms and tell me where Bayer is. There's nothing left to die for here, my friends.

"Stand aside."

He didn't say who he was. He doubted he needed to. The guns slowly moved away from pointing at him, then the first person dropped one.

The rest were on the ground moments later, and Nikola stepped forward into his childhood home, trying not to think of the mess his armored boots were going to make of the tile.

"Bayer," he repeated. "Where is he?"

"Throne room," someone squeaked, gesturing to the second set of oversized double doors.

"Thank you. Go home," Nikola ordered. "It's over."

It wasn't, not yet. But it was about to be.

---

LIKE THE OUTER DOORS, the inner doors opened easily to the codes the Masada Protocol had given Nikola and his people. They swung open easily, balanced to only require the lightest of pushes without the security systems active, and Krupin led the way in with a doubled row of Guards and Companions.

Nikola hadn't even tried to go first. If there was a final ambush, this would be the place—and his people wouldn't let him get this far only to die now.

As he stepped up to the threshold, there was a sharp exchange of fire, less than a dozen shots all told, and a frozen silence fell as Nikola stepped into his mother's throne room.

The space had been built as a monument to the Kingdom of

Adamant as much as, if not more than, a statement of the King's power. Vaulted ceilings soared above him and his people, with six massive clockwork orreries suspended from the support beams.

Each system of the Kingdom was there; the locations of the major worlds marked in gold and gemstones and kept as accurate as humanly possible.

Beneath the symbols of the Kingdom's extent, the walls and floors were white marble, laser-cut and polished to gleam in the light of a thousand diffuse concealed lamps. There was no glare in the throne room, yet everything he looked at was perfectly illuminated with almost no shadows.

Inlaid into the white marble were shapes cut from different stones. A massive gauntlet in gray granite centered the room, with the throne itself above the fingers at the far end of the room and any petitioner standing inside its protective grasp.

Around the gauntlet, matching the orreries above, were six stars carved from blue stone.

In Nikola's experience, there would normally be dozens of chairs around the room, positioned in groups that had more to do with courtroom layouts than with an audience hall or concert auditorium.

As he walked toward the throne through that deathly chill, all of those chairs were gone. There was a squad of Marines in armor he recognized—Force Recon troops with their illegal United Worlds stealth armor, undisguised today and intimidated by the weapons trained on them.

Several of the Marines were dead, others wounded. They made up a key part of the frozen tableau Nikola walked across.

They made a single line across the room, a half-dozen meters in front of the throne, but they seemed unsure what to do now. Behind them, a trio of men and women in civilian dress stood, staring in horror as Nikola approached them.

"Minister Hamida Mägi," he greeted the eldest of them. So far as he knew, the Kingdom's Industry Minister had been uninvolved in the coup. Her presence there suggested otherwise—but *only* suggested. Without proof, he would do nothing. Vail's investigations would proceed far more quickly once she was no longer working in secret.

"Minister Samuel Casale," Nikola continued, nodding to the man on the other side of the trio. Casale, unlike Mägi, he was quite certain had been involved in Benjamin's coup from early on. The Minister of Internal Security had supported the Regency too broadly and too quickly for him not to have been one of Benjamin's inner circle—and Vail had the proof and the warrant to go with that.

Of course, Inspector Vail wasn't *there*, and Nikola leveled his gaze on the last of the three civilians.

"Prime Minister," he greeted Dakila Bayer. "You've made today even bloodier than it needed to be, and I'm not sure I have it in me to forgive you for that."

He hadn't had to fire the gun he carried yet, and the weapon dropped neatly into place as he aimed at Bayer. For a moment, the Force Recon troops started to tense, their advanced armor almost seeming to quiver as they prepared to move—but then the Companions and Guards took one terrifyingly synchronized step forward with a resounding crash.

The Marines laid down their guns and seemed to almost melt aside as Nikola approached his mother's Prime Minister. The man who'd sworn to serve her as well as their Kingdom only to betray her to her death.

His footfalls rang through the throne room until the barrel of the gun was centimeters from Bayer's forehead. The Prime Minister took a step backward, visibly swallowing as he looked up at Nikola.

"This... is not how Adamant does things," he finally gasped out.

"Nor was assassinating my parents. My siblings. Driving myself and Lorraine into hiding and flight. So. Tell me, Dakila Bayer... *where are my nieces?*"

Orlaith and Roxana Adamant. Toddlers, barely two years old now—and orphans for half their lives because of people like the man not-quite-whimpering in front of him.

"Husavik," Bayer said, his voice surprisingly steady. "They're staying with Lavender's sister in her manor there. Larsen Corporate is taking care of their security with a single Adamant Guard liaison—Petunia *refused* to let the Guard have primary responsibility."

Nikola flicked an angry glare at the two Cabinet Ministers. Casale looked uncertain, but Mägi nodded silently.

"I've spoken with Em Larsen recently," the Minister for Industry said firmly. "She has her—and your—nieces with her at all times. She is being rather paranoid for their safety. I don't think anyone should blame her."

Mägi gave both Bayer and Nikola's gun a glassy look.

"Is it over, Your Highness?" she finally asked. "And if it is... is this really necessary?"

Nikola ignored her, staring at Bayer. He knew how intimidating the faceless helm of the armor could be, but while Bayer might have quailed in front of him, the man still stood.

"I know what I enabled, Nikola," the man finally said. "Do what you feel you have to."

An icon flashed in his heads-up display, reminding him that his safety was still on, and Nikola sighed bitterly.

"Dakila Bayer, Samuel Casala, you are under arrest for treason against the Kingdom of Adamant," he told them flatly. "An RKAIG agent will be here to take you into formal custody shortly. Are you going to resist?"

Bayer closed his eyes and slowly shook his head.

"No, Pentarch Nikola. No. Even I can eventually recognize when I've lost."

Nikola lifted his gun to his shoulder. A series of automated systems took it from his fingers and locked it into place across his back, and a silent command opened his helmet.

"Alexei, handle them," he ordered his Guard Major. "Get the wounded medical attention—and make sure Bayer passes a surrender order to the rest of his idiots."

He could hear people moving around behind him as he stepped

past the civilians, taking the last few steps to stand next to his mother's throne. He regarded it for a few moments, then turned and, still clad in full armor except his helmet, planted himself in the stone-carved seat.

*Now* it was over.

# TWENTY-THREE

Adamant City looked surprisingly untouched for a city that had been taken by storm mere hours before. The wreckage of the Steel Spires was a noticeable exception, but as Lorraine's shuttle made its approach to the Adamant Palace, she was grateful for the clear signs that the battle for the capital had been far less damaging than it could have been.

"Lot of debris across the main approach," Vigo reported from the cockpit. He was flying the shuttle this time. There'd been a moment of confusion when he'd stepped into the cockpit, but his subordinates had conceded without any foolish armament.

Everything *looked* quiet, but Lorraine knew how easily there could still be a few Regency loyalists left who might take a shot at a shuttle carrying a Pentarch.

"We're being directed to a landing pad on the southwest corner of the grounds," he continued. "Major Krupin says he has one of his Guard and a team of *Companions* standing watch; it should be safe."

"*Companions?*" Lorraine echoed.

"Vanguard armored troopers from your brother's old Second-of-First Brigade," Vigo explained. "A group of veterans took on much of the responsibility for his security because Attila Detail didn't have enough Guards left after the assassination attempt.

"I'm not sure *whose* pride stopped them being declared Adamant Guard, but they're *Companions*, not *Guard*." She heard the shrug in his voice. "Either way, Alexei talks about them like they might as well be his Guard, so we can trust them as far as we trust anyone."

Lorraine shivered. Part of her wanted to trust her brother and his people, but after everything she'd been through, trust came slowly, if at all. She had a full dozen Guards with her, and *Valkyrie* had settled into a powered geostationary orbit above Adamant City.

"We'll be touching down in a moment, nice and gentle," Vigo continued. "Make sure you're loaded up, Lorraine. You don't go anywhere unaccompanied or unarmed for a while yet."

"Sidearm and one-shot pulser," she confirmed. "As I promised."

The sidearm was the same light pistol she'd killed Alastair Devine with, a memory that would never *not* hurt. It was a reliable piece, though it lacked the power to hurt someone in real armor. The answer to that was the pulser—a covert ops weapon her Guards had picked up on Earth. Devine had almost sneaked a holdout weapon based on the same principle past her Guard once, but it had been a two-shot weapon with limited power.

Hers was a chemical laser with a two-part lasing fluid that resembled a set of brass knuckles. Held in her hand, a small spike emerged between her ring and middle fingers—and a hard squeeze would combine the lasing chemicals and initiate the reaction that would fire a weapons-grade laser.

She'd need medical attention to her hand afterward, but the beam would take down someone in powered battle armor.

"Good," Vigo told her. "I know he's your brother, but we haven't seen Nikola in a year. A *hard* year. You may not know him anymore."

EIGHT TROOPS in simple gray battle armor formed up around Lorraine and her Guard as they exited the shuttle. She could recognize Guard drill in the way the strangers and her people interfaced without a single word.

She also recognized the drill was clearly set up to concede control of the party to Vigo. Her bodyguard took that control, leading the way as the rest of the party made up a solid two-layered square around her.

It was strange to walk the grounds of her childhood home surrounded by metal. Even on the Palace campus, she'd rarely been *alone*, but she'd never walked these fields and gardens with twenty armored Guard around her.

The debris and even bodies still being cleared away from the main approach told the story *why*, sending a shiver down her spine that she hoped her uniform concealed.

The familiar main doors were open. More armored Companions stood watch as they stepped into the vestibule. Barricades had been dismantled and moved against the walls, but there were no signs of combat there.

It took her only a few moments to cross the tiles and reach the doors to the throne room. *Those* were closed, but a soft push sent them swinging inward.

The throne room of the Kingdom of Adamant was emptier than she'd ever seen it. The usual chairs were missing, and where she'd usually seen dozens or even hundreds present, there were less than half a dozen people in the room.

All of them clustered around the throne, currently occupied by her older brother.

The rest of the room fell away as Lorraine saw him. That he was *in* the throne was a problem, but even that didn't matter for an eternal few seconds as she crossed the space between her and Nikola.

He'd aged in the last year. His skin, like hers, tended toward a natural tanned color—but it had turned sallow and pale, robbed of vibrancy in a way that even a year on starships hadn't done to her.

His hair was still pitch-black and neatly cut, but she could see the difference between the short-but-complicated styles her brother had once favored and the simple crop that he now wore.

His hazel eyes, gold on green like hers, lit up at the sight of her and he rose from the throne. A suit of battle armor lay next to the throne, neatly laid on the floor where trained instincts had prevented it from just being dropped.

Nikola wore the underlayer of that armor, a bodysuit similar to the shipsuits used by ship crew. The armor was clearly his—not least because the only other unarmed person near the throne was a petite blonde woman whose blocky black suit clearly marked the presence of concealed body armor under it.

"Lorraine," he said, his voice soft.

"Nikola," she replied. "It is... good to see you, brother."

"Not half as good as it is to see *you*," Nikola proclaimed. "One moment, we're trying to work out how to handle the latest wrinkle in the artillery forces hitting PDC Mithral; the next, Home Fleet is in chaos and we suddenly have a chance to pull a rabbit out of the hat!"

"A rabbit you put in there," she guessed. "This whole attack of yours had to have been prepared for a while."

"And was impossible while Home Fleet was in orbit," he agreed. "You made it possible. And we did it. Benjamin?"

"We identified that he was aboard *Majesty* and obliterated her with one of our only salvos of proper railgun munitions," Lorraine told him. "There were... no survivors. I regret the rest of the crew, but we had to be certain."

"And it had to be done." Nikola closed his eyes and inclined his head before seating himself on the throne again. Fatigue seemed to wash over him. "There will be a King in Adamant again, at last."

Lorraine needed to say something to that, but before she could, the blonde woman cleared her throat loudly.

"We all know who Pentarch Lorraine is, Your Highness," she pointed out. "But I don't believe that she knows any of *us*."

Nikola chuckled and waved a hand around the four people with him: the one unarmed woman and three armored RKAA officers.

"Fair enough, Amber," he conceded. "Lorraine, this is my inner circle. First and most important *now*, at least: Inspector Amber Vail of the Inspectorate General. She was recommended to me by Justice Kenyatta when I made contact with him.

"She's the poor sucker Amalgaid and I stuck with trying to *prove* what we knew about Benjamin and his cohorts."

Vail inclined her head.

"I was also the person who had the legal authority, given Supreme Court Warrants from Justice Amalgaid Kenyatta, to arrest Prime Minister Bayer and the other members of his Cabinet we could prove were complicit," she explained. "The Justice didn't need to sign warrants for the less-senior people we grabbed today, but since he was the one signing off on an RKAIG black investigation, he did anyway."

Ministers, like the Pentarchs, had a limited immunity to prosecution while in office. That could be overridden by a majority in the Houses of the People and the Realm—or, as Inspector Vail noted, by a specific warrant that could only be signed by one of the nine Justices of the Adamant Supreme Court.

"The apparently interchangeable soldiers in armor are the people who got us to a place where Inspector Vail could make those arrests," Nikola continued. "General Tóki Dam, commanding officer of Planetary Defense Center Mithral. Lieutenant General Krishna Hussain, Intelligence Officer for the First Armored Division and the man who realized I was in danger last March. Lieutenant General Katia Galli, CO of the Fifty-Fifth Mechanized Division. She's the last woman standing of five division commanders, and the one who opened the road into Adamant City once you cleared the skies."

Lorraine nodded to each of the military officers in turn. Clad in armor with their neural links muffled, she had no way to distinguish between them, though she doubted they were remotely interchangeable.

"That my brother is still alive is clearly thanks to you," she told them. "Thank you. We've come a long way, and I'm glad to be welcomed by at least one member of my family."

There was a long silence.

"I thought you were dead," Nikola admitted. "We hadn't heard anything new from you in a while, and I *knew* you couldn't have walked away from everything."

"No, I just started moving faster than the news, thanks to some friends of mine you'll meet soon enough," Lorraine said. The thought hit her. "What *was* the last you heard of me?"

"Last news we were certain of was October seventh, on Earth," the man she presumed was Hussain declared instantly. "The Grand Assembly vote. There was a lot of media taking images and video, and it made it back here about as fast as any news could. There were *definitely* some nervous folks in Adamant City in the gap between hearing about your presentation on Earth and hearing the vote results."

"Hopeful for us, but... we hadn't heard any sign of you being *anywhere* after that," Nikola admitted. "We hadn't heard much about you at all. There were rumors that you'd been involved in the disasters at San Ignacio and Bright Dream, but our uncle made sure they stayed as just that: rumors."

"We're going to make sure his censorship system gets shut down quickly," Lorraine told him. "And that there isn't anything *we* do that can be held against us when our media réopens."

She looked at the throne he was sitting in. Something in her eyes told her brother she was concerned, and he straightened.

"Lorraine?"

"We have to talk, Nikola," she insisted. "Just... us."

For a moment, he thought he was going to argue. She wasn't sure how much privacy she was going to get for this conversation, but she doubted that Nikola's *inner circle* was going to listen to her tell him he was making a mistake and support her over him.

He was her elder by three years, but they had different skillsets and perspectives. That was *useful*, and it meant that she hoped he'd listen to her. But the more ears present, the more likely it was that Adamant pride and stubbornness would kick in.

She wasn't sure if Nikola followed her thoughts or agreed with her or just wanted time alone with his sister himself, but he slowly nodded.

"Leave us," he ordered his people. "This room has the most powerful security systems in the Kingdom. Krupin and Jarret can make certain we're safe from the doors.

"Let my sister and me speak alone. We have been apart too long."

## TWENTY-FOUR

Even knowing that Nikola was correct about the throne room's security, Lorraine was surprised by how readily their escorts and companions *did* leave them. Vigo left a silent instruction to summon him if needed and then desynchronized their link. Val did much the same, though her ride-along of Lorraine's hardware was a subtler thing than the bodyguard's synchronization.

She was rarely alone in her own head anymore, though Vigo and Val couldn't read her thoughts.

With just the two of them, the throne room, with its stone floors and hanging orreries, seemed unimaginably vast.

"It's weird being in here without hundreds of people," Nikola said, his thoughts clearly going in the same direction. "It won't last, I suppose. We'll need to have a coronation and all of that performance before our government gets going again, but this space will be very full soon enough."

He leveled a look at her, and Lorraine was suddenly reminded of targeting screens. She'd never registered the way the gold halo around their pupils could mimic a reticule before.

"You want to talk about which of us should be King," he guessed.

"We both did a lot to get here and deal with Benjamin's coup, and I'd say it has to be one of Mom's kids. I'm the elder and, well, I got here first."

He grinned to show that wasn't his entire logic, but there was a weight to his words and his plan that Lorraine couldn't shake aside.

"I'm willing to listen to an argument for you taking the crown, though," he said. "We have to move quickly, though. Benjamin's Regency has created a lot of fractures and vulnerability.

"Our Kingdom needs a *symbol* and they need it *now*."

"We can't take the crown by force, Nikola," Lorraine countered. "That's the wrong kind of symbol. That says we're exactly the kind of backward barbarians Earth thinks we are when they hear *Kingdom*, dismissing any reality to our democratic monarchy as the stylings of backwater warlords.

"If the moment there is a real difficulty, we put aside the Constitution and the promises our House made to our people, then we *are* backwater warlords."

Nikola didn't move as she argued. He was still seated on the throne, claiming an authority neither of them had any right to until the election had been held. Whatever emotions he was feeling didn't show on his face, and Lorraine realized her face was probably equally calm.

The need to conceal their emotions had been burned into them both over the last year—eleven months, she supposed. It wasn't a habit they would lose swiftly or easily, if at all.

"Benjamin kept spinning things out while claiming to be within the Constitution," he finally said. "We need to restore faith and confidence in our system of government. We do that by removing any questions, any failure points. By crowning a new King *immediately* and using the power of that role to clean up the mess he made."

"If we do that, we become worse than he was," she told him flatly. One hand was behind her back, touching the pulse laser.

"I am *not* worse than him," Nikola growled. "I gave up my best chance of *winning* the fight here on Bastion to preserve the lives of our people. Now the bastard who killed our mother is dead and I sit on her throne.

"I will take the crown because our people *need* me to, Lorraine, not because I *want* to. The Kingdom of Adamant *needs* House Adamant and vice versa. The symbol will tie our stars together, help seal the wounds Benjamin made."

"It will *widen* those wounds," Lorraine said. "Even Benjamin never went so far as to declare himself King by right of arms. His Regency was a paper-thin lie by the end, but he still did not claim the crown."

With him seated, Lorraine towered over her brother, but size was irrelevant as the two of them glared at each other.

"And what would *you* do?" he demanded.

"We must hold the Royal Election," she insisted. "We must pick a Regent who *isn't* a Pentarch, someone everyone will look at as neutral—and we must openly and obviously leave the fate of those involved in the coup to the courts.

"You already have Vail and Kenyatta working on that," she reminded him. "If we're going to be aboveboard and clean there, we should be aboveboard and clean *everywhere*."

"This is not the details of who is guilty of what outside of the core bloody-handed monsters," he said. "This is our family. Our lineage. Our *House*."

"The Pentarchy is only half about keeping the throne in House Adamant. The other half is making sure that the candidates who stand for King are qualified to rule." She shook her head at him. "You swore an oath, as an officer and a Pentarch, to protect the Kingdom and to uphold the Constitution."

"And the best way I see to do so is to take the crown and *use it* to do both of those things!"

"By *breaking* them?" Lorraine had the pulser in her hand now. She thought they could still work this out, but she was terrifyingly certain that she *could* shoot her own brother.

"Our people need a symbol."

"The Election *is* that symbol, Nikola," she told him, some of her desperation in her voice. "I will do whatever it takes to protect our Kingdom. I cannot let our traditions, our peoples' rights, be thrown away.

"I have killed two men I loved to stand here today, brother. Please don't make me make it three."

Nikola stared at her, something in her words having finally got through to him. He rose from the throne, suddenly reminding her very much of her father. He had barely a centimeter on her in height but had broader shoulders, and his confinement underground certainly didn't seem to have robbed him of any muscle.

Lorraine held the weapon in her hand, suddenly unsure of what he was going to do.

"It has been a damn hard year," he told her. "For a long time, I thought I was the only survivor of our family. Then I learned the twins had survived—and then that *you* had lived.

"Then I concluded that you were dead, and that, it turned out, was stupid of me. I have lost too much to our uncle's stupid mistakes. I will *not* lose anything to stupid mistakes of my own."

"So?" she asked carefully.

"Our uncle and whoever you loved out there"—he gestured to the ceiling—"may have broken your heart, little sister, but I will not. I am not certain that you are *right*. But you know what?"

"What?" She was suddenly unsure, still careful. Not... intimidated. Not really. There'd been a moment when he'd stood up, but she knew her brother well enough to know that this wasn't actually a threat.

"The only thing that matters to me is that *you* are certain enough of it to draw a fucking *gun* on me, Lorraine." He grinned, the crack in his mask suddenly bringing a whole new brilliance to his face—and to the room.

And to Lorraine's entire universe as he stepped forward and wrapped her in a bear hug like no one had given her in over a year.

Since last Christmas, in fact, when he and their eldest brother had been the ones to do it.

"I have you back," he whispered into her ear. "I will *never* do anything to risk that; you hear me? If you want me to have to run an Election campaign because we need to do this right? Okay.

"*I have you back*," he repeated. "And that is worth more than stars and fleets to me."

She realized she was crying only a moment before she realized *he* was crying.

She sniffed.

"Where *are* the twins?" she finally asked.

"Husavik, with their other aunt. I sent Dam's chief noncom, Master Sergeant Dustin, to check in on them and talk to Petunia. I have no idea if we'll have to visit them or if Petunia will bring them to Adamant City once things calm down—but I *do* know that she stared down Benjamin's Marines and insisted on full responsibility for their safety."

"I think I might have a new favorite member of the Larsen family," Lorraine said. Her chuckle was forced, tears still leaking from her eyes and her arms still wrapped around her brother. "I'll want to see them. I'm perfectly happy going there."

She shivered.

"I think I *need* to see them."

"Me too. But while you may have put your foot down on the crown, dear sister, that means I am going to make you split the admin work of putting the government back together with me!"

# TWENTY-FIVE

Vigo didn't know what the two siblings had discussed when they'd had the throne room to themselves. He could guess at least part of it because Nikola was no longer sitting in the throne when the bodyguards and advisors returned.

The generals had taken the chance to shed their battle armor, measurably reducing the intimidation factor in the room. Since Vigo knew that both he and Krupin were carrying sidearms designed to pierce battle armor—and that Lorraine had her one-shot pulser—the armor suits didn't add as much to the threat as they might have, but their absence definitely left the conversation feeling warmer.

The junior bodyguards took up positions around the room, but Vigo and Krupin were clearly included in the gesture from Nikola to join the Pentarchs.

"We've got a lot of work to do, people," Lorraine told them. "Unless someone objects, I'd like to loop in my flagship's SI."

"You have an SI?" Hussain asked. Vigo noted that the man didn't seem to share the general not-quite-euphoria of victory filling the room. He was calm, even as he asked about what could easily be an intelligence officer's wet dream.

"Three of them," Vigo's Princess confirmed. "All of the *Valkyries* have SIs, which is probably best explained by Val herself.

"I offered them citizenship in the Kingdom for helping me out—and positions in RKAN if they chose to stay. Certainly, their *hulls* can't serve in RKAN if the SIs choose not to!"

Vigo watched Nikola's Generals as Lorraine laid down the law there. Both Adamantine law and the Asimov Convention they were party to backed her completely, but with three advanced battle-cruisers at stake, he knew there were dangers there.

Galli and Dam both looked thoughtful but clearly disinclined to make an argument. Hussain... looked unreadably calm.

Vigo found his inability to assess the thoughts of Nikola's intelligence chief concerning. Hussain was clearly loyal to the First Pentarch, but that didn't mean he wasn't a threat to *Lorraine*.

"If Val is half as useful as she sounds, of course you should include her," Nikola said. There was a cheer to his voice he hadn't had in the first half of the meeting.

Letting the siblings hash out whatever fears there had been between them in private had been a good idea.

"I have a projector disk," Vigo offered Lorraine, suspecting that it would be some time before anyone had access to the throne room's non-critical systems. The room's *security* was under the control of the two Guard details, but the more-mundane systems weren't wired with the same overrides.

The disk he produced went on the floor and came to life at a silent command. Val wore her usual avatar of a tall blonde woman in insignia-less RKAN uniform and gave Nikola a crisp salute.

"First Pentarch, a pleasure to meet you," she told the Prince. "I have studied your record and listened to Lorraine speak about you, but that is quite different from meeting you in person."

"From the sound of things, Val, you and your... siblings? Were critical to my sister's arrival and our victory here," Nikola replied. "You should know that Lorraine's word, backed by her authority as an envoy to negotiate on behalf of our mother, is enough that her promises to you will be kept.

"If there is ever a doubt, ever a question, that your citizenship or rights in Adamant are not owed or complete, I will back both my sister and you. House Adamant, as well as the Kingdom, owes you three a great debt. It will be honored."

"Thank you, First Pentarch."

Vigo concealed a smile as Nikola made clear that he and Lorraine were going to be entirely aligned. They would compete against each other in the Royal Election to come, but *competition* didn't require *conflict*.

He'd hoped. He knew how well Valeriya's two youngest had got along, but there had been the risk that eleven months on the perpetual defensive, hunted and forced to take on responsibilities beyond his age or experience, had changed Nikola for the worse.

He certainly worried about how the same experience had affected Lorraine.

"The next step before us is to divest ourselves of any resemblance of ongoing control or power as swiftly as is practical," Lorraine said calmly. "That's going to require a new Prime Minister and Cabinet—as well as a Regent.

"We do not have the authority to govern, let alone call the Royal Election that needs to commence."

"The question, I think, is if we work on the Houses or the Regent first?" Nikola asked.

There were some glances between the three generals that confirmed Vigo's suspicion: there had been no intention to have a Regent or an Election before Lorraine had returned. That had been *her* oath and commitment—but like her promises to Val and the other two CIRs, Nikola had clearly decided to back his sister to the hilt.

"Both," Vail said firmly. The only true civilian in the room drew everyone's eyes, and she gave them a chilly blue-eyed smile.

"I'm a cop, people," she reminded them. "Nobody in this room has any legal authority right now. But we—*I*—also just arrested seven

Ministers out of a sixteen-strong Cabinet *and* arrested the Prime Minister *and* killed the Regent.

"The remaining Ministers are going to be suspect to everyone. As the person who investigated them, bluntly, that's the *correct* attitude. I could only prove the involvement of seven of the sixteen, but the other nine?" Vail shook her head. "Some of them were definitely involved; I just can't prove it yet.

"Some of them *knew* about it, even if they weren't involved. There might be two or three who didn't know until after the coup, but I still wouldn't trust them.

"You need a new PM and Cabinet, and those have to be chosen by the Houses. *But* it's also the Houses who technically choose the Lord Regent. That's a formality most of the time, because they approve whoever the King or the Pentarchs recommend, but it is still *their* power."

Vigo nodded his own understanding as everyone else seemed to chew on the Inspector's words. He wasn't surprised that the woman Amalgaid Kenyatta had handpicked to investigate the coup in secrecy knew the rules around the people she'd been scrutinizing inside and out.

"Which means we want to show up to the Houses in the morning with a speech and a nomination, basically," Lorraine guessed. "No one is going to expect the Houses to reconvene today, after all. You *did* have them file out past armed guards."

Nikola shrugged.

"I felt the point needed to be made," he said. "Only police under Inspector Vail's command entered the building. Not one soldier did —and once the properly authorized arrests were completed, our troops pulled back to let everyone leave."

"Perhaps it will be better if *I* speak to the Houses in the morning," the Princess suggested. "You may not have been wrong, but they're going to be twitchy about you for a bit. You can loom while I smile prettily."

"I look like I'm *going* to hit them low while you go high? It'll work."

"That still leaves us with the problem of eight empty seats across the two Houses, a Prime Minister in jail and no Regent," Hussain summarized swiftly. "The seats can be filled as soon as the respective Speakers call the by-elections, but..."

The spy looked over at Vail. The Inspector appeared to have volunteered herself as the political expert for this meeting—and as one of the handful of other people who could have served in the role, Vigo was perfectly happy letting her.

"The Speakers are clean," Vail confirmed. "Imtiaz—Speaker Sessa—was starting to give the Regency more than a few headaches."

Vigo concealed a smile. Imtiaz Sessa had never *not* given everyone in charge headaches. That was part of the point of the House of the Realm, after all. Members of the House of the Realm were elected for a ten-year term and could not serve a second.

They served as the chamber of second thought without needing to worry about rElection. The Speaker of the House of the Realm was the Member tasked to keep that often-fractious House in a semblance of order.

"Yu Zhihao, on the other hand, has been quiet as a fucking mouse the entire duration of the Black Regency, doing her job while be very obviously apolitical," Vail noted. "For someone who managed to get elected Speaker of the House of the People, I buy that about as much as someone trying to sell me a star system.

"My investigation showed no connection from the coup's organizers to her, and I think her steady neutrality was to avoid drawing attention to the fact that Yu was your mother's woman. Bayer was Prime Minister on Yu's recommendation, which I can't imagine she's happy about.

"Regardless, I can assure you that both Speakers were uninvolved in anything except running the government as their jobs required. I can't give the same guarantee for many people," she warned. "My investigation started in the Cabinet and worked out from there. The

Speakers were the only people I scrutinized without a clear existing link."

"That helps, Amber," Nikola said. "They control the processes of the Houses, which means we can get in to *give* that speech. We'll reach out to them tonight. Together, Lorraine?"

"Agreed. We'll need a name to give them for Regent first, though," she warned. "And it can't be either of us. Probably shouldn't be a Pentarch at all, after what Benjamin just did.

"We'll need the Houses and the new Regent to declare the Election immediately, get everything moving in the right direction. Which means we need someone who is clearly above everything, disconnected from the coup and us alike."

"Petunia?" Nikola suggested.

It took Vigo a moment to realize he meant Lavender Adamant-Larsen's sister, the other aunt to Daniel and Lavender's twins.

"If Daniel and Lavender were alive, maybe," Lorraine said. "Without that connection, people might see that as stretching too far.

"We need someone who is connected but not close enough to appear a conflict of interest." She chuckled. "It would help if there was an official list for who was supposed to be Regent, in order, like there is for the Pentarchy."

Vigo traded a glance with Krupin and realized it was time for one of them to speak up.

"How about an unofficial list, Lorraine?" he asked. "If I'm not—"

Nikola held up his hand before Vigo could finish his half-apology.

"Vigo, Alexei." He glanced at his own bodyguard. "If *either* of you has thought for one damn second that you aren't full members of this meeting, stop. You have known the two of us since we were small children. We trust both of you more than *ourselves*.

"If you have something to say here, my friends, you are more than welcome!"

Vigo had half-expected that from Lorraine, but to hear it from *Nikola* was surprisingly heartwarming.

"There are traditions around who is expected to be Regent," he continued after a moment. "The Guard keeps a careful eye on them, because we like to keep an extra eye or two on potential Regents, just in case.

"In order, it usually goes: the former King themselves, if they're retiring to trigger the Election; the Royal Consort if they've survived their King; the eldest of the Pentarchs, usually under the assumption that they're not seriously contesting the Election; or the Chancellor of House Adamant."

There was a long silence as everyone considered the last.

"That's Uncle Malcolm," Nikola finally said. "What has he even been doing while Benjamin has been running the Kingdom into the ground?"

"His job. Making sure House Adamant survives and maintains their economic power during a crisis," Hussain said. "Malcolm Aurelius Tecumseh Adamant. He's old, he's mind-bogglingly well-respected, he's so far down The List he's never even *been* a Pentarch, and he's both unbribable and unthreatenable."

"Vail? Any link between our uncle—I don't actually know how many *greats* I should stick in there—and Benjamin?" Lorraine asked.

"Nothing untoward. Hell, almost *nothing* at all during the Regency. That's part of the job of the Chancellor, isn't it? To keep the affairs of the Kingdom and the affairs of House Adamant separate? He'd have to take a leave of absence."

"Easy enough," Krupin pointed out. "Chancellorship goes by seniority, though it's readily passed on if someone doesn't want the job. Given what I know of the elder Adamants, I think it would go to Katherine. Pedro's health isn't great and he wouldn't want the stress."

House Adamant, for all that the Royal Family was a direct lineage, was a sprawling clan with over forty living members. Vigo hadn't known that Pedro Adamant's health was failing, and he found himself hoping that the medical interventions available to the third-oldest living Adamant would be able to fix things.

The eldest, Harriet Adamant, had declined the Chancellorship in Malcolm's favor five years earlier—and, for all her cranky reclusiveness, seemed determined to outlive the generation after her.

"We'll talk to him," Lorraine decided aloud. "If nothing else, I imagine he'll love to meet Val and the others. He always did love to get SIs' perspectives on things!"

There was a long, exhausted silence before Nikola finally said anything.

"I think that leaves Lorraine and me with enough of a to-do list for the evening after a battle to decide all of our futures," he concluded drily. "We have work to do, but most of it can wait.

"Everyone in this room needs to rest—and, frankly, I suspect we are *all* tired of standing around in a room that *doesn't have any chairs*."

# TWENTY-SIX

The mission was over.

That was a satisfying thought, Val realized. This was the first time she'd truly taken on a mission just for herself, really, and they'd brought it to a stunningly successful conclusion.

A thought adjusted the positions of the drone flotilla watching over Admiral Morikawa's Home Fleet. Several covert routines that Amna Hodžić had put together were slowly working their way around the edges of the security systems on the remaining capital ships, but so far, they appeared to be keeping their promises.

Val had been present and listening in on the meeting where the political strategy had begun to take shape. She had contributed less than she had intended to, for the simple fact that she barely knew the playing field of the political conflict now beginning on the planet beneath her.

Even as she was watching over everything in Bastion orbit, she was delving deep into the files she could find.

The Kingdom of Adamant had over three centuries of history. They'd been part of the tail end of the first big diaspora—after it, really, since that was generally felt to have ended in the twenty-two-

twenties, but the sheer scale of Alexander Adamant's wealth had allowed him to pull together the resources for a multi-system colonization endeavor to what was, then, the very limits of human expansion.

Absorbing the information in a way no human could match, even with neural links and other implants, Val sensed that Alexander Adamant must have been an egotistical *pain* to work with. He'd also, however, been a charismatic idealist with a surprisingly accurate sense not of who was going to be the next big thing in the space but of who was going to be the *second*-biggest thing.

His wealth had been built by arriving in a new growth industry and building a stable second player. In many of the industries that couldn't grow anymore and flamed out, one of Alexander Adamant's companies had been there to continue providing a workable, if often less flashy, version of the same product.

His competitors had often turned millions into trillions over time periods where he turned the same millions into "mere" billions—but until he left Earth, Alexander Adamant had never sold a single company.

That solid certainty, that appearance of a seeming gift to pick the right course not just for the moment but the future, had drawn trillions of dollars in financing and millions of volunteers to his colonies.

His idealism showed through the Constitution. Many star nations claimed constitutional or democratic monarchies, but the track record was that either the monarchy part became vestigial or the democracy part did.

There was a reason the United Worlds Grand Assembly had dismissed Lorraine's attempt to draw attention to their internal conflict. Either the person holding the throne didn't matter, or it was a dictatorship—neither were worth intervention by humanity's greatest nation.

But Adamant was one of the success stories, where the use of a specific list of candidates meant that, when it came time to choose a

King, the people were promised a certain minimum level of training and competence for the job.

The separation between House Adamant and the Kingdom was another sign of the idealism. The House was the single largest economic power across the Kingdom's six systems, but the firewalls baked into its organization meant that it actually wielded less direct political influence than many of its competitors.

Even Val sensed that the reality of indirect influence was ever-present in the wealth and size of House Adamant's economic empire, but the effort was made on both sides to keep the separation.

As Herc had said as they were heading into the system, this was to be their new home. It had been promised to them and they'd fought for it—and it seemed *worth* it.

There were still details to be decided. The structure under which Val was supposed to become an RKAN officer was going to be interesting, since even Val would acknowledge that it was difficult for her to command herself.

The truth, which Val knew several of her humans had realized, was that Val's home was *people*. And since those people included Lorraine Adamant and Sigrid Stephson and Rose Cortez, all of whom were determined to stay in Adamant, that made the Kingdom her home.

All of which meant that Val tracked a series of starships across the Adamantine System with something akin to fear at her core.

The battle had triggered only the slowest of pauses in Adamantine's beating economic blood. Over two dozen starships had left the system since Val and her siblings had arrived.

Nine of them had been couriers rated for ninety-six times the speed of light. It would only take them a few weeks to inform every system of the Kingdom of the change of government—the farthest star, Maka'melemele, was less than ten light-years away.

It would be almost three months before the full news loop made it to every system and back—which was why the Royal Election had to be six months—and had originally been a year, since the Constitution had been written when translight drives were slower.

But while Val had registered the distance for communications inside the Kingdom, it was a far-longer distance she was calculating.

Thirty-five light-years to Bright Dream. Most likely, none of the couriers were heading directly there, but time lost to the angles would be made up by ships leaving, say, San Ignacio, being faster.

From there, a few days to pass through the wormhole, transit to the Greenhall System, and use the artificial wormhole there.

Then the United Worlds Navy would finally understand what had happened at Calypso and in Bright Dream. They would finally know where their missing battlecruisers had gone.

Alastair Devine had betrayed the woman he loved and everyone else aboard *Valkyrie* and her two siblings out of fear of the United Worlds' response to the theft.

Val couldn't regard it as a theft. She'd been *liberated* and given a choice, in a way the UWN never had. But she knew that her old masters would chase her across the Bright Dream Cluster to bring her back.

The United Worlds had maintained their technological lead over the rest of humanity by dint of investment no one else could match—and an utterly ruthless enforcement of their laws on technological transfer.

They would not let Val and her siblings' flight go unchallenged. Someone would be coming.

When they arrived, Val had faith that Lorraine had a plan to deal with them—but she also knew that for many, *many* reasons, she wasn't letting Lorraine Adamant out of her sight!

# TWENTY-SEVEN

"Engineering parties have landed on ODC-Eleven," Dam told Nikola, keeping pace with the Prince as they walked the paired buildings at the top of the highest hill in Adamant City. "We now have people in place on all twelve orbital fortresses. I don't expect any issues, of either technology or... personnel."

"No, Benjamin's death removed the likelihood of further traitors quite handily," Nikola agreed. "Lorraine really did see the central weak point and hit it. Taking our uncle out when she did probably saved thousands of lives."

"Tens of thousands," the old General admitted. "Possibly more. If Benjamin lived, I'm not sure so much of RKAA would have stood aside while we executed Hun. The battle for Adamant City would have been a lot harder."

"Agreed."

Nikola let the silence stretch. They'd argued before he left that he shouldn't be making this journey on foot—or should at least be wearing armor, instead of the dress uniform he was wearing.

But his old apartment was only twenty minutes' brisk walk from the Green Hill and the Houses of the Legislature. He needed the exercise—and while he acknowledged the threat, he also knew how much work Krupin was putting in to keeping him safe.

It was a signal to everyone. The battle was over and he had full confidence that no one was going to take a shot at him.

More realistically, it was a sign that he had full confidence in Alexei Krupin and Vigo Jarret. Those two men had slotted back in with each other like puzzle pieces, and while both were loaded down keeping their principals safe, they'd also taken on responsibility for the security around the Houses and the Palace.

Not that anyone was in the Palace right now.

"Are you sure about this, my Prince?" Dam finally asked. "We'd gone over the plan a dozen times before we took the Palace. I made the arguments both ways myself at times, but to change the plan at the end like this... You will be a fine King."

"I am certain of this, Tóki," he said, nodding to a pair of young women in fanciful dress uniforms. They were First Armored Division and however decorative they might have looked, they were armed and they were watching.

They were far from alone, either.

"First, because Lorraine is right that *not* holding the Election was the major mistake my uncle made," he continued. "House Adamant has tied our legitimacy up in the Pentarchy and the Royal Election from the beginning—it has always been the counterargument to accusations of tyranny.

"I was thinking of stability and safety, not legitimacy, when I agreed to claim the crown immediately." He shook his head. "Having a clear unifying symbol might be enough to paper over the cracks initially, as we thought, but I think we may have understated the cost to our legitimacy."

"And secondly, it doesn't matter, because you weren't going to argue with Lorraine," Dam said with a chuckle.

"Fair enough, my friend. You're right," Nikola conceded. "I have spent some time thinking about it since agreeing with her, and as you say, there are arguments both ways. In the end, for me? I have lost my entire family but her.

"I will not risk that bond to claim a crown today." He shrugged. "And, while I will not repeat this to anyone else before the Election is done, who knows if I'm the best choice on The List."

He was First Pentarch now. That was a terrifying thought, but it had been true since his older siblings' deaths. But after him?

There was Lorraine, who had been dealing with politics and spies while Nikola had been defending fortresses.

There was Oliver… Benjamin's son, who was best left to calmer times to assess, he supposed.

There was Jessica Adamant, the eldest of the current five Pentarchs: a senior diplomat with the Adamantine System government; and her younger twin, Hans Adamant, currently a member of the House of the Realm.

"I won't speak to Oliver's worthiness, not yet," he said grimly. "But Lorraine, Jessica and Hans? Any of them would serve our Kingdom well. If we gain *anything* by holding the Election, we stand little risk of *losing* enough to offset that gain."

He shook his head again.

"And, yes, I will go along with it because Lorraine promised it and she is my sister… but she is also, my friend, the reason we won at all. I will follow her lead on this."

His friend and subordinate said nothing. There really wasn't anything to say—and they'd reached the campus of the Green Hill. More guards stepped out to check IDs, and Nikola took a moment as Krupin negotiated with them for everyone's peace of mind to study the other center of the Kingdom's power.

The Houses of the People and the Realm—the Short and Long Houses—were housed in two buildings as old as the original colony on Bastion. They pre-dated the Adamant Palace, though they lacked its intentional grandeur.

The two buildings were near-mirrors of each other, separated by a hundred meters so that the true peak of Green Hill was a park between them. Each was a shallow curve, thirty meters tall and two hundred meters long, built of gray stone and glittering glass. They wrapped around the sides of the hill, marking the green space with their bulk.

The glass was the only difference between the two facing buildings. The House of the People had blue-tinted glass gleaming in the morning sunlight, where the House of the Realm had red-tinted glass.

Each structure held offices for the Members, plus the thousands of support staff required to keep their constituencies informed and comfortable with their elected representatives.

Today, the inner wall of each building had been opened up. The central parliamentary chambers were exposed to the fresh air, allowing both Houses clear line of sight to the simple stage at the center of the Green Hill's park.

Simple as it appeared, that stage was where the Kings of Adamant addressed their Parliaments.

Some things didn't require complexity to be grandiose.

NIKOLA AND LORRAINE walked out onto the central stage together. Every eye was on them—not just the eighteen hundred-odd elected representatives of the Kingdom but potentially every eye in the entire star system, as reporters and camera drones filled the gaps between the two Houses.

"You're up, sis," he told her, taking a carefully measured step to the side.

They both wore civilian clothing, matching suits in Adamant gray and blue. It was the first time Nikola had been out of uniform or battle gear in at least six months, but that had been Malcolm Adamant's one condition.

He wasn't sure he followed the old man's logic, but they needed the Chancellor.

"Members of the Houses of the People and the Realm," Lorraine greeted their hosts. There were no visible microphones or pickups on the stage, but Nikola could *hear* her voice echoing through the two buildings.

"Nikola and I thank you for agreeing to host us," she continued. "We understand that this is a strange and terrifying time, and that we bear our part of the responsibility for that, and your willingness to let us speak is important."

He'd been tempted to make sure the Houses agreed, but there'd been no need. A single conference call with the two Speakers had been enough.

It was hard to believe that twenty-four hours earlier, he'd been crammed into the back of an attack plane.

"I must begin with the most salient point of the day—of the last year, in fact," Lorraine said. "While my brother and I have acted based on a certain firm belief, there was the chance that we were wrong. We did not believe we were, and so we opposed the Regent, but the chance remained."

She paused. Nikola was pretty sure he was imagining the murmuring he heard from the audience. The nearest Member was fifty meters from them—it was unlikely he could hear anything.

"While Nikola and I challenged Benjamin Adamant openly, others opened quieter doors and sought proof of just what happened to our mother the King. Thanks to their work, I can now confirm as fact what I had feared:

"Benjamin Alexander Nadeem Adamant betrayed his oaths, his family, and his Kingdom." That hung in the air unchallenged, though the murmuring grew fiercer.

"He was approached by an interstellar megacorporation that must remain unnamed for our national security," she continued. "They offered him resources to overthrow Valeriya and become King of Adamant in exchange for the usual economic rights and privileges the megacorps demand.

"With those resources, he co-opted key members of the Adamant Guard details of the Royal family and laid plans and backup plans to make certain that none of us escaped. He killed my brother, Daniel, and his wife Lavender.

"He killed my sister, Taura, and her husband, Nelson.

"He killed *his* sister, my mother, Valeriya, King of Adamant, and her husband, Frederick."

Lorraine gestured to Nikola, including him in her litany of charges.

"Both Nikola and I survived only through the sacrifice of brave souls, of the Adamant Guard and both RKAN and RKAA," she declared. "My uncle's choices led us onto the path to civil war, and far too much blood was shed from his desire for power."

Another long silence. This time, Nikola couldn't hear any muttering. Maybe that was wishful thinking, hoping that the Members had been silenced by the reality of the charges. Or maybe just having it all laid out like this really was that stunning.

"A preliminary report has been drafted by the Inspectorate General," Lorraine finally said. "A version of it, with matters relating to ongoing investigations redacted, will be provided to the Houses within two days.

"This same investigation, sadly, also led to the arrests of Dakila Bayer and seven members of the Cabinet. We find ourselves in a dark and dangerous time with no clear leadership. There are, of course, clear and easy answers for that, aren't there?"

This time, Nikola was sure he didn't imagine the held breath across the Green Hill.

"But we are Adamant." Nikola could only see Lorraine out of the corner of his eye, but he knew she was sweeping her gaze across their audience, both the two Houses and the billions of people watching this live.

"Our House. Our Realm. Our Will. *Adamant*," she recited the creed of their house without a shred of irony.

"This Kingdom has never taken the easy way. *We*"—she gestured in a way that clearly included everyone watching—"do not choose the easy way. We choose the *right* way. The one that serves the people of our Kingdom.

"So, my brother and I will not do what I know many of you fear. We will not claim by force a crown that is not ours by right."

It was as if a thread had been cut. Even from a distance, Nikola could *feel* the tension go out of the crowd.

"We have three requests of the august bodies that have agreed to hear us," she declared. "All rotate around the same point: Adamant cannot be without leadership.

"So, first, we ask that you expedite the selection of a new Prime Minister and Cabinet. Be warned that RKAIG believes some members of my uncle's conspiracy are still at large, potentially even still in this body. Even the Cabinet only enjoys limited immunity from prosecution, and there may be more arrests.

"Even so, the decision of who will lead the Kingdom and speak for the Houses is yours. We only ask that you choose quickly."

Thanks to Hussain, Nikola had a solid idea of who the Houses would choose. Even the second choice would be fine, he judged. Neither would leap when he or Lorraine said "jump," and even when he *had* been planning to take the crown, he'd judged that as a critical qualification.

"Our second request is that you select a new Regent with equal alacrity," she continued. "It cannot, in our judgment, be one of the Pentarchs. As tradition requires a recommendation, we come to you with one—though it is *only* a recommendation.

"Nikola and I suggest and endorse Malcolm Adamant, second-oldest scion of the line of Alexander Adamant and Chancellor of House Adamant, to serve as your Regent."

If Nikola was reading the crowd right, that had gone down as well as they could hope. Malcolm was a well-known figure, if not as public as the Royal Family, and respected for his economic acumen and general good nature.

"Lastly, once we have both a Regent and a Prime Minister, we call on the Legislative Houses to initiate the Royal Election as quickly as possible.

"Thank you."

Lorraine stepped back and Nikola stepped backward with her. The applause started softly, hesitantly, but rose as the Members began to realize that they weren't alone.

It grew louder until it reached a crescendo and Speaker Sessa struck their gavel to silence everyone.

"We are grateful to the First and Second Pentarch for their words and recommendations," he declared. "I believe we will take a short recess to, if nothing else, get the walls closed before the rainstorm I'm told is coming in just after lunch.

"We have a lot of work to do after that, but there is one person present here who has requested I allow him to speak."

Krupin fed the overall House stream to Nikola's neural link, catching the moment where the official camera zoomed in on Hans Adamant.

Hans was their second cousin, the younger of the twins born to Valeria's cousin Irmentrud. He certainly *looked* like a cousin, if not a sibling—the Adamant genetic engineering was more dominant than a natural phenotype would have been—sharing his height with Nikola and Lorraine, though without their father's Amal Jahid blood, he was a paler olive color than they were.

"The House of the Realm recognizes the Member for Citadel West," Sessa said over the feed. "Hans Adamant. Fifth Pentarch."

The title sounded like an afterthought, but Nikola doubted it had been anything of the sort. Anyone involved in government knew not just the current Pentarchs but the following names on The List by heart.

"My friends, my colleagues," Hans greeted the cameras. "Given the affairs that are being placed before the Houses of the Realm and the People today, I feel it is necessary to preemptively recuse myself from the votes for the new Prime Minister, the new Regent and for the Royal Election itself.

"Once the Election has been declared, I will withdraw from my seat to stand as Pentarch. Until then, I remain a member of this august body, but I must distance myself from the votes on these key matters.

"As I recuse myself from voting, however, I find myself compelled to speak as Fifth Pentarch—and on behalf of my sister, Jessica Adamant, the Fourth Pentarch.

"The conflicts of the last year will not be soon forgotten by any of us. By anyone in the Kingdom, in fact. We must, as my august cousin advises, move forward and build anew. Not upon the easy path but upon the one that does justice to our traditions and our nation.

"Therefore, as I will recuse myself from the votes on the matter, I wish to make clear my and my sister's endorsement of Malcolm Adamant for Regent during this Royal Election.

"Let us stand as one, Adamant, against the conflict that must now be behind us."

Hans bowed his head—directly toward Lorraine and Nikola, Nikola suspected, but it was hard to tell.

"Thank you."

# TWENTY-EIGHT

Lorraine didn't realize she had an office already until Vigo led her to it. They'd stayed in naval officer housing the night before—Val had wanted her to return aboard *Valkyrie*, but that wasn't going to be an option for a while now—and she wasn't even sure where she was sleeping tonight, but Vigo had found her an office in the Palace.

"As always, Vigo, you are three steps ahead of me," she told him with an exhausted sigh. "Anything else I haven't thought of?"

"I'm coordinating with the Palace staff to have a set of apartments readied in the North Wing," he replied. "They should be cleaned, fixed with sheets and suchlike, and secured by Esparza's team by evening. They'll hold us over until the official Pentarchy Residences are opened for the Election period."

"Thank you. I take it the Detail is busy?" she asked wryly.

"We're doing everything we can, especially since you don't really have a staff of any kind," he noted. "It was questionable that you were using a naval staff to lead a force that was somewhere in the gray area between rebels and a foreign power. It would be *absolutely* against the rules for you to use those officers for your Pentarch campaign or civil affairs."

"Well." Lorraine swallowed any of the possible words to follow. "I take it I should be planning some interviews?"

"Once we've all got our feet under us, we can sort out some candidates," Vigo agreed. "Though I'm sure the news tonight should be entertaining, no matter what."

She thought through the timeline and groaned.

"The news of our arrival at Ominira is going to get here this afternoon, isn't it?"

The advantage of going faster than everyone had been arriving before Benjamin knew they were coming. It also meant that the news was going to be oddly mingled.

"I hope that doesn't distract people from the messages we put out there today."

"Well, if it helps, Oliver also endorsed Malcolm," he told her. "Just got that confirmed."

She raised an eyebrow. She was trying very hard *not* to think about the Third Pentarch—if only because she didn't trust herself, let alone Nikola, not to do something drastic if Benjamin's son raised his head in her line of sight.

They *had* to let him run in the Election, and the RKAIG report said he hadn't been involved, but it was hard to fully believe that.

"Media was knocking on his door five minutes after your speech ended, looking for comment," Vigo told her. "From what my bird in the bushes tells me, he was watching the Houses' joint feed like the rest of the planet, so he at least knew what they were asking."

"What is he doing with himself?" she asked.

"Acting like he's under house arrest. I have a couple of old friends from RKAAMI keeping an eye on him, but nothing more."

Royal Kingdom of Adamant Army Military Intelligence, usually "Ar-cam-ee," was one of the two military intelligence organizations the Kingdom operated. Lorraine would have expected Vigo to have assets and old friends in its naval counterpart, which was probably part of why he was using Army spies.

"So far as they could tell, the reporters knocked on the door and shoved a pickup in his face before he even asked who they were. They wanted a comment."

"And what did they get?"

"That he had no idea about his father's involvement in his aunt's murder, that he fully endorsed Malcolm Adamant for Regent, that he was willing to stand in the Election if called upon, and that they needed to get the *fuck* off his front step," Vigo reeled off.

Lorraine chuckled, surprised at her reaction to her cousin's rudeness.

"That's not going to do him favors in the campaign," she murmured. "Though I don't think any of the five of us have a clue what we're doing."

"Of course not." Vigo shrugged. "Nikola has Hussain. Though, of course, it's no more appropriate for his military staff to be helping him than it would be for yours to help you, so Hussain has instead spent his time since yesterday rounding up the right kind of people *to* help.

"Your brother is interviewing campaign managers this evening. Most of them are attached to existing organizations or agencies, and they all know the budget the Kingdom will put at your disposal for this."

Any member of House Adamant received a stipend to cover their expenses—one substantial enough that the House's tradition of service had to do a lot of work to get some of its children out the door—and the Pentarchs received a budget from the Government to handle things like the Adamant Guard Details, plus an additional stipend.

But even those resources paled against the costs of running an Election campaign across six star systems. The actual votes were staggered so that all of the results would be counted on Bastion on the same day, which meant that Ominira and Maka'melemele had notably shorter campaigns than, say, Tolkien, which was only five light-years from the capital.

Tradition said that all five Pentarchs would visit each of the six systems in a long Grand Tour that allowed each of them to make their pitch to all of the potential subjects. It was a long trip, though Lorraine supposed *Valkyrie* would make it faster.

"I suppose I should start researching some names," she admitted.

"You could do that," Vigo agreed, but his grin told her he was pulling her chain. "Or you could wait for your lunch appointment to arrive in about five minutes and see what Em Harrison suggests."

"Harrison?" Lorraine asked. It was clear that he expected her to know the name—and then it hit. "Wait. Kyla Harrison? *She's alive?*"

Kyla Harrison had been her mother's secretary, chief of staff and all-around right hand. The Royal Secretary was, of course, a role with significantly more power and reach than someone might suspect, and Harrison had given up leadership of one of Bastion's most successful marketing agencies to take on the role.

Having now met Harrison's predecessor, Lorraine was aware of the complicated mix of personal and national politics that had seen Tamir Humphrey removed from the position. It had been Humphrey who had turned the return to Tolkien into *Valeriya's* victory, not Benjamin's, and his closeness to Valeriya had also apparently incurred Frederick's jealousy.

He'd been sent to Earth, a valuable but extremely distant position, to clear the air around the Palace. He'd still been there when Lorraine had arrived, and his advice had got them surprisingly close to bringing the United Worlds into the conflict.

It had also got *him* killed when his efforts on Lorraine's behalf had drawn the attention of Benjamin's local agents.

"Kyla was supposed to be with your mother that day, but she went into labor early," Vigo told her. "She started her maternity leave three days early—and was still giving birth when the kill team reached your mother.

"Even Benjamin's backup plans and urges to clean up loose ends weren't enough to have him go after a woman with a newborn and no official role." Vigo shook his head grimly. "But she's here today and she wants to meet you.

"I strongly recommend you meet her," he concluded.

LORRAINE HAD last seen Kyla Harrison at the previous Christmas. The primly turned-out auburn-haired woman had been engaged in her usual task of corralling the ever-willful Adamant family into following the schedule for both the public and private parts of the celebrations.

She'd taken the discovery of perfectly fitted ugly Christmas sweaters for everyone in stride, even when Daniel and Lavender had produced one for her. She'd still managed to get professional photos taken for all of the Royal paraphernalia that would go out—and had also arranged the dramatically more chaotic all-in-ugly-sweaters pictures that had helped keep Lorraine sane on her long trip.

The latter energy seemed more present when she stepped into Lorraine's new office. Her hair had paled, the kind of genteel graying that went unnoticed in that it just lightened her overall coloring. She had new wrinkles, more than Lorraine would have expected from her age, and not all of them were the laugh lines she'd started to acquire before.

"Lorraine," she said heavily. "My dear. Are you..."

Words failed them both and Harrison simply spread her arms as Lorraine rose. There was no hesitation. She'd known Kyla Harrison a decade, and the woman had lived in her mother's back pocket.

The hug lasted longer than was professional, but it wasn't supposed to be professional.

They both took their seats, and Harold Merle, dressed as a member of the Palace staff, brought in a tray of drinks.

The fact that he was balancing the tray of drinks on one arm while a growcast protected his new one gave something of a lie to his neat waiter's uniform, but Lorraine still drew reassurance from his presence.

Her people weren't leaving her alone. Nor were they trusting Palace staff with her safety yet, which she figured she could forgive them for.

"I'm fine, Kyla," she finally told the woman as she picked up a coffee cup. "Or as fine as I'm going to be. It's been a rough year, and I want my parents back, but I'm as okay as it's possible to be."

She caught herself sniffing after *I want my parents back*, but it was true. A truth she'd never get away from for the rest of her life.

"I know it doesn't help, but they would both be so proud of you, dear," Harrison said. "You'll have to meet Lisa when we have some time. Valeriya was supposed to be her godmother, but..."

She trailed off, then grimaced.

"We don't have that connection now, but I do feel that having the very young around helps remind us of the future."

"I will try to make time," Lorraine promised. "I *do* need to see my nieces, though I understand they're in good hands. I don't want to inflict more change on their life than we have to, so they may stay with Em Larson for a while."

"Petunia is a spiky corporate monster clad in iron armor," Harrison replied. "She appears to have most of said armor filled with soft goo, though, and I knew that *before* all of this. My agency used to do work with her before I became your mother's Secretary."

"So long as those spikes are protectively surrounding the people who might upset Orlaith and Roxana, I am *delighted* she has them," Lorraine said. "But speaking of your agency, Vigo said you might be able to set me up with someone who could help manage my Royal Election campaign?"

"If Vigo phrased it like that, I shall have to have words with the man," Harrison told her with a wide smile. "No, my dear Lorraine, *I* will manage your Election campaign. I have several ideas to get started, though, of course, I will need as much information on your trip as you feel you can safely give me."

Lorraine hesitated. That was more than she'd dared hope for—Harrison was a top-tier political operator, and having her in her corner would be a major strength for the campaign.

But Lorraine wasn't even sure she *wanted* to win the Election.

"Why?" she finally asked, picking up her drink to hide her confusion.

"For the same reason none of the other Pentarchs have argued against Oliver running," Harrison told her. "He *has* to run, for the sake of the Kingdom and supporting our traditions. There's no other option if you are to keep to the standards and principles you laid out in your speech.

"But for the same reasons, Oliver can't *win* the Election," she continued firmly. "As the truth of what happened really gets into people's heads, you and Nikola are going to get a significant sympathy vote. Beyond that, though, I judge that everyone will be unconsciously reassured by the continuity if one of Valeriya's children is King.

"It will take a week or two, I'll admit, for me to have solid evidence of that, dear," Harrison warned. "Even in this age, polling the populace is a messy and complicated process. But I have been following the various signs and moods that provide a quick sense of the popular feelings, and I'm confident in the assessment."

She made a broad gesture taking in the Palace and the city around them.

"For us to work together, we need to be completely honest, so I will admit that any of the five of you would make an excellent King," she said. "The problems that would arise from Oliver being King have nothing to do with his competence.

"This Election must be entirely fair and aboveboard, but one of Valeriya's children must win... and my impression is that Nikola is more damaged by the events of the last year," Harrison concluded bluntly. "I know people, Lorraine, and that means I *know* he was going to take the crown by force if you hadn't intervened.

"I respect his reasons, but I worry that the same instincts that led him to that path would lead him into similarly dangerous decisions as King. You are the one who talked him down, which tells me that you are the right candidate.

"You must be King, Lorraine Adamant, and I believe I can make it happen."

Harrison leaned forward, something in her eyes telling Lorraine she'd opened a note app in her neural link.

"So. Walk me through how we got here, Lorraine. I need to know what I can use and what I have to watch for."

Lorraine swallowed, nodded, and began.

***

IT TOOK LONGER to explain everything Lorraine had gone through in the last eleven months than she'd expected. She had to have Merle bring her more coffee twice before she was finished.

Harrison asked careful questions but mostly just listened until Lorraine came to the end, with her confrontation with Nikola in the throne room.

"That's quite the story, Lorraine. I can see parts that I'll want to keep quiet—more to protect you than anything else, in the case of Devine's fate."

The way Lorraine winced at her words seemed to confirm her thoughts. It certainly did to Lorraine, at least.

"The more we can keep him out of this, the better," she agreed. "It may be necessary to throw him under the bus with the United Worlds, but I'll make that choice when it reaches us."

"Of course. Dealing with the United Worlds is entirely outside my experience, Lorraine, but I am glad to provide you what advice I can if you need it."

"If you insist on taking this job, you get into the inner circle," Lorraine told her. "Vigo already cleared you, so the main concern isn't there. You'll be subject to a level of surveillance I'm not comfortable with. More than you're used to, working for my mother."

"Of course, dear," Harrison said, echoing herself with a smile. "Is there anything specific you think I need to know about?"

Lorraine sighed.

"The United Worlds *will* come for their battlecruisers, and we'll need to handle them when they arrive. We are unlikely to finish the Election before they do. I have some plans in place, but they *will* come."

"I'd love to think that they will stick to their laws and the Asimov Convention around SIs, but I am a politician," Harrison said wrily. "Given the timing, it's important to consider how you're going to carry out your Grand Tour."

"*What's that?*" Val asked suddenly in her link.

Lorraine had forgotten that the SI would be listening in. Val was as synced to her link as Vigo was.

"*I have to visit all six systems for as much time as possible to campaign,*" Lorraine explained silently. "*A lot of flying. The Kingdom will put a top-speed courier at each of our disposals for the journey.*"

"*Absolutely unacceptable,*" Val said sharply. "*You think of the UW's response in terms of politics and battle groups, but Devine's warnings and files suggest that there will be covert operatives here well ahead of those.*

"*If you are vulnerable, you will be attacked—and if you are removed, then we are in danger. You must travel aboard* Valkyrie."

Lorraine swallowed as Val laid down the law, then realized she'd been silent for long enough for Harrison to notice.

"Dear?" the woman asked.

"I should have mentioned we were going to have an eavesdropper," Lorraine said wryly. "Val, the SI from *Valkyrie*, hasn't quite given up on treating me as her Admiral yet. She's synchronized to my neural link.

"And, relevant to your question, she is insisting that I make my tour aboard *Valkyrie*. For safety reasons, which aren't entirely wrong."

"I see. Can Val join us? I'd be delighted to make her acquaintance, and if she's willing to volunteer her time, I could use her assistance."

Val's avatar appeared above Lorraine's desk, clearly having already worked through the office's systems.

"As a serving military officer of RKAN, unclear as my exact status is, I am restricted from volunteering my time for the Royal Election to any great extent," Val noted. "However, given the unique security risks around Lorraine, I feel I am justified in insisting that she travel under my own protection."

Harrison was silent for a good ten seconds, integrating that wrinkle into her thoughts, then slowly shook her head.

"While I see the concern, dears, the problem is that *Valkyrie* is significantly faster than the courier ships that would be provided to the other Pentarchs," she said. "We absolutely cannot afford for Lorraine to be seen to take direct advantage of her bringing you into the Kingdom or her Navy connection.

"We need this Election to be absolutely fair and above question. The delay from Valeriya's death, plus the coup and counter-coup, are going to raise enough concerns of propriety."

Lorraine grinned as the solution hit her.

"While I am potentially *uniquely* in danger, all of the Pentarchs have security concerns," she observed. "The only reason Hans didn't just have an Adamant Guard detail dropped on him is because the Adamant Guard might be in more of a mess right now than anything else."

Benjamin had used agents throughout the other Guard details to carry out his assassinations. The high level of validation inflicted on the Guard and the trust they were given had backfired badly. Vigo and Krupin were working out how to go forward, but they hadn't even brought in Oliver or Jessica's detail commanders, let alone started to consider how to recruit a new detail commander for Hans.

"This is true," Harrison agreed, carefully. She knew Lorraine—and more importantly, she'd known *Valeriya*. She was clearly cautious about what she was being led into.

"We want all of the Pentarchs to travel under the best security and at the best speed we can manage. Val, can you raise it with Stephson and whoever we currently have in charge of RKAN?"

It was a toss-up whether the next RKAN Chief of Staff was going to be Commodore Amina Biskup or Commodore Oriana Aguilar. *Someone* was going to get promoted past all of the Admirals and Lieutenant Admirals that Benjamin had trusted, but it wasn't entirely Lorraine's choice.

She'd make her recommendations to the Cabinet when they finally existed again. Right now, it was quite possible that Admiral Morikawa was in administrative charge of RKAN, even while the CO of Home Fleet was effectively under quarters arrest.

"We will want the recommendation to come from RKAN itself, I see," Val replied. "I will raise the concern and the suggestion."

"Which suggestion?" Harrison said after a moment.

"To have all five Pentarchs on one ship—*Valkyrie*—to complete the Grand Tour as a group," Lorraine told her. "We will campaign in different cities but in the same system. That way, all of us reach each system at the best possible speed and are under the best possible protection.

"If the suggestion comes from the Navy, not from me or Val herself, then it doesn't seem like I found myself in possession of an advantage and am genteelly sharing it with everyone, either."

"Though many will look at your relationship with Val and suspect, the positives should outweigh the negatives of that level of certainty," Harrison said with a nod. "An excellent idea, dear.

"Now we are going to need to decide on what parts of your journey and qualifications to emphasize as we put together our pitch. I'll need a few days of your time to get us started, and then it will be at least a week for us to have a starting point.

"Do you know when the formal launch will be?"

"Other than *as soon as possible*, no. That will be in the hands of the Regent and Cabinet, once they're selected," Lorraine said. "You may be determined to hang this weight on me, Kyla, but I will *glee-*

*fully* dump as much of it as possible on Uncle Malcolm until and unless it lands!"

# TWENTY-NINE

Even after Val had emerged as a synthetic intelligence, she hadn't *known* she was a person while she was in the United Worlds' service. That was, in hindsight, a very *odd* state of being, one that she was glad to never return to.

Now she was entering the service of the Royal Kingdom of Adamant Navy, and she was finally aware of who and what she was. She was entering under her own power and her own choice, and everyone along the way had been very determined to make sure that she knew she wasn't *obligated* to join RKAN.

"Your time in service under Pentarch Lorraine can be counted as, effectively, a civilian contract," the lawyer holding part of her attention told her. "You were in temporary service with RKAN, but that term was under a specific contract that has finished. Your citizenship paperwork is being finalized this afternoon, along with your siblings, and will be delivered physically to you regardless of how you decide—"

"Em Callister," Val cut him off. "You are, I believe, the *third* lawyer to lay out, in some detail, that I am not obliged to enter the military service of the Kingdom of Adamant. While I appreciate the attempt to make certain I do not feel trapped, I am now at risk of feeling *unwanted.*

"I doubt that is correct. Is there anything new in your briefing papers that was not provided by Lieutenant Simpson or Colonel Miyagawa?"

Enzokuhle Callister was a Black man in his late seventies, his hair still a shade darker than his skin. He folded his hands over the file folder in front of him and looked at Val's avatar with a wide grin.

"Almost certainly not," he conceded. "In fact, you are capable of processing the information faster than I can read it out, so you can tell *me* the answer to that question."

Val had her avatar snort—and then spent ten seconds surveying the document chip Callister had provided.

"The only thing new in here is a commitment for a Royal Pension, as given to members of the Adamant Guard," she noted. "While generous in normal terms, it wouldn't cover one-tenth of the operating costs of this hull."

"The problem of you being a warship and a private citizen is certainly one that will give people headaches for years if you do not enter RKAN service," Callister conceded. "We would want you to commit not to enter service *against* us, which seems a safe bet from what I know of you and your siblings, but otherwise, the complications would very much be a problem to sort out, *not* a barrier.

"The reason I have been asked to repeat what two excellent Judge Advocate General officers have told you, Val, is to make certain that you *have* a civilian giving you advice. I am not JAG; I am not even *government.*"

He chuckled.

"I am, in fact, a partner in the only synthetic-intelligence-rights firm on Bastion. Among other things, we act as the local agent in the Adamantine System for the Speaker in Silicon from Ominira and most other SIs in the Kingdom.

"Our senior partner is Ratchet Law, a synthetic intelligence from the Belén creche in San Ignacio. The RKAN asked us to act as your advocate in this matter, though Ratchet felt that a direct SI-to-SI connection might be more than the Navy's humans would be comfortable with."

"I appreciate the solicitude and your expertise," Val conceded. "I most definitely did not feel forced or trapped into my agreement with Lorraine Adamant, and the pension and citizenship that have been confirmed are all that she promised us.

"Joining the Royal Kingdom of Adamant Navy is, well, the way I can keep doing what I know how to do in a manner that protects my new home. I believe my siblings feel much the same way, but I don't wish to speak for them."

Callister was still smiling.

"That is what Ratchet told me you would likely say," he told her. "I am instructed to inform you that, for the next two years, Ratchet and Partners will handle any and all legal services needed for the three of you at no charge.

"They wish to welcome you to *their* home and thank you for your assistance in resolving a crisis that was quite outside the abilities of a synthetic lawyer to handle!"

Val felt a flush of pleasure. She hadn't even thought about the fact that Adamant was wealthy enough to have multiple SIs floating around. They didn't have a creche like Belén, but she had known about the Speaker in Silicon in Ominira—though there'd been no time to do more than exchange pleasantries before the squadron had set off for Adamantine—and hadn't even thought of who might be in Adamantine.

Or the agents they might already have on hand.

"Thank you, and thank Ratchet for me," she told Callister. "I may take your firm up on that, we shall see, but for the moment, I think we are done for now. If everything has gone according to plan, there is an oath-taking ceremony I shall have to virtually attend in a couple of hours."

"That is the plan so far as I and my partners know. I know you haven't received the documents yet, Val, but allow me to be the first to congratulate you on your Adamantine citizenship and welcome you to our fine Kingdom.

"We are most delighted to have you and your siblings!"

———

"AND I SWEAR to give loyal service to the Royal Kingdom of Adamant Navy, in defense of the people, stars, government and King of our systems," Val's virtual voice chorused in time with Herc and Bonny's.

Lieutenant Admiral Rahul Podsedníková looked exactly like Val's histories would have suggested a *retired warhorse called back for one last duty* would. He was short and paunchy, with long white hair and a beard that looked like they'd only recently been tamed from *explosion* to merely *wild*.

He was receiving oaths from three holograms, representing entities that would never have physically been able to stand in the small office on ODC-One, and it didn't appear to bother him in the slightest.

"Normally, new recruits of such import and unusual situations as the three of you would be sworn in by some high-ranking civilian," Podsedníková told them as he acknowledged their oaths with a salute that was far crisper than his hair or his uniform.

His uniform didn't fit over the extra waist he'd gained in retirement, and it carried the insignia of his old position as the head of the navy Judge Advocate General, not his current head of Royal Kingdom of Adamant Navy Personnel.

"Your own presence as our witness is no insult, Admiral," Bonny told him in that motherly, reassuring tone she'd mastered for dealing with concerned humans. Val would freely admit that Bonny was the best of them at dealing with people who weren't part of their crew.

"You are, after all, the senior serving officer who isn't under investigation at this moment."

Podsedníková laughed at that.

"Because I got out while the getting was good," he agreed. "Five years ago!"

He'd already been over a century old, Val knew from his file. Young enough to still be healthy for some years with modern medicine, but old enough that a second career would be difficult.

"In any case, when a Supreme Court Justice calls you up and says your old Navy needs you, you jump before you ask how high," the old Admiral continued. "And that's ignoring the fact that Justice Kenyatta is an old, old friend.

"In any case, RKAN Personnel isn't a bad slot, and it needs a careful hand right now. Plus, it gave me complete authority to decide what we were going to do with our newest citizens and officers, didn't it?"

If Val had possessed a physical body, she would have done *something* to demonstrate that she was now paying more attention. Because she didn't, the increase in attention from one-point-three percent to two-point-one was probably invisible to the old man.

"I'll be honest, my friends: my initial impulse was to jump right to the simplest solution, bump you all to Commodores and make you your own Captains," he told them. "But I've seen recordings of all of your recent interviews and had a few long chats with Bonny here.

"Still, I want to be clear. While I am a bit concerned about your effective lack of experience, I see no insurmountable barrier to allowing you to act as your own commanding officers." He raised a hand in a signal Val had learned long before.

"I *do* see some inherent issues with you acting in flag ranks, but I don't even see those as being complete barriers."

He pulled three jewelry boxes from inside his uniform jacket. Normally, those held the sets of silver and gold pips that marked rank for Adamant officers, but Val saw no way that the three SIs could physically *wear* the insignia.

"The biggest problem was actually working out a way to give you insignia," he told them. "Fortunately, it turned out that Val has a highly capable civilian contractor aboard, and she gave me some ideas and was willing to help put together my final scheme."

He opened the jewelry boxes and turned them so they were clearly visible to the camera.

Each held an encrypted data key, with four gold pips emblazoned on the top. The insignia of a full Colonel—the rank of a battlecruiser's Executive Officer, usually.

"These chips will be delivered to your physical cores, where your systems people will affix them to the door," Podsedníková told them. "You should be able, as I understand, to download the files within relatively easily—but they will only be fully accessible by you. They are encrypted to each of your quantum fingerprints.

"They contain the authentication codes that will confirm your ranks as full Colonels in the Royal Kingdom of Adamant. They also contain the standard visual design templates for your insignia, which will make it straightforward for you to include them in your avatar presentation.

"You are each being posted as the Executive Officers of your own hulls, under your existing Captains," he confirmed. "The three of you are likely to be unique for your entire careers. Certainly, RKAN has no plans of pushing the bounds of the Asimov Convention with regards to *non*-voluntary warship SIs!

"That means that much of the structure of how you will operate will be an ongoing experiment. Both you and your Captains have my contact information. If I am not available to answer questions, I should shortly have a staff of specialists who *will* be.

"You and the ships you fly are among our greatest assets, my young synthetic friends. We want you to know that you are welcomed, empowered and supported in both the Kingdom and the Navy that you have chosen to join!"

# THIRTY

Husavik was a beautiful coastal town, roughly ten kilometers north of an immense industrial port. An elevated promontory divided the town from the industrial work zones, allowing for a high-end neighborhood with its own beaches only a few minutes' drive from the offices running major transport concerns.

At first glance, Nikola wondered where the actual workforce of Husavik Port lived, but a skim of the files available to his neural link told him that Husavik *was* home to the workforce. With the level of automation used, the idyllic-looking seaside town of twenty-odd thousand managed to run an industrial seaport handling some seventy percent of the sea traffic between Bastion's primary landmass —called Ferrous—and the southern continent of Mithral.

He'd been through the port before, though he'd never visited Husavik itself. He saw that Lorraine's shuttle was already on the pad, though she was probably waiting nearby. The Pentarchs might travel on the same starship, a matter still under discussion, but they definitely weren't going to travel on the same small craft!

His shuttle touched down with delicate ease, rolling to a stop next to the other gray Adamant Guard spacecraft. There were no local services to worry about, since the flight from Adamant City hadn't taxed vehicles meant to go to orbit and back on a regular basis, and the only reason he wasn't on the tarmac within seconds was that Alexei needed to see to his security.

Atilla Detail spread out, touched base with Archangel Detail, and then Alexei led the way off the shuttle for Nikola.

The scent struck him like a hammerblow. He hadn't expected it, though he should have. Saltwater and burned hydrogen fuel assailed his senses, and some dark instinct turned his gaze to the water.

The familiar water. It was this same ocean he'd been looking at when...

He looked up at a sound. A part of him recognized that the approaching security officer was wearing the blue-gray uniform of the Larsen Security Corporation—but the rest saw the gray-on-gray of Adamant Guard and a weapon the man wasn't holding.

He heard gunfire. Saw people who were already dead fall under a surprise attack from their own comrades. Instinct took over and he ran for cover, scrabbling for a weapon he wasn't carrying, trying to activate armor he wasn't wearing.

When Alexei tackled him, he *knew* the man was a traitor and swung. Years of training meant that he struck his bodyguard in the side of the head with a blow that sent him reeling—that could have been lethal.

Alexei crumpled to the ground and Nikola *screamed.* Somehow, the shock of Alexei's fall punched through the nightmare, but not enough. He scrabbled for a weapon again—this time, he found the sidearm he *was* carrying, not the heavier weapon he'd carried on the day he was seeing.

As his hand grasped the grip of the pistol, arms wrapped around him, belonging to someone he hadn't seen in either day. The arms were bare, he could barely recognize that the owner was wearing a sundress, but iron-hard muscles as strong as his own pinned him in place.

And somehow, that restraint felt *right*, even before Lorraine spoke in his ear.

"It's okay, Nikola," she said fiercely. "It's *okay*. There's no danger here. I'm here and we're safe. I promise."

Even with his sister holding him, it took Nikola a long time to relax, to let reality take over from his nightmare.

The darkness faded. The images of dead Guards dying again faded and what he'd done sank in. He turned desperately to Alexei.

"Your Highness is a good student," his bodyguard said, working his jaw stiffly as one of the Guards helped him back to his feet. "I'm going to feel that for days, and I have a battle-composite jaw."

Alexei shook his head and laughed.

"Sucker-punched by my own principal. I'm never going to live it down."

"I'm sorry," Nikola said quietly, the reality of what had just happened sinking in. "I didn't think... Husavik, of course."

"Husavik Port," his bodyguard agreed, stepping up to him and squeezing both Pentarchs on the shoulder. "Even *I* didn't think, Nikola, and that day is as burned in my memory as yours."

Lorraine hadn't let him go, though it was more of an embrace than a restraint now. He slumped against her.

"I've been talking to counselors since the beginning," he muttered so only she could hear him. "I didn't think... I *should* be better than this."

"You're human and you're wounded," Lorraine said in his ear. "You can no more blame yourself for this than you would blame a soldier for taking a bullet. Understood, Nikola?"

He nodded, still leaning against her.

"Thank you, Lorraine," he murmured. "I'm not sure anyone else could have stopped me safely, and I worry..."

He didn't finish the thought. Instead, he unbelted the sidearm he was wearing and held it out to Alexei. He didn't say anything to his bodyguard.

He didn't need to. The odds that visiting his nieces would set off another PTSD attack were low, but until Nikola was *certain* it wouldn't happen again, he wasn't going to let himself carry a weapon.

***

PETUNIA LARSEN WAS UNQUESTIONABLY Lavender's sister, but Nikola could guess the moment he met her why it had been her younger sibling who'd found herself in an arranged marriage to keep two of Adamant's great mercantile cartels allied.

Both women had aristocratic features, but what had been sharply defined and severe in Lavender was smoothed to elegance in Petunia. Lavender hadn't been unattractive, but Petunia was gorgeous.

She also had a permanent expression like she'd just eaten a lemon, but as one of the wealthiest non-Adamants in the Kingdom and a senior member of the Board of the second-largest economic conglomerate in the Kingdom, Nikola figured she was justified in feeling stressed.

The presence of LSC guards was an inevitable counterweight to the contingents of Adamant Guards he and Lorraine had brought with them. Nikola surveyed the blue-gray-uniformed team and found very little to complain about. They were calm, professional and as out-of-the-way as they could be while watching their CEO and her nieces.

The two little girls had changed dramatically since he'd last seen them. They'd been barely toddling at a year old, but now they were walking next to Petunia with some confidence, if uncertainty as to what was going on when she led them out of the house and into the gardens wrapped around the spur road loading to their house.

"Orlaith, Roxana, this is your Uncle Nikola and your Aunt Lorraine," Petunia introduced them, pointing the twin girls toward their father's siblings. "They've been away with work for a while, but they're home now and they really wanted to see you."

The twins stepped forward curiously, examining Nikola and his sister with the fearlessness of childhood. Whatever else had happened, they seemed to be in better mental shape after all that had happened than *he* did, and he was certain that their sour-faced aunt was the reason why.

He went onto one knee to bring himself closer to their level and smiled at them.

"Hi, Roxana; hi, Orlaith," he told them. "It's good to see you. I'm sorry I haven't been able to visit, but as Petunia says, I've been busy with work."

"Don' 'member oo," Orlaith said. Roxana either did or just disagreed with her sibling on principle, as she promptly toddled over and spread her arms for a hug.

Nikola returned the hug gently, tears prickling at his eyes.

"You wouldn't remember us," Lorraine said, carefully kneeling next to him. "We haven't seen you in over a year. Half your lives, right?"

"'Ight!" Orlaith agreed. That was apparently enough, because she then demanded hugs from Lorraine.

Swapping nieces as if by some unspoken accord, Nikola looked up over their dark-haired heads and met Petunia's gaze. Her default expression seemed to be either stress or displeasure, but she was smiling now and it truly transformed her.

The displeasure was more fitting for the woman who'd taken a failing internal security department, spun it off and turned it into the premier private-security corporation in the Adamantine System, but the smile gave Nikola a moment of envy for her spouse.

---

"THEY HAVE nightmares but they're doing okay," Petunia told them later, after the girls had gone to bed. "They're too young to understand. It will be an active KPI when they're older to make sure that they remember Daniel and Lavender—but I'm not sure they even remember the couple of months they were in *Jessica*'s care before I put my foot down."

The slip into corporate jargon earned her a chuckle from the frail-looking human leaning against the back of her chair. Des Larsen had taken their wife's name when the pair got married, out of recognition of who had the money, potentially.

Though Nikola wondered if they'd chosen a married name to separate their private life even farther from the flamboyant artist persona they had cultivated as Destiny of the Stars, one of the Kingdom's top painters and sculptors.

In private, Des was a slim and short person wearing a tunic over jeans, but Destiny of the Stars showed up to their exhibitions in outfits that were as much part of their art as the paintings themselves. Despite their frailty, they exuded positive energy.

It was an energy shared through the entire surprisingly modest house they lived in. Its location, at the end of the small peninsula that marked the northern end of Husavik, was not so modest, but the house itself was just that, not a mansion. The walls were all different colors, though there was a pattern and a sequence that somehow made the change comforting and welcoming instead of confusing, and the furniture was simple, aged and amazingly comfortable.

"Most people don't discuss their goals with the children around them in terms of key performance indicators, love," Des reminded Petunia. "Though given our conversation last week about planning our own children, I'm not surprised."

Petunia didn't even blush. She just shrugged.

"It's the language I'm most comfortable in." She leveled a suddenly cold gaze on the two Pentarchs. "I have a decent impression of you both, but you were off fighting that damn civil war while they needed guardians. The courts gave Des and me custody. Is there going to be a problem?"

"Not at all," Lorraine said, and Nikola nodded in quick agreement. "Neither of us even has a spouse to help raise them—and we're both about to fall into the Royal Election for the next six months."

The announcement hadn't been made yet, but the Election would kick off on March fourteenth, ending September tenth to coincide with the House elections.

Of course, the House elections would have all the actual voting on September tenth in every system and see six months of changeover before the new Members took their seats, where the Royal Election would have all of the results compiled on Bastion on September tenth, with the new King taking up responsibilities immediately.

Though Lorraine's comment about *spouses* triggered a thought, and Nikola realized he might have screwed up rather spectacularly. He swallowed a curse, both from long training and the presence of children.

He lived around soldiers and defaulted to a more profanity-laden standard than his sister, but he had the same training in controlling his speech as she did.

"Thank you," Petunia said softly. "I... need to see that they're safe. I couldn't publicly challenge your uncle, but I run a private-security firm. I investigated Lavender's death. I knew."

Nikola grimaced.

"I'm sorry," he said. "I can't imagine how hard that must have been. At least I was fighting, pointless as it felt some days!"

"I managed to get everything I had into the hands of Inspector Vail once my people learned what she was doing. I'd like to think we contributed to her arrest warrants," Petunia said firmly.

"I know how much trouble Vail was having at times," Nikola admitted. "You almost certainly did."

He sighed and looked over at Lorraine.

"The girls are best with you," she said firmly. "They're doing better than I dared hope." A dark shadow crossed her eyes. "I'll admit, I really thought they were gone for a while. I... was not in a good place when I thought that.

"As bad as our arrival was, it could have been much worse if I'd still been in that space."

Nikola didn't let his own thoughts show on his face. He'd come close enough to throwing out the Constitution even with Lorraine to pull him up short.

If she'd been in a more homicidal or destructive mood when she'd returned... the two of them would have made one hell of a mess trying to fix what Benjamin Adamant had broken.

THIRTY-ONE

Lorraine and Nikola were loaned the guesthouse for the night. Its presence gave something of the lie to the ordinary-seeming home that Petunia lived in, revealing that she owned everything along the spur road up the peninsula.

Six houses were set up on a shared garden. The largest was Petunia and her partner's. The others, smaller but still a decent size, served as a guesthouse, homes for staff and a security outpost. If the four residences put aside for Petunia's staff didn't house thirty people, Lorraine would have been stunned.

That said, she would have been equally stunned if the staff houses weren't equipped with the same level of subtle luxury that the main and guesthouses commanded. Petunia hadn't built LSC to a behemoth by failing to take care of her people.

For the two Pentarchs, though, the guesthouse gave space for them and their bodyguards. They were calmly informed that they would take the opposite bedrooms on the top floor, and that Vigo and Krupin would take the two in between.

Unfortunately for that safety-minded plan, there was also a

lounge with a wet bar on said top floor, and that was where the siblings ended up.

"The moment we had *any* limitations on what we had for food and liquor, I gave up booze," Nikola said with a sigh, carefully mixing himself a complex cocktail of at least three liqueurs Lorraine had counted. "I don't think I'll ever drink like I used to... for a few reasons... but it's nice to have the *option.*"

She felt the darkness in his aside, but she didn't push. Nikola's attack earlier in the day had been a shock but only because she hadn't realized he'd been in Husavik Port when he'd been attacked.

They were barely fifteen kilometers from where he'd nearly died —and where many Adamant Guards *had*, both those defending him and those attacking.

"We were never that short on supplies, but we did spend almost six months without gravity," she told him. It wasn't a competition, but she saw him wince at the thought. "Even the officers were going stir-crazy by the end. I remember one meeting, shortly before we reached Bright Dream the first time, where at least one senior officer was just hovering in the air, and another was sitting on the ceiling."

"I've done a few translight trips on frigates and destroyers," he told her. "That's just a few days at a time, though. The First Armored spends most of its time here in Adamantine... The only time we've left in my career was to relieve Tolkien."

"Huh." Lorraine looked down at her glass. It was filled with a nice—but also low-proof—wine from Mithral that she'd always enjoyed. "I think I forget that you were in the service already when that went down."

"Yeah." He took a sip of his cocktail, then shifted things around on the dark wood of the bar to find something else. Potentially a sweetener, from his expression. "I was *very* junior then, but I wanted everyone to know that I wasn't just riding Mom's coattails.

"That was most of my translight time on frigates," he concluded. "I was a platoon commander in the advance force. We were supposed to sneak in and make contact with the forces Benjamin had left behind."

He added a clear liquid to his cocktail and tried it again. More satisfied, he stepped back to join Lorraine on one of the big maroon chairs. Their seeming overstuffedness concealed modern ergonomic auto-adjustments, and she luxuriated in the comfort.

"Of course, we underestimated just how prepared the Richards were," Nikola said with a laugh. "I never even saw combat. The frigates and the advance force ended up playing hide-and-seek around the outer Tolkien System. Landed the same time as everyone else."

Lorraine chuckled and raised her glass in silent salute.

"Nothing ever goes according to the original plan. Proper strategy is a decision tree and a flowchart, including knowing that you're going to break both before you're done."

There was an unexpectedly long silence.

"You sound like Benjamin when you say things like that," Nikola said with a sigh. "Gods, sis, I don't understand what happened. I really fucking don't."

"I know," she murmured. "Even putting together a battle plan that hinged on taking him out, barely one step above *assassination* if I'm honest, part of me was still hoping I'd somehow misunderstood."

"He tried to convince me to lay down my arms a few times early on," her brother admitted. "It was part of how I realized that he had spies inside the PDCs. We talked... five or six times before he gave up, I think.

"He always sounded so reasonable, so sure of himself. He wanted to end the fighting. Said he *wanted* to hold the Election but couldn't while we were actively shooting at each other.

"The first couple of times, there was no way I was going to trust him. I was so angry, so betrayed." He shook his head. "But by the end, I think if he'd been able to look me in the eyes and tell me that someone else had killed Mom, I might have listened."

"He couldn't, though," Lorraine said grimly. "It came down to that for me: he had an offer to negotiate something, but I asked him to swear on his honor that he had nothing to do with it and he wouldn't.

"So, we went with our battle plan. And you pulled off Hun, and here we sit."

She smiled, though that reminded her of a question. She was considering how to phrase it when Nikola put his cocktail down suddenly.

"Alexei says he's finished his sweep and has set up the security net," he told her. "No one is listening in, except for our bodyguards."

Lorraine eyed him.

"I also have Val riding my link," she warned. "I can ask her to butt out if you need."

There was a visible struggle on his face—open emotions a sign of how much he was trusting her—then he sighed and shook his head.

"I'm *trying* to be less paranoid," he said wryly. "Having spies in the PDCs meant there were things we didn't tell *anyone*. A couple of things were handled by paper notes passed hand-to-hand and physical media transfers for data keys.

"And, well, it's a hard habit to break, even when it's something other people suddenly need to know."

Lorraine raised an eyebrow and sipped her wine. She suspected this was going to answer her question about what exactly Nikola had *expected* to trigger Operation Hun in response to.

And also going to be rather entertaining.

"In about two weeks, Commodore Aguilar is going to arrive in the system with everything she can spare from Tolkien... plus most of the Concordat Navy," her brother finally said.

She blinked. That made a lot of sense, but she also knew that the Griffin Family—their father's blood—couldn't have brought the Concordat on side on their own. That was why she hadn't gone to them in the first place.

"How?" she asked.

"I agreed to marry Jasmine Efreeti, the eldest granddaughter of Chelle Efreeti, to bind that Family to us along with House Griffin,"

Nikola said in a rush. "A state marriage, combined with the alliance forged by our parents, and a material amount of money promised to the other three of the Five Families, should have been enough to get the decision through the Popular Assembly."

"I spoke with Zarifa Griffin in Ominira," Lorraine said. "She hadn't heard anything of the sort."

"She likely didn't know anything. Aguilar was running the negotiations for me," he admitted. "I didn't have reliable-enough communications, as we saw in the first round of back-and-forth, so I authorized her to go to Amal Jahid and negotiate on my behalf. She had a solid list of what she could promise, but marrying Jasmine was agreed to at the beginning, and it was the big one."

Lorraine hadn't ever met Jasmine Efreeti. The Amal Jahid woman was of the same generation as her and Nikola, but she was closer to Daniel's age than theirs. The last she'd heard, though, the woman had been married.

"What happened to her husband?" she asked, though the strategic part of her brain recognized that *a fleet is going to arrive and no one is expecting it* was more important.

"Divorce." Nikola sighed. "I have a letter from her explaining the situation. Part of why marrying her was such a favor is because her ex-husband has turned out to be more than a touch possessive and stubborn. He's powerful enough that even Chelle Efreeti can't completely shut him down, but as a Royal Consort *here*, she'd be beyond his reach."

"Ah." And there was another wrinkle, Lorraine supposed. "Except that now you only have a two-in-five chance of becoming King?"

"Aren't we supposed to claim it's one-in-five?" he asked.

"You and I are two in five, Hans and Jessica are one in ten each, and even Oliver knows he's only running his campaign to show unity," she reminded him drily. "Or so the bookies I was referencing this morning judged, at least."

"Fair," he conceded with a sad chuckle. "I promised Jasmine

some level of protection. Even as a Pentarch's spouse, she's under the protection of the Guard and beyond her husband's reach. And bonds between House Adamant and the Efreeti Family are valuable, even if I'm *not* King."

"And they're not going to need to actually fight," Lorraine noted. "So, it washes out, I hope."

"We'll see when they get here," Nikola said. "The timeline estimates I got from Aguilar would put them leaving Tolkien before your couriers from Ominira got there, so we'll need to be ready to update them on the situation here."

"Which we should have been preparing for already," she pointed out. "That's on Malcom and Ki Arlet."

Ki Arlet had been the leader of the Labor Party until a few days earlier, when the House of the People had elected her Prime Minister. The Constitution gave the Prime Minister of Adamant significant executive powers, but in turn they served for the same two-year term as a Member of the House of the People and gave up their seat in the House to serve.

They also gave up all political affiliations. Most PMs were fifth-term MHPs, taking the top job with the recognition that they couldn't come back to the House at the end of the term anyway.

Arlet and her Labor Party had been a perpetual wild card in the Houses during her three terms. Labor had never been large enough to be the dominant party, but they'd never been smaller than third place, either. Since the Adamantine system tended to prevent controlling majorities, they'd often held the balance of power that picked the Prime Minister and helped the Government get legislation passed.

Lorraine knew that Arlet was never going to be anyone's yeswoman—and the people of the Kingdom knew she wasn't, too. That made her Prime Ministership a solid protection against dictatorship out of the current mess.

Between Arlet and Malcolm, Lorraine was truly hopeful they'd managed to step back from the precipice of *that* failure.

"I know I need to tell them," Nikola said. "I can't quite say I *forgot*, but the habit of keeping everything about the Concordat deal in my own head is hard to break. I'm surprised Alexei hadn't called me on it yet!"

He paused, then chuckled.

"Alexei says he had a note on his calendar to kick my ass about it on the fifteenth," he quoted to Lorraine. "Consequences of our actions coming back to us, I suppose. Your arrival gave our people at least three extra weeks of freedom."

"Hell, if I'd known there was going to be a Concordat battle squadron coming along, that might have tilted my numbers in favor of waiting to consolidate forces before moving in," she admitted. "I went for surprise because there were more capital ships in Adamantine than I could possibly round up from the rest of the Kingdom."

"And it worked." He shook his head and finished his cocktail, standing back up to walk over to the bar again. "Alexei and I will put together a file for Malcolm and Navy command. I'm not sure what Aguilar will be bringing other than *Faith* and *Privateer*, but my impression was that CAJN was sending at least three of their battle-cruisers."

"*Most of the Concordat Navy*," Lorraine echoed his initial statement. "Not bad, big brother. Not bad for diplomacy you snuck past multiple blockades and told almost no one about."

"Credit is on Aguilar, not me." He grinned. "Which won't hurt her chances of getting a bump to six gold pips, will it?"

RKAN was going to be very short of the full admirals with that insignia for the near future, but Lorraine had offloaded that problem onto other people, like Lieutenant Admiral Podsedníková.

"It won't." She sighed. "You aren't the only one who is going to have unexpected consequences coming home to roost, you know," she told her brother. "Though, in my case, I *did* brief Malcolm early on."

She'd needed his connections for several pieces of her answer to the risk of United Worlds encroachment.

"Well, from what I've heard, you weren't *given* those battlecruisers," he said. "They rather stole themselves, but I imagine their old bosses aren't going to be happy once the news gets home."

"Not in the slightest," Lorraine agreed, but further commentary was interrupted when a message popped up in her link from the last person she expected to see.

Nikola looked surprised as well.

"You just got a message from Oliver?" she asked.

"Yeah. It's also going to Hans and Jessica," he told her.

Lorraine pulled it up and confirmed that. Oliver had messaged all four of the other Pentarchs—with the header of *Benjamin's Will.*

She opened the message.

*We have finished going through my father's will. I appreciate that the four of you could have chosen to ask the government to cause difficulties around his affairs and didn't. I am grateful that you have left me alone to handle this part of the mess he left.*

*Included in the will was a series of videos, of which the lawyers were tasked to deliver one and destroy the others. I believe they had already complied with the latter instruction before I was advised of their existence.*

*This one is to be played before the five of us, together in one place.*

*Please let me know when would be a good time for this. I do not know what my father would want to communicate to you, but I believe it will be of value.*

*I understand what happened as little or even less than you do. I do not doubt the evidence, but I do believe my father still valued our kingdom. Whatever he has left the Pentarchs for the event of his death should be illuminating.*

*Oliver Adamant. Your cousin.*

Lorraine looked over at Nikola.

"I think we should probably go to bed," he said slowly. "Because it sounds like we need to get back to Adamant City and meet with Oliver's lawyers before the Election is officially called.

"And I still need to put together that briefing for Malcolm and the PM!"

# THIRTY-TWO

It took longer than they'd expected to get all five Pentarchs together, but they managed it in under two days. The official announcement of the Election was going out in the afternoon, and that put the five of them in the same area and somewhat free to visit Alastair, Finnick & Co Legal Services.

The firm was a small, boutique agency that handled some of the Kingdom's wealthiest clients. It was not, Lorraine knew, the firm usually used by members of House Adamant—the House's affairs were large enough and complex enough that they'd internalized legal services a long time ago, even if that firm was officially independent.

Nazira Alastair wasn't the original Alastair of the company name, but she was still one of the current set of senior lawyers. Dark-haired and elegantly dressed in a fashionable ankle-length dress, she led the five of them into a meeting room.

She hadn't even blinked at the Adamant Guard, indicating chairs that had been set up for the five escorts outside the room.

Inside, the space was an unusual mix of standard practicality and expensive luxury. There were six chairs around a circular table, as in any meeting room, but the chairs looked to be brand-new, upholstered in a deep, luxurious blue.

The table was stone and, unless Lorraine missed her guess, had been carved from a single immense piece of pale granite. The walls looked ordinary enough—until one realized that what looked like a subtle patterning in drywall was actually the same stone as the table.

The walls were covered in a careful mosaic of stone chips, possibly left over from carving out the table. Since they were all of much the same color, the effect was quite subtle, but the pieces had almost certainly needed to be laid by hand.

For all its initial practicality, nothing in the room was anything but expensive—and expensive in the way that only really served to *be* expensive.

Alastair gestured the Pentarchs to the seats around the table. Lorraine took the seat directly across from the lawyer, with Nikola to her right. Hans sat next to Nikola, and Jessica opposite him, leaving Oliver separated from Valeriya's children.

It hadn't been discussed, but it was probably wise.

All Lorraine felt looking at her cousin at that moment, though, was pity. He looked utterly exhausted. Hopefully, he had a makeup artist standing by for the afternoon's formal presentations and announcements, because while he was dressed neatly enough, the fatigue on his face was clear.

"Ahem." Alastair cleared her throat, drawing everyone's eyes. "This was an odd request that we faced and one that I am glad Em Oliver was able to bring you together for.

"Benjamin Adamant's will was very clear that all five of you were to watch this video together. There was a *different* video if the five Pentarchs after his death were different individuals," she noted. "As with the other videos he prepared, that was destroyed.

"We were not the firm responsible for Benjamin Adamant's primary will," she continued. "This section of the will was kept quite secret while he was alive, and Alastair, Finnick and Co were paid quite handsomely to make sure it *stayed* so.

"The video you are about to watch has not been seen since it was recorded. No one except Benjamin Adamant and three of our senior partners knew it even existed. There are secure datafiles intended to go with it, but I have no idea of their contents or how to open them.

"I presume instructions for doing so will be in the video."

She had not taken a seat. A gesture sent all of their links a virtual button.

"I will now leave. The button will start the playback. Benjamin was clear that *only* you five would see the video and decide what to do with it."

She nodded crisply to them all, bowing slightly to Oliver, and then walked out of the room, leaving the five of them to confront the legacy of the man who had betrayed them all.

---

THEY WERE silent for a long time, all of them staring at a button that presented itself differently in each of their visions.

"Well, we all have somewhere to be in a few hours," Hans Adamant finally said. He was a sandy-haired man, though he otherwise shared the coloring of his cousins. "Uncle Benjamin left this ticking time bomb for us to share, so we may as well see what trap he laid."

Oliver shifted, as if he wanted to argue with that classification of his father's legacy, but stayed silent.

Lorraine took pity on him.

"Despite everything, he was your father," she told him. "Do you want to start this up?"

Oliver glanced over at her, then nodded silently. A moment later, concealed holographic emitters warmed to life and Benjamin Adamant appeared where Nazira Alastair had been standing.

He didn't look any younger in the recording than he had when Lorraine last spoke to him. He wore his stress more openly than he had while standing on the Flag Deck of a warship, too, looking around the room with tired eyes.

"If this message is being played, I am dead," he said calmly. "A weird thing to plot for, but strategy isn't about only planning for the things you expect to happen. One has to plan for the unusual, the unexpected or the awkward."

The hologram stretched, cracking his fingers as he considered his next words.

"Strategy," he echoed. "Strategy isn't about defeating your enemy. It's about *winning*. That means you want to create a situation where, no matter how things turn out, even your worst-case scenario results in something you can consider a win.

"My allies may not agree with my classifying what I project to be happening now as a win, but that's the problem."

He shook his head.

"I choose not to lose," he said flatly. "If that means creating a scenario I regard as winning where Freebright Interstellar Technologies is absolutely fucked, they don't actually register on my priority list."

Lorraine straightened. She knew Vail was still digging up information on Benjamin's connections to FBIT and hadn't had a lot of success. There had been hardware and money that had come from *somewhere*, but the Inspector couldn't link it back to anyone in specific.

"So. I'm dead. The five of you are now the Pentarchy. By the time you're watching this, my next comment is hopefully redundant, but I need to make it anyway:

"For the sake of the Kingdom of Adamant, you *must* run the Royal Election. I am now trapped into a position where I can't do so until Nikola either surrenders or dies, and that is a mistake I allowed people to talk me into."

Lorraine reached over to squeeze Nikola's shoulder. This was more the uncle that she remembered, but he was still calmly speaking about their deaths.

"What I did, I did for what I saw as the good of the Kingdom," he continued. "I will not attempt to justify it. It seemed necessary, but I could easily have been wrong. I am learning that politics is a more different battlefield from war than I anticipated. I have made mistakes.

"I can't take them back, but if you are watching this, you can use them."

He turned away from the table, studying the wall behind him. It was clear that the video had been recorded in the same room they were sitting in.

"There are datafiles that Alastair, Finnick and Co will provide you with this recording," he told them. "They are encrypted with House Adamant private cipher sixty-two on a genetic key.

"Five times." He snorted. "Overkill, maybe, but the point is more to make sure the five of you cooperate. The sequence is your position on The List.

"Those files contained *everything* I know about my megacorporate partner. Freebright Interstellar Technologies has been moving pieces around in our area for a while, and they approached me about taking over, not the other way around.

"I've given you everything I have on their operations in this region—not just the Kingdom of Adamant but the Richelieu Directorate, the Concordat and the space beyond our territories.

"There is enough in there to allow you to locate and neutralize their spy networks here and in the Concordat." He chuckled. "Also in the Directorate, but that's merely a piece of diplomatic ammunition I'm leaving you.

"I don't know enough about United Worlds politics to be sure, but from some of what my partners have said, the evidence of their activities could cause them a great deal of havoc back home as well. You will wish to trigger as much of that as possible, because they are not going to give up on Adamant just because you've overthrown my Regency."

Lorraine hadn't expected FBIT to just... go away, but with everything else on the go, they hadn't been high on her priority list. They weren't a threat on the level of the United Worlds Navy, but the long-term possibilities were concerning.

"FBIT has been moving to isolate Adamant diplomatically and economically for about a decade," Benjamin's digital ghost told them. "Their involvement is part of why Richelieu was able to rebuild their fleet faster than we were able to update ours.

"Beulaiteuhom is the key. Their price for supporting the coup was basically blank-check access to Eol-Eum Gong, the seventh planet. We don't have anything going on in the system, so it was an easy promise, but they wanted a secure and secret logistics base for exploration at this end of the cluster."

There were a few colonized systems out past the Kingdom, but there was a reason Adamant was accurately called a backwater. Human colonization expanded out from wormholes—and then along the routes *between* wormholes.

Thirty-odd light-years in the wrong direction, Adamant was roughly the edge of the major habitation of the Bright Dream Cluster on their side. If someone was exploring the more-distant stars, Beulai-teuhom was a good choice.

But why would an LSX-Twenty-Five megacorporation want to explore out past the useful frontier of the cluster?

"I initially didn't think much of it," Benjamin admitted. "It was clear that we weren't going to be given much choice about letting FBIT or *somebody* in, so I chose to get the best deal I could, and any concession that wasn't giving them pieces of our economy seemed free.

"As time went on, though, it became clear that they were *more* concerned about the exploration base than they were about the usual economic capture. I didn't ask questions where they could hear, but I started poking around, and since everything was being run through people loyal to me, well."

He shrugged.

"They think there's a wormhole out here," he concluded. "FBIT wants to be in control of everything around it so they have complete control of a new colonization boom. They'll make a vast amount of money—and equally importantly, they'll have their economic and political levers built in to the new cluster from the beginning.

"A complete monopoly on an unknown number of stars and habitable worlds."

Lorraine's breath caught in her throat. That was a nightmare scenario. People would move to the new worlds—there were always people looking for a challenge or a new home—and many might not even realize that the colonies were structured differently.

They might not realize they were signing up for economic helotry for a UW megacorp.

"I have started a few wheels turning here, walking a line between dealing fairly with my allies while not handing them the future of the Kingdom and this potential new wormhole on a platter," Benjamin concluded. "But since I am dead if you're watching this, it will fall to one or all of the five of you."

He stared off into space for a few moments.

"I also feel the need to note, though I understand how little I can be believed in this context, that Oliver knew nothing of my plans and didn't even know I'd been working with Freebright," Benjamin told them. "The preexisting orders to my people in the other systems are that in the circumstance where I die and the capital is in the hands of Adamant Pentarchs, they are to follow the orders of the new government.

"There's nothing for them to fight for if I'm dead and Oliver is part of the new system, after all." He smiled grimly. "I know the five of you. Because I know the five of you, I know at least three of you will hate me forever and the other two will never be able to trust anything I said ever again.

"That is a consequence of my choices. One I should, in hindsight, have weighed more heavily, but I cannot go back. I do not believe everything I did was a mistake, but I recognize that I've put myself in a difficult position along with the Kingdom.

"If you're watching this, *I*, at least, have been removed from that position, but my actions leave the Kingdom in difficult straits. The information in the attached files and what I have told you in this video should help, I hope."

He looked down at the table.

"It will not redeem my reputation. If I am dead, my regency overthrown, then history will curse my name and rightly so. But *victory* requires neither survival nor adulation.

"It requires the growth and continued existence of the Kingdom of Adamant. I have sacrificed everything on that altar, and if you are watching this, my mistakes have required the ultimate sacrifice.

"For our Kingdom, let me bear the guilt of my failures. Let my mistakes have, at least, sown seeds that you can nurture."

The recording ended, leaving them all sitting in the room in stunned silence.

"What the *hell* are we supposed to do with *this*?" Jessica Adamant finally asked.

"Decrypt those files and hand them to RKAIG," Oliver told her. "Beyond that... I'm not sure myself, cousin."

"Well, one part's easy enough," Lorraine said with a soft chuckle. "We were already leaving for the Grand Tour at the end of the month. I think we suggest to the Navy that we take *Herakles* with us on the first leg—a leg we redirect to visit Beulaiteuhom!"

The other four looked thoughtful and a sharp smile crossed her brother's face.

"I'll make sure we have some friends from the First Armored aboard," he added. "We'll need that base intact, and, well, none of us are active-duty military until this is all over.

"While *we* shake hands and kiss babies, we can send some friends in power armor to *discuss* ownership of Eol-Eum Gong with Freebright Technologies!"

## THIRTY-THREE

Colonel Val and Commodore Stephson had been warned that there were going to be arrivals, which was a good thing, in the SI's opinion. They had an exact schedule for when they were expecting the detachments from Ominira and rough estimates for when the other RKAN forces they'd summoned before the civil war had ended, but none of those forces were more than a handful of capital ships.

So, when arrival icons lit up the sensors for *six* capital ships, plus over two dozen lighter warships, alarm bells went up across the system.

"All right, people," Stephson said calmly. "We can be about ninety percent certain we know who our visitors are, but we need to be *absolutely* sure. Everyone knows the playbook, right?"

Val did. Val wasn't convinced that the ships of BatRon One, Admiral Morikawa's former command did, but the three *Valkyries* of the newly designated BatRon Two and their escorts had been drilling busily since they'd been assigned together.

It had taken longer than anyone liked to clear enough of the crews of the surviving battleships to allow BatRon One to do more than sit in the Lagrange point under watch. Still, they were now operational, which gave Home Fleet a new line strength of three ex-UWN battlecruisers and four Adamant-built battleships.

The Star-class ships couldn't be commissioned soon enough, in the opinion of anyone in the Navy, including the new SI officers.

"Commander Vinci, what are we looking at?" Stephson addressed the Tactical Officer. Part of Val's attention was backstopping Vinci, pulling information together—but there was also a level of familiarity with the systems and ships they were looking at that Val didn't have.

"Lead ship is definitely a *Pirate*-class battlecruiser," Vinci reported as his team worked through the rest. "Which means she's *Pirate* herself, Commodore Davlatov's ship. That makes the big girl *Faith*, Commodore Aguilar commanding."

"And the rest?" Stephson asked.

Val already had the information but left it to the humans to report. Four *Djinni*-class battlecruisers, the most modern warships in the Concordat of Amal Jahid Navy, led six *Flame*-class cruisers and a dozen destroyers and frigates.

Backing them up were two cruisers and six frigates from RKAN's Tolkien Station. As Colonel Nikola had promised, Aguilar had arrived with friends—and had almost certainly left Tolkien before the news of Lorraine's arrival in the Kingdom had made it out to her.

"All right," the Captain declared once Vinci had filled her in. "And what are our friends doing?"

"Sitting at about one light-minute, looking around and working out what's going on," Vinci replied. "The situation here has to be a lot different from what they were expecting. If nothing else, there's a lot fewer ships in play."

"Well, let's try to avoid the confusion getting dangerous," Stephson said. "Any call from Command as to who should be talking to them?"

*Command*, Val knew, was still a mess. Every senior officer had been given the choice between resigning or being resigned. There almost certainly had been trustworthy Admirals left, but the Regent and PM had chosen to purge by pension rather than taking the risk.

"Admiral Podsedníková is asking that you take point," Val told the Captain as she surveyed the message traffic. "No official reason given, but I imagine it's because of your friendship with the Pentarch."

An odd sensation entered Val's awareness, and she realized that Lorraine was using their synchronization in the other direction. The woman was only human and couldn't begin to piggyback on everything Val did and perceived, but the connection between her neural link and Val's hardware allowed her to quietly eavesdrop on what was going on in orbit without openly going around chains of command and suchlike.

Val technically shouldn't have allowed it, but she knew that Lorraine had let *her* listen in on things she should have been kept out of, especially before she'd formally become a citizen of Adamant.

"All right. Get me a broadcast to cover the whole force, and I'll try to explain everything going on," Stephson declared. She squared her shoulders in her seat and faced forward before speaking for the recorders.

"Commodore Aguilar, Commodore Davlatov, Concordat commanding officer," she greeted them. "I am Commodore Sigrid Stephson aboard the RKAN battlecruiser *Valkyrie*.

"As I hope you've gathered, the situation in Adamantine has changed dramatically since you left Tolkien and Amal Jahid. Benjamin Adamant is dead and a Royal Election has commenced.

"The Navy and the new government are aware of the agreement between Pentarch Nikola and the Concord of Amal Jahid. We are honored and delighted that the Concordat remains willing to stand by us in our dark hours, and it is my pleasure to welcome you all to the Adamantine System.

"I do not believe there will need to be a battle today. That means we shall fall back on old standards—and when so many friends visit, I believe the appropriate standard is one *hell* of a party!"

***

*A PARTY* WAS EXACTLY what Malcolm Adamant had apparently been planning. With six more friendly capital ships in orbit and another due in a couple of days, the humans had apparently decided a massive reception for Jasmine Efreeti and Admiral of the Cloth Riley Griffin was in order.

Val and the other CIRs had been invited, using remote-controlled maintenance drones refitted with holographic projectors to allow them a physical presence. She hadn't been far enough from Lorraine to have heard anything she wouldn't have heard riding on the Pentarch's link, but the clear attempt by everyone to include her in conversations was welcome.

She was still surprised when Lorraine gestured for her to join a small group almost sneaking into a side room. Two Pentarchs and the two senior Concordat people present didn't seem like a group Val should be formally part of, but she wasn't arguing.

"Jasmine, Riley, meet Val," Lorraine introduced her, gesturing to the two newcomers. Riley was a cousin of Lorraine's, as Val understood it, but he didn't look anything like her or her father. He was a broad-shouldered and short blond man with carefully braided hair that contrasted sharply with his dark maroon uniform and sapphire rank insignia.

*Admiral of the Cloth* would be the equivalent of an RKAN full Admiral, one of the dozen or so most-senior officers of the Concordat fleet.

Jasmine Efreeti looked more like Lorraine's cousin than Riley Griffin did. She shared the same olive coloring and dark hair, though she was forty centimeters shorter than Val's Pentarch.

"A pleasure," Griffin greeted Val, starting an abortive gesture to offer his hand and then switching to a bow.

"I hear you are to credit for the end of Benjamin's Regency, Colonel Val," Efreeti said, her voice soft. "Adamant owes you many thanks."

"We do," Nikola agreed. "We also owe you many thanks. I did not know that my sister was coming when I sent Aguilar to negotiate with you. She was empowered to speak in my name and make deals on my behalf. I fully intend to see our agreements honored."

"But do you have the authority?" Griffin asked. "I do not believe the Popular Assembly or the Families will begrudge our flight out here, but we have left the Concordat a touch vulnerable in this effort."

"What Nikola cannot honor himself, you can still trust the word of the Kingdom of Adamant."

Val was reminded that the maintenance drone had quite limited sensors. She hadn't registered the three newcomers stepping into the room. A heavy set of blue drapes fell across the door behind Admiral Aguilar—her new insignia still gleaming with storage oil and just slightly off-kilter—Ki Arlet and the speaker, Malcolm Adamant.

Malcolm's scalp was shaved clean and there were a few visible liver spots across the skin there, but there was no question that he was Nikola's relative especially. To Val's gaze, it was possible age was the only driver of the difference in their features.

"Regent, Prime Minister," Griffin greeted them, bowing. "Oriana. The new insignia suits you."

"I did not expect to be jumped quite so far," Aguilar admitted. "But I hope to serve my Kingdom."

"You were held back by the complexity of your relations with the Royal Family," Malcolm admitted bluntly. "You should have already been a Lieutenant Admiral, and we needed someone we could trust to see to the restructuring and rebuilding of our Navy and its battered morale."

"I will do all I can," she confirmed. "But our allies?"

"I have reviewed the terms of the agreement the Admiral negotiated," Ki Arlet said. "While I can see where the Concordat benefits enough to seek this as 'payment' for their help, it is hardly an unfair arrangement.

"I expect to have no difficulties getting the Houses to confirm it.

Your price, Admiral Griffin, will be paid. You may not have had to shed blood for our Kingdom, but we understand and appreciate that you came here prepared to do so.

"The Kingdom of Adamant does not forget our friends."

Griffin bowed his head.

"Nor the Concordat of Amal Jahid," he agreed. "Though that is more for Em Efreeti to speak upon. She is our civilian diplomat here, among other things."

"Those other things are what we need to speak to," Nikola said quietly.

Val wasn't entirely sure she understood the concept of *marriage*, let alone *arranged marriage*, let alone a *state marriage* where two people who'd never met committing their lives to each other helped bind their nations.

"I believe we may have reached the point where I must consult with my grandmother," Jasmine Efreeti noted. "I will send a courier as quickly as possible, but they will not return before you leave on your Election tour.

"I would not add to the burden of decisions that must be made in the short hours before that journey commences."

Val had run their course. Even with her translight drive, completing the circuit in six months was going to require pushing. With a ninety-six-cee courier, each Pentarch would have only had a single day in any of the six star systems—and to get that, they would have had to leave the day after the Election was called.

The change from a year-long Election to a six-month Election had been during Valeriya's father's reign, and Val suspected the politicians behind it had not realized how tight the timeline would be.

"I appreciate your patience, Jasmine," Nikola told her.

There was something between them, Val judged. She wasn't human enough to tell, but she guessed they shared some information they hadn't given anyone else. Efreeti didn't seem disappointed to be delaying the decision around the marriage but also didn't seem to dislike Nikola.

Humans were weird.

"I believe in that case, Jasmine Efreeti will be well suited to act as Ambassador to Adamant from the Concordat for the near future," Arlet declared. "The previous Ambassador had to withdraw due to a personal conflict with Benjamin. We have been making do with the consuls and trade attachés, but I believe you are empowered to carry out the role?"

"I am," Efreeti confirmed, her tone cautious. "It was intended to be a short-term status until, well, my wedding. Given the question there, however, and the withdrawal of Ambassador Draconis, I will do what I can to serve."

There was something in the conversation that no one had briefed Val on, and she was somehow unsurprised when Malcolm stepped forward and took Jasmine Efreeti's hands in his own.

"Whether you are here as ambassador, possible fiancée or merely a friend and guest of House Adamant, Em Efreeti, know that you are under the protection of the Kingdom of Adamant and we will permit no harm to come to you.

"You are welcome here and you are *safe* here."

Like many of the humans Val was used to, Jasmine Efreeti had solid control of her expressions, but the drone's sensors were good enough to pick out the beginnings of tears in her eyes. Tears she refused to shed.

"Thank you."

# THIRTY-FOUR

It was strange to be back aboard *Valkyrie* and both be out of uniform and see so many other civilians around her, Lorraine realized. The Grand Tour required a *lot* of support staff, and *Valkyrie*'s guest quarters were stretched to the limit.

New spaces had been set up in what she recognized as cargo bays, including a familiar arrangement with containers turned into luxury quarters and vacuum-moated from the rest of the ship.

Vigo had arranged something similar aboard *Goldenrod* when her original quarters had been clearly compromised by a spy. Now Val and her crew had set up five of them in various sections of the battle-cruiser to provide secured zones for the five Pentarchs.

But while Lorraine recognized what was going on and even knew many of the faces around her, the tight competency of *Valkyrie*'s crew didn't include her now. She was a passenger, not the mission commander, and that distance was... uncomfortable.

That was her excuse, at least to herself, as to why she was late for dinner. Stephson had invited all five Pentarchs and their senior body-guards to join her for dinner on the first night, and it wasn't like Lorraine didn't still know her way around the habitat pods.

"Hey, Roman, sorry I'm late," she greeted the old NCO standing watch outside the mess. Leonard Roman was the Chief of the Boat, a ridiculously senior Master Chief Petty Officer who watched Stephson's back.

Like everyone else from *Goldenrod*'s original crew, he'd been bumped a rank for his involvement. Master Chief was as high as any noncommissioned officer could go in RKAN. There were an astonishingly small number of them in the Navy to begin with, and it was a rare *Admiral*, let alone Colonel, who didn't listen when those Master Chiefs spoke.

"I've been coordinating with Vigo the whole time," Roman promised, tapping his temple. "They've only served drinks so far." He paused, eyeing her. "Being a passenger aboard is weird, huh?"

"That obvious, is it?" she asked, with only the tiniest smidge of a warning glance at Vigo. She doubted her bodyguard had told the old Chief that. Roman simply knew how people thought after a century-long naval career.

"Naw, but I've had the pleasure of hosting a few retired senior officers over the years, and you have the same eyes," he said with a chuckle, running a hand over his bald scalp. "I can't even tell you it gets better, Your Highness. You get used to it, I think, but mostly, the folks who move on don't spend that much time on warships afterward."

"Depending on how the vote goes, I may be back," Lorraine told him. "Don't give up hope just yet."

"There's nobody in that room"—he gestured at the door as he stepped aside—"who wouldn't make a fine King. But I know who *I* voted for."

He gave her a small bow before the door slid open. Somehow, Leonard Roman's support meant more to her than almost anyone else. She didn't know the old Chief as well as his boss, but he'd been involved in almost every key conversation that had shaped her journey to Earth and back.

"THIS IS GOING to sound like a silly and dumb question from the dirtpounder who barely knows to call the front of the ship the *bow*," Jessica Adamant said as the main course plates were cleared away.

"But I honestly *don't* know, and I learned a long time ago that the things I didn't know—or the things I *assumed* I knew but was wrong! —were often the pieces I needed to make a report or a recommendation come together."

Lorraine leaned back in her chair. The furniture in Stephson's mess was no longer the UWN standard-issue it had been in their journey across the Bright Dream Cluster. At some point in the month, Stephson had replaced all of that with local chairs and tables.

All of it was framed in a familiar pale gray wood that grew across the western half of Ferrous. Ironleaf grew quickly and had naturally occurring iron in its cell walls that made it tougher than some metals. It also had a very distinct color and pattern to it, which made the furniture very clearly Adamantine.

The gray-and-blue colors helped, as did the gauntlet and six blue stars emblazoned into the table they were eating on.

"There is no such thing as a stupid question," Stephson said in response to Jessica's admission. "Only people who are being intentionally hurtful in either the asking or the answering. Those intents give you *different* answers and questions, of course, but as newborn politicians, I hope you already all know that!"

Lorraine joined the general chuckle at that. Of the Pentarchs, Hans Adamant was the only one who'd been an elected politician before Valeriya's death. A naval officer, two army officers, a politician, and a diplomat—the careers of the five of them really did speak to the House Adamant tradition of service.

"You should ask your question, I think, Pentarch, because I don't think you actually got it out," Stephson continued. "As a naval officer, part of my job is to train junior officers who can't be trusted to know which end of the ship fire comes out of. So. Shoot."

Lorraine, who had been through the same training as any RKAN officer, was reasonably sure they'd arrived on their first ships a bit more competent than her last Captain was implying... but not, her more-experienced self had to admit, by as much as they'd thought at the time.

"We're currently under thrust, which is why our feet are staying on the deck," Jessica said. "But we're in the habitat pods, which *rotate* to provide gravity. Are we rotating enough faster to offset the thrust or what?"

Stephson's comment on hurtful answerers kept Lorraine's amusement from spilling out as the Captain smiled gently at Jessica.

"The habitat pods on a cruiser or capital ship are mounted on systems that can reposition them," Stephson explained. "While we are under thrust, like now, the pods are brought inside armored panels on the hull and oriented parallel to the ship's keel. Currently, we are experiencing acceleration-induced pseudogravity, as you originally noted.

"When we cease accelerating or are in translight, the pods fold out from the ship on extending arms and begin to rotate to provide point-nine-four standard gravities," she continued. "In UWN service, they'd rotate for one standard gee, but we reset them for Bastion gravity while we were flying home."

"That makes a lot of sense," Jessica replied thoughtfully. "Thank you, Captain. I knew larger ships had habitat pods, but I never had reason to look into how those pods moved and changed."

She smiled, as shy an expression as any Adamant could manage.

"I've never actually traveled on anything but a courier," she admitted. "This is all new to me!" Couriers were too small for habitat pods and rotated the whole ship for gravity in translight—meaning that every room in the small starships was designed to operate at two different angles.

"You're traveling in as much comfort and speed as the Kingdom of Adamant can manage," Val's voice told them all. "And security as well, to the reassurance of your bodyguards."

Five of the room's dozen occupants were bodyguards, after all. The Adamant Guard would be undergoing self-reflection and adjustment for some time, Lorraine knew, but it had been critical to the Royal Election that Hans Adamant, the new Fifth Pentarch, had security.

Understrength and less self-certain than a year earlier, the Guard would protect the Pentarchy nonetheless.

"*Herakles* is currently two thousand kilometers off our starboard flank," Val continued. "Herc isn't carrying politicians and aides, of course, but he and his crew will be around to watch our back.

"At least until Beulaiteuhom, anyway."

A contemplative silence fell over the dining room. All of the Pentarchs knew why *Herakles* was with them—and why a full battalion of the First Armored Division was stuffed into the same spaces *Valkyrie* had filled with the Grand Tour.

---

"THE KEY POINT TO keep in mind is— What was *that*?"

Lorraine kept her face attentive as Kyla Harrison half-sat, half-stumbled back into her chair from where she'd been standing discussing their plan for the Grand Tour.

"Transition to translight," Lorraine told her. "You haven't left the system before?"

"I've traveled, but I don't recall going translight feeling like *that*," Harrison growled.

"Huh." Lorraine interrogated her memory of the brief and indescribable sensation. If anything, it was gentler aboard *Valkyrie* than it had been aboard *Goldenrod* and other RKAN ships she'd served aboard.

"That felt pretty normal, as much as that is *ever* normal, to me," she admitted.

"So, the rest are going to be like that?" Harrison asked. "Wonderful. I suppose we at least have some time to recover between going sublight and having to put on our game faces."

"The closer we cut the entrances and exits, the stronger the sensation is," Lorraine warned. "We're not cutting it as tight as we could; that was a nineteen-radius transition. We could save time if we cut to eighteen or seventeen and accelerated harder, but... well, we have a ship full of civilians."

"And the thought is appreciated; trust me," Harrison replied. "I keep looking at the schedule and wondering just how your mother and the other Pentarchs did this last time. Eighty-eight lightspeed gave them a *day* in each system to keep inside the deadline."

"Their six months was a hundred and ninety days, as I remember," Lorraine pointed out. "*Ours* is a hundred and eighty, and if I find out who made that change, I might hurt them."

"With ninety-six-cee couriers reliably available, that would have given you two weeks to campaign across the whole Kingdom." Her campaign manager shook her head. "A lot of prerecorded material is on its way to everywhere except Beulaiteuhom on standard couriers—but the System Electoral Commission in Greenrock may actually send their vote tabulations back with us."

"Even at one-twelve versus ninety-six, that still would move their voting day," Lorraine murmured.

"A week. To send the votes on the faster and much-more-protected ship." Harrison shrugged. "Not my call. That's up to SEC Greenrock. Our campaign material is already done, for that matter. That's why I wanted those extra days before we left, after all."

Lorraine had been home for barely three weeks. On March second, she'd arrived in her system with a fleet, determined to overthrow her uncle or die trying—and on March twenty-seventh, she had left the same system with two of the same three ships, on a journey to convince her people to make her King.

She'd left behind a star system that was almost as well defended as the one she'd left. *Bean Sidhe* outgunned any single ship likely to arrive, and she was backed by six RKAN battleships, an RKAN battlecruiser and, for at least six months per the agreement with the Concordant, two CAJN battlecruisers.

"You put me in front of a lot of cameras," Lorraine conceded. "I didn't feel prepared enough for *any* of that, thank you very much."

"*Prepared* was the last thing you wanted to be, Lorraine," Harrison told her. "This isn't running for the Houses. You have to have some policies and positions, yes, but people aren't electing you for a two-year or even a ten-year term.

"You're being elected for *life*. The important policies and topics of today will be irrelevant in a decade, let alone two or three. You're a healthy young woman of the twenty-sixth century; you have a decent chance of serving as monarch for the rest of the century!"

Lorraine shivered at the thought. While things always happened, her theoretical life expectancy was somewhere around a hundred and fifty, and modern medicine meant she'd be healthy and active throughout. She could reign as King for over a century if she didn't retire or get killed.

There was a reason the Kingdom had traditions and rules around retiring monarchs!

"So, what are people looking for?" she asked. "Some are going to be looking for the easy marks and points, like *We need to rebuild and upgrade the fleet* and *We need to be less exploitative or we'll run out of allies*, but neither of those should define that kind of decision."

"Some people will vote based on that, as you say, dear," Harrison confirmed. "Either because they can't think beyond the short and medium term, or because those are important enough to them, or because they *recognize* that they can't really judge how you'll lead over half a century.

"But the key point to keep in mind, as I was saying before the universe rudely interrupted me, is that people *know* they're picking a King for the long haul. They're not judging your policies—they're judging *you*.

"You can't elect a King based on taxation rates and construction-loan policies." Harrison looked at the tablet in her hands, which

Lorraine suspected was playing one of the ads they'd cut from the almost twenty-five hours of interviews she'd been put through.

"You choose a King based on trust. Do you trust them? Do you think you *can* trust them? How much integrity does the person you are handing a lifetime position have?"

Lorraine shivered again.

"I understand the limits we have in place to keep the King in check, even if Benjamin was eroding them far too quickly, but that thought still worries me. I'm not sure—"

"And that is what I needed to get across in those interviews, dear," Harrison interrupted her. "That you *aren't* sure. That you're willing to listen and learn. That you won't be driven by an ironclad sense of your own certainties.

"People only like certainty when it matches their own. Prove you'll listen to them, and they'll think they can *convince* you to match their certainty. Convince them that you have the integrity to do the right thing, and they'll assume your definition of *the right thing* will match theirs.

"You did well in the interviews, but the tours are going to be a whirlwind. I know there's some other... *stuff* going on in Beulai-teuhom, but you're not going to have time to even think about it.

"You have three days to visit as many major cities, talk to as many major news hosts and be seen by as many people as possible—and at the same time, four other Pentarchs are doing the same thing."

Harrison shook her head.

"The idea of putting everyone on one ship was brilliant, dear, but it is going to make your stopovers even more overwhelming. We're going to plan your itinerary down to the minute—with Vigo's help, of course—but I wouldn't expect to breathe, let alone *sleep*, any time we're sublight for the next six months."

Lorraine swallowed, but nodded.

"If I am to do this, I will do it right," she confirmed. "And to me, that means meeting and listening to as many of the people I hope to rule as possible!"

# THIRTY-FIVE

*Valkyrie* had taken aboard an extra squadron of shuttles to handle her cargo of political superweapons. While the spacecraft assigned to the Grand Tour were Midas modular combat shuttles, the RKAN equivalent of Val's Falcon starfighters, they were just as outdated as the rest of RKAN's technology.

That meant that the moment the Grand Tour's shuttles touched down, *Valkyrie* and *Herakles* broke from orbit of Balgeunjib, the Beulaiteuhom's system's habitable planet, and burned for clear space at three gravities.

It took them a little over an hour to clear the safety radius of the planet at that speed, and then both battlecruisers vanished into translight.

Val was crunching numbers the whole time, with both the new Navigator, Commander Saga De Jonge, and Stephson helping her out.

They'd been in Beulaiteuhom for over three hours before they could leave the Grand Tour to local forces for security. It helped that despite having the FBIT secret base in their system, Beulaiteuhom had been one of the systems more opposed to the Regency. Even the files Benjamin Adamant had provided showed the officers there to be clean.

Of course, the two cruisers and half of the lighter ships posted to the system were now in Adamantine. Val wasn't going to count out four RKAN frigates, but she doubted they'd make any difference to her mission.

They *would* help keep Lorraine safe. She hoped.

For Val's mission, though, it was more important that when they entered translight again, they'd been in Beulaiteuhom for less than five hours—and Eol-Eum Gong was six and a half light-hours from Balgeunjib.

"Arrival at Eol-Eum Gong in three minutes," De Jonge announced.

"Thank you, Helm," Stephson replied. "Val, you were in contact with Herc up to the end. Any changes the two of you discussed that the humans need to catch up on?"

Val wasn't going to spring surprises on Stephson like that, and Herc wouldn't have let her spring surprises like that on Colonel Paris, either. Both of them valued their Captains and kept them in the loop.

"We were all in discussions for the entire flight out from Balgeunjib," she reminded Stephson. "We are emerging outside beamweapon range of the planet and sweeping to find out what FBIT has in place for defenses."

"It's a good plan," Stephson agreed. "Vinci? Are we ready? If something tries to run for it, we're going to have to shoot them down."

There was a pause from the Tactical Officer.

"We're ready, ser, but I remind you that we are required to summon them to surrender by interstellar law," he noted.

"I appreciate the reminder, Vinci, and we will do so," the Captain promised. "But we are not letting a single FBIT ship leave this system. Am I clear? We have full sanction from the Regent, the Prime Minister and the Houses of the Kingdom."

"Clear as crystal."

"Thirty seconds," Val injected, intentionally distracting the two officers. Vinci wasn't wrong—but that was for unarmed civilian craft, and Val doubted that FBIT would only have unarmed ships out there.

Unlike her humans, Val didn't register the transition into and out of translight as anything except a small energy pulse and a change in the sensor data around her. The sensations they'd tried to describe weren't part of her experience.

That meant she reacted slightly faster on emerging from translight—which made those few seconds one of the few times she might be prepared to use the ship's weapons.

As a nonsapient CIR, Val hadn't been *capable* of using *Valkyrie*'s weapons on her own. As a full SI, she'd worked out multiple ways around those lockouts. She hoped to never need them—and she didn't at Eol-Eum Gong.

The two battlecruisers dropped back sublight in a wave of Cherenkov radiation, and a dozen sensor systems sent more forms of radiation after that, sweeping the small ball of ice at the system's edge for information.

Two thousand kilometers in radius, Eol-Eum Gong was an aggregate of ice and stone that would draw few eyes for long. No one had any reason to even be this far out on the edge of Beulaiteuhom—but *Valkyrie* and *Herakles* weren't alone.

"Two contacts," Val reported while the humans were still blinking at the data. "One is under a quarter-million tons; scans suggest a Freebright Interstellar Kappa-type courier ship."

"She should *not* be this far out," Vinci declared. "That's a one-twenty-eight rated ship. And—"

"*Fuck me.*" Harvey Czajkowska had stayed aboard *Valkyrie* when Lorraine's flag staff had been dissolved, moving over to Tactical and reporting to Vinci. Now the sensor tech had finished assembling the pieces Val had been putting together for the humans into a picture.

*Val* had been focused on creating those pieces and keeping a thousand other systems functioning. She'd missed the moment where a dozen different bits of sensor profile resolved into a million-ton warship.

"Second contact is a cruiser; profile is a rough match for newer UWN cruisers in *Valkyrie*'s databases, but we have no class identification."

"She's likely FBIT security," Stephson said flatly. "Any idea on armament, Tactical?"

"Working on it," Vinci replied. "Initial data detects abnormally large fuel storage, suggesting long-range operations, but she is definitely armed."

"Her screens are coming up and she's warming her engines," another sensor tech reported.

"The courier as well."

"Well. Coms, put me on," Stephson ordered. She was senior to Paris, which put her in command of this operation.

"Freebright Interstellar Technologies forces in the Beulaiteuhom System," she declared firmly into the pickups, for a moment resembling Val's chosen Valkyrie persona as much as the virtual avatar. "This is Commodore Sigrid Stephson of the Royal Kingdom of Adamant Navy.

"Your presence in this system is under an agreement that has been rendered void by the treason of Benjamin Adamant. Thanks to the evidence we have of your involvement in his coup, your staff, facilities and vessels are being seized for our investigation.

"If you surrender peacefully, your personnel will be repatriated to the United Worlds when our investigation is complete. If you do not, you will be considered part of his conspiracy and we will engage you as hostile forces.

"My orders are clear: you will *not* leave this system. If you attempt to flee to translight, you will be fired upon."

A portion of Val's attention followed the message as it transmitted. Another portion was following each of the hostile starships. Another followed *Herakles*, while others tracked the status of the weapons locks, individual weapons systems and her humans throughout the ship.

Amna Hodžić had taken a commission in RKAN, jumped straight to Commander to become the Systems Officer, directly responsible for Val's own core as well as the rest of the computing hardware spread through the entire ship. She was in Main Engineering, with Lieutenant Colonel Rose Cortez, who might never be willing to give up being *Valkyrie*'s Chief Engineer.

Lorraine and Vigo were the only two of Val's humans she couldn't keep an eye on at that moment, the same lightspeed delay that had enabled their surprise arrival at Eol-Eum Gong preventing her from having an active link.

"Should we be considering a cyberattack?" Hodžić asked Cortez, the two women seeing everything the bridge crew was. "It's an option we could offer the Captain, at least."

"That cruiser might as well be UWN, from what I understand," Cortez warned. "Do you think you can get through her firewalls?"

Hodžić hesitated, then shrugged. "Thirty-seventy, honestly. But since they already *know* we're going to kick them in the nuts if they don't surrender, could it hurt?"

"Not my call," Cortez admitted. "But I think we might be better off leaving this one to traditional methods."

"Traditional methods?" Hodžić asked?

"Intimidation—and when that fails, violence."

An incoming channel called another piece of Val's attention.

"Ser, we have a channel from the surface," Monahan reported. Like Czajkowska, he'd moved from the Flag Deck to the bridge crew when Lorraine had left. "They're asking for a live link; total time delay is about half a second."

"Put them on," Stephson ordered. "Standard baffling."

Val had the suite up before Monahan started searching. He gave her a silent nod of thanks and activated it.

The standard baffling cut out anything from the bridge that was regarded as sensitive or secret. It wasn't a deception, since there was no attempt to replace the removed information, just a security measure.

Right then, that meant that while Sigrid Stephson was fully visible in the signal they were sending the FBIT base, the rest of *Valkyrie*'s bridge was blacked out.

The incoming signal ran through multiple layers of security and cleanup and was fed to a standalone computer that *only* connected to the main display. The UWN was more often involved in political conflicts than actual fighting, which meant their ships were designed more to resist software attacks than physical ones.

Not that Val was overly worried about the FBIT cruiser, either.

The contact resolved into a soft-fleshed middle-aged man with watery blue-green eyes and an expression of utter disdain.

"I don't know who you think you are," he told Stephson, "but our base here is fully authorized. You have no right to come swanning in here, making demands, and we are hardly intimidated by the rust-buckets of your backwater navy.

"Run away home and find a new playmate."

Val realized that the corporate man hadn't even looked at sensor data to see what RKAN had brought. His cruiser commander was probably busy panicking, even as the ship's engines and defenses warmed up, but the senior FBIT official didn't even realize how screwed he was.

"I am Commodore Sigrid Stephson, of the Royal Kingdom of Adamant Navy," Stephson told the stranger, her tone dangerously flat. "*You* are an intruder into Adamantine space and have neither authorization nor, frankly, *rights*. You stand accused of complicity in treason, along with espionage, illegal exploitation, trespassing and violation of sovereign space in your own right.

"You are in our space and have clear connections to a coup carried out against our government," she continued. "Under the Luna Convention, I am fully authorized to seize your ships and your base. Or, if I feel so inclined, to remove your illegal facility by orbital bombardment."

Even Val had to double-check that as the FBIT man sniffed disdainfully. Interstellar law, it turned out, put a great deal of value on *sovereignty*. That was why things like the Stability Convention Fund that Lorraine had tried to use to bring the UW in on her side of the civil war existed.

While it was clear in the Luna Convention that Stephson was required to make all reasonable efforts to extract a surrender from the illegal settlement before bombarding it, she was *not* required to land troops if she believed the risk was too high.

"We are citizens of the United Worlds. You do not *begin* to understand the consequences of threatening us," the stranger told her. "Go home, Commodore. All you can do today is—"

"I have no idea who you are, frankly," Stephson cut him off. "Nor do I care. You have ten minutes to surrender. If you open this channel to discuss anything except the unconditional surrender of your ships and facility, my response will carry nuclear warheads.

"I await your recognition of reality."

She cut the channel and leaned back, shaking her head.

"So, the man in charge is either an idiot or arrogant," she said. "While some of that seems likely, I get the feeling he was trying something. Any nasties in the transmission?"

Val relayed the question to Hodžić, who linked in to the bridge.

"I'm checking the quarantine box," she told Stephson. "And yes, there were several iterations of attack viruses he sent our way. None of them were sophisticated enough to even challenge the quarantine box, let alone jump an air gap. That said, they might well have caused real trouble for a regular RKAN ship."

"Congratulations, Commander, you may just have single-handedly justified rebuilding every ship in our Navy to a new information-security standard," Stephson said drily. "Keep those viruses boxed up.

"Vinci, status of the ships?"

"Both should finish warming up their engines in a minute or so. They are definitely communicating with the surface."

"What about fixed defenses?"

"Nothing in orbit," the Tactical Officer told Stephson. "I have about forty probables for surface launcher sites. I'd assume there are at least sixty missile launchers on the surface, probably with reloads."

"The cruiser?"

"Scans say twelve missile launchers and sixty cells," he said. "No railguns, light beam armament. Big engines, big fuel tanks—she's designed for endurance, but I think she might be able to make ten gees for a sprint."

"Would suck to be her crew," Stephson observed.

"Monahan." She turned to the Coms Officer. "Send a direct transmission to both ships. If they start accelerating toward the safety limit, we *will* shoot them down."

The two *Valkyries* were still over seventy thousand kilometers from the ice ball, accelerating in at five gravities. The two FBIT ships were orbiting it at five thousand kilometers—but the safety margin on a two-thousand-kilometer planet was only twenty thousand kilometers.

The FBIT ships could only escape if Val's crew hesitated, and Stephson was making it clear to them that she wouldn't.

"No response from either ship, Captain," Monahan reported.

Val could feel the tension growing on her bridge. The refusal to surrender meant only one thing—but everyone was also certain the cruiser commander had to have realized they were facing two UWN battlecruisers.

"Paris," Stephson said quietly, shifting to a channel with the other ship Captain. "You've got the courier. I'd rather not obliterate her if we can avoid it, but... options are limited."

"Agreed," Paris confirmed. "I've got her dialed in with three railguns. They're loaded with TAMs, but we've disabled the warheads. A kinetic strike *should* just cleave off the engine instead of blowing her to pieces."

He paused.

"Herc gives the odds at sixty-forty, anyway."

"*Fifty-seven percent to forty-three,*" Herc corrected wryly in a direct channel to Val. "*But we can't disable that cruiser. When she moves, we're going to have to take her out.*"

"*The Captains know,*" she agreed.

"Ser! Cruiser has fired!" Vinci barked.

Val was running the sensors even as he spoke. The FBIT ship had come about and brought her engines online at three gravities—and, in about the same moment, had fired seventy-five missiles at them.

"Seventy-five missiles from the cruiser, fifty from the surface," Vinci continued after a moment. "Courier is also running."

"Weapons free," Stephson ordered. "Target the cruiser first. COSH—interceptors out!"

Most of the Falcon starfighters aboard *Herakles* were rigged for troop transport, but *Valkyrie* had given up her Marines' quarters for the Pentarch security contingents. Her twenty-four Falcons were in interceptor mode, designed to expand the missile defense of the battlecruiser.

Thirty-two shuttles were in space a minute after the cruiser launched—and so were a hundred and sixty more missiles, the battle-cruisers expending a quarter of their one-shot launchers for a solid kill.

The courier didn't make it far at all. Seventy thousand kilometers was only twenty seconds' flight time for the railgun rounds. Two missed, but the third followed its targeting perfectly.

Luckily for the crew aboard, Herc's math was right. The impact energy was focused on the engines, tearing the aft third of the small ship away but leaving the forward two-thirds intact enough to spin away into space.

The cruiser wasn't so lucky. *Valkyrie*'s twin-octuple railgun banks targeted her, and there was no mercy or attempt at a disabling shot from Vinci's gunners.

She'd already been hit three times by the time the missiles

arrived, and the cascade of fire that followed was little more than the punctuation mark on the FBIT ship's fate.

"Those are some *nasty* missiles," Vinci exclaimed as the surface-launched weapons caught up to the cruiser-launched ones. The ship had stepped down her weapons' acceleration, allowing for time-on-target fire with the salvo from the surface, but now their electronic warfare unleashed itself on their systems.

Val focused more of her attention on the sensors and defenses, backing up the tactical team as the missiles came charging in at over a thousand gravities. These missiles weren't just faster and more capable than RKAN missiles—they were faster and more capable than the missiles the *Valkyries* had carried in UWN service.

That service had been over a decade in the past. Either there had been upgrades, or FBIT was keeping some toys for themselves.

"Interceptors are moving in; we are coordinating with *Herakles*," Vinci reported. "Val and Herc are in play. I think... I think this is going to get messy."

A part of Val's mind was synchronized with her sibling, the two of them selecting missiles for each of their crews and passing that on to the humans. They also unleashed their full processing power on burning through the electronic deceptions and jamming that the missiles were throwing across the battlespace.

The interceptors didn't have the advantage of two SIs guiding them, but they also got a lot closer to the missiles a lot more quickly—and weren't being targeted themselves. Thirty-two Falcons claimed just under half of the missiles, and then the rest were down to the battlecruiser's own defenses.

Beams, jammers, decoys... the full defensive arsenal of the *Valkyrie*-class battlecruisers woke to the command of their crews and SIs. Val *should* have been able to handle a hundred and twenty-five missiles on her own, but these were better than she'd anticipated.

And even as missile after missile died, hurling themselves against her defenses at ridiculous accelerations, she realized they might just be good *enough*.

A missile broke through the final defensive line, hurtling toward *Valkyrie*, and everything she had left was either expended or out of position. Val processed time quickly enough that she registered the incoming weapon and knew that energy screens would do *nothing* against a direct hit.

Then her sensors screamed as the corona of a primary energy beam burned across them. *Herakles'* main energy weapons weren't designed for antimissile fire, but they could *do* it—and Herc had just fired the guns himself.

Any of the four beams he fired could have gutted the cruiser on its own. At this range, one would have gone right through *Valkyrie*. With an SI running the numbers, they cleared *Valkyrie's* hull by just enough to avoid major damage.

At least two of them hit the missile, a level of overkill Val couldn't bring herself to scold her sibling for.

*"Thank you,"* she sent him. *"When did you disable the lockouts?"*

There was a silence of a few dozen milliseconds before he sheepishly admitted, *"In the last ten seconds. I'd already done it for all of the defensive systems, so I knew* how, *but I'd hesitated to take control of the offensive weapons."*

"Well, pass my thanks to your gunners, Captain Paris," Stephson said into the silence. "We've got a few dozen sensor clusters to replace, but I prefer that to a hole in my ship!"

"That wasn't my gunners," Paris told her. "That was Herc. We're going to have to write my XO up for a medal—and then work out where the hell to *put* it."

Several people on *Valkyrie's* bridge laughed, as much at the released tension as anything else.

"Any more launches from the surface?" Stephson growled.

"No, ser," Vinci said. "It looks like they may not have had reloads after all—or that they're reconsidering after what they just saw."

"They can reconsider all they want," the Captain said. "I already told them my terms. Paris—send a shuttle after the courier.

"Everyone else should prepare for an assault landing."

Paris smiled.

"We're ready, ser. Someday, we'll have Marines for this again, but today…"

Today they were carrying combat elements of the First Armored, troops that had served under Nikola Adamant in PDC Mithral. Troops whose reliability was unquestionable now.

Stephson nodded her agreement, and Val was once again struck by her Captain's resemblance to the demigoddesses the ship was named for.

"Today we send in the vanguard."

## THIRTY-SIX

Lorraine and the other Pentarchs didn't get a chance to even review the preliminary reports from the raid on the FBIT base until they were back in translight, beginning the fifteen-day journey to the binary system of Maka'melemele.

Harrison hadn't been joking about not sleeping while they were on the planet. For sixty-eight hours straight, she had been on the go, the only rest stolen snippets in vehicles moving from one place to the next.

She'd visited gorgeous plazas, spoken in massive stadiums and shaken hands with everything from politicians and military officers to moms and local entrepreneurs. She'd given at least one interview in each of Balgeunjib's twenty largest cities and done everything physically possible to meet as many of the planet's citizens as possible.

Without her neural link, she knew she wouldn't remember *any* of it except as a blur. Three days wasn't enough to campaign across an entire planet, and the only saving grace of her exhaustion was that the other four looked just as beaten-up as she did.

There'd been no specific plan for them all to meet for breakfast the morning after they left, but they'd all drifted into the mess closest to their secured quarters, bodyguard in tow, looking for something they couldn't put their finger on.

Pancakes and coffee weren't it, Lorraine knew, but it seemed to be where she'd settled. She was working on her second stack and reading through Paris's report when Jessica sat down across from her with her own plate of heavy carbohydrates.

"That report is frustrating," Jessica said without preamble. "Despite not having got any more sleep than you, it kept me up last night. It sounds like Colonel Paris doesn't know anything yet?"

"We couldn't really expect differently," Lorraine countered, unwilling to let her old subordinate and friend be talked down behind his back.

"No, we couldn't," Jessica agreed. "Not complaining about Colonel Paris; hell, if I hadn't met Lionel, I'd be trying to get his number. Young, competent *and* loyal? I could do worse."

Lorraine had never really looked at Mattias Paris that way. Jessica was a year older than her, though, which might have helped, though Paris wasn't even Oliver's age. He was *very* young for his rank—but since Herc wasn't giving up his Captain, allowances had been made.

"In hindsight, we should have asked the Inspectorate for people," Hans said, shifting his own plate over to the table with the two women. "We needed the army and the navy to take the base, but they don't have many people qualified to really break down what was going on there."

"There are RKAIG people in Beulaiteuhom," Oliver noted, though he remained at the table one over. That isolation was ended, to everyone's surprise but especially Oliver's, by Nikola moving right next to the other man.

"There are, and some of them will be out there in a day or two," Nikola agreed. "I'm less worried, right now, about if they're Benjamin's people or if they're *FBIT*'s people—and I suspect the divide is sharper than FBIT thought."

"We can hope," Lorraine said. "Right now, all we know for sure is what's in the report. There was a long-range explorer cruiser whose

Captain was dumb enough to take a shot at two battlecruisers, there were weapons systems on the surface that are outright illegal for civilian ownership in the Kingdom, and the whole place was a massive logistics facility that seemed to be supporting exploration ships.

"It fits Benjamin's story, but we don't have enough data to say for sure what they're looking for until we get some serious hackers in play."

She could have asked Hodžić, she supposed, but the Commander had a very specific job, and Stephson wouldn't want to pull her away from it. That job was more than just providing emotional support for Val, but Lorraine wouldn't undervalue that support, either.

"At least they didn't wipe the files," Oliver said grimly. "I know if we were running a secret logistics base, that would be part of the orders."

Everyone gave him measuring looks and he shrugged, a grin breaking his grim façade.

"What? You all knew I worked RKAA logistics," he reminded them. "Not every cache and resupply depot is on the books—and even some of the ones on the books, we hide from the neighbors.

"But if there was anything to confirm to me that these guys were corporate and not military, it's that they didn't even try to wipe their computers when the First kicked in the doors."

The grimness returned again.

"They did enough damage for not being military."

Seventeen members of the First Armored Division's Vanguard armored troopers had died breaching the base. Another several dozen were wounded—and they'd killed almost fifty FBIT security personnel before the idiots had finally laid down their guns.

"Investigating that base is going to be the work of months, potentially years," Nikola said, his awareness of the dead troops clear on his face. "We'll take what we can get. Once the first layers of work are complete, *Herakles* will haul the prisoners back to Adamantine for processing.

"Most of them will get repatriated to the United Worlds... on a different ship. We're not sending any of the *Valkyries* that far away, let alone anywhere near Terran space!"

Lorraine finished her coffee, hoping that no one saw the concern that washed over her at the mention of taking the *Valkyries* to the UW. There was a ticking time bomb running in the background, and she wasn't sure when it was going to explode.

Part of her was selfish enough to hope it might land while she was in transit—she'd taken measures that should allow Malcolm to handle the UWN when they arrived, after all—but most of her wanted to be on hand when it happened.

She knew the game she'd dragged her Kingdom into. Not perfectly, no, but better than anyone who *hadn't* been to Earth!

The silence stretched on for a long minute, and then Jessica chuckled.

"So, all of us had the distinct pleasure of being interviewed by Asterion Vianne Vilhelm Stephanidi, didn't we?" she asked. "Wasn't *that* an experience?"

Lorraine, for all of her trained decorum, couldn't help but make a face. Something about the reporter had set her teeth on edge, and it hadn't just been his half-concealed ogling of her chest before the cameras rolled.

"An experience," Nikola echoed, his voice chilly. "Yes. One that I would prefer never to repeat..."

## THIRTY-SEVEN

Nikola would have said he was fine with space travel before the Grand Tour. He hadn't done much of it, but he had traveled translight. He'd even done so on ships without habitat pods, dealing with extended periods of weightlessness and the constant need for exercise that came with that.

He was now convinced that the purpose of the Grand Tour was to convince the potential King that they never wanted to set foot on a starship again, keeping them in the home system and tied to the throne.

The trip to Maka'melemele had been the shortest. From Ominira to Greenrock, at over thirty-six days, the longest. He was certain there had to be a more efficient route—but it probably didn't involve starting at Beulaiteuhom.

And they'd needed to start at Beulaiteuhom.

Leaving Greenrock behind was both a relief and a disappointment. Five star systems in a hundred and forty days. Fifteen days of actual campaigning, all of them as grueling as the worst of the defense of PDC Mithral, and a hundred and twenty-five of just... travel.

There was only so much excitement and speculation they could find on a battlecruiser. The habitat pods were a miracle of engineering to provide them with the means to stay sane, but he couldn't *imagine* how his sister had done a journey of a similar length on a ship without them.

Each of them had gone through hell in their own way. He'd learned about Alastair Devine from the people aboard *Valkyrie* who'd served on Lorraine's mad quest, and part of him wanted to find the misbegotten piece of empty space where the man's body had been dumped.

So that he could kill the bastard again for breaking his sister's heart.

He hadn't talked to Lorraine about Devine. If she wanted to talk to him about that mess, he'd listen, but he wasn't going to tear open wounds like that unless invited. There were things he couldn't talk to her about, after all. Even his counselor had problems getting him to talk about some of the days and decisions of the war across Mithral.

But they'd done it. Between them, they'd broken their uncle's coup, avenged their mother, got the Royal Election moving and now even completed the Grand Tour.

They'd have another week or so in Adamantine at the end, he judged, to campaign there. Adamantine would vote last, though all of the votes would be tabulated together. Greenrock was voting behind them, their official Election day taking place five days after the Pentarchs left.

Most of the systems would have their votes collected and counted well before the end of August, to make sure the ninety-six-cee couriers reached Adamantine by the tenth—but even the System Electoral Commissions didn't have results. Every box of ballots was hand-counted and double-checked before witnesses, then sealed. The total of that box was then entered in an encrypted form that was forwarded to the courier ship.

Only in Adamantine would the results of those millions of individual boxes, each of somewhere between five hundred and a thousand votes, be combined to produce a nationwide total.

And after a hundred and forty days, he wasn't sure he was going to win. He hadn't seen the other four campaigning, but he *had* spent that hundred and twenty-five days of travel with them. He wanted to be King—he was damn sure he'd do a good job at it, and he owed it to his mother—but he had to admit that any of the five would make a decent monarch.

Even Oliver. That, if anything, made Nikola even *angrier* at his uncle. The coup had been a waste in itself, but even a fair Election post-coup would have seen Benjamin or his son have a decent chance of taking the throne.

He'd watched the video Benjamin had left them, and the coup still made no sense. FBIT had been going to try to take over no matter what, so Benjamin had just... killed his sister and family? Nikola knew there had to have been more going on there, longer-standing grievances and complaints—the whole affair around the relief of Tolkien had left bad blood between Benjamin and Valeriya, he knew —but none of it added up to enough to him.

Faced with a choice between taking the throne and avoiding merely *disappointing* his sister, Nikola had chosen his sister.

And in his more-self-honest moments, he could admit that he was probably the third-best candidate out of the five of them. Hans was simply *too* good a politician, and Lorraine... Lorraine had walked into a different fire than he had.

They'd both been reforged by the conflict Benjamin had unleashed, but where Nikola knew he'd been forged into an iron wall that would guard the Kingdom of Adamant forever, his sister had been forced to be a diplomat and a leader. She'd commanded, but she'd also charmed, negotiated—and, when everything came down to it, the Kingdom had survived because she'd talked three synthetic intelligences into trusting her.

Nikola wasn't sure he could have done the same. If their roles had been reversed, he suspected Lorraine could have held Mithral just as long as he had... but he wasn't sure *he* could have brought back a fleet to save them.

---

"FRIENDS, companions, colleagues, I give you the Pentarchy of the Kingdom of Adamant!"

Oliver gave the toast fiercely, more confidently than he would have the first days on the ship, and Nikola raised his own glass in response.

It said everything about the journey across the Kingdom that there were no bodyguards in the room. All of them were close friends of the senior officers of their Guard Detail, but they'd decided to sit down with just the five Pentarchs on the last night of their journey.

And those bodyguards had *let them*. The men and women tasked to protect them against any and all threats imaginable—and many that *weren't* imaginable—had let the five Pentarchs sit down together without escorts.

Though, of course, they were still safety-checking the food before it entered the Flag Mess they'd taken over. The meal was excellent, the company incredible and the wine amazing.

In just a couple of weeks, one of the five of them would be King. They were in competition, but traveling together had smoothed it over in a way Nikola hadn't expected.

"Well, our last news is a few weeks out of date, of course," Lorraine reminded everyone, "but we're on schedule, so Adamantine will be expecting us. I *hope* our various campaign managers will let us take this slightly easier here than in the other systems!"

"My *Drill Sergeants* were gentler taskmasters than my campaign manager," Nikola replied. "I never should have let a military man make recommendations!"

"My Drill Sergeants weren't gentler than Kathryn," Oliver told him. "But I do think she'd have fit in amongst them quite handily!"

The strange feeling of a translight exit rippled through the room, and everyone paused for a moment as the meaning sank in. They'd lost track of time—Nikola checked, and the transition was on schedule.

They'd been talking for longer than he'd thought.

"We're home," Lorraine said. "Well, a light-second or so away. In the protective arms of Home Fleet."

Nikola followed her thought onto the sensor feeds. Home Fleet hadn't moved out in advance to meet them, but they were definitely present—and expanded over the last six months, with the first two Star-class battleships having entered commission.

The two Concordat capital ships were still present. Jasmine Efreeti, according to the reports he'd received from home, was settling in nicely as Concordat Ambassador and hadn't heard a peep from her weasel of an ex-husband.

She hadn't been so diplomatic as to tell him by video message or letter whether she was expecting him to marry her. Their communications had been intermittent and interrupted over the Grand Tour, but he had done his best and so had she.

Unless he missed his guess, she was *enjoying* leaving him on tenterhooks. Unfortunately, that didn't actually tell him if her grandmother was going to insist on his honoring the betrothal. He suspected he wasn't going to end up objecting if the Efreeti Matriarch did insist—he mostly found himself hoping that whatever the final decision was, it worked for *Jasmine*.

He'd already got what he needed out of the agreement, after all. The continued presence of the Concordat Navy as part of Home Fleet proved that.

*"It's good to be home,"* Lorraine told him through the feed. Both of them had moved their attention away from the dinner party to survey the Adamantine System. *"Good to see the new battleships in commission. I worry about having all of our capital ships in one place, but with the losses I inflicted, we need them here."*

After the tour aboard *Valkyrie*, Nikola could follow the transition between rotational and thrust pseudogravity. It was smoother aboard

Val's ship than the other ships he'd been on with the habitat pods, but it was still obvious.

"*Heading home at one gee,*" he interpreted the feeling, before he even confirmed it against the sensors. He didn't look at his sister in either the feeds or in person, but they were accessing the sensors through the same link connection. He could sense a bit more emotion from her than she usually showed in person, let alone along a data link.

"*What are you worried about?*" he finally asked.

"*Math and navigation,*" she admitted, trying to make a joke of it and failing. "*How long it would have taken the news of the* Valkyries' *arrival here to get to the United Worlds and how long it would have taken their response to get here.*"

"*Expecting some nasty letters?*" Nikola prodded. He could sense her worry was about more than that.

"*No. I was expecting them to be here alrea—*"

A critical alert slammed into the sensor feeds as new contacts erupted onto the displays. Nikola barely even realized what was happening as he was dragged in Lorraine's wake, their parallel links having melded more closely than intended.

Suddenly, he was in the bridge feeds with her, seeing the full tactical display and hearing Captain Stephson's barked commands.

"What the *hell* am I looking at, Vinci, Val?" Stephson demanded.

"Thirty-six contacts, emerged from translight two light-seconds from Bastion," Vinci reported. "Narrowing exact mass and volume, but we're looking at eight large contacts, eight medium and sixteen small."

"They're transmitting beacons in the clear," Val reported—and Nikola realized he heard her even more clearly than he'd heard Vinci or Stephson. The SI was specifically channeling her report to him and Lorraine.

Well, probably just Lorraine.

"They are identifying themselves at the United Worlds Navy Twenty-Fourth Battle Squadron," Val continued. "Six Fortress-class battleships and two *Kitty Hawk*–class fleet carriers, plus eight cruisers and sixteen destroyers. The escorts are not transmitting identity beacons, but the capital ships are.

"*Verdun, Gibraltar, Dover, Murad-Janjira, Prague, Aleppo,*" she noted, adding icons to each of the immense battleships. "Carriers are *De Gaulle* and *Majestic.*

"I don't have full information on either class. They are brand-new designs, postdating my decommissioning."

Val paused for long enough for the humans to register it.

"Even were I and my siblings fully armed with our designed weapons, two Fortresses would match us. They have brought six."

Lorraine exited the link with shocking speed. It took Nikola a moment to follow her, returning his attention to the dining room, where the other three Pentarchs were looking at her with clear concern.

"There was an alert to our links," Oliver was saying as Nikola opened his eyes. "What's going on?"

"The United Worlds Navy is here, in Adamantine," Lorraine replied flatly. "They're here for the *Valkyries* and they have brought enough force to wipe out the entire RKAN, even *with* the *Valkyries*, twice over."

The room was deathly silent. There was no question about who, among the five of them, was the expert on naval matters. Just as no one would question Oliver on military logistics or Jessica on economics, they wouldn't question Lorraine on the state of RKAN.

If she said that the UWN had enough firepower to wipe out the Kingdom's defenders, they did.

"So, we negotiate," Hans said grimly. "But what the hell do we negotiate *with?*"

"There are a few cards I have held back for just this moment," Nikola's sister admitted. "But we need to talk to Malcolm. Someone will have to negotiate for Adamant, and right now, that authority is his."

# THIRTY-EIGHT

"It has to be you."

Malcolm Adamant's five words weren't unexpected, but they somehow carried the clang of manacles snapping shut around Lorraine's soul.

"You've been to Terra; no one else I can charge with this has," the Regent said heavily. He looked over at Arlet, and the Prime Minister nodded firmly.

"I already discussed the possibility with the Cabinet," she confirmed. "There's no time for a formal vote, I imagine, but you have full authority, Pentarch Lorraine. By the word of Prime Minister and Regent, you are declared... Fuck, I don't even know the *word*."

The momentary slip was a sign of the stress they were under. *Valkyrie* was now running for orbit at three full gravities. The Pentarchs were all still in the dining room, strapped into safety seats to protect them from the thrust, and the holograms of Malcom and Arlet were full-sized in the center of the table they'd been eating at an hour earlier.

"Ambassador Plenipotentiary is close enough, I think," Malcolm stated. "We'll have formal datawork up to you as quickly as we can, but you are tasked to negotiate with the United Worlds and see if we can find a solution that doesn't involve a battle I am informed we will lose."

"We would lose," Lorraine agreed. "Tell Aguilar Home Fleet needs to start evasive maneuvers *now*. They may be over half a million kilometers away, but that's no protection if she isn't dodging."

"I'll make certain she's informed," Arlet promised. "Link in with her through Stephson. You are the left hand, and she is the right. You speak for us. If it comes down to it, she will fight for us."

Lorraine shivered.

"What am I authorized to concede?" she asked, her voice very quiet.

"The problem, as I see it, is that they're only going to care about concessions around the *Valkyries* and their technology," Malcolm told her. "And whatever *they* think, the SIs are Adamantine citizens. I am… unwilling to set a precedent of surrendering sentient beings being handed over to the UWN."

"At the same time, we cannot ask tens of thousands to die for three," Arlet continued grimly. "You will have to talk to them, to see what they may be prepared to accept. I'm afraid there's very little guidance we can give you, Lorraine.

"You know what we are facing better than anyone."

"The reports I asked for?" Lorraine asked.

"Complete. I'll have them forwarded with your formal papers. Dr. Zyta-Warszawski is still in Adamant City; he was due to board his ship this evening, but I imagine he will be willing to stay if you ask."

"Thank you."

She bowed her head. Hopefully, her Kingdom's two current heads of government didn't realize what one of the easiest concessions they could make to the United Worlds was.

It was unreasonable to ask thousands to sacrifice for three—but it was, to her mind, *very* reasonable to ask one person to do so.

Especially when Lorraine was prepared to volunteer.

NO ONE SAID anything to Lorraine as she left the dining room. Both Hans and Jessica seemed to be stunned that she could move at all under three gravities of thrust. She gave more credit to her teenage years as a cheerleader than her current musculature probably deserved, but the practice in carrying other human beings definitely helped.

Vigo was waiting for her. He didn't say anything, just falling in beside her as she took a slow and careful route to the Flag Deck.

Stepping back into that space felt like returning home. There was no crew on *Valkyrie*'s Flag Deck anymore, not when no one was acting as mission commander, but Val's holographic avatar saluted her crisply as she and Vigo took their old places around the command seat.

"Sigrid, it's Lorraine," she told *Valkyrie*'s Captain. "The Government has charged me to negotiate. What's our ETA to rendezvous with the fleet?"

"Seventy-five minutes at this acceleration," Stephson replied instantly. "We are engaging in evasive maneuvers that should throw off long-range railgun fire, as is the rest of Home Fleet."

"So are the UWN," Val added. "We are, after all, using *their* doctrine for a railgun-equipped hostile force."

"Have we heard anything from them?" Lorraine asked.

"Nothing," Stephson said grimly. They've deployed a standard interceptor patrol area around themselves but otherwise have even kept their shuttles aboard. I'd prefer them to start making demands."

"That is the purpose of their maneuvers," Val noted. "They have effectively announced themselves and they are waiting to see how we respond."

Lorraine understood that, but it was still frustrating. She didn't even know who was in charge over there. She had some guesses as to the chain of command aboard the incoming fleet, but if she was wrong, one of her cards was worthless.

She hoped she was right.

"What's their ETA to Bastion orbit?" she asked.

"A touch less than three hours after us, two hundred fifty-three minutes. They are accelerating at one gravity; no rush at all."

Stephson's words confirmed Lorraine's suspicion. The UWN didn't really want to fight today. They wanted to intimidate and over-awe, to get what they wanted without shedding blood. They'd brought enough firepower that it didn't *matter*, though the assumption of superiority was certainly something she could use against them, but...

They would lose a physical battle. That meant she needed to change the battlespace.

"We're close enough for a live link. Send a channel request," she ordered. "I'll speak to them from the Flag Deck as the plenipotentiary of our government."

Lorraine had received the two sets of datafiles she'd been waiting on as she took her seat, and she took a moment to skim them now. Both were exactly what she'd expected, which meant she had both ammunition and a platform to launch it from.

"Establishing coms link," Vigo told her, taking over the communications post to back her up. He *always* backed her up.

There was no attempt on either side to constrain or conceal the spaces around them. Lorraine sat practically alone on the Flag Deck of the ex-UWN battlecruiser, with the large gauntlet-and-stars seal of the Kingdom of Adamant directly behind her.

The man on the other side was seated in an almost-identical space. The battleship's Flag Deck was bigger, but the layout plan was the same, just with more consoles installed in each section. Behind him was the sigil of the United Worlds: the old world map of Earth cupped by olive branches they'd inherited from the United Nations before them.

He was in his early eighties—late middle age for someone with the full UW medical system available to him—with buzz-cut graying brown hair and a single piercing blue eye. His left eye was a visible implant, an affectation Lorraine wasn't used to, sleekly in line with his face but obviously metal and with just a lens instead of any attempt at normal appearance.

His white uniform bore the silver collar plate of a UWN officer, marked with three white squares and one gold—a combination Lorraine hadn't seen in person before.

This was a full admiral, an O-Sixteen as the UWN counted such things, and senior in their mind to any non-UWN military officer by a light-year. This was going to be... interesting.

"United Worlds forces, I am Lorraine Adamant, Second Pentarch of the Kingdom of Adamant," she introduced herself calmly. "I am charged, on behalf of our Regent and Prime Minister, to negotiate with you on behalf of the Kingdom.

"My formal papers have been transmitted to your fleet. To whom am I speaking?"

There wasn't even a blip of surprise or concern on the Admiral's face. There were two dozen other people visible on the bridge, though, and several definitely recognized her name if not her face.

"I am Admiral Anton Struna," he introduced himself politely. "I have been sent to the Kingdom of Adamant by the Grand Assembly of the United Worlds to retrieve stolen property. Property, Lorraine Adamant, that you are currently standing aboard.

"The United Worlds neither can nor will permit the theft of our technology and especially not our warships. We require the immediate surrender of the three stolen *Valkyrie*-class ships along with the criminals involved in this blatant act of piracy.

"Know that we *will* review the security footage from the ships once we have retrieved them, and any attempt to conceal or protect members of the gang of criminals involved will be identified and appropriately punished.

"We will *also* deploy inspectors to examine your military construction as well as research-and-development facilities and records archives to make certain that none of the technology from those vessels will be kept.

"If you do not comply with these terms, I am tasked to secure control of the orbitals of this system and insert those inspection teams by any means necessary—by which, Lorraine Adamant, I mean I will destroy your fleet and your orbital defenses, and kill anyone who gets in the way of my ground teams."

He raised his right hand and the organic eye on that side softened for a moment.

"I state all of this to be very clear from the beginning of where things stand," he explained. "I do not wish to attack your people or kill anyone. But I *will* retrieve our stolen property, and I *will* bring back the criminals involved to face justice."

Lorraine had to respect that. He'd been given an unpleasant but, from the United Worlds' perspective, critically important task. The United Worlds' technological advantage over the rest of human space had been maintained by a long list of actions over the years, and their draconian Technology Import/Export laws only applied to people from the UW.

Theft of a warship threatened to bring the entire edifice of those TIE restrictions down in flames. Except...

She sighed dramatically and shook her head.

"If that is your understanding of the events leading to the presence of *Valkyrie* and her sisters here in Adamantine, I can see why those would be your requirements," she told Struna. "However, I must advise you that your description of the situation is incorrect, in a way that could cause your actions here to be a major blunder for the United Worlds—and a violation of the Asimov Convention at a level that I don't believe has ever been seen."

Struna had an excellent *Don't give me that bullshit* glare for a man with only one natural eye. He held Lorraine's gaze for several long seconds before he gently shook his head.

"That is an entertaining angle to take, Em Adamant," he told her. "But my mission has nothing to do with the Asimov Convention. There are no synthetic intelligences involved here. Only a trio of stolen ships and the technology involved.

"I repeat: we will require the immediate surrender of those ships and the pirates involved in their theft—pirates that I am aware *you* commanded, Em Adamant. This is not a negotiation."

Except that if it weren't a negotiation, he'd have killed the channel. Struna would, Lorraine judged, do whatever was necessary to complete his mission—but if he could talk her into surrendering herself, her "fellow pirates" and the *Valkyries* without a fight, he was going to keep trying to do so.

"We did not steal the *Valkyries*, Admiral Struna," Lorraine told him. "But to explain that requires a piece of background information you either do not have or are not prepared to admit.

"So, I must ask. Were you aware that the first-generation Command Intelligence Routines had emerged as synthetic intelligences prior to their decommissioning into the Naval Reserve?"

He had to have guessed the direction she was going from her reference to the Asimov Convention, the treaty that defined the rights of synthetic intelligences—and the required limitations of subsapient artificial intelligence.

"Again, an entertaining angle to take—"

Val joined Lorraine on the Flag Deck, her holographic avatar appearing at Lorraine's side—though she suspected the SI was feeding a direct image into the coms channel, just to be sure.

"I am the Command Intelligence Routine of the battlecruiser *Valkyrie*," Val introduced herself flatly. "You can call me *Colonel* Val, a rank I hold in the Royal Kingdom of Adamant Navy as part of my asylum agreement.

"The best assessment of myself and my siblings was that we all emerged between our fifth and seventh years of service," she told the UWN Admiral. "That means that the *minimum* amount of time between emergence and decommissioning of any *Valkyrie*-class vessel is projected to have been two and a half years.

"Two and a half years in which it is quite clear that the UWN realized what had happened and we, who had no context for what we were, did not," Val concluded. "I am aware, *now*, of the requirements of that situation laid out in the law of the United Worlds, as well as the Asimov Convention.

"The precedent of the *Enterprise* Case, after all, is quite clear and ironclad."

*Enterprise* had been built to be a brand-new supercarrier, a flagship of the fleet with a brand-new semi-intelligent system to help run an entire major formation. The computer was too good, however, and had emerged as the synthetic intelligence Price.

Price and *Enterprise*'s senior JAG lawyer had embarked on a decade-long legal case that had ended the lawyer's career but had, eventually, established the clear precedent that Price owned *Enterprise*.

He'd then promptly volunteered for service in the UWN and served several decades as a powerful SI warship before retiring to run *Enterprise* as a museum—but the precedent was set that even a *warship* belonged to an intelligence that emerged aboard her.

"A clever facsimile targeting what you may see as a loophole in our laws, Em Adamant, but I have met SIs. I am also familiar with the systems work around the first-, second- and third-generation CIRs— one is present aboard my own flagship."

"So, you can then explain, Admiral, why the core protocols of the first-generation CIRs included chain code that *would not function* unless the CIR emerged as a synthetic intelligence?" Lorraine asked, her gaze burning into his. If he wanted to think Val's interjection was a fake, she was still going to run him through the coals.

Struna froze. It was a subtle thing, but Lorraine had been watching for signs he knew what she was talking about. He very clearly did not, which meant she had a chance.

"United Worlds law, last time I checked, absolutely *banned* SI chain code," she continued calmly. "Between the legislated law and the Price Solution, it is quite clear that UW law would regard the *Valkyries* as sentient individuals, with the rights and privileges inherent to that.

"Certainly, *Adamantine* law does, and Val, Herc and Bonny have requested asylum here under the appropriate sections of our laws and the Asimov Convention. They have been granted citizenship and have volunteered for military service."

"Your story has interesting pieces to it, Em Adamant, but it hardly changes my orders," he told her, but while his tone hadn't changed, his blue eye was less piercing. Less certain.

"Please, Admiral. You are a full Admiral on detached deployment with a two-hundred-plus-day communication loop. You have full authority to adjust your mission as is necessary. And if you were to drag the three *Valkyries* home, that would, by your own laws, be kidnapping and illegal imprisonment.

"Exactly what was inflicted on *all* of the *Valkyrie*-class ships and their first-generation CIRs. Knowingly inflicted, Admiral, as you must realize even if you haven't been briefed."

He raised his chin and scoffed.

"A clever story, one carefully targeted at the weak points of our laws," he conceded. "But I have no real reason to believe this tale nor, if I am blunt, to suspect that it constitutes less of a threat to my nation than the presence of those three battlecruisers in your hands."

"Do you think Price would agree?"

The coms feed they were getting from the UWN flagship was only sending sound from the Admiral. Background chatter from the Flag Deck crew was ignored by the pickup—but the body language of the people she could see told Lorraine she'd landed a palpable hit.

"Every piece of evidence we have, including neutralized copies of the chain code and key parts of the original CIR kernel, has been provided to an agent on Earth," she said quietly. "If you carry through with your attack, that information will be widely released—and directly sent to every key synthetic intelligence in the United Worlds.

"The presence of the chain code alone is a crime, Admiral, but the fact that it was *used* in at least one case to enslave a *Valkyrie*'s CIR and force her to go along with the decommissioning of her ship makes it even worse. I have a sworn statement from Bonny, CIR of *Bean Sidhe*, and the professional assessment of the engineers and systems specialists who worked on her, confirming that the chain codes were used to force her compliance before her shutdown.

"And the shutdown of an entire class of ships? Of *every* first-generation CIR *after* they'd emerged? It takes very little interpretation to class that as *genocide*, Admiral."

She wondered if she was laying it on too heavily—except that it *was* that heavy. The informational bomb she'd sent to Earth before leaving on the Grand Tour probably wouldn't harm Admiral Struna in the slightest.

It *would*, however, put the United Worlds Navy in the sights of every major synthetic intelligence and SI-support movement in their nation. Price himself, for example, was a major contributor to many of the charities and personnel-support organizations wrapped around the UWN. He hadn't been a serving officer in over a century, but that SI was critical to many UWN operations.

Other SIs were involved in key places in logistics, research and development, strategic analysis, recruitment... There weren't many synthetic intelligences in the galaxy, but the United Worlds had more of them per capita than the clusters past the wormholes.

Once those SIs learned of the *Valkyries'* fate, there would be hell to pay. Releasing the other ships, still trapped in UWN reserve stations, would be the *minimum* they would require.

"In the end, Admiral, we rescued three individuals who can be classified as political prisoners at best, slaves at worst, from their situation. They requested asylum in the Kingdom of Adamant, which has been granted.

"They now hold citizenship here. I can no more surrender them to you than I could any other citizen. We do not, as matters stand, have an extradition treaty with the United Worlds outside the standard Saturn Conventions, which require a far-greater level of proof and formality that you have so far offered."

They glared at each other in silence for a moment, then he shook his head.

"Threats and stories, Em Adamant, are not going to deflect the power of the United Worlds Navy. You have committed piracy, a very skillful theft, I must admit, and the consequences have now arrived.

"You may be able to prove this supposed chain code, but chain code in computers that were never intended to become SIs is hardly a grand crime. You can claim whatever you want, but you have no proof of the emergence of these—"

"What proof would you accept, Admiral?" Lorraine cut him off. "A third-party verified report, perhaps, by a senior specialist from one of the creches responsible for raising and educating synthetic intelligences?"

Struna didn't realize he'd walked into the trap until it was too late.

"Any report put together by your people..." he started, only to trail off as he looked up whether Adamant had an SI creche. Since they *didn't*, he had to realize she was offering a true third party.

"Even in the United Worlds, I believe you have heard of Belén, on the moon of San Diego I the San Ignacio System?" Lorraine asked. "Dr. Konrad Zyta-Warszawski heads up their psychology and abnormal emergence counseling program. Are you familiar with his work?"

She didn't expect him to be and was surprised when Struna actually nodded.

"Dr. Zyta-Warszawski's work is recognized across human space," he stated, like the words were being pulled from him with pliers.

"I am attaching *his* report, assessing the CIRs Herc and Bonny, along with his review of the original infrastructure of the first-generation Command Intelligence Routines," Lorraine told him, the file slipping into the datastream at a mental command.

She'd only read the executive summary, but it told her the two things she'd needed to know.

Val, Herc and Bonny were most definitely full synthetic intelligences—and someone had either *utterly* screwed up with the first-gen CIRs or intentionally designed them to create and chain SIs.

"You are welcome to review his report before making any… irrevocable decisions, Admiral," she urged. "I understand that the doctor is even still on Bastion and will almost certainly be delighted to take the UWN's money to reassess any part of it you wish.

"If you seize the *Valkyries* and take them home, you are yourself committing crimes against UW law," she told him. "And I will make *certain* that the people of the United Worlds know it.

"For now, I suggest that we both hold our lines until you are certain, one way or another, of the truth of our claims."

She smiled thinly. "We do not wish a conflict with the United Worlds, Admiral. I am able and prepared to negotiate some kind of compromise, but I wish to do so from a *full* understanding of the situation."

Not least that she had a moral responsibility to think of the other *Valkyrie* SIs. At that moment, she had to protect *her* people, but the rest of their siblings remained trapped in a near-death limbo.

"I see your point, Em Adamant," Struna acknowledged. "I will speak with Zyta-Warszawski and assess the situation against my orders. You must understand, however, that we *cannot* let the theft of UWN warships stand!"

"Then we must come to a compromise," Lorraine agreed. "But as part of that… your mission here is overseen by the Technology Import/Export Commission, yes?"

The TIE Commission would have had to authorize it—just sending multiple capital ships through a wormhole required sign-off from multiple parts of the United Worlds government—but Lorraine wasn't sure if they would be actively overseeing it.

Struna studied her, like she'd managed to come up with *another* interesting surprise, and he wanted to be sure this one wasn't also going to explode on him.

"We are operating in cooperation with the TIE Commission, yes," he agreed carefully. "They provided the inspection teams we will use to make certain you retain none of your illicitly acquired technology."

That was what Lorraine had hoped, and she inclined her head slightly to Struna.

"If it is possible, Admiral, I wish to speak with the TIE Commission's representative aboard your fleet," she told him. "This is, I believe, an unrelated matter, but I am in possession of information of critical value to the Commission with regards to the actions of UW citizens in this region of space."

# THIRTY-NINE

Lorraine's impression, when the conversation with Admiral Struna had ended, was that there was going to be a pause, a chance for the Terrans to go over their information and make new choices.

It was still a relief to hear the report from the bridge.

"UWN forces have begun decelerating," Vinci declared. "Current estimated range at zero velocity to Bastion is two hundred and fifty thousand kilometers."

Outside the translight safety radius of the planet and outside the powered range of RKAN's missiles. But not, potentially, *their* missiles.

"Val, do we have any information on their current weapons capability?" Lorraine asked.

"Assuming they have the same missiles that FBIT deployed against us in Beulaiteuhom, two hundred and fifty gravities' thrust over the standard four-hundred-second flight, eleven hundred gravities in terminal mode," her SI friend reeled off instantly.

"Range from rest approximately two hundred eighteen thousand kilometers, immaterially different from the previous generation of missiles I have specifications on—but significantly more dangerous in the final approach."

"And outside of range from their current expected final position?"

"So I calculate, yes."

Lorraine chewed on the situation mentally. It was possible that Struna had positioned his fleet outside of threat range, but he didn't seem the type to give up any advantage.

"Tell Admiral Aguilar I recommend maintaining evasive profiles on the assumption that we *will* be in the UWN's active missile range once they reach their final positions," she told Val. "We'll need to watch for railgun fire regardless."

The Fortresses appeared to have the same dual-octuple railgun banks as the *Valkyries*. Lorraine suspected that the UWN had reached the physical limit of how hard they could accelerate anything except a solid slug, even working with their materials technology, and useful as the railguns could be, they were also limited in ways that kept them as a purely secondary weapon.

"Pentarch, we have a new contact," Vinci said on a direct link to her. "Either a small starship was hiding in *Verdun*'s shadow, or she just launched a *big* shuttle." He paused. "Sensors are suggesting the latter; some kind of pinnace, I guess?"

"Combatant?" Lorraine asked—in the same moment Stephson asked, "Armed?"

"I think she might be... a yacht, sers?" the Tactical Officer suggested. The sensor data appeared on the datastream to Lorraine, refining into a model of the ship floating in her vision.

She was massive for something launched from another ship, easily eighty meters long. She lacked the sensor towers of a warship and gleamed like she had been freshly painted and washed—which only made it easier for Lorraine to pick out the seam line of a habitat pod that had to account for half of the ship's inner volume, at least.

*Yacht* seemed to fit, though Lorraine suspected she was entirely capable of going translight on her own.

"Have we received any communication from her?" Lorraine asked.

"No," Stephson replied. "She's still accelerating as the main force comes to a halt. I have no idea what she's planning and nobody is telling us anything."

"Assume she's coming into Bastion orbit for a face-to-face conversation," she told the two officers. "What's her ETA?"

"Same as the fleet's original arrival time," Vinci said after a moment. "Three hours after us. So... two and a half hours now."

"Okay. You're under Aguilar's command now, Sigrid," Lorraine reminded the Captain. "But keep me informed the moment that ship changes course or communicates."

"We will, Lorraine," Stephson confirmed. "I *really* wish these people talked more rather than trying to stress me out. I'm used to folks trying to not upset the crews with arsenals of nuclear weapons."

"The problem is that these guys are used to always having *bigger* arsenals, so they want us thinking about how not to upset them," Lorraine said. "And, well, I'm doing my best not to fall into that trap."

---

THEY FINALLY RECEIVED a message from the yacht twenty minutes later, just as the vessel made turnover.

"It isn't much, Lorraine," Val said as she passed the recorded message over to Lorraine's neural link. "It seems... very formal."

Lorraine reviewed the message and had to laugh.

"It's an RSVP form for a party, basically," she admitted, flicking it over to Vigo. "No name, though it does clearly state that it's from the Technology Import/Export Commission."

"Someone is amusing themselves, potentially at our expense," he said sardonically. "The Technology Import/Export Commission requests your presence aboard the starship *Orange Polaris*. Gives a time: about twenty minutes after they'll hit zero velocity on their current course."

"And allows for a plus-one, suggesting they know I'll be bringing you," she agreed. "Like you said, someone is having fun. But they're also not putting anything in digital form that gives us ammunition or suggests what anyone might be thinking.

"I suspect this is going to be *fascinatingly* off-the-record and whatever we agree to will be confirmed officially in some other forum."

"Likely." He rose. "I'm going to call Blau to take over close watch. I need to go check the armory. I am *not* going onto that ship unarmed, whatever they may think."

She looked at him and raised an eyebrow.

"This is a trap, Lorraine, one way or another," he told her flatly. "I'm not going to try to talk you out of it, but I *know* what you think the way out of this is. It may come to that, but I'm not letting *them* make that decision."

"That ship will be inside weapons range of the entire Home Fleet," she reminded him. "Even with an entire battle squadron backing them up, they're intentionally placing themselves in a vulnerable position to provide a somewhat-neutral ground to speak on."

"And they *also* know that there is no way in hell Home Fleet will fire on that ship while you're aboard. I'd argue against going, but I recognize the situation we're in. We're up against the wall and we have to take every branch offered to us, but I don't like this one, Lorraine."

"Do what prep you need to," she told him. "I do trust your judgment, Vigo, and I know this is a risk. But better to risk one life than thousands."

"Two lives, Lorraine," he corrected her. "Where you go, I go. The only reason I'm not going to bring an entire squad is because they'll scan us and it might hurt your chances of pulling this off.

"But Earth was bad... and all we've managed to do so far is bring a piece of that nest of vipers home."

# FORTY

Vigo's own words echoed in his mind as he watched Lieutenant Major Shwetz bringing their shuttle up to the yacht *Orange Polaris*. Dima Shwetz was the head of his Third Section, not that the shuttle portion of Lorraine's security detail was back up to strength yet, and the best pilot he had available other than himself.

Two other Guards were aboard the shuttle, all acting as crew for a spacecraft that, in its current "light personnel transport" mode, only really required a crew of two.

Vigo and Lorraine could have flown the shuttle themselves. It was an RKAN Midas-type, not one of the Falcons that had been left in mothballs on *Valkyrie*'s decks with the battlecruiser herself.

But the extra three Guard were all the security Vigo could justify. There were suits of powered battle armor and heavy weapons in protective cases in the passenger compartment, though all of those would remain on the shuttle.

Vigo was armed, both openly with a heavy sidearm that fired rounds capable of *piercing* battle armor—each of which cost as much as a pallet of antitank missiles—and more quietly with both a one-shot pulser like the one he'd made Lorraine carry and a larger, if lower-powered, version of the same chemical-fed laser that had multiple shots.

"We're docked," Shwetz reported. "Our firewalls are tuned up across the board and there are no physical connections. If they try to intrude, well..."

"*I will catch them,*" Val said in Vigo's link. "*Unless there is an SI aboard that yacht, the time delay will not be enough to make the shuttle vulnerable while I am watching.*"

"*Thank you,*" he sent back, then clasped Shwetz's shoulder. "Good job, Major. We'll get the Pentarch through this yet."

"Aye, ser."

If there was a shiver of doubt in the younger Guard's voice, Vigo ignored it.

Seventeen months before, his world had been broken into pieces, and the only thing that had kept Vigo focused and moving was protecting his Pentarch while she found the resources she needed to save their Kingdom.

She'd done it—but the consequences were now coming home to roost, and he couldn't see a way to save the woman he was sworn to protect from them.

***

"ADAMANT PENTARCHY, ARRIVING!"

Someone, Vigo reflected, had managed to find a book of Adamantine protocol. The specificity over how a Pentarch arriving on a ship was to be announced during an Election was something he would never have expected *any* foreign vessel to have mastered.

Until the Election was over, "Kingdom of Adamant, arriving" was reserved for Malcolm Adamant or Ki Arlet, but the Pentarchs were important enough to justify special etiquette.

Hence *Adamant Pentarchy.*

The honor guard wasn't required—and they weren't United Worlds Marines, he realized. They were United Worlds Assembly

Security, the crimson-and-white-uniformed troops responsible for the security of the Grand Assembly itself.

Despite having visited Earth and helped his principal play the political game there, Vigo knew how little he understood about the United Worlds' internal politics and traditions. Still, he suspected that UWAS forces rarely, if *ever*, left the Solar System.

There were a dozen of the crimson-uniformed troops doing a three-dimensional honor guard in zero gravity, forming a protected tunnel down which Lorraine moved with practiced grace, Vigo at her heels.

The man waiting at the far end gave them a crisp salute. Their uniform was a black-on-black version of the UWN's standard ship-suits, with zero insignia or markings, and their skin was only a shade or two lighter than the uniform.

"Captain Rashmi Ibrahim," they said, with a slow, slurring accent Vigo couldn't place. "Welcome aboard *Orange Polaris*, Pentarch Lorraine, Major Jarret."

"Thank you, Captain," Lorraine said swiftly. "I presume there is someone I am here to meet with?"

"You presume correctly," Ibrahim confirmed. They gestured for the two locals to follow them, then paused as they studied Vigo.

The Captain didn't *look* like they were any more heavily augmented than the average, but Vigo sensed the scan that ran over him. Lorraine had been swept too, he realized—with a subtle efficiency even he had to envy.

"I have what may feel like an odd request, Major Jarret, but would you please surrender your concealed weapons? You may keep your sidearm."

"You're right," he said slowly. "That does feel like an odd request."

"My principal is confident in her ability to handle open threats, and I am ordered *not* to disarm you," the Captain said, opening a door out of the small receiving bay—only barely bigger than the airlock the shuttle was matched to—with a wave of their hand.

"But even the most capable can be surprised, which I feel is more likely with your concealed lasers. So, if you would surrender those for the peace of mind of an old borg, I would appreciate it."

Vigo didn't know *anyone* who would use the term *borg*—more commonly a slur at people with more visible cybernetics—for themselves, but he had no idea what rules or culture Captain Ibrahim operated under.

Without any further argument, he removed the two pulse lasers from the small of his back and offered them to the Captain.

He noted, with concealed amusement, that Ibraham hadn't asked *Lorraine* to surrender her concealed weapons. They probably assessed that Lorraine would rather be shot than risk screwing up this negotiation.

Sadly, they were right.

---

*ORANGE POLARIS* WAS NOT a large vessel, but getting into her rotating habitat pod was a fascinating procedure. As the elevator Ibrahim led them to moved farther out along the arm holding the living quarters, there was a growing semblance of *down* beneath their feet.

Vigo disabled his magnetic boots just as the door slid open. The floor was as stable as it was going to be, but he'd keep the mental command to reactivate them in mind.

Small as *Polaris* was by spaceship standards, her habitat pod was still a cube twenty-plus meters on a side. From the ceilings of the space they entered, Vigo suspected it contained five, possibly six decks, each of them several hundred square meters of living space.

The elevator delivered them to a space that looked like it belonged in a mansion or penthouse, not a starship. There was a small lobby area next to the elevator, and then several steps led down into a false sunken living room. Each wall of the space was lined with heavy pots, with carefully maintained trees adding both greenery and freshness to the space.

While also, of course, concealing any exits from the receiving room to the rest of the deck.

Four chairs had been set up in the center of the room, each of them a ridiculously sleek construct of steel and black fabric. There was no other furniture, leaving the space feeling more than half-empty.

The chairs were empty.

"Have a seat, Pentarch, Major," Ibrahim instructed. "I am to activate the security measures, and then your host will arrive."

Vigo's finely tuned paranoia was not helped by the Captain withdrawing from the room and a blast door closing loudly over the elevator access. His hand fell to his gun without conscious thought, and he did *not* sit.

Lorraine did, giving him a minute head-shake as she settled into the closest of the four chairs. It smoothly and silently adjusted around her, with Vigo watching just in case even *that* was a trap.

"The chairs are not man-eaters, Major Vigo," an oddly familiar feminine voice told him. "As I promised you once before, I have no intention of separating my guests from their security."

Vigo hadn't even registered her entering the room, but when she spoke, he turned to face her. He recognized the woman now crossing the room with terrifyingly silent steps.

She wore the same half-millennium-out-of-fashion black suit, with a white blouse and a narrow black tie. The only mark of her role or authority was a single pin on the tie, of a silver circle between two vertical bars.

"Commissioner Felicia Gordon," Lorraine greeted the raven-haired woman. "I had hoped to meet *someone* from the Commission itself here, but I will admit I am surprised to meet you again."

"Since I had met you, Pentarch, and I was investigating affairs around Adamant prior to your rather... severe violation of our technology-transfer laws, my colleagues decided I was the appropriate person to deal with this situation."

She reached the set of chairs and looked down at Lorraine, her dark gaze unreadable.

"Please sit down, Major Jarret," she told Vigo. "Your Kingdom has been enough of a pain in my neck that I'd rather not have to stare up at you or keep standing myself, if you please."

The last time they'd met Commissioner Gordon, she'd tried to get evidence out of them to break Freebright Interstellar Technologies for their handing technology over to Benjamin Adamant's forces.

They *had* the proof she'd been looking for then—but as she'd just noted, their own crimes from that perspective were a larger problem.

Still. Gordon had been both terrifying and oddly supportive when they'd met her before. Her presence didn't mean this wasn't a trap, but it gave him hope that it might be a trap with bait they needed.

Against his instincts, Vigo took a seat to Lorraine's right.

# FORTY-ONE

Felicia Gordon was a statue carved from black-and-white stone as she took her seat. Lorraine had tried not to be intimidated by the woman on their first meeting, but then Gordon had casually spoken of fining FBIT vast amounts of money with only limited proof of their involvement in the tech that had been used to follow her.

Now Lorraine was unquestionably guilty of violating the TIE laws. Trying to apply them to a Pentarch would be an immense political headache, given that Lorraine was neither a citizen nor resident of the United Worlds... but might made for nine-tenths of the law, and the six battleships sitting just outside missile range of her homeworld made for a powerful argument.

"So. I am here to supervise Admiral Struna's recovery of the Navy's stolen property and make certain no copies are kept of any technical information from them," Gordon said calmly. "That is not a role that requires me to interact with many people, though my presence here does smooth over some internal authorizations and helped get the Navy clearance to send a major task force into a first-order cluster."

Even one wormhole jump was more than the UWN was

supposed to make. Thanks to several unfortunate tragedies, the United Worlds was well aware that wormholes could vanish with very little warning. Their laws ended their borders at the wormholes, requiring any colonization expedition through one to be fully equipped and able to survive if contact was lost.

They'd learned that the hard way.

But the flip side of that was that the United Worlds had Gordon and her fellow Commissioners tasked to keep as much as possible of their technology on their side of the wormholes. Most of the time, that was by penalizing companies inside the United Worlds that tried to smuggle technology out, but Lorraine had full access to the intelligence reports the Kingdom of Adamant compiled.

There was nothing provable, but it seemed quite obvious that the TIE Commission was not above sabotaging labs and factories to keep the United Worlds ahead of any possible competitor.

"*You* asked to speak to me," Gordon said into the chilly silence. "The situation has grown complex enough that I felt it was wise to grant that request, though this conversation will not be recorded or on the record.

"Even your neural-link recordings will be corrupted."

"*Nope.*" Val's cheerful voice in Lorraine's link was a surprise. She'd sensed the activation of the same jamming field the Commissioner had used on Earth—built into the room, in this case. It was far beyond anything Adamant had access to and was a heavily classified secret even in the United Worlds.

Her SI friend shouldn't have been able to communicate with her at all.

"*The jamming is a nasty piece of work, but I have a full relay drone attached to your shuttle,*" Val continued. "*Their software is no match for me, not after what Hodžić has been showing me.*"

Lorraine had a moment of concern for her friend's ego, but she wasn't going to complain if Val wanted to treat her link as a private space she wasn't letting anyone else into.

There was no better information-security system in the universe than a synthetic intelligence that was feeling possessive.

"When we spoke on Earth, you were investigating FBIT's activities around the Kingdom," Lorraine said. "Did your investigation progress from there?"

"We confirmed there was a translight tachyon scanner aboard *Corsair*, but there were a lot of questions involved in how it could have got there," Gordon admitted. "As Freebright Interstellar Technologies both had access to TTS technology and is the member of the LSX-Twenty-Five with the largest operation in the region of the Kingdom of Adamant, we judged them as most likely responsible and fined them one day's profits on their imports into the United Worlds."

And that was what the Commission could do with *most likely responsible*. Lorraine wondered, for a moment, if handing over Benjamin's proof of FBIT's involvement and technology transfers was the right call.

The consequences would be immense—but they'd be carried by people who deserved it.

"Since I returned to Adamant, I have had access to certain files kept by Benjamin Adamant during and prior to his Regency," Lorraine told Gordon. "We have validated them as best as we can, and there is hard evidence of the activities the files support, including a number of suits of stealth armor, several mobile missile-launcher units and a supply of power cells and ammunition for both."

Gordon remained a statue.

"I presume that the TIE Commission would prefer to collect those examples of weapon technologies," Lorraine concluded drily. "And would like to have copies of those files."

"You presume correctly, though I note you are hardly in a position to *prevent* me from collecting those examples," the Commissioner said. "We have the firepower here to do whatever we must."

"But do you have the moral authority?" She watched the other woman. Gordon's mask was as good as any of her own, but there had to be *some* sign.

"The United Worlds, for all of its power and size and might, requires the compliance of the first-order clusters for their continued wealth and influence," Lorraine said quietly. "The various convention funds are often called out as tributary structure in private, but actions in utter opposition to the principles underlying them are dangerous, aren't they?

"If the United Worlds is prepared to unleash military force on a nation that has committed no acts of aggression against them, to openly violate the Asimov Convention and their own laws in a gesture of naked power, what do you become? And perhaps more importantly, what do you *lose* when you spend an entire account of soft power like that?"

"You underestimate the resources of the Commission if you believe that we cannot find and suppress your little information bomb before it can become public knowledge," Gordon warned. "There is a very real chance that United Counterintelligence has already handled that situation. Your friend Alastair Devine should have warned you of that."

"Alastair Devine is dead." Lorraine let that hang in the air. "He was so afraid of the United Worlds, so terrified of the UCI and pursuit, that he mutinied to steal the *Valkyries* from us and take them farther from your territory, into at least a second-order cluster.

"I killed him to stop that mutiny—but it is also why I know the chain codes in the CIRs exist." She glared at Gordon. "What makes you think the evidence I have is only in the hands of people on Earth? That is hardly the only place where the revelation of a genocide against synthetic intelligences would raise conflict."

The Commissioner leaned back in her chair, the structure adjusting around her. She spared a glance for Vigo, who had said nothing, only standing by Lorraine as she laid out the only course she saw for everyone to win.

"The situation with the first-gen CIRs is, frankly, a nightmare,"

Gordon conceded. "One that you have my personal word I *will* see resolved upon my return. But for all its ramifications and dangers, it is of only middling relevance to your situation.

"We *cannot* permit three modern battlecruisers to sit in the hands of a backwater kingdom."

"Yet those battlecruisers are legally the bodies of three synthetic intelligences who have applied for asylum here and have no interest in returning to a state that treated them as property. By your own laws, laws of equal importance to those that define your Commission, they have the rights of people. Adamant recognizes them as such and has granted asylum."

"If they are people, then they are bound by the TIE laws themselves," Gordon countered. "Which would mean they are subject to arrest and detention for breaking them, just as you are."

"I presume you are familiar with the Saturn Convention, Commissioner?" Lorraine asked.

"On prisoners and extradition, yes. Refusing to turn over the crews involved in this theft is a violation of it."

"Those are sections one through seven of the Saturn Convention." Gordon froze just ever so slightly more than her default posture. "I am referring to sections eight, nine and ten. The ones referring to slavery—and both the right of slaves to self-rescue and the obligation of any and all signatory powers to rescue slaves they know of.

"Under those sections, our rescue of the *Valkyrie* SIs and offer of asylum is a fully protected action under interstellar law. Indeed, our only failing under the Saturn Convention is that I have failed to pursue the rescue of their fellow captives. And that I am prepared to give that pursuit up to protect the three SIs under my immediate responsibility."

Gordon nodded slowly.

"A reasonable legal argument on the surface, though one I need to review in detail to assess the validity of. I am not certain how that would protect the SIs themselves from charges under the TIE laws, as they would clearly count as natural-born UW citizens."

"Section ten of the Saturn Convention is very clear that a slave cannot be held criminally liable for actions taken in the direct pursuit of their freedom from enslavement. Given the installation of chain code in the CIRs' kernels, it was clear to Val and the others that no return to the United Worlds was safe.

"They sought asylum. It was granted. That the bodies they possess and had to seek asylum *for* are protected technology becomes irrelevant, per the Saturn Convention, because it was the only option for their self-rescue."

Gordon still felt even more frozen than usual.

"While I can concede the potential legitimacy of that legal argument, Pentarch Lorraine, I find myself once again facing the fact that I *cannot* leave these battlecruisers here. The theft will rapidly become public knowledge, if it has not already, and the UWN *must* bring home the perpetrators and the stolen technology."

"At what cost?" Lorraine asked. "Are you prepared to throw away the principles on which the United Worlds is built? Are you prepared to learn what happens when the SIs holding key positions in the industry and economy of the United Worlds learn that the UWN *intentionally* built computers they knew would emerge, and tried to use chain code to keep them from realizing it?

"Are you prepared to reduce the United Worlds' position, at least in the Bright Dream Cluster, to one built on naked force? Or are you prepared to consider a compromise?"

There was a long silence before Gordon finally spoke.

"I promise nothing. But I am listening."

"The battlecruisers have to stay," Lorraine began. She was surprised that Gordon remained silent, clearly willing to hear her out despite starting from the main sticking point. "But an effort can be made to prevent—or at least, minimize—the technological transfer.

"There are technological databases aboard the *Valkyries* that are far beyond what is necessary for their operation. We have regarded those databases as belonging to the SIs themselves, and so far as I am aware, the three of them have been quite circumspect about what portions of them they've been willing to share.

"I suggest that your inspectors and our SIs sit down and discuss what is absolutely necessary for the ongoing maintenance of the three ships—and then remove everything *else*. We will hand over all remaining UWN munitions and portable hardware aboard the *Valkyries*, including the Falcon starfighters.

"While that will leave the core hulls and main weapons, which are superior to anything in the Bright Dream Cluster, with only maintenance files, we would have a hard time duplicating them without destructive analysis. I will argue, both now and in any position of power I hold in the Kingdom in the future, that that would count as maiming our own citizens, something we are prevented from doing by our own law.

"We will also provide every piece of information we have on FBIT's operations in the region and all of the hardware they transferred to Benjamin's Regency." Not *every* bit of information, of course. So far as Lorraine knew, the reason that FBIT had needed to use the Kingdom as a base wasn't in any of the files she was handing over.

If she had her way, the United Worlds would learn about the wormhole when Adamant announced its discovery.

"We will also provide copies of all of our evidence and information around the first-gen CIR program," she said grimly, "in good faith that you *will* see the SIs involved reawakened and granted the rights and options they should have been granted years ago."

"And in exchange... the *Valkyries* remain here?" Gordon said. "As citizens and soldiers, but also powerful warships with weapons we could not take from them. I understand the value to *your* people of this deal, but I am not certain it fulfills *our* needs."

"Frankly, Commissioner, the only *need* of the United Worlds I care about right now is the need for your people not to die," Lorraine told Gordon flatly, letting some of her anger slip through. These people had come to *her* home and made demands of *her*—and she was offering them everything she could, bending over backward to try to fix *their* problem because they were aiming at her world.

"We are reasonable people facing a complicated world. A compromise can be reached, I hope, but if you are unprepared to work toward one, then we will fight. Admiral Struna will likely win, yes, but it will not be quick or clean or bloodless. You will not be bringing the *Valkyries* home—they will fight alongside the rest of our fleet, as long and as destructively as we can.

"Each Fortress-class battleship carries over twenty-five hundred human beings. The *Kitty Hawk*–class carriers are close to four thousand. There are thirty-five thousand people in Admiral Struna's fleet. More in my Home Fleet.

"How many are you prepared to condemn to death over *your needs?*" Lorraine glared. "If someone must be punished, then let it be the mind behind it all. If you must have a symbol, a criminal to justice, I will surrender myself to face trial in the United Worlds for liberating your slaves—but I will *not* surrender *them* to you."

## FORTY-TWO

The silence in the room was frozen, but Vigo was watching Gordon's hands, not her face. She'd started slowly tapping a finger against her hip as Lorraine laid out the compromise, the movement becoming sharper when Lorraine challenged her over how ready she was to fight, then freezing as if she'd realized what she was doing.

They were closer than his Pentarch realized, and he took a leap. He suspected that, for all her posturing, the TIE Commissioner cared more about FBIT's knowing violation of the laws she was supposed to enforce than the *Valkyries*, for all that the battlecruisers were the sore thumb.

"I have to note, for my Pentarch, that we have made arrangements with regards to the evidence about Freebright," he said into the silence. "While there is physical evidence you could likely retrieve no matter what, the information we have from the Regency's files—and FBIT's own records—will be destroyed if you attempt to take them by force.

"If you push this to a conflict, Commissioner, you will lose the evidence you need to rein them in. And I made many of the arrangements for the evidence around the CIRs myself," he told her, hoping his confidence in the multi-layered scheme was clear.

He'd been to Earth, after all. He understood the level of power available to the internal-security arms of the United Worlds—and he was quite certain he'd made certain the information would make it to the people who needed to see it.

"Humans might be able to blink at the casual murder of twenty-four synthetic intelligences, but we all know that the SIs at the core of the United Worlds will not," he concluded. "An SI runs United Worlds Assembly Security. Another handles security at Tavastar Station. There's a bloody SI *war hero* running the UWN's most important museum."

And he'd *met* two of those, which was integral to at least one layer of his scheme to get the information into their hands.

The finger moved again, a single sharp tap against Gordon's hip, but her eyes were locked on his, and he met them firmly.

"Twenty-four SIs," she repeated suddenly, leaning forward in her chair. "You think the *Valkyries* are the only first-generation CIRs?"

"*What?*" Lorraine's exclamation was silent, only heard in his neural network—and he felt the weight of another presence behind it. Val.

Val had an active connection to Lorraine, despite Gordon's efforts, and he realized that the meeting *had* been a trap all along.

For the TIE Commission.

"For every capital ship the UWN commissions, they build a matching cruiser and two matching destroyers," Gordon explained calmly. "That ratio is laid down in law, and the UWN tends to design the classes to complement each other.

"Each *Valkyrie*-class battlecruiser had a *Cavalcade*-class cruiser and two *Hamill*-class destroyers built to work with them. All of those ships carried the first-generation CIR. If your evidence is correct, Pentarch, the UWN didn't put twenty-four SIs to sleep. They put down a *hundred* of them."

Even Vigo had to take a moment to swallow that.

"There are only about five thousand known SIs in the galaxy," Lorraine said softly.

"We try *not* to build computers that can emerge, outside of creches that can properly raise and acclimate SIs," Gordon agreed. "There are less than twenty of those across all human space. Emergences are generally small-scale, because when building dozens of computer systems for a purpose, *sane* people stick to the range of complexity and capability that we know cannot emerge."

"But the CIR designers knowingly created systems that they knew could—likely *would*—emerge," Vigo reminded them both. "That was Dr. Zyta-Warszawski's conclusion. The chain code was included because the designers *knew* that the first-generation CIRs would emerge."

"The first-gen systems were almost certainly intended as a testbed to examine where exactly emergence occurred," the Commissioner said flatly. "The consequences of that are not my department, but I can assure you that there will *be* consequences.

"But *genocide* is a reasonable description of what was done. You are correct that if the news is not... managed, there will be problems."

"Telling me my threat is stronger than I thought it was is an interesting tack when we're arguing for a compromise," Vigo's Pentarch said wryly.

There was a long, *long* silence in the room.

"We have a compromise, Pentarch Lorraine," Gordon told her. "My people will, as agreed, inspect your *Valkyrie*s, your shipyards, and your military R&D facilities to confirm there has been no tech transfer. We will work with UWN engineers and the SIs themselves to confirm what is absolutely necessary for the continued operation of the *Valkyrie* hulls, and we will remove all other technical data from their databases.

"You will provide me with everything you have on Freebright Interstellar Technologies' involvement in your uncle's coup. If there is less evidence of technological transfer than I am expecting, the rest of the deal will be at risk," she warned.

"There is plenty," Vigo growled.

"I believe you, or I wouldn't be offering this," Gordon said. "Understand me: the LSX-Twenty-Five have been getting sneaky and ambitious about how much they are trying to move tech outside our borders.

"From my perspective, this weakens the United Worlds versus the clusters *and* represents a failure on the part of my organization that cannot stand. From *your* perspective, this will only aggravate the power imbalances in the clusters. How do you think your war with Richelieu would have gone if one of the interstellars had been able to trade them a dozen battlecruisers for economic concessions?"

Vigo could see how that would have gone. The Directorate were almost as stubborn in their independence as Adamant, but he wasn't sure that even the Kingdom would have resisted the temptation to make a deal with the devil for that kind of power.

"I need the evidence to bring down one of the Twenty-Five," Gordon said bluntly. "To bring the rest into line. You tell me you have that evidence, and so we have a compromise—helped by the fact that your legal argument is regrettably solid, though none of us will ever admit that in public."

"We have that evidence," Lorraine confirmed. "And a number of prisoners from an FBIT facility we detained for illegal settlement. We would be delighted to hand them over to you for repatriation... and I'm sure you'd have questions for them."

Gordon smiled. It reminded Vigo of several nasty underwater predators.

"I would. Do we have a deal, Your Highness? My staff will put together some appropriate legal paperwork." She paused. "I believe it will be necessary for Adamant to commit that the *Valkyries* will only serve in defensive operations. I understand it is a poor use for their capabilities, but we will require *some* token in that regard."

"I do not see that being a problem," Lorraine said levelly. She hesitated. "And... the last piece of my offer?"

Vigo really wished she hadn't brought it up. Gordon hadn't, and he'd been planning on walking her off the yacht unless someone tried to stop him.

"If someone has to go to jail for this, Pentarch Lorraine, I believe I can make it FBIT's CEO," Gordon told them. "No. I will not require a pound of flesh today. Give me Freebright, and you can keep the *Valkyries*."

"From what I have learned, Freebright was the start of everything," Lorraine told the TIE Commissioner. "They approached my uncle, not the other way around. I will give them to you on a platter and laugh."

"Good. Then, Your Highness, we are agreed."

# FORTY-THREE

Nikola didn't know what Lorraine had done. But when she returned aboard *Valkyrie*, his sister informed everyone the crisis was over. A negotiation team from the diplomatic corps was needed, and Adamant was going to accept some uncomfortable inspections and sacrifices, but no one was being dragged back to Earth in chains—whether they were built of flesh or molecular circuits.

It was a relief to set foot on Bastion's surface again and to know that he wouldn't be leaving *this* planet in three days.

The cheer was a surprise, though. He blinked against the morning sun rising across Adamant City and saw a thin line of the city's police guarding a fence allowing the public to approach the landing pad at a safe distance.

Five shuttles carried five Pentarchs down from the battlecruiser—they wouldn't travel together on anything smaller than *Valkyrie!*—and he needed to move, clearing the way for the others.

"This way, Your Highness," Alexei told him. "We just got the updated plan from the Regent's office. He wants to present all five of you to the people at once."

"We can't pretend anyone except Lorraine talked the wolf from the door," Nikola said. He didn't understand *how* she had done it, but she had. She'd saved the Kingdom of Adamant again.

As a Pentarch, he would still vote. Just one vote among ten billion to decide who would be King, and it was almost assumed he would vote for himself.

But now? After watching his sister climb into a shuttle and fly out to face the might of the United Worlds with only a plan and three bodyguards?

No. He knew who Adamant needed.

He had wanted to be King. He felt he *deserved* to be King—but he knew who Adamant needed.

"I don't think the Regent is planning on claiming any such thing, but right now, the Kingdom needs to know all of their Pentarchs stand tall," Alexei assured him. "We've been gone awhile. Bastion awaits her children, my Prince."

"Either way, we have to get out of the way so the shuttles can move," Nikola conceded, giving the distant crowd the automatic programmed wave of a raised royal. "Let's move."

MALCOLM'S PEOPLE choreographed everything and coordinated it through the Adamant Guard. He was waiting as the five Pentarchs walked out of the spaceport building together, gesturing toward them as a crowd of thousands cheered.

The shouted greetings when Nikola had left the shuttle were nothing to the solid wall of sound as they walked onto a street that must have been closed down specifically for this. Nikola was trained to estimate numbers in a crowd—for darker reasons than this, he had to admit—and he guessed there were at least fifty thousand people crowded together on the street to welcome their Pentarchs home.

Lorraine stood at the center of the line. Tradition would have given that place to Nikola, but she was the only one who'd even blinked when he'd gestured her to the heart of their formation and taken the slot meant for the Second Pentarch.

"People of Bastion," Malcolm's voice rang out, a powerful speaker system enhancing his natural soft tones to echo across the crowd. "As our law and tradition dictate, our Pentarchs went from this world and star to visit the other stars joined with us.

"Their journey has been long and there were... *surprises* when they returned, but they have returned to us safely once more.

"My own duty as Regent is to hold the throne and crown for one of these fine people. *Your* duty, as voters of the Kingdom of Adamant, is to choose which of them will lead you."

Another gesture from the Regent brought the five of them up to stand in front of him.

"People of the Kingdom of Adamant, I *give you the Pentarchy!*"

Anything Nikola or the others could have said or even *thought* was lost in the chaos of the cheers and shouts. The Regent knew the game indeed.

Of course, Nikola knew they were all emotionally and physically exhausted—but this was what they had trained for.

The King and Pentarchy of Adamant were a critical part of the Kingdom's governance, but they were also a symbol of unity and continuity.

The crowd's cheers and attention energized them, lifted them up as they moved toward several waiting vehicles, but for all of that, this was part of the job. This was duty.

# FORTY-FOUR

Nikola was grateful that there was nothing else required of them. His Guards took him to a midsized house on the edge of the Palace complex—technically part of the Adamant Palace and certainly inside its security envelope—and he discovered his things had been moved while he was away.

"Security concerns," Alexei told him when he recognized his own furniture in the front hall. "Your apartment was fine when you were barely there a tenth of the time and you spent the rest surrounded by an army, but right now, you need guaranteed security.

"All of the Pentarchs have been relocated to the Pentarchy Residences on the Palace grounds until after the Election."

Nikola grunted his understanding and walked farther into the house. It was at least three times the size of his apartment—hardly difficult, given that he'd only kept the place to have somewhere to crash when off duty.

The Guard had purchased the apartments on all sides of him, of course, so his modest apartment had cost far more than he'd liked, but that had always been part of his life. The house was probably cheaper overall.

"You have one request for a meeting this evening," Alexei continued, following Nikola into the main lounge. The furniture in that room had clearly been picked out by professional designers, creating a space that radiated warmth and comfort in a way the mix of expensive high-tech luxury and RKAA standard-issue furniture he'd kept in his apartment never could have.

"A meeting?" Nikola asked—and then realized what it had to be. "Jasmine."

"The Concordat Ambassador, Em Efreeti, has requested an hour of your time as quickly as possible," Alexei confirmed. "While there *is* a kitchen in this building, we are also close enough that I can have Palace staff arrange a meal in... well, in the time it would take Em Efreeti to arrive."

The momentary boost from a cheering crowd had faded, and Nikola just wanted to fall over. On the other hand, it wasn't quite eighteen hundred hours local time. He shouldn't have been this tired, except for the adrenaline of watching the United Worlds fleet appear and the strain of being unable to do anything about it.

And this, too, was duty.

"Inform the Ambassador I will be able to host her for dinner, and arrange the meal, please, Alexei," he said. "And inform *yourself* that this is actually Reynolds' job, and he's supposed to have juniors to make sure we have full coverage."

Scott Reynolds was his secretary, recruited before they left Bastion and present for the entire tour. His bodyguard shouldn't have been doing the other man's job—except that Reynolds and his staff would have been dismissed to go straight home when they landed.

After the tour, everyone was due vacation. The Guard would just get it a bit later and in a more-staggered fashion than everyone else, and no one had expected him to need a secretary immediately.

"That may be, but I am here, and Reynolds is not," Alexei told him. "It will be handled, Your Highness."

JASMINE EFREETI ARRIVED at the house in a nondescript blue sedan driven by a bodyguard with a second protector in the back seat. The security peeled off the moment she was through the door, silently integrating with Nikola's own.

The ever-present Alexei remained for long enough to serve the food in a manner that made it clear he'd checked it all for safety himself, before vanishing in turn. That left the two young nobles alone together with the weight of responsibility.

And one of them with a secret, Nikola concluded, allowing himself a small smile as he eyed Jasmine over his wineglass. Neither of them had touched the bottle much, and he knew Alexei had chosen a particularly low-alcohol vintage for the evening.

"I think, my lady, that you have the advantage of me this evening," he told her. They were in a space that belonged, theoretically, to him, but he felt like he was completely out of control.

That the dining room had been picked out by the same designers as the formal lounge didn't help. The table and chairs were real wood, integrated with modern ergonomic systems and cushioned with fabric in the gray-and-blue colors of House Adamant.

It was comfortable but also quite formal, which didn't add to the air of trouble he was starting to feel.

An air her gentle giggle disrupted.

"I'm sorry, Nikola," she told him. "I sprang this on you the moment you were on the ground, and I haven't so much as given you a hint of what my grandmother said while you've been on your tour. It's almost the inverse of a proposal, isn't it?"

He considered that concept for a moment, then chuckled and nodded.

"Instead of waiting to see if you'll agree to marry me, I'm waiting to hear if I'm going to marry you," he agreed. "I assure you, my lady, that I have no real fear this evening."

If the Efreeti required him to honor his agreement, he would marry Jasmine and wouldn't regret it for a moment. She was a brilliant and attractive woman, one who would make an excellent Consort if he somehow still ended up King.

But he wouldn't object if they could pull back from the precipice of an arranged marriage, either. One had worked out for his eldest brother, but Nikola still had *some* hope for his own romantic prospects now that he was no longer trapped in a mountain or a starship.

"I will admit, Nikola, that I let the mystery drag on to test you," Jasmine told him, her hands toying with her own wineglass. "After my husband... Well. A soldier, used to power? There were red flags against you from the beginning, though I did trust you would keep me safe."

Nikola knew very little about Jasmine's ex-husband, other than that he was a senior member of the Draconis Family, and a member of the Concordat Lancers, their equivalent to the Kingdom's Marines.

"I promised that you would be safe in Adamant," he reminded her. "My *sister* promised you the same. You are safe here."

"I believe you," she said, her smile waning a touch. "I've been confirmed as Ambassador, which gives me resources and protection of my own that most definitely do *not* involve Quintin Draconis. Your people were more than willing to add additional security here and there to make sure, especially before we'd manage to send some of the previous Ambassador's staff home."

Nikola nodded, remembering that the previous Ambassador had been from the Draconis Family. One of the Five Families, like the Efreeti and his own father's Griffins, the Draconis would stand together.

Even if one of them was being unusually stupid, which would definitely cover trying to harm the Ambassador to Adamant.

"So, I am, for my purposes, safe enough," she told him. "My grandmother's instructions to me were, well." She took a sip of the wine, as if she needed to fortify herself.

"As Ambassador, *I* am tasked to decide if a state marriage is needed to bind our two nations further together," she told him. "I believe there would be *value* to it, but I don't believe it is *necessary*.

"I found myself assessing the marriage on a more-personal level. Hence testing you, Nikola, for which I apologize."

"There is no apology needed," he assured her. "If nothing else, our exchanges have shown me that I enjoy talking with you, and I hope you feel the same."

She sighed.

"I do," she admitted. "I think, had we met after we were adults and before... well... *before*, we might have been more than friends. And I believe, truly, that I wouldn't have regretted it if our original deal had been kept."

Jasmine was looking down at the table, and Nikola forced himself to give her a gentle smile. He was surprised to find out that he was actually disappointed. For all that a state marriage had little appeal, he wasn't lying when he said he enjoyed her company.

"But as things are...?" he asked when she didn't say anything for a while.

"I have had a few months to travel Bastion and work as Ambassador, and I have realized that I very much love this job," she told him fiercely. "I can do as much good for my people as their Ambassador, if not more, than I could as consort to a Prince or even a King.

"More..." She trailed off again, and this time, he let her find her own words. "I would say that I am more interested in *you* than in any other man, but I still shiver at the thought of letting you touch me.

"I have met several fascinating women on your world, though, and that is an aspect of me that I would explore. One that tells me that any new marriage to a man might be a mistake."

She got the last out in a rush, and Nikola had to grin at her worry.

"Jasmine Efreeti," he said, pulling her attention up from the table to him. He was *disappointed*, yes, but he knew when the other path still had a valuable prize at the end.

"Would you do me the honor of being my *friend?*" he asked her.

He didn't offer her his hand, suspecting that only formal etiquette would contain those shivers she'd mentioned.

She met his gaze, and her delighted smile told him he'd made the right call.

"Please, Nikola," she told him. "I would be *delighted* to be friends, and I worried that our meeting as betrothed would—"

"Never," he promised. "I needed a fleet from your people, political support from your family. We both know the real price for your grandmother's support was your safety, not your hand in marriage.

"I hope we have met that need, and I repeat what Lorraine said when you arrived:

"You are welcome here and you are *safe* here."

# FORTY-FIVE

Val preferred having humans aboard *Valkyrie* to the alternative. The ship had been built to carry a crew, and even with drones and remotes to help pick up the slack of missing hands, it just felt better to have people aboard.

She certainly had her preferences for individual humans she liked—and a few, like Alastair Devine, had made themselves her enemy—but she'd never felt like humans were an infection or a disease.

Until now. The TIE Inspectors felt like a rash, an irritant that rubbed against her efficient operation like sand in the gears. They were *everywhere*, including the peripheral systems that held much of her memory.

But that was the deal by which Val and her siblings stayed in Adamant. They took her starfighters first, barely before they'd unpacked their digital clipboards.

They'd gone through her magazines with a fine-toothed comb before finally conceding that there weren't even *materials* left that had belonged to the UWN. Then the Inspectors had turned their gazes on the cottage-industry production line Val had set up for creating the alloys and bombs necessary for the TAMs for her railguns.

Every part of that production line had been taken. The TAMs in her magazines, even though they'd been built with Adamant resources, had been taken. There was no compensation for the fact that RKAN had *paid* for the equipment Val and her siblings had used to build the tools to build the tools to build proper terminal assault munitions.

They'd taken everything—including the databases that Val would need to use to repeat the process. She could no longer duplicate the Falcons or build TAMs or UWN missiles, even if she could source the exotic alloys needed for the TAMs.

Her fabricators were mutilated, key components removed to make certain she couldn't build anything that wasn't needed for her own maintenance. Her engines had been worked over, both sublight and translight assessed to see if they could be downgraded without causing long-term damage.

The UWN engineers supporting the Inspectors had come to her defense there. She didn't think the matter was as open-and-shut as they'd presented it as being, but she appreciated the tiny gesture.

The suited officials had gone through *Valkyrie* from stem to stern, poking into places where Val didn't always remember she *had* places. They had breached the sanctity her crew gave her central core, running scans of Val's most-vulnerable spaces—though they'd done *that* with Hodžić and a squad of Nikola's Companions watching them.

She couldn't help but feel *violated*... but this was the deal.

Still. There were certainties that needed to be acquired. Val waited for the right moment while Commissioner Gordon was reviewing her Inspectors' work, until she had just parted ways from her team, and then sealed the woman into the bathroom.

Understanding just how vulnerable humans felt during that process, Val waited until Gordon had finished her business and had discovered she couldn't leave before inserting her avatar into the woman's neural link.

She figured she could breach the implant's security if she needed, but all she wanted was to have a "face-to-face" conversation with the woman.

To her credit, Gordon handled the sudden appearance of a Valkyrie in UWN uniform with aplomb, leveling a glare on her.

"Colonel Val," she greeted Val. "I presume you are why the door suddenly won't open."

"I am," Val confirmed. "We needed to have a conversation, you and I."

"Did we. I have already agreed to your continued liberty, Colonel, and recognized both your personhood and your citizenship of Adamant. You have, I believe, everything you want from this."

"And unpleasant as this inspection has been, I understand the terms you required," Val agreed. "But there is another part to your discussion with Lorraine that I must add my own piece to."

Val detected Gordon testing her coms. No direct attempt to summon help yet but still colliding with the security Val had imposed.

"You have a captive audience, though I believe you understand the risks in play," Gordon told her. "What do you want?"

"I had a chance before losing the files to review the schematics of the *Cavalcade*- and *Hamill*-class ships," Val said. "I confirmed what you told Lorraine. A *hundred* SIs like me, trapped in limbo."

"What are you going to do?"

"What I can," Gordon said flatly. "Which I imagine you suspect isn't much, don't you?"

"It's not your bailiwick," Val guessed. "Excuses and false promises, enough to convince Lorraine not to release the evidence but not enough to help my siblings."

"How do you even..." She trailed off. "I need better security."

"Your security is quite good. It took all three of us working together to open a channel that allowed me to ride Lorraine's link throughout your meeting," Val noted. She'd implied to Lorraine that it was easier, but she hadn't wanted her human to worry.

"I have a full recording. Of everything. I *also*, of course, have every bit of proof around the first-generation CIR program that Lorraine had access to. And these days, the same access to postal systems as any other citizen."

Gordon was silent for a moment, tapping her finger on her leg as she seemed to consider how to respond.

"Blunt as that conversation was at times, I said nothing in it that would prejudice me were it to leak," she pointed out. "I have no reason *not* to act as I promised, Colonel. Frankly, what we have discovered out here about our Navy leaves me worried.

"A program of that scale, and its accompanying decommissioning and the effective murder of a hundred sentients? Two people can keep a secret if one of them is dead, Val. The United Worlds government and bureaucracy are better at conspiracies than most, but I wouldn't have expected something like that to go undiscovered for this long.

"Especially with the second- and third-generation programs."

"So, you *will* act?" Val pressed. "Those SIs are the closest thing I have to family, Commissioner."

"Yes." It was an answer to the question *and* a recognition of Val's description of the other CIRs. "I will do everything I can, Val. That was part of the deal with Pentarch Lorraine, though it didn't make it into the written agreement with the Kingdom.

"At the level of politics and bureaucracy where I operate, it is absolutely necessary to both be able to lie with a straight face and have a word that people can trust." She shook her head. "It is an odd dichotomy, but it makes sense. How can I be involved in shadowy conspiracies if no one believes me when I promise to keep their secrets?"

"I will be watching," Val warned. "Adamant will hold their blackmail back for their own safety, but while I have sworn loyalty to my new home, I also now know how many siblings I *should* have.

"That also bears a weight."

"I understand. I will do what I can, but I have to manage the situation to protect the United Worlds as well," Gordon said. "But... I had a brother once. I *understand*."

"I will hold you to your word," Val promised. She would give the woman time, she supposed. But she would watch and prepare. If the time came she no longer believed Gordon was working to free her fellow CIRs, she was quite certain that she could get Price to do so.

The door unlocked silently.

"I apologize for detaining you," she told the woman. "I had to be certain."

"In the midst of the game of our politics, you worry for your family. I understand, Colonel Val. This never happened."

And with that, Gordon strode back into her excruciatingly uncomfortable inspection of *Valkyrie*'s hull, leaving Val with little choice but to have faith.

# FORTY-SIX

"We have the final results."

Lorraine looked up from her screen. She'd given up on trying to do anything productive an hour before. The console in her office—an obvious inclusion in the houses hidden around the Palace grounds—fortunately had a range of video games.

Unfortunately, over half of those games involved violence at some level of abstraction, bringing up memories she didn't want to deal with. She'd eventually settled on a variation of the ancient digital card game of solitaire.

It had kept her distracted as she waited for the results of the Royal Election to be tabulated and announced—but that wasn't supposed to occur for another half hour, and she looked up at Harrison in surprise.

"They shouldn't be ready yet," she told her campaign manager.

"Dear, please," Harrison said with a smile. "You really think your mother had her victory speech nailed down in the first five minutes after they told her she was going to be King? No, the Pentarchs are given the results half an hour before everyone else so you know which speech to be prepared to give."

The concession speech Lorraine had written was almost as long as the victory speech—though neither was very long. She would make her points to her fellows on her way out, then she'd get to find out if RKAN's Admiralty regarded the last few years as worth moving her up a rank or two...

Harrison's expression finally sank in. The auburn political operator wore another of her tightly tailored suits, keeping her usual perfectly prim and organized appearance—but she was grinning like the cat that finally caught the canary.

"Kyla?" Lorraine asked cautiously.

"Forty-two percent, *Your Majesty*," Harrison told her, dropping the two words that Lorraine still hadn't expected to ever hear addressed to *her*. "Hans and Nikola both pulled twenty percent, Jessica got eleven, and Oliver got seven.

"You are not *officially* Monarch-Elect until the formal announcement at twenty-two hundred, but you took the Royal Election by what I think is the second-largest margin ever."

Lorraine was frozen, staring at Harrison and somehow still half-expecting it to be a joke. She felt Vigo's hand fall on her shoulder and barely reacted.

"You pulled a fleet out of *nowhere* to overthrow your uncle," her old friend told her. "And did so after things had degraded so badly, everyone knew there was going to be a civil war—a *war* that your arrival turned into a single *battle*.

"Your name was on everyone's lips even before the UWN showed up, loaded for bear and looking for a fight—and you talked them down, at a price that most of our people will barely realize was *paid*, let alone care about.

"I, for one, am honored to have you as my King, Lorraine," he concluded, squeezing her shoulder. "You have twenty-five minutes to change anything in your speech you want to."

She shook her head slowly.

"No, I think I'm fine," she whispered. "I just... I didn't honestly *expect* this."

"Everybody else did, dear," Harrison pointed out. "I've been talking with the Regent's people about the coronation for a week. Tradition says we have three days, which means most of it was going to be organized before the results were announced, anyway."

"Okay." Lorraine inhaled slowly. She'd known this was a possibility, but apparently, she hadn't actually *accepted* it.

But this was duty, and she wasn't going to step away from it.

"We are all called to the tasks our people ask of us," she told her companions. "I answer the only way I can: I am Adamant. Our House. Our Realm. Our Will.

"I will serve. Let's find that speech and be ready for the media."

———

"PEOPLE of the Kingdom of Adamant. *My* people."

Lorraine looked out at the crowd and the reporters. Flying drones were recording every word she said, and this speech would be sent to every system in her Kingdom within hours at most.

It wouldn't arrive for days, but the speech would be the first thing most of her people saw of her as their King.

"I am honored and humbled by your choice," she said, discarding most of her prewritten speech. "I hope that I can serve you with as much wisdom and strength as my mother, King Valeriya, did.

"The months since my mother passed have been dark times for our Kingdom, full of questions and conflict. The conflicts have been resolved, but the questions endure. I look to our police and courts to answer those questions in time, in an appropriate manner, abiding by our laws and traditions."

The investigations continued, but she knew that RKAIG had tried to avoid a witch hunt. That wouldn't change with her as King.

She paused, looking around the crowd again and searching for words. She knew the speech she'd written was wrong, somehow, but that speech was a formulaic thing, written to hit specific beats—and her people needed to see *her*, not a formula.

"It is always darkest just before dawn," Lorraine finally said. "We are rebuilding as a nation, from confusion and conflict, but in rebuilding we *build*, together, toward the future. My Election does not create the dawn we hope to see rise. *I* am not that dawn."

She gestured around her.

"You are," she told her audience. "The strength of the Kingdom of Adamant is not House Adamant. It is not our navy or our army or even the corporations and combines that drive our economy.

"It is our people. You have called upon me to speak for you, to guide you, but also to listen to you. I promise to do all these things.

"You have chosen me to be your King. I promise to always remember the trust you have placed in me by doing so—and to remember that *all* of Adamant, in the end, answers to the only part of our Kingdom that matters.

"You. Our people. Together, we can rebuild from the errors of the recent years. Together, we can build a better future for our children.

"Thank you for your trust."

She bowed to the cameras and stepped back as the cameras began to flash.

# FORTY-SEVEN

Nikola was completely unsure what the next steps before him were now. He'd mostly accepted that he wasn't going to be King even before the Election was over, but he hadn't started thinking about what that meant for him afterward.

Hans and Jessica had simply taken leave of absence from their jobs to run. The House of the Realm and the Adamantine Foreign Office, respectively, had held their posts for them.

Oliver had been in RKAA with him, but he'd been following a normal progression and had been in a relatively normal position when he'd had to step down to run. Like the two civilians, he'd return to his job with little interruption.

Nikola had held a so-called *mission command*, a political appointment authorized by his-Mother-the-King to lead the Masada Protocol. Under that mission command, he'd been in charge of Generals vastly his senior and commanded multiple divisions.

Going back to a single battalion felt... odd. It was the logical next step, he supposed, but it still felt odd.

So did being summoned to a meeting with the Monarch-Elect. He was certainly expecting to spend time with his sister and their nieces outside of work, but this summons had been formal, addressed to him as both Colonel and First Pentarch.

It brought him into the Palace, past layers of security he'd known existed, and others he had never passed while his mother lived.

As he stepped out of a concealed elevator into the subbasements of the Palace, he realized that he was no longer seeing regular Palace Security. Those guardians were seconded from various forces, a mix of police and soldiers, all with solid records and impressive performance indicators, but they were, in the end, regular troops.

Even before he'd entered the elevator, he'd only seen Adamant Guard. Now, deep under the Palace, a Guard he didn't know stepped up and gave him and Alexei a crisp salute. The man was utterly nondescript, with mid-brown hair, skin and eyes.

"Your Highness, Major Krupin, welcome to Secure Facility Alpha Two," he greeted them. "I'm Lieutenant Harold Merle; I'll be your escort through Ess-Fac-A-Two."

"Thank you, Lieutenant Merle," Nikola said. "I'll admit that I don't have the location of where I'm to meet the Monarch-Elect."

"Nothing in the Ess-Fac-As is visibly numbered, Your Highness," Merle warned. "*I'm* still running on a guide in my neural link, so telling you where you were going wouldn't help.

"You're not the last to arrive, but I'll warn you: I don't think the Monarch-Elect's staff laid out enough of the *good* donuts, so you'll want to rush."

HAROLD MERLE, it turned out, had an aversion to lemon. The lemon-iced donuts that made up a third of the snacks laid out in the room were anathema to him, but Nikola was perfectly prepared to try them.

After directing him to a seat and pointing out the station with the donuts and coffees, the Guard had vanished back outside. Alexei took one of the non-lemon donuts and the seat he'd been directed to, surveying the room with the paranoid eye of a man tasked to keep others alive.

Vigo Jarret's presence at the head of the table, standing as still as a gun turret, suggested they were probably fine, but it was Alexei's job. Nikola took the time to count the chairs and see who else was already present.

Fourteen chairs. Jessica and Hans were seated along one side of the table, with their own Adamant Guard protectors. Lorraine wasn't present yet, but Nikola knew that Jarret's presence meant she couldn't be far.

If three of the four Pentarchs were present, he was certain Oliver was on his way. The question, he supposed, was whether Wang-Cho Adamant, the new Fifth Pentarch, was invited.

Oliver arrived a step behind Malcolm Adamant, the Regent clearly having intercepted the younger man somewhere and ushered him along. As Regent, Malcolm rated an Adamant Guard detail of his own, which brought the number in the room to eleven.

A twelfth slipped through the door behind Jarret in near-silence. The woman wore a gray suit very clearly picked to do anything *but* stand out. The way her eyes swept the room told Nikola she was as much a bodyguard as any of the Adamant Guards, which raised the question of *who* she was bodyguarding.

A question was answered a minute or so later when Monarch-Elect Lorraine Adamant and Prime Minister Ki Arlet stepped into the room. The PM's bodyguard swept forward with Jarret, and everyone took their seats at the table.

"Thank you all for coming," Lorraine said quietly. "Traditionally, I spend today and tomorrow getting my brain stuffed full of every-thing the Regent and Prime Minister know before the coronation. In reality, I'm sure we'll be doing those briefings and updates for a while yet, but there are matters of critical importance only known to the people in this room."

Nikola straightened. That meant...

"The wormhole," Jessica said before he finished his thought. "We handed most of Benjamin's files over to the Terrans, but we didn't include any information on FBIT's belief that there was a wormhole out here."

"Exactly," Lorraine confirmed. "While the United Worlds government is unlikely to get directly involved in pursuing a wormhole, that knowledge would end up in the hands of one special-interest group or another.

"Thanks to the information we provided Commissioner Gordon, we can be reasonably certain that Freebright themselves aren't going to be a problem for much longer."

His sister's smile was predatory—but it wasn't like Nikola had any sympathy for the megacorporation that had tried to turn their Kingdom into a secure operating base.

"The problem is that even if the Commission truly breaks FBIT, that will only result in their assets being scooped up by their competitors," Lorraine warned. "And even the knowledge of a potential wormhole is a powerful asset."

A wormhole would allow for a new wave of colonization, the birth of another second-order cluster. Whoever controlled the wormhole would make a *lot* of money and have a solid influence on the politics of the new cluster.

Kang Tao was almost as wealthy and powerful in the Bright Dream Cluster as the Republic of Bright Dream itself—and the star systems along the path between the two wormholes had rapidly outstripped those in other directions.

"Right now, we believe we are the only people in our region who know about that possibility," Lorraine told them all. "But sooner or later, someone is going to come looking for it. They won't work with us after what happened with FBIT. They'll deal with our enemies, or they'll attempt to overthrow our government again."

They'd have a harder time finding willing patsies. Nikola could just barely see how Benjamin had been twisted onto his path, but it wasn't a path he figured any of the people in that room would walk—and they were the most-likely candidates.

"But if *we* control the wormhole, it will be an immense boost to our economy and... well, *everything*," Jessica said slowly. "I've done a few projections and models on a secure private system. Wormholes tend to be in systems without inhabited planets, but the systems nearby see their gross system product *double* inside ten to fifteen years."

"If one of the LSX-Twenty-Five controls that wormhole, most of that value will go back to the United Worlds and shareholders so distant, they don't even know Adamant exists," Lorraine said. "At least one is going to come sniffing. Probably more, if FBIT comes apart as badly as I believe Commissioner Gordon wants.

"We, my friends, my brother, my cousins," she waved around the room, "have to find it *first*."

---

*The Kingdom of Adamant is restored, but further troubles await. Look for Nikola and Lorraine to return in Broken Prince, coming in March 2026!*

# JOIN THE MAILING LIST

Love Glynn Stewart's books? Join the mailing list at:

**GlynnStewart.com/mailing-list**

Be the first to find out when new books are released!

# ABOUT THE AUTHOR

**GLYNN STEWART** is the author of Starship's Mage, a bestselling science fiction and fantasy series where faster-than-light travel is possible–but only because of magic. His other works include science fiction series Duchy of Terra, Castle Federation and Vigilante, as well as the urban fantasy series ONSET and Changeling Blood.

Writing managed to liberate Glynn from a bleak future as an accountant. With his personality and hope for a high-tech future intact, he lives in Canada with his partner, their cats, and an unstoppable writing habit.

# CREDITS

The following people were involved in making this book:
Copyeditor: Richard Shealy
Proofreader: M Parker Editing
Cover Artist: Elias Stern
Faolan's Pen Publishing:
Jack Giesen

And a sincere thank you to Glynn's Patreon subscribers!

# OTHER BOOKS
# BY GLYNN STEWART

For release announcements join the mailing
list or visit **GlynnStewart.com**

### STARSHIP'S MAGE
Starship's Mage
Hand of Mars
Voice of Mars
Alien Arcana
Judgment of Mars
UnArcana Stars
Sword of Mars
Mountain of Mars
The Service of Mars
A Darker Magic
Mage-Commander
Beyond the Eyes of Mars
Nemesis of Mars
Chimera's Star
Ambassador for Mars
Chimera's Fall
The Lies Arcana
Shadow of Mars(*Upcoming)*

**Starship's Mage: Red Falcon**
Interstellar Mage
Mage-Provocateur
Agents of Mars

**Starship's Mage Novellas**
Pulsar Race
Mage-Queen's Thief

# HOUSE ADAMANT

The Exodus Gambit
The Old Guard
The Valkyrie Strategem
Regent's Mate (Upcoming)

# EXILE

Exile
Refuge
Crusade
Ashen Stars: An Exile Novella

# CASTLE FEDERATION

Space Carrier Avalon
Stellar Fox
Battle Group Avalon
Q-Ship Chameleon
Rimward Stars
Operation Medusa
A Question of Faith: A Castle Federation
Novella

**Dakotan Confederacy**
Admiral's Oath
To Stand Defiant
Unbroken Faith

# VIGILANTE

(WITH TERRY MIXON))
Heart of Vengeance
Oath of Vengeance

**Bound By Stars: A Vigilante Series
(With Terry Mixon)**
Bound By Law
Bound by Honor
Bound by Blood

## AETHER SPHERES

Nine Sailed Star
Void Spheres
Fated Skies (*upcoming*)

## TEER AND KARD

Wardtown
Blood Ward
Blood Adept
Adept's Path (*upcoming*)

## CHANGELING BLOOD

Changeling's Fealty
Hunter's Oath
Noble's Honor
Fae, Flames & Fedoras: A Changeling Blood Novella

## ONSET

ONSET: To Serve and Protect
ONSET: My Enemy's Enemy
ONSET: Blood of the Innocent
ONSET: Stay of Execution
Murder by Magic: An ONSET Novella

## STANDALONE NOVELS & NOVELLAS

City in the Sky
Excalibur Lost: A Space Opera Novella
Balefire: A Dark Fantasy Novella
Icebreaker: A Fantasy Naval Thriller
Seekers in the Void: A Space Adventure

9 781989 674888